UNDER PASSION'S SPELL

What was there about his eyes, his voice, that captivated her so? It was easy to believe he was a magician. He certainly seemed to be casting a spell over her.

She stared up at him, relieved that he hadn't kissed her, disappointed that he hadn't even tried.

"Cara?"

It was wrong. It was foolish. Maybe the most foolish thing she had ever done, yet she leaned toward him, her face uplifted, her heart beating a crazy rhythm she had never heard before as he bent down and captured her lips with his.

She had been kissed before, and often, but never like this. There were no words to describe the incredible wonder of his kiss, nothing in her past experience to compare it to. It was as if he had invented something entirely new, something no one had ever thought of before. As if he had taken a simple kiss and reinvented it.

Other *Love Spell* books by Amanda Ashley:
A DARKER DREAM
SUNLIGHT, MOONLIGHT
DEEPER THAN THE NIGHT
EMBRACE THE NIGHT

LOVE SPELL BOOKS  NEW YORK CITY

LOVE SPELL®

January 1998

Published by

Dorchester Publishing Co., Inc.
276 Fifth Avenue
New York, NY 10001

ISBN 0-505-52243-8

Printed in the United States of America.

This book is dedicated to *all* my wild, weird, wacky, wonderful on-line buddies, especially . . .
Chip, who always makes me laugh, proving that laughter is the best medicine. Thanks, Doc.
Julie, cause she's fun and she loves me.
Paul, my favorite "masked" man.
Wayne, for the sexy "got mail" war.
Melissa, for sharing Wayne.
Mike, for being so sweet.
Cyndi, who keeps me up-to-date on what DG is doing.
Michael, for his slightly off-kilter e-mails, and for reminding me that *he* is also sweet!
Gloria, who sends me jokes, and takes good care of my favorite doctor.
AJ, who has *awesome* talent even though he thinks he doesn't.
Pat, who sends me "goodies" via snail mail.
Chris, who answers all my tech questions.
Patti, because she's hopelessly addicted to AOL and hopefully to John, as well.
John, because he's a great guy and a wonderful son.
James, because he's a fellow Phantom Phan.
And for **Preston,** because he sings "Music of the Night" to me online.

Shades of Gray

Memories of daylight
fall warm upon my mind
teasing me
tormenting me
with all I've left behind

My heart beats cold
all hope is gone, and
I live in shades of gray
the moon my sun, the sun my death
should I surrender to the day

The sun's light, once a blessing
now drives me to my lair
where I dream of its warmth,
yearn for its light
and pray it ne'er finds me there

Now a creature of darkness
I am every nightmare come true
fears made flesh
the terror of the night
and I have come
for you.

Chapter One

The Roskovich Carnival was the smallest, seediest looking excuse for a circus Marisa Richards had ever seen. The owner's main claim to fame was his boast that, inside the largest of its three rather shabby-looking tents, he had the body of a genuine Transylvanian vampire.

Marisa paid the wizened ticket-taker six-fifty and then, bypassing the usual carnival rides and games, entered the large blue-and-white-striped sideshow tent along with the other hardy souls who had ventured out in the rain on this cool and windy Halloween evening.

She wandered from one attraction to the other, pausing to look at the bearded lady, at a two-headed man who was so obviously a fake it was laughable. Moving on, she saw a sad-faced giant clad in a leopard-skin costume that reminded her of Fred Flintstone. There was a morose-looking dwarf, a man who had skin like that of a reptile, a diminutive woman who was covered from head to foot with psychedelic tattoos.

The air was thick with the scent of rain-damp clothing, cotton candy and buttered popcorn, mustard and onions. A vendor wearing a yellow apron was calling, "Get your hot dogs! Get 'em while they're hot!"

Marisa stopped when she came to a smaller tent set up within the big one. A hand-lettered sign read

COUNT ALEXI KRISTOV
OLDEST VAMPIRE IN EXISTENCE

Marisa felt a sudden chill skitter down her spine as she stepped into the small tent. Good special effects, she mused. She glanced over her shoulder, expecting to see some sort of fan, but saw nothing.

And then she saw the coffin. It was the old-fashioned kind, bigger at the top than at the bottom. Dull black in color, it rested on a raised wooden dais in the center of the sawdust-strewn floor. The closed lid was covered with a large spray of fake, bloodred roses.

There were perhaps a dozen other people in the tent. They stood in a loose semicircle around the casket, talking in hushed whispers. A little girl tugged on her mother's hand, begging to go on a pony ride. Two teenage boys stood together, teasing a pretty teenage girl by making jokes about the undead and creatures of the night.

The crowd fell silent as a tall, cadaver-thin man dressed in a dark brown suit and old-fashioned cravat entered the tent and took his place at the head of the coffin. He stood there, his pale hands folded, his expression somber, while the lights dimmed.

"Welcome," the man said, executing a courtly bow. "I am Silvano."

He spoke with a heavy accent, though Marisa

could not place it. Hungarian, perhaps, or Russian?

"What you are about to see may shock you, but, be assured, it is quite real. Hundreds of years ago, Count Alexi Kristov was a ruthless monster, a scourge who decimated many small villages in my native Romania. In his time, he preyed on my family, devouring them one by one until my ancestors were almost completely destroyed."

Marisa took a step forward, drawn in by the man's words. She had never been one to believe in ghosts or goblins. She wasn't afraid of the dark. She didn't believe in witches or warlocks or vampires.

But something in this man's voice, his words, made her believe. She felt the hair rise along her arms as Silvano took a deep breath and began to speak again.

"Over a hundred years ago, one of my ancestors discovered the count's resting place. He rendered the vampire helpless by binding him with silver chains."

Very slowly, Silvano removed the plastic roses from the top of the coffin. He hesitated, for dramatic effect, Marisa surmised, and then, with a flourish, lifted the lid, which was lined with white satin.

"Though he looks dead," Silvano went on, his tone somber, "I can assure you that Count Alexi Kristov is very much alive. A century without nourishment has rendered him helpless and virtually powerless."

Silvano extended his hand in invitation. "Please, do not be afraid to come forward for a closer look. There is no danger."

Marisa hung back until everyone else had taken a good look at the count, and then, on legs that suddenly felt like limp spaghetti, she climbed the two steps up to the dais and looked down into the casket.

The bed of the coffin was lined with the same white satin that lined the lid. A silver cross, perhaps a foot tall, was secured to the foot of the coffin. Similar crosses were placed on either side of the vampire's head.

The vampire, attired in an old-fashioned shiny black suit, was laid out with his arms at his sides. She thought it odd that his hands were tightly clenched. A thick silver chain was wrapped around his body from his chest to his ankles. His skin, which was almost as white as the satin beneath him, was drawn paper-thin over his skull-like head. Pale brown lashes lay against his sunken cheeks. His hair was long and limp, the color a dull reddish brown.

He definitely looked dead. A long time dead.

Feeling Silvano's gaze, Marisa looked up. "Why didn't your ancestors kill him?"

"They felt death would be too merciful."

"Merciful?"

"This—" Silvano gestured at the vampire. "How can I explain it? He is very much alive. Without human blood to sustain him, he is in constant torment." A smile that was not really a smile twisted Silvano's thin lips. "He cannot escape the chains. The crosses render him powerless. His soul is trapped within this body. This dead body."

Marisa shivered as she looked at the vampire again. Almost, Silvano had her believing the vampire was real. But, of course, it was just some extremely skinny man and some impressive stage makeup.

She stared at the vampire's chest, silently counting the seconds. One minute passed. Two. The man never took a breath. Three minutes. Four.

A cold chill ran up her spine. Maybe it really was a corpse.

Silvano turned away as a pretty girl wearing a short red skirt, a white off-the-shoulder blouse, black net stockings, and ballerina slippers called his name.

Marisa watched Silvano leave the tent with the girl. Glancing around, she saw that everyone else had left, too.

Heart pounding with trepidation, she realized she was alone with the vampire. She stared at the body. Maybe it wasn't human at all. Maybe it was made of wax, like the figures at the Movieland Wax Museum.

She laughed with relief. That was it, of course. Why hadn't she thought of that before? It was just an elaborate hoax.

She glanced over her shoulder. There was no one in sight. Feeling foolish, she ran her fingertips over the links of the chains. They felt real, solid. A small fortune in silver.

And then, unable to resist the temptation, she touched the vampire's hand.

It wasn't made of wax. The skin was cold. Smooth and dry, it reminded her of ancient parchment. She gasped as the papery skin grew warm beneath her fingertips. And then, very slowly, the skeletal fingers of the vampire's left hand uncurled and spread out to lie flat against the smooth satin lining.

With a shriek, Marisa jumped away from the coffin. She tripped as she stumbled backward, cried out as she tumbled down the steps. She scraped her leg on the rough wood, landed in the sawdust on her hands and knees.

Shaken, she glanced over her shoulder, at worst expecting to see the vampire climbing out of the coffin, its fangs bared in a hideous grin, at best expecting to see an ordinary man sitting up, laughing uproariously because he had scared her out of ten years of her life.

But all was quiet within the tent.

Deathly quiet.

Marisa scrambled to her feet, wincing as she did so. Looking down, she saw blood dripping from a shallow laceration just above her right ankle.

Pulling a handkerchief from her purse, she mopped up the blood; then, with a grimace, she tossed the hanky in a trash can and hurried out of the tent.

Blood. Warm and sweet and fresh. The scent of it filled the air, teasing his nostrils, tantalizing his senses, awakening a thirst that had lain dormant for a hundred years.

Blood.

The woman's blood.

His hand tingled as he remembered the touch of her hand, her fingers warm and soft, the throb of her pulse beckoning him.

He fought through layers of blackness, a century of darkness, all his senses honed on the irresistible scent of the woman's blood.

He flexed his hands, his shoulders, licked his lips as the Hunger roared to life.

With an effort, he opened his eyes. A cry of outrage rumbled deep in his throat when he saw the crosses. Three of them, all silver.

With the return of awareness came pain—the pain of the silver chains that bound him, the raging Hunger that had not been fed for a hundred years.

Ignoring the pain and the Hunger, he reached deep inside himself, calling on the strength of a thousand years. . . .

Marisa came awake with the sound of her own screams ringing in her ears. Breathing heavily, she switched on the bedside lamp and glanced around, relieved to find herself safe at home, in her own bed.

Her hand went to her neck, her fingers anxiously probing the skin beneath her left ear. There didn't seem to be any bite marks. There was no blood.

"A dream," she murmured, "it was only a dream."

But it had seemed so real. The creature bending over the bed, his gray eyes glowing an unholy red in the darkness, his hands like claws as they clamped over her shoulders to hold her in place, his long reddish brown hair brushing against her cheek as he leaned over her, his fangs poised at her throat.

So real, she thought, so real.

Leaving the light on, she drew the covers up to her chin, afraid to close her eyes, afraid to go back to sleep for fear the nightmare would find her again.

Chapter Two

Marisa returned to the carnival the following Monday evening after work, hoping that by seeing the vampire again, by assuring herself that it was still there, she would somehow be freed of the nightmares that had been plaguing her dreams for the past three nights. Why she thought seeing the creature again would put an end to her bad dreams instead of causing more remained unclear as she parked her car on a side street and ran through the light drizzle that had started falling at sundown.

She paused when she reached the lot, surprised to see that the food booths were gone. Several of the rides had been dismantled; in the distance, she could see three men taking down the Ferris wheel. Another man was trying to load a skittish horse into a trailer. No one paid her any attention.

The ticket-taker's booth was empty. A black-and-white sign was propped in front of the window. It read:

CLOSED UNTIL FURTHER NOTICE

For a moment, she stared at the sign; then, glancing around to make sure no one was watching, she ducked into the big tent. It was empty. She could hear her heart pounding in her ears as she approached the smaller tent.

Taking a deep breath, she stepped inside.

This tent was empty, too. The dais stood in the center of the floor, but the ebony coffin was nowhere to be seen.

"May I help you?"

The sound of a woman's voice startled her. Whirling around, Marisa recognized the girl she had seen on Friday. The girl had been wearing a short red skirt, ballerina slippers, an off-the-shoulder blouse, and long, dangling red earrings then. Today, she looked as though she had just returned from a funeral. The severe black dress made her look older than her years. She wore a black scarf over her hair. A filigreed silver crucifix hung from a thick silver chain around her neck. Wide silver bracelets adorned both wrists.

"I came to see the vampire."

The girl frowned at her a moment. Her eyes were red, as if she had been crying.

"Ah, yes," she said, "you were here on All Hallow's Eve, weren't you?"

"Yes." Marisa glanced at the center of the tent where the coffin had been. "Where is it?"

The girl looked around the tent, her fingers worrying the crucifix.

Was she imagining it, Marisa wondered, or did the girl's movements seem furtive, fearful?

"Is something wrong?" Marisa asked.

"What? Oh, no. I regret the . . . the count is no longer available for viewing."

"No longer available? Why not?"

The girl hesitated before answering, and Marisa

had the distinct impression that she was choosing her words with great care. "The body is being . . . restored."

"I see," Marisa said. "Do you know when he . . . when it will be finished?"

The girl's hand tightened over the cross. "I'm sorry, but I couldn't say."

"Is Silvano here?"

The girl looked at Marisa sharply; then, expelling a deep, shuddering sigh, she shook her head.

"It looks like you're packing up."

"Yes, I'm afraid unexpected business has called us away. I'm sorry you made the trip out here for nothing. Good evening to you."

"Yes, good night."

Marisa watched the girl leave, then walked to the center of the tent and stared at the empty platform. The girl had said the body was being "restored." What, exactly, did that mean? How did one go about "restoring" a body that wasn't quite dead?

She felt a sudden coldness at the base of her neck, an eerie sensation that she was no longer alone. She glanced at the doorway, thinking the girl had returned, but there was no one there.

"You came to see the vampyre?"

Marisa whirled around, her heart leaping into her throat. "Good Lord, you startled me!" She stared at the stranger, wondering how he had gotten into the tent. She had been facing the doorway. Surely she would have seen him come in. He was not a man who would pass unnoticed.

His long black hair was wet from the rain. His brows were thick and straight. He was tall and broad shouldered, with the trim build of an athlete, yet his skin was pale, as if he didn't spend much time in the sun. He wore a bulky gray sweater; tight black jeans hugged his long legs. There was mud on his boots.

"Forgive me," he said. "I didn't mean to frighten you."

His voice was low and deep, and it slid over her skin like warm satin.

"That's all right."

He glanced at the place where the coffin had been and she saw a muscle twitch in his jaw. And then, like a wolf sniffing the air, he lifted his head, his nostrils flaring.

Marisa shivered as his eyes met hers, deep black eyes that seemed to probe the very depths of her heart and soul. The devil would have eyes like that. The thought came out of nowhere.

"Did you come to see it, too?" she asked. "The vampire, I mean?"

"Yes."

She took a step backward, uncomfortable standing so close to him without knowing why. "They told me it's being restored, whatever that means."

A smile so faint she wasn't sure it even qualified as a smile touched his lips. Full, sensuous lips. "Is that what they said?"

Marisa nodded, enchanted by his voice. Never had she heard anything like it: low, mellifluous. An angel's voice.

Grigori studied the woman for a moment, noting that she was quite lovely. Her shoulder-length hair was dark brown with a slight curl; her eyes were bright and green, like fine-quality emeralds. Her lips were finely sculpted, warm and generous.

Inviting. A pink sweater and faded black Levi's revealed a petite figure with softly rounded curves in all the right places.

"And do you believe in vampyres?" he asked.

"Of course not. He was probably just some old guy they hired for a few days." Yes, she thought, that was it.

"Yet you came back. I wonder why."

"I'm not sure." She met his gaze, a challenge in her eyes. "You don't look much like a man who believes in vampires and things that go bump in the night, either, but you're here."

He lifted one black brow. "Indeed? You would be surprised by what I believe in."

"No doubt," Marisa retorted. "Well . . ." She settled her handbag on her shoulder. "Good night."

He stared after her a moment, watching the gentle sway of her hips as she exited the tent. Then, remembering his reason for being there, he crossed the floor and delved through the trash can until he found a wadded-up handkerchief. Closing his eyes, he took a deep breath, a quiver of longing running through him as he inhaled the scent of blood.

His eyelids flew open as he recognized the scent. It was the woman's blood that stained the cloth.

Shoving the handkerchief into his back pocket, he hurried after her.

Standing in the rain, he watched her climb behind the wheel of a late-model Honda Prelude. And then, hands shoved into the pockets of his jeans, oblivious to the lightning that split the clouds, he followed her home.

* * *

Marisa took a long, hot shower, sprinkled herself liberally with dusting powder, then pulled on a pair of stretch jeans, a sweatshirt, and a pair of thick socks and curled up on the sofa. She flipped through the TV channels for a minute, then switched off the set. Reaching for a book, she tried to read, but after she found herself reading the same page for the fourth time, she tossed the book aside.

Too restless to sit still, she went into the kitchen to fix something to eat and then, on a whim, decided to go out instead.

She pulled on a pair of boots, and then, grabbing her purse and an umbrella, she left the house. The rain was no more than a fine mist now, though the clouds still hung dark and ominous in the sky. She contemplated taking her car, but decided a walk in the fresh air would do her good.

Angelo's was her favorite restaurant, a cozy little Italian place with red-checked tablecloths, candles in old Chianti bottles, and a relaxed atmosphere. It was located a couple of blocks away, and Marisa went there often. The owners were friendly and the spaghetti couldn't be beat.

Standing under the restaurant's awning, Marisa shook the rain from her umbrella, then went inside and took a seat at a booth in the back. She smiled at the waiter who handed her a menu.

She was trying to decide whether to have rigatoni or ravioli when she realized she was being watched.

Lowering the menu, Marisa glanced around the restaurant, felt her heart catch in her throat as she saw the dark-haired man from the carnival walking toward her.

He smiled as he reached her table. "Hello again."

"What are you doing here?"

"Seeking company on a stormy night, perhaps. I see you are alone. Would you mind if I joined you?"

Of course she'd mind. She didn't know a thing about the guy, not even his name.

The prudent thing would be to tell him to get lost. She knew that. Still, for no reason she could think of, she found herself inviting him to sit down.

Graceful as a leaf falling from a tree, he slid into the seat across from her.

"Do you come here often?" Marisa asked.

"No, this is my first time." He smiled at her. It was a totally disarming smile, revealing teeth white enough for a toothpaste commercial. "Fortuitous, don't you think?"

At a loss for words, Marisa nodded. She was glad when Tommy came to take her order.

"Hey, sweet cheeks," the waiter said with a wink, "how's it going?"

Marisa shook her head. Tommy was a hopeless flirt. He was studying accounting in college, and worked at the restaurant four nights a week. He was under the delusion that he was irresistible.

"So," Tommy purred, "what'll it be?"

"Rigatoni, I think."

"Excellent choice. Rigatoni and a glass of Chianti."

Marisa grinned. "You know me too well."

"Not as well as I'd like," Tommy replied, waggling his eyebrows at her. "And what can I get for you, sir?"

"A glass of red wine. Very dry."

"Coming right up," Tommy said.

Marisa spread her napkin over her lap. "You're not eating?"

"I dined earlier. I only stopped in for a drink."

"Oh."

"You must come here often," he remarked.

"Yeah, usually once or twice a week. Cooking isn't my favorite thing, and the food here is good, and inexpensive."

She looked up and smiled as Tommy brought their wine.

The stranger picked up his glass. "A toast?"

"What shall we drink to?"

"New friends?" he suggested.

Marisa picked up her glass. "New friends."

He watched her over the rim of his glass as she swallowed.

"I'm afraid I don't know your name, new friend."

"Forgive me. I am Grigori." He extended his hand.

"Marisa Richards."

He took her hand in his. His grip was gentle, yet firm, his skin cool.

"It is my pleasure, Marisa Richards."

His words slid over her, richer than dark chocolate, more intoxicating than the wine in her glass.

"So, Grigori, what do you do for a living?"

"Magic, mostly. And you?"

"Magic!" She cocked her head to one side, and then nodded. Yes, she could easily imagine him standing on a stage clad all in black, a silk cape billowing around him. "You're a magician?"

He shrugged. "Among other things."

"Are you performing here in town?"

"Not at the moment."

"Oh, that's too bad. I don't suppose you'd show me one of your secrets?"

"I'm afraid not."

"I didn't think you would. There's some sort of magician's oath or something, isn't there?"

"Yes," Grigori said, smiling faintly. "A very ancient oath not to reveal our secrets. You did not tell me what it is you do," he reminded her.

"I'm a legal secretary at Salazar and Salazar. The elder Mr. Salazar is my boss. A tyrant if ever there was one." She smiled. "Maybe you could make him disappear."

She had expected him to laugh, or at least smile back. Instead, he regarded her for a moment and then said, quite seriously, "If you wish."

Not certain how to reply, she changed the subject. "What do you do when you're not working?"

"I like to take long walks in the moonlight."

"Oh, a romantic."

He shrugged. "Perhaps I just prefer the night."

"Do you? Prefer the night, I mean?"

"Yes." He made a vague gesture with his hand. It was a graceful movement, airy, light. "My eyes are quite sensitive to the sun."

"Oh."

"And what do you like to do when you're not working?"

"Oh, I don't know. Read. Go to the movies." She grinned at him. "Take long walks through the park."

"In the evening?"

"In the morning, I'm afraid. I don't like walking in the park at night."

"Perhaps you would take a walk with me some evening and give me a chance to change your mind."

"Perhaps." She regarded him for a moment, trying to think of a tactful way to pose the question uppermost in her mind. In the end, she just asked it, straight out. "You're not married or anything, are you?"

A hint of sadness passed behind his eyes. "Not anymore."

"Divorced?"

"No. My wife and children are . . . are no more."

It was an odd way of putting it, she thought. "I'm sorry."

"It happened a long time ago."

Tommy brought her dinner then, and she was glad for the interruption, glad for the chance to change the subject.

She had thought it would be awkward, eating while Grigori watched, but he sat back in his seat, sipping a second glass of wine. They made small talk while she ate. She declined dessert, protested when Grigori reached for the check.

"You don't have to pay for my dinner," she said. "After all, you didn't eat anything."

"I wish to," he replied, and something in the deep timbre of his voice, in the sultry glow of his eyes, made her blush.

Outside, he placed her hand on his arm in a gesture that could only be called old-fashioned. "I should be honored if you would permit me to walk you home."

She stared at him, suddenly alert. "How do you know I walked?"

A good question, Grigori mused. "I was behind you on the street."

Marisa chewed on her lower lip. She didn't remember hearing anyone walking behind her. Of course, the rain could have muffled the sound of his footsteps. Her hand tightened on her umbrella. Not much of a weapon, she mused ruefully, but better than nothing.

His dark gaze met hers. In the glow of the street lamp, his eyes seemed fathomless, compelling. There was a hint of danger, of mystery, in those eyes.

"You do not know me," he said quietly. "I am a stranger you are reluctant to trust."

"Well, this is the nineties, you know. A girl can't be too careful."

"I understand." He stepped away from her. "Perhaps another time, then."

"Wait, I—"

"I would not want you to be uncomfortable, Marisa."

"I'm not, really." She shrugged. "It's just that, well, you know . . ."

"It is the nineties." He smiled at her. A beautiful megawatt smile that left her momentarily breathless. "Shall we?"

He offered her his arm again, and she took it without a qualm, still mesmerized by the effect of his smile, and the rich, sexy sound of his voice.

"How long have you lived in the city?" he asked.

"All my life. What about you?"

"I've been here only a few weeks."

"Oh. Business or pleasure?"

His gaze rested lightly on her face. "Definitely a pleasure now."

He smiled again, and it washed over her like sunlight. "Are you on vacation?"

"Vacation?" A slight frown furrowed his brow. "No. I am looking for . . . an old friend."

"How long will you be here?"

"As long as it takes me to find him."

"How do you know he's here?"

"I know."

The tone of his voice, the sudden tensing of the arm beneath her hand, made her glad he wasn't looking for her. She had the distinct impression this wasn't going to be a happy reunion.

"Tell me about yourself," he urged. "Do you like being a secretary?"

"Yes. It's a good job, even if my boss can be a bit of an ogre at times. I get a three-week vacation and paid holidays. And I get my birthday off."

"And when is that?"

"February 26th. When's yours?"

"November 20th."

"A Scorpio, eh?"

"You don't believe in all that nonsense, do you?" he asked, obviously amused. "It is, after all, the nineties."

"Well," she said, laughing, "not really."

"But you read your horoscope in the paper every day."

"Well, not *every* day."

"And you avoid black cats, and throw salt over your shoulder for good luck, and never walk under ladders."

"Are you making fun of me?"

"Of course not."

He smiled at her again, that wonderfully amazing smile the likes of which she had never seen. And his eyes, he had the most beautiful eyes, deep and dark beneath short, thick, sooty lashes. He was quite the most attractive man she had ever met.

For a time, they walked in silence. Marisa swung her umbrella in her free hand, listening to the sound of raindrops dripping from the leaves of the trees. She was surprised that the silence between them didn't make her uncomfortable, but it was an easy, companionable silence, as if they had known each other a lifetime instead of a few hours.

"Well, this is it. Where I live. Thank you for walking me home."

"It was my pleasure, Marisa Richards." He bowed over her hand and kissed it in a manner that could only be called grand. "May I call on you?"

"Call on me?" She grinned at his use of such an old-world term. "Yes, I think I'd like that."

"Tomorrow evening?"

Tomorrow was Tuesday and she had no plans for the evening other than to curl up on the sofa to watch an old Cary Grant flick. "That would be fine."

"What time would be convenient for you?"

Marisa shrugged. "Is seven too early?"

"No."

His gaze moved over her, wrapping around her like a fine, silken web. "Until tomorrow evening, *cara mia.*"

"You speak Italian?"

"*Si.* And Russian and French. And even a little Greek."

"I've always wanted to learn to speak a foreign language."

"Perhaps I shall teach you."

"I think I'd like that."

"As would I. *Buono notte, cara.*"

His voice moved over her, sending little shivers down her spine.

"Good night, Grigori."

He bowed, then turned and walked away, leaving her feeling suddenly cold and bereft.

Chapter Three

Alexi Kristov lifted his head and sniffed the wind. Chiavari was here, in the city.

He glanced up at the apartment where the woman lived. No one was home, but he knew Grigori had been here, in this very place, not long ago.

The other was in the city, too.

Kristov grinned wolfishly. All the players in one place, he mused.

And only one of them would leave the city alive.

Chapter Four

"You see," Grigori said, "there's nothing frightening about walking through the park in the evening."

Dressed in a black turtleneck sweater and black jeans, he looked like a part of the night he loved, Marisa thought, dark and mysterious and a little dangerous.

"Well, I must admit, it doesn't seem scary when you're with me."

Grigori smiled down at her, pleased that she felt safe in his presence, wondering what she would think if she knew she had never been in more danger in her life.

"I find walking in the evening soothing," he remarked.

"Maybe," Marisa replied, "but I still like the daytime better. Everything looks gray at night. I miss the colors of daytime."

Grigori shrugged. "Life is less harsh in the hours of the night. Flaws are less clearly defined. Ugliness can be hidden in the shadows."

"Well, I guess that's true. But things are also scarier at night, don't you think?"

"Perhaps." He paused, turning the full force of

his gaze upon her. "What is it that frightens you, Marisa?"

His voice was as rich as chocolate, as dark and mysterious as the shadows that surrounded them.

"I don't know. The usual things, I guess. Spiders and snakes. Being alone in a strange place." She grinned. "Vampires."

She expected him to laugh, but he didn't.

"Have you ever wondered what it would be like, to be a vampyre?"

"Well, not seriously. Why, have you?"

"Once, a long time ago."

"Well, vampires are only fiction. I'm more afraid of the unknown than the unreal."

The unknown . . . She looked up at Grigori. *He* was certainly unknown. She laughed self-consciously, glad that the darkness hid the blush she could feel heating her cheeks.

"You have nothing to fear from me, Marisa. I will let nothing harm you while I am here."

"You say that like you're expecting someone to come along and try to murder me or something."

"Or something," he murmured softly.

"What?"

"Nothing."

He reached for her hand. His skin was smooth and surprisingly cool. She could feel the strength of his long fingers as they wrapped around her hand. It made her feel like a teenager again, walking hand in hand in the park with her latest boyfriend, her insides churning with excitement as she waited to see if he would kiss her.

They walked along a twisting concrete path. Stone benches were placed at intervals along the way. There was a bridle path along the outer edge of the park. A variety of trees grew at irregular intervals. Several narrow wooden bridges spanned the shallow stream that cut through the center of the park.

The moon was bright overhead, shining on the water so that it looked like a ribbon of silver stretching between the grassy banks. The stars winked down at her, as if they knew a secret.

"Come," he said, "let us walk down by the water."

They left the path and made their way across the damp grass. They stood at the edge of the stream, listening to the whisper of the water as it tumbled over the stones of the riverbed, always moving, always changing in its quest for the sea.

"It is pretty here at night," Marisa remarked.

"As are you."

Just three words, yet she felt her heart turn over in her chest. "Thank you."

"You have the most beautiful eyes I've ever seen," he went on. "Your skin is smooth and unblemished, your hair like a waterfall of chestnut silk."

Marisa looked away, her cheeks growing warm with pleasure at his flattery. She could feel him standing close beside her, so close their thighs were almost touching. Would he try to kiss her? Should she let him? He was a stranger. The thought made her feel suddenly vulnerable and she let go of his hand. There was no one else in sight. It was dark, and they were alone, quite alone.

"Marisa." Just her name, nothing more.

His eyes were as black as ebony, enigmatic in the light of the moon. Hypnotic eyes that seemed to be as deep as the ocean; eyes that could see into the most intimate part of her soul, divine her innermost secrets, grant her every wish if she just let herself fall into their depths.

She blinked up at him, feeling suddenly lightheaded. "We . . . ah, we should go back," she stammered. "It's getting late."

"If you wish, *cara*."

What was there about his eyes, his voice, that captivated her so? It was easy to believe he was a magician. He certainly seemed to be casting a spell over her.

She stared up at him, relieved that he hadn't kissed her, disappointed that he hadn't even tried.

"Cara?"

It was wrong. It was foolish. Maybe the most foolish thing she had ever done, yet she leaned toward him, her face uplifted, her heart beating a crazy rhythm she had never heard before as he bent down and captured her lips with his.

She had been kissed before, and often, but never like this. There were no words to describe the incredible wonder of his kiss, nothing in her past experience to compare it to. It was as if he had invented something entirely new, something no one had ever thought of before. As if he had taken a simple kiss and reinvented it. And he wasn't even holding her in his arms, wasn't touching her at all except for his lips pressed to hers.

When he drew back, she felt as if someone had stolen the strength from her limbs, the stars from the sky, the very breath from her body.

Bereft, she stared up at him. Almost, she asked him what he had done, what it was they had shared. But she didn't know how to ask such a question without sounding either incredibly stupid or incredibly naive.

"Come," Grigori said, offering her his hand. "I'll take you home." *Now,* he thought, *before it is too late. For both of us.*

"What? Oh, yes, home."

Feeling dazed, she put her hand in his. They didn't say much on the way home. She was acutely aware of his nearness, of his hand holding hers. His grip was gentle; his footsteps seemed extraordinarily light for such a big man. She had the fleeting impression that he was floating over the sidewalk.

All too soon, they reached her apartment building.

"Will I see you tomorrow?" she asked as they walked up the stairs.

"Perhaps."

"Oh." She opened the door, and then glanced over her shoulder. "Well, good night."

"*Buono notte, cara.*"

"Good night."

She stood looking up at him, wondering if he would kiss her again. For a moment, she thought he would. Hoped he would. Prayed he would.

Instead, he bowed over her hand. "Thank you for walking with me, Marisa."

"I enjoyed it, too."

She waited another moment; then, with a smile, she stepped inside and closed the door. It was probably just as well he hadn't kissed her again, she mused as she got ready for bed. If one kiss could affect her like that, she didn't even want to think what making love to him would be like.

But later, lying in her bed, unable to sleep, she could think of nothing else.

She couldn't think of anything else at work the next day, either. Staring at her computer, all she could see were Grigori's depthless black eyes. She recalled the sound of his voice when he called her *cara*, the incredible touch of his lips against hers. Just thinking about it made her feel warm and tingly all over.

Later, fighting the traffic on the freeway, she could hardly remember how she had gotten through the day.

At home, she changed into jeans and a Jekyll and Hyde sweatshirt, then went into the kitchen. Rummaging in the fridge for something to eat, she was still thinking of Grigori, of the strange effect his nearness had on her. It was more than just his good looks. His voice, perhaps? She had never known a man with such a deep, rich baritone. But even as she considered it, she knew it was more than that. There was something about the man himself. He radiated . . . what? Charm? Charisma?

She shook her head as she ladled fruit salad into a bowl. No, it was more than that. She had met other men who were charming and charismatic. It was power, she realized, a sense of latent power mixed with a potent dose of raw sex appeal. Even just sitting across from him at Angelo's, she had been aware of an undercurrent of tightly leashed power and sensuality radiating from Grigori.

He might have called her, she thought, annoyed with herself for being disappointed that he hadn't called, and then she realized that she had neglected to give him her phone number. Still, she had told him where she worked. If he had wanted to call, he could have looked it up, or called information. She might have been tempted to call him, but she didn't have his number, either. And then it occurred to her that she didn't even know his last name.

Pouring herself a glass of orange juice, she went into the living room and switched on the evening news, noting that, as always, the news was all bad.

She frowned as the cameras zoomed in on four shrouded bodies being lifted into an ambulance. Leaning forward, she turned up the volume.

"Police today were summoned to the hills behind the Los Angeles Zoo, where the bodies of four women were found by a couple of local teenagers. At this time, the cause of death is unclear. There were no signs of a struggle. Both robbery and rape have been ruled out as a motive. A preliminary investigation by the coroner listed severe blood loss as the probable cause of death. You may recall that the body of Silvano Roskovich, owner of the Roskovich Carnival, was found in a similar condition in a ditch behind the carnival on Halloween night. Two other bodies, as yet unidentified, were found in an alley late last night. In other news . . ."

Feeling numb, Marisa stared at the screen. Silvano was dead. She might have been one of the last people to see him alive. It made her feel responsible somehow.

She switched off the TV, then went into the kitchen and put her dishes into the dishwasher. Going into the bedroom, she gathered up her dirty clothes and headed for the laundry room that was located on the first floor in the rear of the building.

For once, she had the place all to her herself. She was adding soap to one of the machines when she had the sudden, unmistakable feeling that she was no longer alone.

Whirling around, she glanced at the door, which she had shut behind her. The windows on the far wall stared back at her like black, empty eyes. There was no one there, but she couldn't shake the feeling that she wasn't alone, that something was watching her, something evil. . . .

She stood there for several minutes, her heart pounding in her ears, wishing gossipy old Mrs. Patteri or one of the other tenants would join her.

As abruptly as it had come, the sense of evil vanished. She heard footsteps approaching, and then Mr. Abbott, the landlord, entered the room carrying a mop and pail. He was a tall, thin man in his early sixties, with lank gray hair, brown eyes, and an easy smile.

"Evening, Marisa," he said.

"Hi, Mr. Abbott."

"Didn't think anyone was in here," he said. "I'll come back later."

"I'll be done soon."

"Take your time." He smiled at her. "Give me a chance to watch the end of *M*A*S*H*." Leaving the mop and bucket in a corner, he left the room.

In the space of a heartbeat, Marisa was out the door behind him. Her laundry could wait until tomorrow.

Grigori stood outside Marisa's apartment complex, his senses testing the night. He could hear voices coming from the apartment building—an old couple arguing about whether they should visit their son in jail, a baby's hungry cry, a man snoring, the blare of a stereo, a half dozen television sets, each tuned to a different station. The strong scent of fried food and human waste stung his nostrils. And, over all, the scent of blood and warm living flesh, the low thrumming of beating hearts, calling to him . . .

He had come here simply to make certain she was safe. He refused to admit, even to himself, that he had any other motive.

She was home. He could sense her life force, smell the warmth and the heat of her. And then, just as he was about to climb the stairs to her apartment, he felt Alexi's presence.

With preternatural speed, he followed Marisa's scent to the back of the building. His sense of the other vampyre was stronger here. Rage rose up within him, bringing with it the fear that he might be too late.

The sense of evil grew stronger still as he neared the back of the building. He saw a shadow separate itself from the darkness, heard the faint sound of mocking laughter, and then the specter vanished from his sight.

With a wordless cry of frustration, Grigori gave chase. He followed the vampyre down dark alleys and over rooftops, never able to catch more than a glimpse of his quarry. He chased him for hours, never able to get close enough to catch him, though he often heard the mocking sound of his laughter. Anger and frustration burned within him as he realized Alexi was toying with him.

Refusing to give up, he continued to chase Kristov until the dawn threatened to steal the darkness from the sky.

Cursing softly, he turned back, heading for his resting place lest the sun find him.

Marisa felt foolish in the morning, and more than a little irritated that the blouse she had planned to wear to work that day was still in the washing machine.

Muttering about being a foolish, over-imaginative idiot, she ran down to the laundry room and tossed her clothes in the dryer.

Returning to her apartment, she ate breakfast, combed her hair, and brushed her teeth, then went down to the laundry room to take her clothes from the dryer. She folded what was necessary, leaving the rest in a heap on the bed. Dressing quickly, she grabbed her keys and drove to work.

In spite of herself, she found herself thinking of Grigori, wondering whether he would have called if she had thought to give him her number, or if she had read more into their brief encounter than was there.

The day passed quickly. Mr. Salazar was handling a high-profile case, and that always meant a ton of paperwork. Today, she had been glad of it, glad she had been too busy to give much thought to a man with dark hair and sinfully black eyes.

It was late when she finally left work. She had just unlocked her car door when she saw Grigori striding toward her. She frowned, wondering what he was doing downtown and, more specifically, what he was doing in the parking structure of her building. He wore a black leather jacket over a white T-shirt, snug black jeans, black boots.

He looked tall and dark and dangerous, and she felt ridiculously happy to see him.

"Good evening," he murmured.

"Hi. What are you doing here?"

"Looking for you."

"Oh."

"I wondered if I might impose upon you for a ride in exchange for dinner."

"I suppose that could be arranged," Marisa replied. Slipping behind the wheel, she reached over and unlocked the passenger door. "Get in."

He settled into the seat, arms folded across his chest. His presence seemed to fill her small car. Once again, she was aware of the power that radiated from him like heat off a stove.

She started the car and drove toward the exit. "What were you doing downtown?"

"Taking care of some business." The lie rolled smoothly off his tongue. He was here because she was here. "It is a remarkable city. So many big buildings, so much concrete and glass. So many people wandering around with no purpose in life . . ."

"I know," Marisa said. She glanced in the rearview mirror before changing lanes. "There are an awful lot of homeless people living on the streets. It's so sad."

"Yes. It makes me yearn for my old home," Grigori murmured.

"Where's that?"

"Italy."

"Were you born there?"

"Yes. It is a beautiful country." Sadness flickered in the depths of his eyes. "I've not been there for many years."

"Where do you live now? I mean, when you're not working. I guess you must do a lot of traveling."

"Yes. I have a small villa in Naples, and an apartment in Paris. When I'm . . . on the road, I stay in hotels."

"That can't be much fun. I think I'd like the traveling part, but living out of a suitcase must get old fast."

"It does, indeed. Where would you like to eat?"

"You don't have to take me out," Marisa said.

"It would be my pleasure."

"Well . . ." She considered for a moment. She knew a wonderful little restaurant uptown, but somehow the thought of sitting beside Grigori at a small table in a dark, intimate café was too unsettling. "How about the North Woods Inn?"

"Whatever you wish."

"Have you ever eaten there?"

A faint smile tugged at his lips. "No."

"It's one of my favorite places."

She exited the freeway, and he noted she drove with ease and skill. He sat back in the seat, admiring her from the corner of his eye. She wore a pale yellow blouse under a dark green jacket, and a matching skirt that was long enough to be businesslike and modest, yet short enough to show off a pair of very shapely legs.

A few minutes later, she pulled into the parking lot. The building had been designed to look as if it were made of logs. The roof was painted to look like snow.

Grigori held the door for her, then followed her inside. There was a bar to the left. The restaurant was located at the end of a long hallway to the right.

A pretty brunette in a very short red dress and black stockings led them to a table in the back room. She brought them a bowl of peanuts, a menu, and two glasses of water.

Marisa reached for a peanut, shelled it, and tossed the shells on the floor. She laughed softly at Grigori's expression. "It's all right. It's expected."

"Ah." Glancing around, he noticed that peanut shells did, indeed, litter the floor at every table.

Marisa studied the menu. "What are you going to have?"

"Steak."

"Hmmm. I can't decide whether to have the seafood platter or a turkey sandwich."

She was still trying to decide when the waiter came to take their order.

Grigori ordered a steak, very rare, and a glass of red wine.

"The seafood platter, I guess," Marisa said.

With a nod, the waiter took the menu and left the table.

"Do you come here often?" Grigori asked.

"Not really. So, when are you performing again? I'd love to see one of your shows."

"I'm afraid that won't be possible. The show closed last week."

"Oh, that's too bad. Where are you going next?"

His dark gaze moved over her and she flushed, wondering if her words betrayed her disappointment at the thought of his leaving town.

"I'm thinking of taking a vacation," he replied.

"Here?" She couldn't disguise the hope in her voice. "In L.A.?"

"Yes." His gaze swept over her in a most disconcerting manner. "There is still much I haven't seen."

She looked away, her cheeks suddenly warm. The arrival of their dinner couldn't have come at a better time.

"You weren't kidding when you said rare, were you?" Marisa asked when he cut into his steak. "I think it's still moving."

He glanced at the rich red juice that oozed from the meat. "It is the only way to eat a steak." He speared a chunk and offered it to her.

"No, thank you. I prefer mine to be at least a little bit cooked."

"You do not know what you are missing."

She wrinkled her nose with distaste. "To each his own," she murmured, and felt his gaze move over her again.

"Yes," he replied quietly, "to each his own."

She had the distinct impression he wasn't talking about steak.

Chapter Five

There was a man waiting for her on the landing outside her apartment when she got home from work the next night. At first, she thought it was Grigori, but then the man stepped out of the shadows and she realized the only thing the two men had in common was that they were both tall.

"May I help you?" Marisa asked.

"I hope so." He had short blond hair, ice blue eyes, and looked to be in his mid-forties. A thin scar ran along his right cheek. A large silver crucifix hung from a thick chain around his neck. "You are Marisa Richards, are you not?"

"Who wants to know?"

"Forgive me. My name is Edward Ramsey."

Marisa shook her head. The name meant nothing to her. "What do you want?"

"To save your life."

Marisa stared at him in astonishment. Save her life? "I'm sorry, I think you must be looking for someone else."

"I'm looking for two—" A dark shadow appeared in the man's eyes. "Two men. I think you may have seen them."

"Are you a police officer?"

"No."

"You must have me confused with someone else."

"I don't think so." His clear blue eyes met hers with a directness that was disconcerting. "You were at the Roskovich Carnival on Friday last, were you not?"

"Yes, but how did you know?"

His thin lips curved in the slightest of smiles. "I have my ways."

Marisa crossed her arms over her chest. The man had done nothing to frighten her, yet she was frightened just the same. "I think you'd better go now."

Ramsey held up his hands, as if to put her at ease, and she noticed there was a cross tattooed on the palm of the right one.

"Miss Richards, I don't want to worry you, but I fear your life is in danger. Grave danger."

"Maybe you should stop all this cloak-and-dagger stuff and just cut to the chase," Marisa said.

"Very well. If what I suspect is true, Alexi Kristov is following you."

Marisa frowned. "Who?" she asked, wondering why the name sounded so familiar.

"Alexi Kristov. Count Alexi Kristov."

Marisa blinked at Ramsey, and then started to laugh. "Who put you up to this?"

"I beg your pardon?"

"This is a joke, right? Did Grigori send you here?"

"Grigori? Grigori Chiavari?"

"I don't know his last name."

"Is he here?" Ramsey's gaze darted past her to the front door. "Now?"

"No." She took a step backward, wondering if it was safe to open the door, or if he would try to force himself inside.

She glanced over the landing, hoping to see Mr. Abbott watering the front lawn, as was his wont in the evening, but there was no one in sight.

"What's all this nonsense about Alexi Kristov, anyway?" she asked, feeling irritable after a long, hard day at work. "He's dead."

Ramsey nodded. "Indeed, he is."

"You want me to believe that a dead vampire is following me?"

The faintest of grins curved Ramsey's lips. Tiny lines crinkled near his eyes. "I'm afraid there are no other kind."

Marisa stared at him. "What? Oh, right, I guess vampires are dead, aren't they?" She let out a sigh of exasperation. "Listen, you're too late for Halloween and too early for April Fool's, so, if you'll just excuse me—"

"Miss Richards—"

"I don't believe in vampires."

"That does not make them less real, nor does it make the danger to you less great."

"Listen, I don't know what you're up to, or what you're selling, but I find it to be in incredibly bad taste. Now, if you'll excuse me, I've had a long day."

"Miss Richards, please, you must listen to me!"

"I've heard enough." Not willing to turn her back on him, she took a step backward, her hand tightening on her key ring. "If you don't get out of here, I'll scream bloody murder."

Ramsey stared at her a moment, then sighed in resignation. "As you wish." Reaching into his coat pocket, he withdrew a business card. "If you need help, you can reach me at this number. I only hope you call me before it's too late."

He turned and started down the stairs. "If I were you," he called over his shoulder, "I would not leave the shelter of my house after sunset, nor would I go walking in the dark with Grigori Chiavari again."

"What? Wait a minute!"

Ramsey paused on the steps, and then turned to face her.

"What do you mean? Why shouldn't I see Grigori again?"

"He's one of them."

"One of them? You mean a vampire?"

Ramsey nodded. "Good evening, Miss Richards. I hope I see you again."

She was fixing dinner when the phone rang. She knew, even before she picked up the receiver, that it was Grigori. Ramsey's warning flashed through her mind, and for just an instant, she was tempted to hang up. And then she shook her head. Vampires, indeed. The whole idea was ludicrous.

"Marisa?"

"Yes, hello."

"I was wondering if I could interest you in a movie."

"A movie? Tonight?" She hadn't believed a thing Ramsey had told her, yet she was suddenly reluctant to see Grigori again.

"Is something wrong?"

"No, nothing. I'm, ah, just surprised to hear from you."

There was a moment of silence, and she had the eerie feeling that he was reading her mind, that he knew exactly what she was thinking, and why. But that was ridiculous.

She stared at the receiver. "Are you still there?"

"Yes. I should very much like to see you tonight." His voice was warm and thick and sinfully rich, like hot fudge poured over chocolate ice cream.

"I'm really not in the mood for a movie."

"I see."

There was a long silence. Before she quite realized what she was doing, she found herself inviting him to dinner.

"Thank you, I've already eaten, but I'd love to come by and share a glass of wine with you, say, in an hour."

"Okay, see you then."

She replaced the receiver in the cradle, very gently, then stood there, shaking her head. She'd had no intention of inviting him over. Why had she agreed to see him?

She ate quickly, dumped the dishes in the dishwasher, wiped off the sink, then hurriedly straightened up the front room. When that was done, she changed out of her worn jeans and sweatshirt into a pair of white slacks and a short-sleeved blue sweater.

She had just finished putting on her lipstick when she heard a knock at the door.

Smoothing a hand over her hair, she took a deep breath and went to the door. She looked through the peephole to make sure it was Grigori before unlocking the door.

"Hi, come on in."

She stepped back, acutely aware of him as he stepped into the room.

He was wearing black, and she thought she had never seen a man who wore the color so well. But then, all vampires wore black, didn't they? His hair fell past his shoulders. Long and dark, it seemed to emphasize the planes and angles of his face. All he needed was a long black cape, she mused, then shook the thought aside.

With a smile and a flourish, he offered her a bottle of merlot.

"Thank you. Would you care for a glass now?"

"Please."

We're so formal, she mused. Going into the kitchen, she took two glasses from the cupboard. He stood in the doorway, watching her pour the wine. She handed him one of the goblets, wondering if her smile looked as forced as it felt.

"What shall we drink to?" he asked.

"I don't know. Is a toast necessary?"

He shrugged. "Perhaps not." With a slight nod in her direction, he took a drink. "An excellent vintage," he mused.

Marisa took a sip. It was good, far better than she was accustomed to. "Shall we sit down?"

She went into the living room, aware of him behind her, following her. His nearness sent a shiver down her spine.

She sat down on the sofa and sipped her drink.

He sat beside her, close, but not too close, yet she was aware of every line of his body, every breath he took. Never before had she been so aware of another person. Even sitting down, he seemed to tower over her.

Grigori drank his wine slowly, savoring the taste as he savored the woman's nearness. She was lovely. And nervous. He could sense the tension radiating from her. He sat back on the sofa, one arm draped along the top edge, as he glanced around the room. His gaze flickered over the newspaper on the coffee table.

VAMPIRE KILLER STALKS CITY.
BODY FOUND IN DUMPSTER.

Grigori frowned as he quickly scanned the story, which was very short and filled with speculation. This was the eighth body that had been found drained of blood. The press, with its usual flair for the overly dramatic, had labeled the murderer "the vampire killer" because it made good headlines, Grigori mused. If they only knew . . .

"What do you make of that?" Marisa asked, gesturing at the newspaper with her wineglass.

Grigori shrugged. "The noble press," he said with an easy smile. "Surely you don't believe all that nonsense about a bloodthirsty vampire terrorizing the city?"

"No, but . . ."

"But what?"

"Well, it's kind of scary. I mean, the body of the supposed vampire disappeared from the carnival, and then the owner was found dead. And now someone's going around killing people and draining their blood."

She thought of Silvano. She had met him only once, but it was the first time someone she had known had been brutally killed. It made it seem personal somehow.

"I know it's probably another serial killer, but—" She shivered. "It gives me the creeps."

"You'll be safe enough if you stay inside after dark."

"You're the second one who's told me that today."

"Oh?" He looked at her sharply, his eyes narrowing.

"Would you like some more wine?"

Grigori nodded.

Marisa took his glass and stood up, and he followed her into the kitchen.

Resting one shoulder against the doorjamb, Grigori watched her move around the small room. The walls were white, the cabinets of light oak. A small round table and two chairs sat in one corner. There was a green plant in a red clay pot in the center of the table. Cheerful yellow curtains hung at the single window.

"Who else told you to stay inside?"

"I don't know who he was. Some nut named Ramsey."

"What, exactly, did he say?"

"What difference does it make? I told you, he was just some nut."

She handed him one of the goblets, then went into the living room and sat down on the sofa again.

"Tell me, Marisa."

His voice was soft, powerful, compelling.

"He was waiting for me when I got home from work. He said Alexi Kristov was following me and that I shouldn't go out after dark." She laughed, but there was no humor in the sound, and none in her eyes. "Is that the craziest thing you ever heard?"

She looked up at Grigori, hoping he would laugh and tell her she was right, it was just nonsense. But he wasn't laughing.

"What else did he tell you?"

"He said—" Her fingers tightened around the stem of her glass. "He said I shouldn't go walking in the dark with you anymore."

Grigori went very still. She had the impression that he'd even stopped breathing. "Did he say why?"

"No." It was a lie, but she couldn't bring herself to repeat what Ramsey had said. She didn't believe in vampires, but she did believe in evil. Carefully, she put her glass on the coffee table. "I want to know what's going on."

"I'm sure I can't say."

"Can't, or won't?"

Grigori shrugged. "Can't. Won't. What's the difference?"

"Ramsey said he knows you. What else does he know? Why did he tell me not to see you again?"

"You have nothing to fear from me, Marisa."

"That's no answer." She stood up and moved to the other side of the room. "I think you should go."

"As you wish."

Placing his goblet on the table, he turned and walked toward the door. She had never seen anyone who moved the way he did. He moved effortlessly, as if gravity had no control over him, as if there were a cushion of air between his feet and the floor.

He stopped at the door and turned to face her. "Good night, Marisa. Lock the door after me."

"Stop it! Just stop it." She wrapped her arms

around her body in an age-old gesture of self-protection. "I want a straight answer, and I want it now. Who are you? Who's Edward Ramsey? How did he know we went walking in the park? Is he a friend of yours? Why did he say I shouldn't see you again? Dammit, I want to know what's going on!"

He looked at her speculatively. "Do you?"

Not trusting herself to speak, afraid she might change her mind if she reconsidered, Marisa nodded.

"My name is Grigori Chiavari. That much is true."

"And the rest?"

"I'm not here on vacation. I'm hunting the vampyre."

She wanted desperately to laugh but she had a terrible, sinking feeling she might never laugh again. "You're serious, aren't you?"

"Quite. I've been hunting Alexi for a long while."

"But he's . . . he's . . ."

"He's a vampyre, Marisa. A very old, very dangerous vampyre."

She made her way to the sofa and sat down hard. "It's impossible. There's no such thing—"

"I'm afraid there is."

"Are you working with Ramsey?"

"Not exactly. But we both want Alexi dead."

"Why?"

"I have my reasons. You'll have to ask Ramsey about his."

"Ramsey said the vampire was after me. Why? He doesn't even know who I am."

"You cut yourself at the carnival, did you not?"

"Yes, I scratched myself. How did you know?"

He shook his head, his thick black hair swirling around his shoulders like a cloud of dark silk. "It doesn't matter. It was most likely the scent of your blood that awakened him."

"But how?"

"Old vampyres often sleep for a century or two. Perhaps it wasn't your blood that awakened him at all. Perhaps he'd simply rested long enough. I don't know."

"But the man at the carnival . . . Silvano . . . said the vampire was helpless, that he couldn't escape the chains, or the crosses." She looked up at Grigori, desperate for some small measure of reassurance.

"Silvano was right, as far as he knew," Grigori replied thoughtfully. "But Alexi is far older than Silvano knew. I'm not sure anything can defeat Kristov. As for the chains, I'm guessing that Alexi mesmerized Silvano, then ordered the man to free him."

"He could do that?"

"That and more."

Grigori looked past the woman, gazing into the distance, his thoughts turned inward. Even without feeding for a century or two, it would have been a simple thing for Alexi to bend Silvano's will to his own, to compel him to remove the crosses and the chains that imprisoned him. And while Silvano was still enthralled, Alexi would have drunk from him, drunk until nothing remained of the man but a dry husk.

Even as he considered it, Grigori knew that was how it had happened. He could picture it all in his mind, the vampyre's eyes opening, his hypnotic gaze meeting Silvano's, his mind bending the mortal's will to his own, compelling Silvano to remove the holy relics, to release him from the chains that bound him. He would have climbed out of the coffin, his skeletal fingers clamping over Silvano's shoulders, tilting the man's head to the side, burying his fangs in the soft flesh of Silvano's throat as he fed a hunger that would have been growing for a hundred years. . . .

"You're really serious about this, aren't you?"

Marisa's voice brought him back to the present. "Quite."

Marisa glanced around the room. The dead bolt on her front door seemed woefully inadequate; the windows made her feel exposed, vulnerable.

"Be sure to lock your door after I'm gone."

"Wait!" She didn't believe him, couldn't believe him. It was completely impossible. Yet she was loath to spend the night alone. "Please stay."

"You should be safe, so long as you don't invite him inside."

"Why? What's to keep him out? If all those chains couldn't keep him locked up, I'm sure the puny locks on my door won't give him any trouble."

"There are a great many beliefs about vampyres, about what they can and cannot do. Most of them are fables told to frighten children; a few are true. Alexi cannot enter your house unless you invite him inside. He must seek shelter from the sun, although, as old as he is now, he may no longer succumb to the dark sleep. A cross will offer only as much protection as the wearer's faith in it. Silver will burn his flesh, but he will heal quickly. He must have blood to survive, although he can go without it for long periods of time." He paused, as though considering what else to tell her. "Some vampyres have the power to change shape; others have the power to fly."

"What about crossing running water and not casting a reflection in a mirror?"

"Nothing but fables, as is the ridiculous notion that if you wrap a vampyre in a net or fill his coffin with seeds, he will be forced to untie all the knots or collect all the seeds at the rate of one a year before he can leave his grave."

"What about garlic repelling vampires?"

He shook his head. "It bothers them no more than you."

She looked at him suspiciously. "How do you know all this?"

He glided across the floor toward her. Standing there, he looked tall and dangerous and invulnerable. "I told you, I've been hunting him a very long time."

"Ramsey said—" She took a deep breath, wondering if she was making a fatal mistake. "He said you're one of them, a vampire."

"Indeed?"

She waited for him to deny it, her heart pounding fiercely. "Is it true?"

He considered the truth and opted for a lie. "No."

She laughed, tension flowing out of her. Of course he wasn't a vampire.

"Why don't you join up with Ramsey?"

Grigori's expression softened to one of wry amusement. "In a way, we are working together. He hunts the days, and I hunt the nights."

"Would you mind spending the night here? I really don't want to be alone."

Grigori looked at her for a long moment. She was a pretty woman, soft and curvy, beautiful in a quiet way that he found most appealing. "If you're sure."

She looked up at him, aware that he was little more than a stranger, and wondered if she'd done the right thing.

He sat down in the big, overstuffed chair next to the sofa and stretched out his legs.

His presence dwarfed the room, made it suddenly difficult to draw breath. Discomfited, she reached for the remote and switched on the TV.

". . . bodies found earlier this evening in a ravine in La Habra Heights. Police are holding identification of the two women pending notification of next of kin. In other news . . ."

Marisa stared at the television screen. "No," she whispered. "Not again." She looked at Grigori. "It's all my fault."

"No."

She nodded, her eyes filling with tears. "It is," she said emphatically. "I know it is."

She waited for him to say something, hoping he could ease her guilt, but he wasn't looking at her. He was staring at the front door, his whole body tense, as if poised for flight.

And then she felt it, that same sense of evil she had experienced once before. "What is it? What's wrong?"

He rose to his feet in a single, fluid movement. "Lock the door behind me."

"Where are you going?"

"Just do as I say," he said brusquely, and then he was gone.

Heart pounding, Marisa locked the door, and

then slid the safety chain in place. Too nervous to sit down and wait, she went from room to room, checking to make sure all the windows were closed and locked. She closed the curtains in the bedrooms and kitchen, drew the drapes in the living room, checked the lock on the front door again. And then, at a loss for something to do, she sat on the sofa, pulled a furry Mickey Mouse blanket up to her chin, and stared at the door.

She had convinced herself that the evil she had sensed in the laundry room the other night had been nothing more than the product of her imagination, but she knew now that it had been real. And that it had a name.

Alexi Kristov.

Chapter Six

Grigori walked swiftly down the stairs to the street, then paused on the sidewalk, all his senses alert.

"Alexi, show yourself." He whirled around as the sound of soft laughter was carried to him by a sudden gust of wind. "Alexi, damn you, show yourself!"

"I'm here."

Grigori spun around, his whole body tense, poised for attack.

A fine gray mist materialized out of the deep shadows of the night, then coalesced into the form of a man, a man Grigori recognized all too well.

"Alexi."

The count bowed from the waist. He looked like an old-world aristocrat in a full-sleeved white shirt open at the throat, tight black breeches, and soft black leather boots.

"Grigori, my old friend. We meet again."

Grigori nodded curtly. He had not felt fear in over a hundred years, not since the last time he had encountered Kristov.

Alexi's cold gray gaze ran over him, like ice running down his spine. "Will you never give up?"

"Never."

Mocking laughter rose in the count's throat. "I fear that foolish tenacity that you call honor will be the means of your destruction."

"Perhaps. How did you escape Silvano?"

A sound of derision rose in Kristov's throat. "An easy task, I assure you. I rested for a hundred years, closely guarded at all times so I had no worry of being destroyed." A cruel smile twisted his lips. "He was a fool to think he could hold me against my will. Stupid mortal. He paid dearly for his foolishness. Did you know Ramsey is in the city?"

Grigori nodded.

"I shall have you," Kristov said, his eyes glowing with confidence. "When I am ready, I shall have you both."

"No."

"Oh, yes," Alexi said with complete and utter assurance. He glanced up at Marisa's apartment and licked his lips. "And the woman, as well."

"No. Leave the woman alone. This is between you and me."

The count shook his head. "It was the scent of her sweet blood that roused me from my sleep. I will not rest again until I have had her, until her blood feeds my hunger and burns in my soul. She will serve me well, don't you think?"

"Let us end it now!"

"No, it is too soon. I feel the need for some amusement after my long rest, and you and Ramsey will provide it for me. And the woman—" Alexi licked his lips—"she will provide amusement of another kind."

"No!" A low growl rose in Grigori's throat as he

lunged forward, his fangs bared, his hands like claws reaching for Alexi's throat. He felt a sharp pain as Kristov lashed out, his nails raking across Grigori's face, opening five deep lacerations that stretched from Grigori's hairline to his jaw.

Grigori shook his head, flinging the blood out of his eyes.

"Alexi!" He roared the vampyre's name, unleashing his pain and anger, but Kristov was gone as if he had never been there.

Swearing under his breath, he went back up the stairs to Marisa's apartment.

After asking who it was, she opened the door, her eyes widening in horror when she saw the blood dripping from his face. "Grigori, what happened?"

"Alexi happened."

"He was here?" She slammed the door and shot the bolt home.

"He's gone now."

"You're sure?"

Grigori nodded.

On legs that felt none too steady, Marisa made her way into the bathroom. Pulling a washcloth from the shelf, she soaked it in cold water, then went back into the living room. Grigori was sitting on the sofa, staring at the door.

Sitting beside him, she began to wipe the blood from Grigori's face. "You'll probably need stitches," she remarked, yet even as she watched, the deep gashes that scored his cheek began to close. It was like watching a film in fast forward, she thought, the way muscle and tissue knit together.

"This—" She stood up and backed away from

him, the washcloth falling, unheeded, from her hand. "It isn't possible."

"I'm afraid it's very possible," Grigori replied.

"It's true, then," she murmured. "All true. Everything Ramsey told me. Everything he said."

"Are you all right?"

"I don't know." She stared at his face. "It's true, isn't it? You are one of them."

Grigori nodded. He would have preferred she not know the truth, but there was no help for it now. He considered erasing the memory from her mind, but as he considered it, he decided it might be better if she was fully aware of the danger that surrounded her.

"You look a trifle pale," Grigori remarked. "I think you'd better sit down."

"Yes," she replied, "I think you're right."

He caught her just before she hit the floor.

Grigori sat on the floor in Marisa's bedroom, his back against the dresser, watching her sleep. She had roused from her faint and he had insisted she go to bed. She hadn't argued. He knew it was the mortal way, to seek refuge in sleep.

The mortal way. He had been Vampyre so long, it was hard to remember a time when he had been anything else, a time when he had been a mortal man, with a home and a family. . . .

Rising, he went to the window and drew back the curtains.

The darkness waited outside, silently beckoning to him. Come, the night wind seemed to say, come and share the night with me.

It was tempting, but he had promised Marisa he would stay with her.

He stared into the distance, his thoughts traveling back through the centuries, back to the time when he had been a husband and a father. He closed his eyes, and Antoinette's image rose in his mind, as fresh and vivid as if he had seen her only hours ago—hair as black as a midnight sky, eyes that were blue-green, as changeable as the sea. And his children—Antonio and Martina—so young, so innocent.

His hands curled into tight fists, his nails digging into his flesh, as he recalled the last time he had seen them, their bodies sprawled like rag dolls across their beds, drained of blood, of life. Alexi Kristov had stood in the doorway, his mouth stained crimson, his eyes red and feverish from the kill.

"It's true, then," Grigori had said, horrified. He had heard all the stories, listened to the rumors and whispers that had been rife in the village, but he had not believed it was true. Alexi had been his friend, and Grigori had found a logical explanation for every accusation made against Alexi. "All true," he had said again. "You are a vampyre."

Kristov had nodded, his gray eyes cold and distant.

"Antoinette . . ."

Grigori reached toward her, but Alexi waved him off.

"She is mine now."

"No." Yet even as he denied it, he knew it was true. Antoinette looked at him through pale, soulless eyes while drops of blood oozed from two tiny wounds in her neck. Not human, not vampyre, she was no longer his wife, no longer the vivacious girl he had fallen in love with. She had become Alexi's creature. Had the vampyre commanded, Grigori knew she would have killed him.

"Why?" Just that one anguished word, torn from the depths of his heart and soul.

Alexi did not answer. Taking Antoinette by the hand, he turned as if to leave. With a cry, Grigori lunged forward, his only thought to destroy the creature who had killed all he loved.

With a hiss, Alexi whirled around, a wicked gleam in his eye, his hands pinning Grigori's arms to his sides. "Are you so eager to die, Chiavari?"

"I'll kill you for what you've done!"

Alexi laughed. "You? Kill me? I think not."

Grigori struggled to free himself, but Alexi held him effortlessly.

"You have no strength against me," Alexi taunted. With blinding speed, he wrapped his hands around Grigori's throat, lifting him off his feet as his fingers slowly squeezed the breath from his body. "Perhaps I should bring you over," he hissed. "Then you would understand."

Grigori glared at the vampyre. "I understand you're a monster."

Alexi's gray eyes changed then, smoldering, until they glowed a hideous red. His lips drew back, revealing his fangs.

He should have been afraid, but he was too filled with anger and despair to feel anything but hatred. "Go on, do it!" he screamed. "Make me what you are so I can kill you!"

"I think not," Alexi replied. "Were you Vampyre, I think you would pursue me through eternity. But killing you now would be too kind."

Grigori struggled to free himself as Alexi's hands tightened around his throat, choking the breath from his body, until he felt himself falling, falling, into darkness. As from a great distance, he heard Alexi's mocking voice.

"I shall let you live for now, Chiavari. Life will be far more painful for you than death."

When he had awakened, the vampyre was gone. He had never seen Antoinette again. . . .

Grigori opened his eyes as he felt the dawn approaching. It was time to go.

He checked to make sure Marisa was still asleep. She looked beautiful, vulnerable, lying there, her lashes like dark crescents against her skin, her lips warm and pink. He took a deep breath, inhaling her scent—sleep-warmed skin, a faint trace of the flowery cologne she preferred. His gaze lingered on her throat, on the pulse beating there.

Hunger stirred within him. Bending low, he brushed a lock of hair from her neck, felt the anticipation grow as his fangs lengthened. Just one drink . . .

A soft sigh escaped her lips as she came awake, and he found himself gazing into her eyes.

"Go back to sleep, Marisa," he murmured, his voice low. "Go back to sleep."

With a soft sigh, her eyelids fluttered down once more.

Moments later, he was gone.

Marisa blinked, closed her eyes, and opened them again. It must have been a dream, she thought, or a nightmare. She sat up, her gaze darting around the room, but there was no one there. Yet she would have sworn that Grigori had been at her bedside, bending over her. Had it all been a dream? She had a hazy recollection of his voice telling her to sleep. She had felt the brush of his mouth against her neck, a warm intimacy, a sense of fulfillment. . . .

With a shake of her head, she got up and padded into the living room. "Grigori?"

He wasn't there. She went into the kitchen, but he wasn't there, either. Perhaps he'd had an early appointment, she thought as she fixed herself a cup of coffee. And then, in a rush, everything that had happened the night before came back to her.

Grigori telling her that Alexi Kristov was after her, that vampires were real. She recalled feeling that same sense of evil she had felt once before. Grigori had rushed out of her apartment, only to return a short time later, his face cut to ribbons.

She drew back the curtains and stared out the kitchen window, but it wasn't the building next door she saw; it was the long scratches in Grigori's face, healing before her very eyes.

Maybe she had dreamed it, as she had dreamed he was bending over her. That had to be it. What she'd seen, what she *thought* she had seen, was impossible.

She drained her cup and poured another. Going into the living room, she sat down on the sofa, felt a sudden chill as she saw the washrag on the coffee table. The reddish brown stain looked very dark, very ominous, against the white terry cloth.

It had been real, all of it.

Feeling light-headed, she put her cup on the coffee table. There had to be a logical explanation. There simply had to be.

She just wished she knew what it was.

* * *

Edward Ramsey was waiting for her when she stepped out of the elevator after work that night. Dressed in brown slacks, a white shirt, and a paisley tie, his brown hair neatly combed, he blended in with the other men heading home after a day at the office.

"Miss Richards."

Marisa glanced around, hoping to find a security guard. "What do you want?"

"I wondered if you'd thought about what we discussed."

"I don't want to talk about it." She swept past him, reaching into her pocket for her car keys as she went.

He fell into step behind her.

Her hand was shaking as she unlocked the car, then slid behind the wheel, slammed the door shut, and locked it.

She glanced in the rearview mirror as she pulled out of the parking lot onto the street. A dark blue Chevy followed her out of the driveway. Ramsey was in the driver's seat.

She thought of going to the police, of driving around until she lost him, but there seemed no point in it. He knew where she lived, and she had to go home sooner or later.

She pulled into her parking space, noticing, as she did so, that Ramsey parked at the curb in front of the building.

He was waiting for her when she reached the stairs.

"Mr. Ramsey, what is it you want?"

"Nothing, Miss Richards. I simply wanted to see you safely home."

"Oh. Well, I . . . thank you."

"And to give you this."

Marisa stared at the cross on a chain he offered her. It was about an inch wide and an inch and a half long. She knew without asking that both the cross and the chain were made of pure silver.

She wanted to refuse it, knowing that, if she took it, she would be admitting she believed in vampires, believed what Ramsey had told her.

"Please wear it," Ramsey said. "If not for your own protection, then for my peace of mind."

"Oh, all right."

"Here, let me put it on for you."

She turned around, feeling foolish, as he fastened the heavy silver chain around her neck. The metal felt cool against her skin.

"I shall be in my car if you need me. You have my number?"

Marisa nodded.

"Have a good evening, Miss Richards."

"Thank you."

Conscious of his gaze on her back, she climbed the stairs and went into her apartment. Tossing her handbag on the sofa, she went to the window and drew back the drapes, one hand fingering the chain around her neck. She could see Ramsey sitting in his car.

With a shake of her head, she changed out of her work clothes into a pair of jeans and a T-shirt. She started to remove the cross, but it gave her an odd sense of security, so she tucked it out of sight beneath her T-shirt, and then went into the kitchen to see about dinner.

She went to the window several times. It made her feel funny, having Ramsey sitting out there, guarding her. But, as night began to steal across the city, she was suddenly glad of his presence.

When dinner was ready, she picked up the phone and dialed the number he had given her.

"Mr. Ramsey? This is Marisa Richards. Would you like to come up and have something to eat?"

There was a slight pause. She could imagine him staring at the receiver in surprise.

"Mr. Ramsey?"

"Yes, thank you."

A few moments later, he was knocking at her door.

Marisa opened the door, wondering if she had done the right thing. "Come in. Dinner's ready. I hope you like pork chops and scalloped potatoes."

Ramsey followed her into the kitchen, sat down at her invitation.

Marisa sat down across from him. He was a nice-looking man, she decided. Not one you'd notice in a crowd, but handsome in a quiet sort of way.

For a time, they ate in silence. It made her nervous, having a stranger in the house.

"Why are you hunting the vampire?" she asked when the silence grew too loud.

"A vampire destroyed a young woman I once held dear."

"You can't mean Kristov. He's been helpless for a hundred years."

"No, it wasn't Kristov."

Marisa swallowed the lump rising in her throat. "You mean there are more of them?"

Ramsey nodded, his expression somber. "I destroyed the vampire who killed my friend, and I shall destroy Kristov, as well. They are evil, all of them."

"You think he'll come here again, don't you? Kristov, that is?"

"He has been here."

"How do you know?"

"I know." His pale blue eyes met hers. "Am I wrong?"

"No, he was here last night."

"Have you seen Grigori again?"

"Are you going to kill him, too?"

"Yes," he replied mildly, "when the time is right."

She blinked at him, amazed that he spoke of it so calmly. "Why?"

"Why?" Ramsey looked surprised by the question. "Why, because he's a vampire, of course."

Marisa shook her head. In spite of what she had seen last night, in spite of everything Grigori had said, she didn't want to believe it.

"It's true." Ramsey looked at her sharply. "Chiavari's been here again, hasn't he?"

"Last night."

Briefly, she told him what had happened the night before, how Grigori had gone out after Alexi and come back, his cheek gouged and bleeding, how the bone-deep cuts had healed before her eyes.

She waited, hoping that Ramsey would tell her she must have imagined the whole thing.

"You saw," he said, "and you still don't want to believe."

"It just seems so impossible." She shook her head. "How long have you been hunting vampires?"

"Since I was sixteen."

"Sixteen! What did your parents say?"

"It is what we do," Edward said. "Ramseys have been hunting vampires for hundreds of years. It is our gift, our curse. Our destiny."

"Your gift?"

"To be able to sense their presence."

"Then why haven't you been able to find Alexi?"

"I don't know. It troubles me." He speared a piece of meat, chewed it thoughtfully. "Is Grigori coming here tonight?"

"I don't know. He didn't say."

Ramsey lifted his head. "He's here."

"Who's here?" Marisa asked, her heart pounding, though she knew it wasn't Alexi. She would have recognized his evil presence.

"Chiavari."

"Are you sure?" Even as she asked the question, there was a knock at the door. "What should I do?"

"Let him in," Ramsey said. "He's on our side."

Marisa stared at the man. The words *for the time being* seemed to hover, unspoken, in the air between them.

He's a vampire. The words screamed in her mind as she went to open the front door.

"Good evening," Grigori said.

"Hi." She looked up at him, wondering how a man who was so handsome, who exuded such vibrant masculinity, could be one of the undead. He was dressed in a pair of gray slacks, a white shirt open at the collar, black loafers.

"May I come in?"

A burst of hysterical laughter bubbled up inside Marisa. It was too late to refuse him entrance to her house. She moved aside, then shut the door after him. "I have company," she said.

"Oh?"

Marisa nodded. "We just had dinner. Would you care to join us for coffee?" She couldn't help it; she giggled. "I guess you don't drink coffee."

"No." Grigori's eyes narrowed as he studied her.

Marisa swallowed hard, then turned and headed for the kitchen.

Ramsey was standing beside the table, one hand fisted around the crucifix that dangled from a chain around his neck.

Grigori grunted softly when he saw the vampire hunter.

Marisa stood at the counter, glancing from one man to the other. Whoever said looks were deceiving had certainly been right. Ramsey, pale and mild mannered, looked more like a bank teller than a vampire hunter. And Grigori—tall and dark and confident, always well dressed—looked like he should be on the front cover of *GQ*.

"I guess you two know each other," Marisa said.

Grigori nodded curtly. "Ramsey."

"Chiavari," Ramsey replied, his tone equally blunt. "Miss Richards tells me Alexi was here last night."

Grigori stroked his cheek absently, and Marisa noticed the gashes had healed without a trace.

"Yes," Grigori replied. "He knows you're in the city. Be careful."

"He was here, and you let him get away!"

"I didn't *let* him get away, and you know it. He's more powerful than the last time we met. I'm not sure he can be destroyed."

"Have you lost your courage after all these years, Chiavari?"

"I've lost nothing," Grigori replied quietly. "No one wants him dead more than I."

Ramsey's hand tightened around the cross, his knuckles going white. "We must find where he rests during the day."

"That's supposed to be your job."

"Stop it, both of you!" Marisa stepped between the two men. "This isn't solving anything."

"You're right, Miss Richards; forgive me."

"You can go home now, Edward," Grigori said. "I'll keep an eye on Marisa."

Ramsey's gaze rested on Grigori for a long, speculative moment, and then he turned toward Marisa. "Do you wish me to stay?"

"I'll be all right," Marisa said, hoping she was telling the truth. "Thank you."

"Very well. Good night, Miss Richards. Thank you for dinner."

"You're welcome."

Ramsey glanced at Grigori again, then nodded at Marisa. "I can find my way out."

Marisa watched Ramsey exit the kitchen, then turned to face Grigori. "I thought you two were supposed to be working together."

"We are." Grigori grinned wryly. "I'm afraid we're both a little on edge."

"A *little* on edge," Marisa muttered. "That's got to be the understatement of the year."

Chapter Seven

"Well," Marisa said, suddenly ill at ease to find herself and Grigori alone in the house, "do you want to watch some TV?"

As soon as the words were out of her mouth, she felt a flood of color climb up her neck into her cheeks. Did vampires watch TV? Did she really believe he was one of the undead? Looking at him made the idea seem ludicrous. She had never seen anyone, male or female, who looked more vital, more alive.

He grinned at her, as if he knew what she was thinking.

Marisa brushed by him, eager to have something else to focus on. Picking up the *TV Guide*, she thumbed through the pages, scanning the listings for Friday night.

"Bruce Springsteen was right," she muttered, "fifty-seven stations and there's nothing on."

She jumped as the TV crackled to life. She hadn't turned it on; the remote was on top of the set. "How did you do that?"

He lifted one brow, and shrugged. "I told you, I'm a magician."

She sat down on the sofa, as far from him as

she could get, her hands tightly clasped in her lap. The theme for *The X-Files* provided a momentary distraction.

"Is it true? Are you really a vampire, like Ramsey said?"

He hesitated only a moment, but there seemed no point in denying it, not after what she'd heard, what she'd seen. "Yes."

The world seemed to shift somehow, and she knew, in that instant, that her life would never be the same again.

"Do you . . . do you drink blood?"

"When I must."

He spoke so calmly, as if his reply were an ordinary answer to an ordinary question.

She stared at him, speechless. He was a vampire. Dead but not dead. He drank human blood. . . . It was beyond comprehension. She tried to tell herself it couldn't be true even though she knew, deep in her heart, that it was.

"And do you . . . do you sleep in a coffin?"

He lifted one brow. "Would you?"

"Of course not. What are you going to do with me?" Visions of sharp fangs piercing her throat rose up in her mind.

He lifted one thick black brow. "Do with you?"

She raised a hand to her throat, the gesture more eloquent than words.

"Afraid I'm going to drink you dry?" he asked, a slight smile curving his lips.

"Are you?"

"Not tonight." He shook his head at her look of horror. "I was joking, Marisa. I'm not going to hurt you."

"I'd like to believe that," she muttered under her breath.

"Believe it. I mean you no harm."

His voice seemed to wrap around her, caressing her skin, light and soft as dandelion down. His eyes . . . she had never seen eyes so deep, so dark, so mesmerizing. Black flames burned in his eyes, threatening to scorch her, to engulf her until there was nothing left but smoldering ash. They seemed to call to her, promising her the secrets of eternity.

Marisa took a deep, shuddering breath. She could hear her heart pounding like thunder in her ears, feel herself succumbing to the dark power that blazed in his fathomless black eyes. She tried to look away, her heart beating triple time when she discovered she could not draw her gaze from his.

"Stop it," she said with a gasp. "Please . . ."

The twin flames in his eyes burned brighter, then vanished.

Grigori took a deep breath as he broke the connection between them. Sensing she would welcome some distance between them, he stood up and walked to the far side of the room.

"I'm sorry."

Had he said the words aloud, or had she only imagined them?

Marisa crossed her arms over her chest. She was alone in the house with a vampire. Silence stretched between them. What was he sorry for? Had he been trying to hypnotize her? What did one say to a vampire? A thousand questions tumbled through her mind. She grabbed the closest one. "Where did you meet Ramsey?"

"He seemed to turn up in all the same places I

did," Grigori replied. "One night I approached him and asked him why he was following me. At first, he refused to tell me anything." He shrugged. "Eventually, he decided to tell me what I wanted to know."

Marisa shuddered as she imagined how Grigori had "convinced" Ramsey to talk.

Grigori looked at her and sighed. No doubt she would always expect the worst of him, but then, he couldn't blame her. He was, after all, a vampyre. No doubt she considered him a threat to her very existence. With reluctance, he admitted she had every reason to think so. Never, in two hundred years, had he bequeathed the Dark Gift to another, but Marisa tempted him sorely.

"When Ramsey discovered we were after the same thing, he decided to work with me."

"Silvano told me that Alexi had been in their family for generations."

"That's true. At one time, they kept him deep in the vault of a church. The burden of looking after him fell to the oldest male member of the family. Last year, their family fell on hard times. As head of the family, Silvano decided to take Alexi on tour. Not a very wise decision. I didn't know they had left the country until six months ago." A muscle twitched in his jaw. "I found Alexi three days too late."

"Do you think you'll be able to destroy him?"

"I hope so."

"Ramsey said he's destroyed other vampires."

"He told you about Katherine?"

"Was that her name? All he said was that a vampire had killed a friend of his." Marisa shook her head. It was so unreal, sitting here having a conversation about vampires. Until a few days ago, she would have sworn there was no such thing. Vampires had been nothing but fiction, creatures of legend, the things scary movies and nightmares were made of.

Her gaze slid over Grigori. How could someone—something—that was so outrageously handsome be one of the undead? "Are there lots of vampires running around?"

"Not many." He sat down in the overstuffed chair across from the sofa. "To my knowledge, there are only two of us in the city."

"That's two too many, if you ask me," Marisa muttered. She risked a glance at Grigori, felt her cheeks grow warm as he lifted one brow in an expression she was beginning to recognize as wry amusement.

"If Ramsey has his way, your city will soon be free of us both."

"You know he's thinking of destroying you?" Marisa exclaimed, surprised that he seemed so unconcerned.

"Of course. It's what he does. Our liaison is quite temporary."

"You're not worried?"

"No."

"Why not? If he's killed other vampires, what makes you think he won't kill you, too?"

Grigori shrugged. "The vampyre who killed Katherine was newly made. The young among us are vulnerable; sometimes they foolishly believe they cannot be destroyed. Sometimes they forget to be careful who they trust, where they choose to take their rest. Such carelessness is usually fatal."

"But that's not the only one he's killed. He must know what he's doing."

"Can I hope this concern means you are worried about my safety?"

"Of course not. Well, maybe a little." She blew out a deep breath. She didn't know what to think. It was all so confusing. True, yet beyond belief.

Clutching one of the sofa pillows to her chest, Marisa stared at the TV screen, thinking this sort of thing would be right up Fox Mulder's alley. She only wished she knew how to cope with it.

She slid a furtive glance at Grigori. He seemed engrossed in the program. How long had he been a vampire? Had it been a choice he'd made? Did he like it?

Questions, so many questions. They made her head ache. "I'm going to bed." She stood up, eyeing him warily. "Are you going to spend the night?"

"If you wish." He rose to his feet in a fluid motion that reminded her of water flowing over a dam.

She chewed on the inside of her lip, wondering which posed the greater threat, the vampire inside the house, or the one who might even now be prowling the shadows of the night.

"I'll get you some blankets," she said.

"Don't bother." His voice held a note of amusement.

"It's no bother."

"The night is my day," he reminded her softly. "Sleep well, Marisa."

"Right," she muttered. As if she could sleep at all, with a card-carrying, bloodsucking vampire in the house.

Grigori grunted softly as he watched her leave the room. Bloodsucking vampire indeed, he mused, and felt his fangs prick his tongue at the image that thought conveyed. He had not yet fed. Crossing the floor, he gazed out the window and let his supernatural powers peruse the night. The darkness beckoned him. A thousand beating hearts called to him.

With a sigh, he sank down on the sofa, his head resting on the back, his eyes closed. He could hear Marisa getting ready for bed, could track her movements by the sounds she made as she brushed her teeth, washed her face, brushed her hair. He heard the rasp of cloth as she removed her clothes, the whisper-soft brush of silk sliding over skin as she put on her nightgown, the rustle of crisp cotton sheets as she slid into bed. He could hear the sound of her breathing, the steady beat of her heart.

He took a deep breath and his nostrils filled with a plethora of odors—the food she had cooked for dinner, the soap she used to wash her dishes, the scent of the flowers on the kitchen table, the dirty clothes in the hamper, the clean clothes in her closet. And, over all, the smell of the woman herself—the fear she tried to hide, the perfume and hairspray, shampoo and soap and toothpaste she had used during the day, the warmth of her body. Her blood . . . it was a temptation he was hard-pressed to resist, an enticement that pulsed and glowed with every breath she took.

He drew his thoughts from her and concentrated on Alexi Kristov instead. As always, thoughts of Alexi brought Antoinette to mind, and renewed the pain of not knowing how she had died. Had Alexi killed her quickly, mercifully, or had he left her alone, a soulless creature with no will, no mind of her own? Left her to wander in darkness, lost and alone? Had she died of hunger and neglect? Had she been stoned by a mob of frightened villagers? Burned as a witch?

"Antoinette . . ." He groaned deep within himself as the grotesque images filled his mind.

Rage flowed through him, burning white-hot, searing him from the inside out. Anger fed the hunger within him, driving him to his feet, out of Marisa's apartment, and into the night.

Marisa woke with a start, her body drenched in perspiration, the sound of her own scream echoing in her ears. With a trembling hand, she switched on the bedside lamp, her gaze darting around the room as she drew in several deep breaths. Only a dream, only a dream . . . but it had seemed so real, and been so horrible.

Disjointed images flooded her mind . . . a woman walking along the beach under a full moon . . . a dark shadow swooping down on her like some monstrous bird of prey . . . the woman's cry of terror . . . bloodred eyes . . . sharp fangs piercing the fragile skin of the woman's throat. . . .

Marisa shook her head to clear it. Knowing she'd never get back to sleep, she went into the kitchen and brewed a pot of tea. She was pouring herself a cup when she remembered Grigori.

Taking the cup with her, she went into the living room and turned on the light. The room was empty, the door was locked, the safety chain in place. The windows were closed.

She checked the spare bedroom, but he wasn't there, either.

Frowning, she returned to the living room and sat down on the sofa. The clock on the VCR showed it was almost three A.M.

"Some bodyguard," she muttered. Where had he gone, and why?

The answer burned itself into her mind, as vivid as the images of her nightmare.

He was a predator, and he had gone out to hunt the night.

Chapter Eight

He blended with the changing shadows of the night. His footsteps made no sound on the damp pavement. The ocean's salty tang filled his nostrils; he could taste it on the back of his tongue.

He smelled the woman before he saw her, and then he was there, walking beside her, smiling at her, mesmerizing her with his eyes.

With a low moan, she tilted her head back and offered him her throat. And he took it, his teeth sinking into her soft flesh, the sound of her scream blending with the sound of the waves crashing against the shore.

And he drank and drank and drank, until she was cold and empty, and he was warm, filled with the essence of her life force.

Chapter Nine

Marisa rose early after a sleepless night, glad that she didn't have to go to work. Last night, she had gone back to bed, only to toss and turn until dawn. Every time she closed her eyes, she had pictured Grigori bending over the woman who had haunted her nightmares, his fangs buried in the woman's neck as he drained her body of blood, of life.

Slipping on her robe, she went out to get the paper. Carrying it into the kitchen, she poured herself a cup of coffee, then spread the newspaper out on the table. The headlines screamed at her:

VAMPIRE KILLER STRIKES AGAIN
ELEVEN DEATHS NOW ATTRIBUTED TO SERIAL KILLER

Even before she read the story, she knew what it was going to say, knew that what she had dreamed hadn't been a nightmare at all. The woman's body had been found in a dumpster near Huntington Beach. There were two puncture wounds in her neck; she had been drained of blood. Time of death had been put at sometime between two and three A.M. No witness had come forward.

Marisa swallowed the nausea rising in her throat as she stared at the grainy black-and-white photo.

Needing something to occupy her mind, she dressed in a pair of sweats, and then turned her attention to cleaning the apartment. She put the soundtrack to *Joseph and the Amazing Technicolor Dreamcoat* on the CD player and set to work. She mopped the floors in the kitchen and the bathroom, dusted the furniture, vacuumed the rugs, changed the sheets on the bed, cleaned out the refrigerator.

And always, in the back of her mind, she could see the image of the woman she had dreamed about, the woman on the beach. What had the victim's last thoughts been before that monster sank his fangs into her neck? Had it hurt? Had she been terrified, or had the vampire clouded her mind with his power?

That monster . . . She rinsed her hands in the sink, and began replacing the refrigerator's contents. It was hard to picture Grigori as a monster. He was by far the most handsome man she had ever met. Tall and dark and mysterious. And dead. Or undead.

She knew it was true, yet standing in her kitchen in the bright light of day, it seemed preposterous. Vampires roaming the streets of Los Angeles.

She wiped her hands, then went into the bedroom and changed her clothes. She had to get out of the house. She needed to be surrounded by people. Needed to be out in the sunshine.

Grabbing her handbag and her keys, she left her apartment. The late-afternoon sun felt delicious on her skin, and she stood on the landing for a moment, basking in its warmth.

"Afternoon, Miss Richards."

She peered over the balcony to see her landlord watering the lawn. "Hi, Mr. Abbott."

"Pretty day," he remarked, glancing at the sky. "Thought it might rain this morning."

Marisa walked down the stairs and went to stand beside him, careful not to get her shoes wet. "Hard to believe it's November already."

Abbott nodded. "Be Christmas soon. Where does the time go?"

"I don't know."

"So, where you headed this fine day?"

"Nowhere in particular. I think I might do a little shopping."

Abbott nodded again. "Christmas seems to come earlier every year."

"Ain't it the truth. Talk to you later."

"So long."

The mall was crowded. Marisa felt her spirits lift as she joined the holiday throng. Christmas music came over the speakers; the stores were decorated with the usual Santas and reindeer and snowmen. She bought a lavender pantsuit for her mother, a gray sweater and a couple of conservative ties for her father, a Cross pen and pencil set for her boss. It was dark when she left the mall.

She was singing "Have Yourself a Merry Little Christmas" when she climbed the stairs to her apartment.

The words died in her throat when she saw Edward Ramsey waiting for her at her door.

"Good evening, Miss Richards."

"Hello, Mr. Ramsey. Is something wrong?"

He lifted one brow as he regarded the gaily wrapped presents bulging from several shopping bags. She read the silent condemnation in his eyes. A murderer was stalking the city, and she had been out shopping as if it were a day like any other.

"Is it possible you haven't heard the latest news?"

A shiver ran down Marisa's spine. "Not another one?"

He nodded, his expression somber. "They found another body less than an hour ago."

"Another woman?"

"A teenage girl."

"That's twelve in little more than a week."

Ramsey nodded. His eyes, usually so mild, blazed with impotent fury. "I can't believe it's all Alexi's doing."

"What do you mean?"

"Do I have to spell it out for you, Miss Richards?"

She stared at him, remembering her nightmare. Whether she liked it or not, whether she wanted to admit it or not, Grigori was a vampire. And like Alexi, he needed blood to survive.

"You don't think Alexi is the only one involved in the killings." She felt suddenly, utterly weary. "You think Grigori's responsible for some of them, don't you?" Unlocking the door, she entered her apartment. "Come on in." She dropped her shopping bags on the floor and went into the kitchen.

Ramsey closed and locked the door, then followed her into the room. He stood in the doorway, his arms crossed over his chest, watching while she filled the coffeemaker with water.

"Twelve deaths in a week is a lot," Ramsey remarked. "Even for a fiend like Kristov."

"Is it? I wouldn't know."

"I would."

Marisa went into the living room and sat down on the sofa. She had been alone in her apartment with Grigori for the last two nights. Alone with a man who was really a monster in spite of his handsome facade.

She practically jumped out of her skin when the doorbell rang.

"Are you expecting Chiavari?" Ramsey asked.

"No."

"Wait here. I'll get it."

"All right." She clasped her hands to still their trembling, her whole body tensing with trepidation as she heard Grigori's voice.

And then he was there, looming over her. As always, his presence seemed to fill the room. It took all the courage she possessed to meet his eyes.

"What's wrong?" he asked, his voice sharp. "Has Ramsey been filling your head with more nonsense?"

"I don't know. Has he?"

"Do you think I'm responsible for the killings in the city?"

"Are you?" She stared up at him. What was she doing, saying?

Ramsey sat in the chair across from her, but his nearness offered little comfort. She lifted a hand to her chest, felt the solid shape of the cross beneath her sweater. If Grigori attacked her, did she have enough faith to believe the cross would protect her?

"Would you believe me if I said I was innocent?"

"I don't know."

Grigori looked at Ramsey. "Do you think I'm involved in these killings?"

Ramsey nodded. "Damn right. Alexi doesn't need that much blood to survive, not after all these years."

"Alexi doesn't kill because he needs to," Grigori retorted. "He kills because he enjoys it."

Ramsey snorted softly. "And you don't?"

Grigori glanced at Marisa. Her face was pale, her eyes wide with interest and revulsion. "I haven't killed anyone in this city. I never hunt where I live."

"Yeah, right," Ramsey muttered.

"It's true, whether you believe it or not." His words were for Ramsey, but he was watching Marisa. For reasons he didn't care to examine too closely, it was important that she believe him.

Marisa shifted in her seat. Grigori's probing gaze made her decidedly uncomfortable. "I'm going to get a cup of coffee. Edward, would you like some?"

"Yes, thank you."

Grigori watched Marisa and Ramsey walk into the kitchen. He felt a twinge of jealousy that they could share something as ordinary as a cup of coffee. For the first time in a long while, he was keenly aware that he was no longer a mortal man.

Keeping his face impassive, he went to stand in the kitchen doorway. Ramsey and Marisa were sitting at the table. Ramsey held a cup to his lips;

Marisa was staring out the window, the cup in her hand untouched.

"Do you have any idea where Alexi goes to ground?" Ramsey asked.

"No."

"Well, I've looked in all the places I can think of. He's not in any of them."

Marisa drew her gaze from the window. "What kind of places?"

"Old graveyards. Deserted buildings and houses. Empty lots." Edward shrugged. "I've started checking the local hotels, but that takes time."

"I've sensed his presence on more than one occasion," Grigori remarked. "But he always eludes me. I think he's playing with us. Sometimes I can almost hear him laughing."

"He'll be laughing out of the other side of his face when I drive my stake into his heart." For all his soft-spoken words, there was no mistaking the hatred in Ramsey's eyes, or the fervor in his tone.

"He may not be resting in the city at all," Grigori mused, thinking aloud. "Perhaps he's just hunting here, in which case we're wasting our time looking for his lair."

Ramsey nodded. "That's always a possibility. Still, I don't think we should start looking into the surrounding areas until we're certain he's not holed up here somewhere."

"He knows we're looking for him," Grigori remarked, thinking out loud. "He may be changing his resting place every day, or every week, and if that's the case, we might never find him."

"I'll find him."

Grigori shook his head. "I think the only way we'll catch him is if he lets us."

Ramsey's hand reached up to curl around his crucifix. "I will see him dead," he vowed. "One way or another. I swear it. Tell me, Chiavari, where do *you* spend the daylight hours?"

"Do I look like a fool, Ramsey?"

"Not at all, but if I knew more about you, perhaps it would make it easier to find Alexi."

"All you need know is that I never hunt in the same city where I take my rest."

"Fastidious of you."

"Quite."

Ramsey finished his coffee, and stood up. "I'm going home. I've had a long day. Miss Richards, thank you for the coffee." He went to the sink and rinsed out his cup, then placed it on the counter.

"Quite fastidious," Grigori murmured.

Ramsey glared at him. "Shouldn't you be out hunting our fanged friend?"

"All in good time. Weren't you leaving?"

"All in good time." Ramsey inclined his head in Marisa's direction. "Good night, Miss Richards."

"Good night, Edward. Thank you for coming by."

A thick silence fell over the kitchen after Ramsey's departure. Needing something to do, Marisa placed Edward's cup in the dishwasher, then poured herself a cup of coffee she didn't want.

"What if you can't find Alexi?"

"I'll find him."

"And in the meantime, he'll keep killing."

Grigori nodded, waiting for her to go on, to ask the questions he read in her eyes.

"You told Edward you don't hunt where you live."

He nodded again.

"But—" She lifted a hand to her throat. "But you do . . . hunt?"

"I do what I must to survive, Marisa. Would it make you feel better if I denied it, denied what I am?"

"Probably." She regarded him a moment. "You don't look like a vampire."

"Indeed? Have you known many of us?"

She placed her cup in the sink, and then folded her arms over her chest. "Of course not."

"How should I look?"

"I don't know." She shook her head as an image of Frank Langella's Dracula formed in her mind: tall and dark and undeniably sexy in a white linen shirt and long, flowing cape. "Maybe you do look like a . . . a vampire, after all."

He smiled, as if he knew her thoughts, and then, as a howl screamed through the night, he froze.

"What was that?" Marisa exclaimed. "It sounded like a wolf."

He looked at her indulgently. "There are no wolves in the city, Marisa."

"It's him, isn't it? Alexi?"

Grigori nodded. "He's calling me."

"You're not going?"

"Would you rather I met him in here?"

"Heavens, no!"

"You'll be safe enough. Just remember, he can't come in unless you invite him."

"That's not much comfort."

"It's the best I can offer you."

His dark eyes moved over her, deep, fathomless

eyes that held secrets she didn't want to know. Awareness hummed between them, its heat licking against her skin, warm and rough, like a cat's tongue. And then, abruptly, he was gone.

Marisa blinked, startled by the sudden emptiness she felt inside, by the realization that he had not left the house by the door, but had simply vanished from her sight.

Maybe he really was a magician.

Chapter Ten

Grigori paused when he reached the sidewalk. He had been quite serious when he'd suggested that Alexi was playing games with them. No doubt the ancient vampyre found their helplessness amusing. And they were helpless against him, Grigori thought bleakly. Unless Alexi let his guard down, they had little chance of catching him. Kristov possessed the knowledge of untold centuries, the strength of a thousand years.

Grigori raked a hand through his hair. Maybe he was only kidding himself in thinking that he could keep Marisa safe. There was little he could do to protect her that she couldn't do herself. If she was careful to remain locked within her own house at night, Alexi could not reach her. But what kind of life was that, being imprisoned from dusk till dawn?

He laughed softly. What kind of life indeed, he mused. It was the life he lived, save that he was compelled to shun the light of day, to hide away in darkness when the sun was high in the sky.

The howl of a wolf interrupted his thoughts, and he spun around, his gaze probing the drifting shadows of the night.

"Still protecting the lady fair?"

Alexi's voice sounded behind him. Grigori whirled around, the fine hairs rising along the back of his neck, his hands curling into tight fists.

"Why don't you fight me, Alexi? Let us end it here and now."

"You don't think you could best me?" Alexi replied with unbridled amusement.

"Try me."

"Oh, I will, I will, have no doubt of that. But not now. I find your puny efforts to destroy me most amusing." Alexi crossed his arms over his chest and regarded Grigori through ancient gray eyes. "Tell Ramsey he need not change his sleeping place from night to night. All the locked doors and all the garlic and crosses in the world will not save him. In the end, he will be mine."

Grigori nodded. Ramsey had not stayed in the same hotel or motel since they'd arrived in the city, foolishly believing that Alexi would not be able to find him.

Alexi laughed, a harsh, brittle sound. "Tell him he is easy to follow. The stink of garlic trails behind him like the smoke from a funeral pyre."

"So, if you have not come to fight me, what do you want?"

"Why, just to say hello to an old friend."

Slowly, like a snake uncoiling, rage rose up within Grigori. "Friend! You dare call me friend after what you did!"

Alexi waved his hand in an elegant gesture of dismissal. "Don't tell me you're still angry because of the woman."

"She was my wife." Grigori bit off each word.

"How can you still be angry? You must admit,

but for me, you would be nothing but a moldering corpse." He laughed softly. "I should think you would thank me. Because of your hatred, you have a gift thousands of mortals would kill for, yet you despise me for it."

"Thank you? You think I should thank you? You killed my children! My wife—"

"She is not dead."

"What?" Grigori froze, everything else forgotten. "What did you say?"

Alexi shrugged. "She is not dead." He smiled, a slow smile of such evil that it sent a shiver down Grigori's spine.

"Did you bring her over?"

Alexi shook his head, his expression one of boredom.

Grigori stared at the vampyre in horror. "You left her as she was all these years?"

"I have need of her from time to time."

"Where is she?"

"Where you cannot find her."

"Damn you, Kristov, where is she?"

"She is mine now, Grigori, as she was always meant to be."

"What are you saying? She was my wife. You never knew her until I made you welcome in my home."

"I loved her! I offered her the world, eternal youth, and she refused me. Me! I would have taken her away from that hovel, given her anything she desired! Made her a queen." Rage glittered in his eyes. "And she refused! Refused to leave you or those brats. Well, she doesn't refuse me anymore."

With a cry of rage, Grigori lunged forward, his

hands turning to claws as he reached for Alexi's throat.

But his fingers closed on empty air. Alexi was gone.

Grigori swore under his breath. Antoinette wasn't dead. He stared blindly into the distance. All these years, he had thought her dead, grieved for her, mourned her, hated Alexi for destroying the woman he had loved, and she wasn't dead.

In the back of his mind, he heard Kristov's parting words: *She is mine now . . . as she was always meant to be.*

As if returning from a dark abyss, he gradually became aware of the world around him . . . the sound of a car passing by, the roar of a jet, the light rain that was beginning to fall.

Feeling numb, he slowly climbed the stairs to Marisa's apartment. A wave of his hand opened the door. He stood inside the entryway, his gaze sweeping the living room, seeing it all in a glance. Seeing nothing but Antoinette as he had seen her last . . . her face as pale as death, her eyes empty and vacant of life, the bright drops of blood that dripped down her neck like crimson tears.

"Grigori? Grigori!"

He looked at Marisa, not seeing her, and then he shook his head as if to clear it.

"What's wrong?" Marisa stared up at him, thinking she had never seen such anguish in anyone's eyes in her whole life. He looked as if he had just escaped from hell, as if he had seen into the heart of the devil himself. "Are you all right?"

He gazed down at her. "Of course."

"Of course," she repeated, her tone skeptical. "What happened out there?"

"Nothing. We . . . talked."

"It must have been some conversation. You look like you've just seen a ghost." She stilled the tide of hysterical laughter that bubbled in her throat. Vampires. Ghosts. What next? The Loch Ness Monster? Little green men from Mars?

"It's late," Grigori remarked. "Why don't you go to bed?"

"It's not late, and I don't want to go to bed."

With a nod, he brushed past her. For a moment, he stood at the window, staring out, and then he began to pace the floor. His footsteps seemed to beat a tattoo to the words pounding in his mind: *She's not dead, not dead, not dead. . . .*

Marisa sat on the arm of the sofa, watching him, wondering what Alexi had said or done to cause Grigori such distress. She watched him pace, his movements fluid, as graceful as a dancer's. His feet hardly seemed to touch the floor. Nothing stirred at his passing, almost as if he wasn't there.

Vampire. The word whispered down the corridors of her mind.

Sitting there, she felt herself grow tense, felt the heavy silence press in on her. Once, she heard him groan, a heart-wrenching sound that was almost a growl.

And still he paced. She imagined that she could see his footsteps wearing a path in the carpet. His anger radiated from him like heat from a campfire.

She blew out a sigh and he whirled around, his dark eyes ablaze with such hatred she felt scorched by the heat. His lips curled back, revealing sharp white fangs.

Terror drove through her heart. With a low cry,

her fingers closed around the cross Ramsey had given her. It felt warm in her palm, soothing.

Grigori muttered a vile oath as he stopped his restless pacing. Taking a deep breath, he willed himself to be calm, felt the tension flow out of him.

"I'm sorry," he said curtly. "I didn't mean to frighten you."

She stared at him, wary and silent.

"Alexi gave me some disturbing news."

Marisa nodded, waiting for him to go on.

"I told you of my wife and children."

"Yes."

"It was only part of the truth. My children are dead, as I said. Alexi killed them. I had thought he killed my wife, as well, but it seems—" His hands clenched at his sides. "It seems he did not kill Antoinette, after all."

"What do you mean?"

"She's still alive." He took a deep breath. "That is, she's not dead."

Feeling suddenly chilled to the bone, Marisa crossed her arms over her breasts. "I don't understand."

"She's a revenant, a creature totally in Alexi's power. She has no mind, no will of her own. She exists in a world between life and death. He can summon her at any time he wishes, and she is helpless to resist him."

"But . . . if she's not a vampire, how can she still be alive?"

"She's not alive!" He ran a hand through his hair, his eyes again blazing with hatred. "She can't die. Won't die, so long as Alexi lives."

"And if you kill him?"

"She'll die, too."

"I'm sorry." She knew the words were inadequate, but she didn't know what else to say.

He looked at her for a long moment. "I have to go out." His voice was raw, scraping over her senses like sandpaper.

She didn't ask why, didn't want to know why.

Moments later, he was gone.

Grigori stalked the dark streets of a small town up the coast, his mind in turmoil as he thought of Antoinette. The knowledge that she was still alive filled him with hope and dread. Where was she? Where had she been during the century that Alexi had been imprisoned by Silvano's family? Had she roamed the countryside, lost and alone, at the mercy of superstitious villagers who would have hated and feared her? Or had she slept the same deathlike sleep as her master . . . ?

Impotent rage rose up within him as he imagined the hell she must have endured these past centuries. All this time, he had thought her dead, and she had been Alexi's creature.

He sought the shadows of the night, but found no solace there. He threw back his head and loosed his rage and anger in a long howl that echoed and re-echoed through the stillness of the sleeping town.

Pausing at the edge of the ocean, he stared out at the gently lapping waves. Moonlight reflected off the water like candlelight off a mirror. He stood there for a long time, listening to the water as it whispered up to kiss the sand at his feet. Seeking some semblance of inner peace, he closed his eyes and took several slow, deep breaths. Unbidden, Marisa's image came to his mind, and he knew a sudden longing to be held in her arms, to feel the warmth of her hands stroking his back, to hear her voice speaking soft words of comfort.

But he dared not go to her now, when anger and hatred for Kristov burned through him like acid, kindling the urge for violence, awakening a thirst for blood that could be satisfied but never quenched.

He sped through the dark streets, his senses searching for prey, leading him to a seedy bar located a few blocks from the ocean.

Cloaked in the shadows of midnight, he waited.

The woman was laughing when she left the bar, weaving slightly as she made her way to the parking lot. On silent feet, Grigori slipped up beside her. She would have run from him then, but he stayed her with a touch of his hand on her arm.

"Who . . . who are you?" she asked. "What do you want?"

He searched her mind and found her name. "It's all right, Michelle. I'm not going to hurt you."

He gazed deep into her eyes, hypnotizing her with a glance, and then he walked her to her car. Slipping into the seat beside her, he drew her into his arms. She smelled of strong whiskey and stronger perfume. For a moment, he thought of Marisa, who smelled always of soap and flowers.

Wrenching his thoughts from Marisa, he turned the woman's face away from him, brushed her tousled hair aside, his lips sliding over the warm, tender flesh of her neck. How many times had he done this? How many women had he called to him in two hundred years, taking from them that which he needed to survive, then leaving them behind?

The woman moaned softly and he whispered to her, assuring her that she had nothing to fear as his teeth pierced her skin. He drank quickly, stilling the urge to drink it all, to consume not only her blood, but her thoughts and memories, the very essence of her life. She was recently divorced. She drank to forget, to ease the pain of a faithless husband, shattered vows, a broken home.

When he started to release her, she clung to him, staring up at him out of dazed blue eyes.

"Don't leave me," she begged, and he heard the raw edge of loneliness in her voice. "Please don't leave me. I don't want to be alone."

"Go to sleep, Michelle," he said quietly. "You're tired, and you must sleep." He looked deep into her eyes. "When you wake, you will remember nothing."

"Nothing . . ."

He ran his tongue over the tiny wounds in her neck, licking away the last of the blood, sealing the wounds. They would be gone by morning.

"Nothing," he repeated, but she was already asleep.

Leaving the car, he locked the doors. He looked at the woman a moment, knowing he would never see her again. She had satisfied his demon thirst, but his soul remained dry and empty.

"Marisa." He shared her name with the night, felt his need to hold her, to be held by her, grow strong within him. What would it be like, he wondered, to share the Dark Gift with her, to spend an eternity at her side?

A thought willed him across the miles to Marisa's apartment. A wave of his hand opened the door, and then he was there, at her bedside, watching her sleep. Though the room was dark, he could see her clearly, hear the quiet sound of her breathing.

"Marisa."

She stirred at the sound of his voice.

"Marisa."

Her eyelids fluttered open. For a moment, she stared up at him, uncomprehending, and then, in quick succession, came recognition and fear. Her eyes widened. Her hand delved beneath her nightgown and reappeared fisted around the cross Ramsey had given her.

Grigori loosed a sigh. Much as he might wish it, he would not take her by force. "You don't need that."

"Don't I?" Suddenly wide awake, she sat up, still clasping the crucifix. "What do you want?"

He shook his head. "Never mind."

Something in his voice tugged at her heart. "What is it? What's wrong?"

"Nothing."

"I'm awake now, so you may as well tell me what you want, unless you just came in hoping to find a midnight snack."

He grinned faintly, surprised by her ability to joke about something that terrified her. "No doubt you'll laugh."

"I don't think so. I haven't felt much like laughing since—"

"Since you met me?"

She didn't say anything, just continued to look at him, waiting for an explanation.

"I wanted to ask you to do something for me."

Unconsciously, she lifted a hand to her throat.

"Not that," he said quickly, but the thought of holding her, of drinking from her, burned within him like a bright flame.

Suddenly aware of what she was doing, she lowered her hand to her lap.

"Never mind," he said. "Go back to sleep."

"Oh, I hate it when people do that." She flounced back against the headboard, her arms crossed over her breasts, and glared up at him. "It's so annoying when someone starts to tell you something and then changes his mind."

Her anger amused him. "Yes, I suppose it is."

"Of course, you can read minds, so I don't suppose that's a problem for you, is it?"

"No."

She was wide awake now. Grabbing her robe from the foot of the bed, she slipped it on, then threw back the covers and got up.

"What are you doing?"

"I'm going to get some hot chocolate. Do you—" She grinned at him, her anger vanishing as quickly as it had surfaced. "Never mind."

He took a deep breath as she swept past him, inhaling the fragrance of her hair and skin, the siren call of the blood running through her veins.

Swearing softly, he followed her into the kitchen, watching while she filled a pan with milk, added cocoa, stirred it with a spoon.

Marisa tried to concentrate on what she was doing, but she was acutely aware of the man standing in the doorway, watching her. She could see him out of the corner of her eye. He stood there, unmoving, unblinking. She wondered if he was breathing, if he needed to breathe. It was quite disconcerting. As surreptitiously as she could, she touched the cross dangling between her breasts, wondering, as she did so, if it would really protect her.

When the milk was warm enough, she poured it into a coffee mug, then sat down at the kitchen table. And still he stood there, as still as a stone, silent as the grave.

He knew her thoughts. She read it in the slight smile that curved his lips, in the knowing look in his eye.

With hands that trembled, she put the cup on the table as he closed the distance between them.

Moving slowly so as not to startle her, Grigori took hold of her hands and lifted her to her feet, then folded her into his arms.

"Hold me, Marisa," he whispered in a voice taut with emotion. "I need you to hold me."

It was the last thing she had expected him to say. She gazed up at him, felt her heart wrench at the pain she saw reflected in his eyes.

There was nothing frightening or otherworldly about him now. He was just a man who was hurting, and hurting deeply. She wondered how he had endured for so long, living only in the darkness, afraid to let anyone know what he was.

Wordlessly, she wrapped her arms around him and held him close. He lowered his head until it was resting on her shoulder, his face turned away from her neck. She stroked his back, her hands gentle. She was surprised at how good it felt to hold him close, at the inexplicable urge to soothe and comfort him.

Time lost all meaning as they stood there, cocooned in silence. His hair was warm against her cheek; she was aware of how tall he was, of the hard-muscled body pressed against her own. She dragged her fingers over his back, across his shoulders. Broad, powerful shoulders.

And then she felt him stiffen in her arms. His head jerked up and he glanced at the kitchen window. She followed his gaze, surprised to see that the sky was turning gray.

"I must go." He took her hands in his and gazed down at her. "Thank you."

"I didn't do anything."

The faintest of smiles hovered over his lips. "You did more than you'll ever know," he replied quietly, and then, like a shadow running from the sun, he was gone.

Grigori raced the sun back to his lair, grateful for the preternatural speed that allowed him to move so swiftly, thinking ironically that he would have no need to fear the sun if he were mortal.

Safe inside, he paced the floor of his bedroom, his every thought focused on Marisa. What a rare creature she was! And how wondrous it had felt to stand within her embrace, to feel her arms around him, her hand stroking his back. Was there anything to equal a woman's gentle touch, any solace more complete?

He had made love to many women in two hundred years. Most had been bought for a price—a sum of money, a piece of expensive jewelry, a costly fur. Others had come to him out of nothing more than lust, drawn by the dark promise of his preternatural power. He had found satisfaction in their arms, but never pleasure. Passion, but never love. They had met the needs of his body, but none had ever touched his heart.

Until tonight. Marisa's sweet acceptance of his need, that basic human need to be held, to be loved, had arrowed straight to his soul. Before tonight, Antoinette had been the only woman who had held him and soothed him with such tenderness. Antoinette, who had loved him heart and soul, mind and body.

Antoinette. Her name seared his soul, shattering the fragile peace he had found in Marisa's arms.

"Damn you, Alexi," he murmured. "Damn you to hell."

And in the back of his mind, like the rustle of dead leaves, he heard the brittle sound of Alexi's laughter, and the words that continued to haunt him: *She is mine now . . . as she was always meant to be. . . .*

Chapter Eleven

Sunday morning, Marisa rose early and went to church. Though her faith in God had always been strong, she rarely went to Sunday services. But now, when her life seemed to be spinning out of her control, she felt a sudden need for the peace and tranquillity the church provided.

Listening to the soothing words of familiar hymns, hearing the minister's fervent prayers on behalf of the congregation, she felt a sense of peace, of renewal, and wondered why she had stayed away so long.

She gazed up at the stained-glass window over the altar. It was a beautiful piece of art, depicting the Savior of the world holding a tiny white lamb in His arms. In the background, a handful of sheep grazed on a hillside.

Sitting there, it was hard to believe the events of the past week, hard to believe that vampires and vampire hunters could possibly exist.

She felt refreshed in mind and spirit when she left the church.

At home, she spent a good hour on the phone, chatting with her parents. They were well, happily involved in bridge games and tennis tournaments.

Her mother wanted to know if she had found anyone special yet; her father wanted to know how things were going at work. She promised to come for a visit over Christmas and hung up, then called her brother in Colorado.

Mike answered the phone, and they talked for a few minutes, catching up on each other's lives. Marisa talked to her nieces and nephews, asked Mike's wife, Barbara, what Nikki wanted for her birthday; then she went into the kitchen to fix lunch.

Humming softly, she mixed mayonnaise with a can of tuna.

She fixed a sandwich, then went into the front room and sat on the floor to read the paper.

VAMPIRE KILLER STRIKES AGAIN,
DEATH TOLL RISES TO 13

That quickly, her sense of well-being was destroyed.

She read what was becoming a familiar story. The body of a young woman had been found in the foothills behind Griffith Park, her body drained of blood. There had been no sign of a struggle, no evidence of foul play save for two tiny wounds in her neck.

Her appetite gone, Marisa put her sandwich aside, hating herself for wondering if Grigori was responsible for any of the deaths.

She didn't like to think of the dark side of Grigori, didn't like to admit she was physically attracted to a man who wasn't even alive in the normal sense of the word. And yet he seemed so alive, so vital. And she cared for him far more than seemed wise.

She had held him in her arms last night, felt his grief and his pain as she comforted him.

She wondered where he slept during the day, if his sleep was interspersed with dreams, or if he was shrouded in the silent darkness of death.

She wondered what her parents would say if she told them she had met a vampire. Kissed a vampire . . .

She glanced at the clock. Almost two. She wondered why Ramsey hadn't called, and then shrugged. Even vampire hunters needed a day off.

Even as the thought crossed her mind, the phone rang.

"Hello?"

"Miss Richards?"

"Hi, Edward. Are you all right?"

"Yes, fine." She heard him yawn. "I was out rather late last night."

"Did you find anything?"

"No. I guess you've heard the news?"

She glanced at the newspaper and shuddered. "Yes. It's awful."

He grunted softly. "I'll be over before dark."

"All right. Bye."

Edward showed up just before sunset. They shared a thick-crust pepperoni pizza; then Edward produced a deck of cards and they played canasta. Marisa kept glancing at the clock, wondering where Grigori was.

At ten, Marisa went into the kitchen and made a bowl of popcorn.

Sitting on the sofa, with the bowl between them,

they watched the news. It seemed that the stories were always the same: trouble in the Middle East, increasing unemployment, politicians making promises they couldn't keep.

"And in local news, the bodies of two teenage boys were found in an oil field near Huntington Beach just moments ago, bringing the number of killings attributed to the vampire killer to fifteen. Police are asking for anyone who might have information relating to any of these killings to get in touch with them immediately by calling the number on your screen.

"Chief Harrison has issued a statement asking everyone to stay as close to home as possible between the hours of six P.M. and dawn until further notice. When asked if he believed the killings were the work of a vampire, the chief stated an unequivocal *No*, but said the department was working on the assumption that the person or persons perpetrating these crimes was quite possibly operating under that delusion. In other news . . ."

"This is all my fault!" Marisa exclaimed. Rising to her feet, she went to the window and drew back the curtains. He was out there somewhere, and it was her fault. Somehow, her blood had revived him, and now he was prowling the city, killing innocent people, and it was her fault, her fault. . . .

A flicker of movement caught her eye. At the same time, she felt again that sense of evil that she had felt twice before, and with it the sense that someone was trying to reach inside her mind.

Marisa . . . open to me. . . .

"No!"

"Miss Richards, what's wrong?" Edward bolted to his feet, and then he went suddenly still, his senses attuned to the knowledge that a vampire was near.

"He's out there!" She yanked the curtains closed, and quickly moved away from the window.

Ramsey went to the window and peered out, his gaze darting up and down the dark street. Was it Alexi, or Grigori, or perhaps another of the undead?

"I . . . I heard his voice in my mind. Alexi's voice. Where are you going?"

"To see if I can find him."

"Are you crazy? You can't go out there."

Ramsey sighed. "No need. He's gone."

She couldn't believe he was really gone; the feeling of evil still felt so strong. But Edward had more experience than she did. "You're sure?"

Edward nodded, then resumed his seat. "Any vampire hunters in your family, Miss Richards?"

"Not that I know of."

"Has he tried to speak to you before?"

"No, but I've felt his presence." She crossed her arms, suddenly cold. "It's so creepy. It reminds me of those old science-fiction movies where aliens come to earth and take over people's minds."

"Except Kristov isn't science fiction," Edward muttered.

Grigori arrived a short time later.

"He was here," Edward said. "Just a few minutes ago."

"I know."

"You saw him?"

"Yes. I chased him for several miles, and then I lost him."

Ramsey shook his head. "I've hunted vampires

before. I've never had this much trouble tracking one."

Grigori nodded, his attention on Marisa. She seemed distracted. "Are you all right?"

"He spoke to me."

"You saw him?"

"No, no, but I heard him. In my mind."

"What did he say?"

"He wanted me to let him in." She looked up at him, her eyes dark with fear. "It was awful. I feel as if I've been violated somehow."

Grigori didn't say anything, but it seemed as if he backed away from her, over an invisible chasm she couldn't see, couldn't cross.

"It doesn't feel that way when you read my mind," she said softly. "It feels, I don't know, right somehow, when you do it." She looked up at him, silently entreating him to hold her, to shield her weakness with his strength. "I'm afraid."

"I know." He crossed the bridge her words had built between them and took her in his arms. "I won't let him hurt you, Marisa, I swear it."

Ramsey cleared his throat. "I think I'll, uh, go home."

"Good night, Edward," Marisa said. "Thank you for coming over."

"My pleasure." Ramsey looked at Grigori, his eyes filled with reproach. "Call me if you need me."

Grigori nodded, keenly aware that Ramsey's blatant disapproval barely masked the man's jealousy. And yet Ramsey had no reason to be jealous. As much as he, Grigori, might wish it, nothing could come of his growing affection for Marisa. There was no way they could have a life together, no reason to think she would want to spend any more time with him than she had to. He could never be a part of her world; she would not want to share his.

And yet, gazing down at her now, seeing himself reflected in the emerald depths of her eyes, he wished, fleetingly, that he were a mortal man again, capable of giving her a home, a family. But there was no hope of that, and he had no right to think there might be, not now, when Antoinette hovered in the netherworld between life and death.

"It's late," Marisa said, disturbed by his silence, by the tension she felt in the arms that held her. "I think I'd better go to bed, too. I've got to get up early for work tomorrow."

With a nod, Grigori let her go. "Sleep well, Marisa."

He watched her walk away, and though he knew it was only a trick of his mind, it seemed as though she took all the warmth of the world with her.

Chapter Twelve

Ramsey came awake with a start, all his senses suddenly alert. And then he heard it again, a woman's soft cry of pain.

Throwing back the covers, he slid out of bed and went to the door.

"Who's there?" He pressed his ear to the wood. "Who is it?"

"Help me. Please help me."

"I can't, I'm sorry."

"Please! I'm so afraid."

Heart pounding, Edward went to the dresser. Picking up a sharpened stake, he slid it in the waistband of his pajamas; then, one hand clutching his cross, he opened the door.

A young woman crouched in the hallway, her face half-hidden beneath a fall of tangled black hair.

"Please," she said with a gasp, her voice heavily accented. "Please help me." She extended a slender hand toward him, a hand covered with blood.

Cautiously, Edward peered up and down the hallway. Seeing no one, he reached for the girl and pulled her into his room, then closed and locked the door.

The girl huddled on the floor, sobbing, her face hidden by her hair.

"What's happened to you?" Edward asked. "Do you need a doctor?"

She did not answer, only continued to sob as though her heart would break.

Kneeling beside her, Edward brushed the hair from her face, gasped in horror as he saw the two telltale wounds in her neck.

Scrambling to his feet, he backed away from her, his hand clutching the cross so tightly it cut into his skin. "Who are you?"

She looked up at him through blue-green eyes that had no doubt once been beautiful, but were now empty of all humanity. And then, moving slowly, she rose to her feet and walked toward him, her steps stiff, like a robot's.

"No!"

He reached for the stake in his waistband. In a blur, she lunged toward him. Grabbing the stake from his hand with a strength that belied her slender build, she broke it in half and tossed the pieces away.

Terrified now, Edward struck out at her, his fist clipping her chin. With a feral growl, she picked him up and threw him across the room.

Ramsey cried out as his head struck a corner of the dresser. Ignoring the pain, he grabbed a chair and smashed it over the woman's head, once, twice, three times, driving her backward until she dropped to her knees, a horrible, inhuman sound emerging from her throat as blood dripped down her forehead into her eyes.

Knowing she would soon recover, he turned and threw the chair through the window. Grabbing his jacket and keys, he bolted over the sill into the gray dawn of early morning, grateful that he had insisted on a room at ground level.

He raced to his car, not daring to look behind him.

"Edward, what happened?" Marisa stood back so he could enter her apartment, then closed and locked the door behind him.

"I'll tell you in a moment." Breathing heavily, he staggered into the front room and collapsed on the sofa.

"You're bleeding!" Marisa exclaimed.

"No," he said with a gasp. "I'm all right. It's not . . . not my blood."

"Then whose?"

He held up a trembling hand to stay her questions. "Wait . . . just . . . wait."

With a nod, Marisa went into the kitchen and turned on the coffeemaker. A glance at the clock showed it was barely six A.M. She drummed her fingertips on the countertop, wondering what had happened to Ramsey. He looked as if he'd seen a ghost. Or a vampire . . . but it was morning. Surely Alexi was asleep in his coffin, wherever that might be.

The thought made her shudder. Thinking of Alexi brought Grigori to mind. He had told her he didn't sleep in a coffin, but she couldn't help picturing him laid out in a silk-lined casket, his arms folded over his chest, dead but not dead.

She closed her eyes against the nausea that roiled in her stomach. She had let Grigori kiss her, had kissed him back, had wondered what it would be like to make love to him. How had she even considered such a thing? How had she forgotten, even for a moment, what he was?

Pouring two cups of strong black coffee, she went out into the living room.

Ramsey smiled faintly as he took the cup she offered him. "Thank you."

She sat down at the opposite end of the sofa, cradling the mug between her hands. It was comforting somehow. "Feeling better?"

He nodded, then, using as few words as possible, he told her what had happened.

"But how could she be out in the daytime if she was a vampire?"

Edward shook his head. "She's not a vampire. She's a revenant. I suspect Alexi sent her."

"To kill you?"

"I don't know. I don't think so. I think she was supposed to take me to him." A sickly smile flickered across his pale face. "I have a feeling I was supposed to be dinner."

Marisa stared at Ramsey. It was too awful even to think about, yet she couldn't stay the awful images his words conveyed.

"A revenant." Marisa spoke the words aloud without realizing she had done so.

"Yes. Fearful creatures. I've only seen a few, but they are even more frightening than their masters."

"Grigori told me Alexi had turned Antoinette into a revenant. You don't think . . . ?" She stared at Edward in horror.

"I don't know." He sipped at the coffee. "It's possible. But I just don't know."

"Did you . . . is she . . . ?"

He looked up at her, his face ashen, his eyes

troubled. "Dead?" Slowly, he shook his head. "No. There are only two ways to kill a revenant. Remove its head and heart, or kill its master."

"I feel like I'm living in the middle of a nightmare!" Marisa exclaimed. "None of this can be true. It's impossible."

"I wish it were."

"What are you going to do now?"

"I shouldn't have run. I should have tried to restrain her, make her tell me where Alexi takes his rest."

"Are you mad? From what you told me, she sounds stronger than the two of us put together."

"I might have been able to subdue her long enough to tie her up." He lifted one shoulder and let it fall. "I panicked. There's no excuse for it."

"I can think of several," Marisa muttered.

"Grigori will see it as a weakness on my part."

"Well, we mortals are allowed to be weak now and then."

Ramsey smiled faintly. "Would you mind if I stayed here today?"

"No, of course not."

"I don't think you should go to work."

"You don't think she'll come after me, do you?"

"I don't know. It seems unlikely that Alexi would send her into the city in broad daylight, but . . . I'd feel better if you stayed home."

"We're really busy at the office," Marisa remarked, "but I've got some sick time coming. I guess it wouldn't hurt to miss one day." She glanced at the clock. "No one will be there yet. Why don't you get some rest?"

"Would you mind if I showered first?"

"Of course not. The bathroom is down the hall, first door to your left."

With a nod, he carried his coffee cup into the kitchen. She heard him place it in the sink. A few minutes later she heard the shower go on.

Putting her cup on the coffee table, she sat back and closed her eyes. She never should have agreed to stay home. She would have been better off at work. At least there, she'd have something else to think about.

Ramsey returned fifteen minutes later. "Thanks."

"You look a lot better."

"I feel a lot better." He regarded her for a moment, his expression thoughtful. "Are you game to go vampire hunting?"

"Me? When?"

"Now. We should be safe enough if we stick together."

"Are you going like that?"

Ramsey glanced down at his T-shirt and pajama bottoms and grinned. "No, I have a change of clothes in my car." He winked at her. "Pays to be prepared."

"Can I have breakfast first?"

Ramsey laughed softly. "Of course. I'll even fix it for you while you get dressed. What would you like?"

"French toast."

Giving her a thumbs-up sign, he went into the kitchen. She stood there for a moment; then, with a sigh, she went into the bathroom and shut the door.

* * *

"So, where are we going to look first?" Marisa asked. It was a little after nine. She had showered and dressed while Edward fixed breakfast; then, while she cleaned up the kitchen, Edward had changed his clothes. She'd made a quick call to work to tell them she wouldn't be in.

Now she was sitting in the passenger seat of Ramsey's car, her heart racing as she anticipated her first vampire hunt.

"I think we'll start at my room." Edward shifted the car into gear and pulled onto the street. "I need to pick up the rest of my things anyway. Perhaps she left a trail of some kind."

Marisa nodded. That made sense.

Edward had been staying at a small hotel located uptown. He paid his bill, made up some excuse about the broken window, then packed his few belongings into a worn brown suitcase.

Marisa stood in the doorway, her gaze sweeping the room. Except for the broken window, there was no sign of a struggle.

"She must have cleaned the place up," Edward remarked. "See here? You can see where she tried to scrub the blood from the carpet. It's still damp." He swore under his breath. "Looks like she got away without leaving a trace."

"Now what?"

Edward rubbed a hand over his jaw. "I've covered practically every mile of Griffith Park and the surrounding area, since most of the murders took place in that part of town. I've also checked most of the nearby beaches. I've never searched around here, but I think he must be nearby."

"What makes you think that?"

"The revenant. I doubt if she'd be able to drive a car. She couldn't take a bus either."

"Maybe a taxi."

"Maybe." He shuddered as he recalled looking into those soulless eyes. No cabdriver in his right mind would have picked her up once he caught a glimpse of those lifeless eyes. "I'm thinking Alexi's resting place must be within walking distance of my hotel."

"So where do we look first?"

"I'm not sure. Maybe I've been operating under the wrong assumption. Maybe he doesn't hide away anymore. Maybe he's rented a house. Come on."

Returning to the car, Ramsey threw his suitcase in the trunk and then headed for the residential section of the city.

"What are we looking for?" Marisa asked.

"A house that doesn't look lived in. Perhaps one that has bars on the windows. Certainly one that has all the curtains drawn. Probably a fenced yard. With a large dog."

They spent the next four hours driving slowly up and down every street. Ramsey spotted two houses that he thought looked suspicious. He wrote down the addresses, as well as the license numbers of the cars parked in the driveways.

They went to McDonald's for cheeseburgers and fries. Marisa ordered a chocolate shake; Edward ordered coffee.

They found a table near the window in the back. "What will you do after you . . . you've dispatched Alexi?" Marisa asked as she unwrapped her cheeseburger.

"Take a long vacation, I think."

Marisa put ketchup on her fries, took a sip of her shake. "Where do you live?"

"Nowhere."

"Nowhere?"

"I have an apartment in Chicago, but I've never really lived there. It's just a place to pick up my mail."

"Haven't you ever wanted to settle down?"

"I've never had time to think about it."

They finished the meal in silence. Edward got a cup of coffee to go, and they left the restaurant.

They drove up into the hills. This was horse property, and the houses were more expensive and farther apart. Often, it was necessary to drive up a long winding road to get to the house. Twice, they came to driveways with locked gates. Leaving the car, they made their way up hillsides to where they could see the houses. Both had been family homes, with children playing outside.

It was near dark when they returned to Marisa's apartment. "Well," she said as she unlocked her door, "that was a wasted day."

"Not really. At least we know where he isn't."

"Where who isn't?"

Marisa's hand flew to her throat as Grigori materialized out of the shadows in the living room.

"Don't do that!" she exclaimed as she switched on the light. "You scared me to death."

"Where have you been?"

She tossed her handbag on the sofa. "Out. I'm gonna grab a Coke, Edward. Do you want one?"

"Yes, please."

Grigori glared at Edward. "Do you want to tell me where you've been?"

Edward sat down on the sofa and let out a weary

sigh. "Where do you think? We've been looking for Alexi."

"You took her with you!"

"It seemed the wisest course."

Grigori studied Ramsey a moment. "He found you, didn't he?"

Ramsey nodded. "He sent someone after me."

Grigori went still. He stood there, knowing the question must be asked, afraid he already knew the answer.

Marisa came into the room. She handed Edward a glass, then sat down on the sofa beside him.

Silence cloaked the room like a shroud. And still Grigori stood there, his gaze fixed on Edward, though he was acutely conscious of Marisa, as well. He could hear the beat of their hearts, smell the blood flowing through their veins. Minutes passed. He was aware of their discomfort as the silence grew unbearable, knew that they, too, were aware of the vast chasm that yawned between them, an abyss that could never be bridged.

Ramsey drummed his fingers on the arm of the sofa.

Marisa toyed with a lock of her hair.

"Who?" Grigori asked, his voice barely audible. "Who did he send?"

"A woman," Ramsey replied in a voice equally soft.

Grigori closed his eyes a moment, summoning the strength to hear it all. "What did she look like?"

"Tall. Long black hair. Blue-green eyes."

He couldn't contain the anguished groan that rose in his throat. "Antoinette . . . Did you . . . Is she—" A muscle worked in his jaw. "Is she still alive?"

Ramsey nodded.

Hands clenching and unclenching at his sides, Grigori groaned again. "Annie . . . Annie . . ."

Marisa shook her head, her heart breaking at the pain she read in Grigori's eyes. She could not begin to imagine what he was feeling, how awful it would be to know someone you loved had been transformed into something that was no longer human.

And then the pain in his eyes was gone, consumed by flames of rage. "Tell me everything that happened," Grigori demanded, his voice gruff. "Everything you did today."

Ramsey complied, speaking in short, crisp sentences, as if he would be penalized for every unnecessary word.

"You've told me everything you remember?"

Ramsey nodded.

"And you found no trace of Alexi?" Grigori asked, his voice harsh and bitter, like acid.

"No, nothing."

"Do you think he'll send her after Edward again?" Marisa asked.

"Yes, and we'll be waiting."

"We?" Edward asked, clearly surprised.

Grigori nodded. "Tonight we'll find you a new place to stay. If he sent her once, he may send her again. And this time I'll be waiting."

"You're not thinking of spending the day in my room, are you?"

"Exactly so."

Edward snorted. "How are you going to do that?"

"Don't worry about me."

"Believe me, I don't."

"Well," Marisa said, discomfitted by the sudden tension between the two men. "I don't know about you two, but I'm hungry."

Ramsey stood up. "Yeah, me too. As long as he's here, I think I'll go get something to eat."

"I don't think that's a good idea," Marisa said. "What's to stop Alexi from finding you?"

"She's right," Grigori said. "You shouldn't be out there alone."

"I've got some steaks," Marisa said, "or we can order something in."

"I guess you're right," Edward agreed.

"So, what'll it be?"

"It doesn't matter to me," Ramsey said, "whatever you want."

"Well, I don't really feel like cooking. Let's order some Chinese."

"Sounds good to me," Edward said. "I'll take care of it."

"Okay."

"You want anything in particular?"

"No. Well, some sweet-and-sour chicken, maybe."

"Right," he said, and went into the kitchen to use the phone.

Marisa looked up at Grigori. He was still standing in the middle of the floor, his thoughts obviously turned inward. She wondered what he was thinking, and then, seeing the dark, haunted look in his eyes, she decided she didn't really want to know.

It had been a heck of a day, she mused ruefully, and the night ahead didn't look like it was going to be any better.

Chapter Thirteen

Marisa sat on the sofa, her feet tucked beneath her, a pillow clutched to her chest. Earlier, they had all gone out to find Edward a room. Tomorrow, the two men would spend the day there, waiting for Antoinette. Edward had muttered something derogatory under his breath about sharing a room with a corpse. Grigori had grimaced, but let it pass. Upon returning to her apartment, Edward had gone to bed, pleading a headache, though Marisa suspected it was just an excuse not to stay in the same room with the vampire.

"What if it is Antoinette?" Marisa asked after a while. "What then?"

Grigori had been standing at the window, staring out into the darkness. She watched him take a deep breath, and then slowly turn to face her.

"It is her," he replied quietly. "I'm sure of it."

"What will you do?"

"Destroy her."

Marisa stared at him in amazement. She heard the torment in his voice. The determination. How could he even think of doing such a thing to the woman he loved?

Grigori let out a soft sigh. "I'll do it *because* I love her," he said with quiet conviction. "It's the only way to free her soul from the hell she's living in."

"I wish you'd stop reading my mind."

"Forgive me."

His voice, low and deep, moved over her like rich black velvet, making every nerve ending in her body tingle. She gazed into his eyes, and then, remembering how she had held him in her arms, how good it had felt to hold him, she quickly looked away, afraid he would see more of her feelings than she wished him to, afraid he would know that he had filled her every waking thought, her every dream, good and bad, since the night they'd met.

"Come to me, Marisa."

Trapped in the silken web of his voice, she rose to her feet, her heart pounding. She could feel his power drawing her across the floor, feel herself yearning to be in his embrace.

His arms folded around her, lightly, carefully. He placed his finger under her chin, tilting her head up until their gazes met, and she felt herself sinking, drowning, in the midnight depths of his eyes.

Feeling as though she were moving in slow motion, she wrapped her arms around his waist and waited for his kiss. His lips were cool as they slanted over hers, yet heat spiraled through her. A little thrill of excitement uncurled in her belly as his hand flattened against her back, drawing her body closer to his. He was hard and strong, yet he held her as if she were made of spun glass. His tongue was like a flame teasing her lower lip, and she opened to him without a qualm, savoring the taste of him. Time slowed, stopped, and she was aware of nothing but the wonder of his kiss, the welcome touch of his hands stroking her back, threading through her hair, the husky tremor in his voice as he whispered her name.

It was like being in another world, a place where time had ceased to exist, where there was no night or day, no wrong or right. Caught up in the wonder of his kisses, she clung to him, reveling in the feel of his hands gliding over her skin, his long fingers awakening a hunger deep within her soul, a need to be held and touched, to feel his hands upon her. Tremors of delight rippled through her. Her hands roamed over his back and shoulders, restless, eager to explore, to touch and be touched in return.

She was breathless when he took his mouth from hers. Slowly, she felt the earth stop spinning, felt time slip back into place.

Confused, she looked up at him, her gaze searching his. "Am I here because I want to be, or because you've . . . you've mesmerized me?"

Grigori smiled down at her, his expression infinitely tender, infinitely sad.

"Ah, Marisa," he murmured softly. "If you were under my power, you would not think such a thing, let alone ask it." He brushed a lock of hair away from her face, caressed the curve of her cheek. "Do you think to deny the attraction between us?"

"No, I don't deny it, but I don't intend to let it go any further, either."

"Because I am Vampyre?"

Heart pounding, she nodded, wondering if he

would exert his power and take her against her will.

His arms fell away from her, and he took a step backward. "Do you think I would take you that way? Want you that way?"

"I don't know."

He wanted to tell her he would never do such a thing, but he couldn't. There had been times when the desire of the flesh could not be denied, times when he had used the glamour of being Vampyre to seduce a woman he fancied. But he had never employed such tactics on a woman he cared for, and he had not truly cared for a mortal woman for more than two hundred years. Not since Antoinette . . .

He turned away from Marisa. Thinking of Antoinette filled him with a bitter rage, and rage fueled the Hunger, a Hunger that had not been fed for several days.

Without a word, he left the apartment.

Marisa blinked in astonishment. One minute Grigori had been there; the next he was gone. Maybe he really was a magician, she thought with a wry grin. And then a voice inside her head whispered, *No, he's a vampire.*

How could she be attracted to a vampire? Why did she want to hold him and comfort him, to be held by him? Why did the thought of what he was no longer repulse her, sicken her? Why didn't she cringe at his touch? The answer was simple. She was falling in love with him. She shook the thought away, refusing to acknowledge the possibility.

She went to the window and stared out into the darkness of the night. Standing there, she reminded herself again that he was a vampire, undead. He had gone hunting, gone looking for a victim who would feed his lust for blood. . . . How could he drink the blood of another human? The thought died, half-finished, as she reminded herself that Grigori was no longer human, and she wondered again if he had been made into a vampire against his will. Surely no one became a vampire willingly.

She was about to go to bed when she felt the sinuous threat of evil rise up like oily black smoke. She closed the curtains with a jerk and darted away from the window, clutching the cross dangling around her neck.

Go away! Her mind screamed the words.

I will have you. She heard the vampire's voice in her mind. *You cannot escape me. Do not think Grigori will keep you safe.*

"Go away, damn you!" she cried. "Leave us alone!"

"Marisa!" Ramsey ran into the room, a wooden stake clutched in one hand. "What's wrong? Is—" He paused, felt the short hairs rise along the back of his neck. "Dammit, it's Alexi. He's here."

"Edward, no!" She grabbed his arm as he started toward the door. "You can't go out there! He'll kill you."

Ramsey hesitated. She was right. It would be the height of foolishness to stalk Alexi Kristov during the hours of darkness. And yet he could feel the vampire's presence, sliding over his skin like the papery fingers of death.

"He's gone." Marisa released her hold on Ramsey and sank down on the sofa, her whole body trembling.

Edward nodded. The night felt whole again, unsullied by evil.

Marisa pressed her hands to her temples. He had been in her mind and she felt dirty, defiled.

Ramsey went into the bedroom, returning with a blanket, which he draped over Marisa's shoulders. "I'll fix you something hot to drink," he said. "What do you want?"

"H-hot . . . chocolate." She couldn't stop shaking.

"Try to relax."

She nodded, wondering if she would ever feel clean again. Alexi had invaded her mind, her thoughts, threatened her. . . .

"Here." Ramsey thrust a mug into her hands. "Drink it; you'll feel better." He glanced around the room. "Where the hell is Chiavari?"

"He . . . he went out."

"Was he going to look for Kristov?"

"I . . . I don't think so."

Edward grunted softly, his expression saying he understood where Grigori had gone.

Feeling restless, Edward walked through the apartment, checking to make sure the windows were locked, the curtains drawn.

When he returned to the living room, Grigori was sitting on the sofa beside Marisa. The vampire looked up as Edward entered the room.

"Enjoy your dinner?" Edward asked in a voice heavily laced with sarcasm.

"Tread softly, Ramsey, lest you have two vampyres seeking your destruction."

The words were spoken without malice but were no less threatening because of it. Edward's face went pale, then flushed with anger. "I'm not afraid of you, bloodsucker."

"No?" Grigori regarded him a moment. "Then you're a bigger fool than I thought. Marisa tells me Kristov was here."

Edward nodded.

"I thought I felt his presence when I returned." Grigori swore under his breath. If only he had come back sooner! "Marisa, I think you should go to bed. Ramsey will drive you to work tomorrow. Stay inside the building until he comes to pick you up."

"All right."

"I'll see you at dusk."

She nodded, too weary to speak, to think.

"Everything will be all right."

"Will it? Alexi seems very sure of himself."

"I won't let him hurt you." Effortlessly, Grigori swung her up into his arms and, in spite of her protests that she could walk, carried her down the hallway to her bedroom and tucked her into bed.

He stared down at her a moment, and she felt herself caught up in his gaze again, felt the attraction that was ever between them hum to life.

Grigori blew out a deep breath. "Sleep well, Marisa," he murmured, and, bending down, he brushed his lips across her brow.

With a contented sigh, she closed her eyes, instantly asleep.

Grigori regarded her for a long moment, admiring her quiet beauty, the sweep of her dark lashes against her cheeks, the lush fullness of her lower lip. His gaze drifted to the rise and fall of her breasts, and he felt the stir of desire, the longing to hold her in his arms, to make love to her until the sun stole the night from the sky.

But Ramsey waited in the other room. And Alexi stalked the streets of the city, seeking prey to quench his monstrous thirst.

And somewhere, lost in a world of endless darkness, Antoinette waited.

He drew the covers up to Marisa's chin. The simple act stirred the memory of other nights, long ago, and he felt a sharp pang as he recalled the nights he had put his children to bed, told them a story. How, before he sought his own rest, he had always gone in to make sure they were safely tucked in. Marisa was not a child, yet, compared to him, she was young, so young. And so vulnerable. The protective instincts he had harbored for his children rose up within him now, and he vowed again to keep her safe, no matter the cost.

"Rest well, *cara,*" he murmured.

Edward glanced up from the newspaper he was reading, a flicker of unease in his eyes, as Grigori entered the room.

Reaching into his pocket, Grigori withdrew a key and tossed it to Ramsey. "I'll be waiting for you after you take Marisa to work."

Ramsey nodded uneasily, clearly not liking the idea of sharing a room with a vampire. "You really think he'll send her after me again?"

"Nothing's certain in life except death," Grigori replied. "You should know that by now."

"Did you ever stop to think that he's only using Antoinette as bait. For you?"

"Do you take me for a fool?" Grigori snapped. "Of course I have."

"Why is he doing this?"

"I told you, it's a game, one he feels certain of winning."

"A game—" Edward shook his head. "He's playing with people's lives."

"He has no regard for humanity," Grigori said, "or for anything else. He's existed for a thousand years, maybe more. Eternity can be very boring, even for a vampyre, and so he's devised a game, and you and Marisa are the pawns."

"And what are you?"

"I'm the prize."

"And what of Antoinette?"

"As you said, she's the bait."

"But he must care for her. He's kept her with him for two hundred years."

"He cares for nothing, and no one." Grigori lifted his head, nostrils flaring as he tested the air. He could sense the night changing to day, feel the first teasing warmth of the sun. "It's time for me to go. Don't leave Marisa alone for a moment."

Edward stared at the key in his hand. "Won't you need a coffin to rest in?"

Grigori lifted one dark brow. "You watch too many movies, Ramsey." He bared his fangs in a wolfish grin. "But I thank you for your concern."

Edward muttered something obscene under his breath.

"Take good care of Marisa," Grigori warned, and left the apartment.

Outside, the sky was turning gray. He could feel the dawn approaching, the promised heat of the sun in the sudden itching of his skin, in every nerve ending.

With preternatural speed, he traversed the city.

The door to the motel room opened at a wave of his hand. After locking the door behind him, he stripped the blankets from one of the beds and used them to cover the room's single window. He checked the bathroom, noting the bars on the narrow window over the tub.

Returning to the main room, he observed his surroundings in a long, sweeping glance. It was remarkably ugly, from the drab brown carpet to the pale beige walls and matching drapes. A cheap painting hung over the bed. There was a dresser, a chair upholstered in a hideous plaid.

Sitting on the edge of the bed, he switched on the TV, turning to a local morning-news show. As he feared, another body, drained of blood, had been found near the zoo.

Sitting back, he stared, unseeing, at the television screen, his senses probing the surrounding area for some indication that Antoinette was nearby. Antoinette . . .

. . . She gazed up at him, her blue-green eyes radiant. "We're going to have a child, Grigori," she whispered tremulously. And he swept her into his arms, his heart swelling with love for his wife, for his unborn child. He was at her side when their daughter was born, humbled by the miracle of birth, by Antoinette's willingness to walk through the valley of the shadow of death to bring a new life into the world. And a year later, she gave him a son. . . . Life was perfect, better than perfect. He adored his wife, his children, and knew their love in return, until that fateful night when he came home to find his children murdered in their beds, and his wife a mindless shell of a woman. . . .

"Damn you, Alexi," he murmured. "I thought we

were friends. You could have had any woman you wanted."

Even now, more than two hundred years later, he cursed himself for bringing Alexi home that first night. People had warned him there was something peculiar about Count Alexi Kristov, but he hadn't seen it. Maybe he hadn't wanted to see it. He had liked having Alexi Kristov for a friend. Alexi had often been a guest in their home. Always, he had been polite, well mannered. In spite of Alexi's idiosyncrasies, Grigori had never suspected him to be other than what he seemed, a gentleman from a far country who kept peculiar hours. How had he been so blind? Why hadn't Antoinette told him that Kristov had asked her to go away with him? Had she been afraid of his reaction? Afraid he wouldn't believe her? And what would he have done if she had told him? He had been a mortal man then, no match for a thousand-year-old vampire.

He remembered the first horrible days after he had buried his children. He hadn't eaten, or slept, had not been able to bring himself to leave the graveyard that held their remains, could not bear to leave his son and daughter there, alone, in the darkness of eternity.

He had been sitting there, late one foggy night, when he felt a sudden coldness creep over him. Turning, he had seen a slender figure in a dark cloak moving soundlessly among the headstones.

Grigori had gasped, certain, for one dreadful moment, that he was seeing a ghost. Only it had been far worse than a ghost. Between one blink of his eye and the next, the shadowy creature was standing before him. He saw then that it was a woman with waist-length silver-blond hair and skin as white as the shrouds that enfolded the bodies of his children.

What are you doing here? she had asked, though he had never been certain if she spoke aloud or if he heard her words in his mind.

Held captive by the twin flames that burned in her pale blue eyes, he had told her what had happened to his wife, his children.

And do you wish to join your children in death? she asked.

No! he had declared vehemently. *I want to avenge them, but how can I?* His voice broke as he fought back his tears. *How can I?*

How, indeed, she replied softly. *Shall I show you how?*

The tone of her voice, the gleam in her eye, had sent a shiver of unease down his spine. *Only show me,* he replied with a bravado he did not feel, *and I will do whatever you ask.*

She smiled at him then, a smile filled with compassion. Even so, he had seen the fangs she didn't bother to hide.

He recoiled in horror. *You're one of them!*

Will you not join me, my handsome one? It is the only way you will ever be strong enough to find the vengeance you seek.

You're asking me to become the same kind of monster he is! Grigori exclaimed.

We are not all monsters, she replied calmly. *Look at me. Do I appear a monster to you?*

No, he replied slowly. She didn't look like a monster. She looked like a queen, with her regal bearing and alabaster skin. *Who are you?* he asked.

Khira, she replied. She held out a slender, gloved hand. *Will you join me?* she asked again, her voice soft and gentle and filled with compassion.

And he cocked his head to one side, offering her easy access to the large vein in his neck. There was a sharp prick, a fleeting moment of pain, followed by bliss and blessed forgetfulness. And when next he woke, he was a newly made vampire with all of eternity stretching out before him.

The wonder of it had astounded him, so much so that, for the first few months, he forgot everything but the wonder of his new abilities. He saw the world through new eyes, eyes that could penetrate the darkest night, see details overlooked by mere mortals. Colors were brighter; he spent hours watching dancing flames and flickering candles. He heard sounds mortal ears never heard: a spider crawling across the floor, a leaf falling from a tree. His sense of smell was heightened, and every breath carried the rich, sweet scent of blood . . . ah, how he craved the taste of it, lusted for it, certain he could never drink enough.

He was never sick. He had the strength of ten strong men. He could move with incredible speed, read mortal thoughts if he put his mind to it.

And then, late one evening, he saw Khira bending over a lost child, her fangs bared, her eyes glittering with blood lust.

With a low growl, he had grabbed the boy from her grasp. *No!* Clutching the frightened child to his chest, he screamed the word at her, and in that terrible moment, when he saw his own death reflected in her bloodred eyes, he remembered why he had wanted to become a vampire.

That very night, after returning the boy to his home, he had gone in search of Alexi. . . .

The past fell away as a scent he had carried with him through the centuries wafted toward him on a vagrant wisp of air.

Rising, he watched the door swing open, felt his heart turn cold at what he saw there.

She was as beautiful as he remembered. Slender as a willow, her olive-hued skin clear and unblemished. Hair as soft as eiderdown fell past her waist like a river of black silk. Her eyes, as blue-green as the sea, stared at him without recognition.

"Antoinette." Pain slashed through his heart and gouged his soul. Had he been a living man, he thought he might have died of it.

He waited, hoping that the love they had once shared would somehow bring her back to herself.

"Antoinette, it's me, Grigori. Remember me, love," he begged. "Please remember."

She stared at him for a long moment while he hoped, prayed, for some glimpse of humanity. And then she raised her arm, and he saw the long, slender blade of the knife she held. A ray of sunlight crept through the open door, glinting off the finely honed silver blade, illuminating the large crucifix that nestled between her breasts, shimmering like moonlight on the silver. She wore wide silver bracelets on her wrists; a thick silver collar protected her throat.

Summoning all his power, Grigori caught her gaze, but he could not touch her mind, could not influence her thoughts, for she had none of her own. Mindless, soulless, she belonged to Alexi, heard no voice but his.

She took a step toward him and he looked past her, wondering if he could make it out the door before she struck him down. The sunlight seared his eyes, momentarily blinding him.

A thin, humorless smile pulled at her lips as, seeing his distress, she kicked the door wider.

Grigori swore under his breath. What the hell was keeping Ramsey? He felt the sun's heat penetrate his clothing and he took a step backward, seeking the darkest corner of the room.

Wondering which would be worse, the shock of silver slicing into his heart or the burning rays of the sun igniting his skin and turning him to ashes, he stared at her, watching, waiting.

She moved with a quickness that startled him, lunging across the floor, her lips peeled back in a horrible grin as she struck out at him with the knife. He jerked to the side, and the blade, meant for his heart, pierced his right shoulder, then sliced across his chest, leaving a long, bloody furrow that oozed dark blood. She struck out at him again and again, and each time the blade found its mark.

In desperation, he grabbed for her knife hand, his fingers burning as they closed over the silver bracelet on her wrist. Grimacing with pain, he tried to wrest the blade from her grasp.

With a feral growl, she grabbed the crucifix and thrust it into his face. The silver burned through his left cheek like the fires of hell, and he stumbled backward, his nostrils filling with the scent of his own burning flesh.

She was on him again, the knife flashing in the

sunlight. He had not expected her to be so fierce, or so strong. They toppled backward onto the bed, and his mind filled with a sudden image of the two of them lying in each other's arms on a wintry morning long ago, and then he looked into her eyes and knew that the woman he had held and loved no longer existed.

She thrashed wildly beneath him, upsetting the lamp on the bedside table, as she stabbed him again and yet again.

Teeth clenched against the pain that engulfed him, he drew back his fist and drove it into her face. Blood spurted from her nose, spraying over him like drops of crimson rain.

With a cry that could only be called a snarl, she lashed out at him with the knife, and he struck her again, and then again, until she lay still beneath him, her clothing and the bedding awash in his blood.

It was an effort to stand up. He could feel the sun climbing in the sky, feel the darkness probing at the edges of his consciousness as he stared down at the woman who had been his wife. He needed blood, but could not bring himself to take hers, knew he should kill her now and knew, just as surely, that he could not do it.

Going to the closet, he reached for the blankets folded on the shelf. With hands that trembled, he shrouded himself in the smothering folds of the thick wool, then staggered outside. It took every ounce of his rapidly waning strength to propel himself across town. Had the sun been higher in the sky, he knew he never would have made it. Even so, he could feel the sunlight seeking his flesh through the heavy cloth. In spite of the heat that engulfed him, fear that he would not reach her house in time chilled him to the core of his being.

It seemed as though hours passed before he reached Marisa's apartment. Barely able to stand, lacking the strength to break down the door and unable to summon the concentration needed to open it with the power of his mind, he threw a flower pot through the window, then leaned forward and let himself go limp so that he fell across the sill onto the floor, hardly aware of the shards of broken glass that nicked his skin.

He lay there a long moment, while the pure white heat of the sun burned through his clothing and scorched the preternatural flesh of his back and legs. He lay there for a long moment, watching his blood seep onto the carpet, leaving a dark, ugly stain on the blue rug.

The instinct to survive, the need to see Marisa one last time, provided one last burst of energy. Dragging himself across the floor, he made his way into her bedroom. It was an effort to open the closet door, to crawl inside, to close the door behind him.

Racked with pain, he huddled under the blankets, wondering, in a distant part of his mind, if there would be anything left for Marisa to find when she got home.

Chapter Fourteen

Ramsey felt the hair rise along the back of his neck as he stood in the doorway and surveyed the motel room. She hadn't made any effort to clean up this time. The sheets on the bed were soaked with blood. A broken lamp lay on the floor.

Moving cautiously, he entered the room and stared down at the sheets. So much blood. Was it hers?

He went into the bathroom, and then returned to the main room. Pulling his handkerchief from his pocket, he wiped off everything Grigori might have touched, and then left the room. He locked the door behind him, wiping off the doorknob.

Where was Grigori?

Getting into his car, he drove to Marisa's apartment.

He swore under his breath when he saw the broken window. Had Antoinette come here looking for him? He swore again as he opened the door with the key Marisa had given him.

Holding his cross tightly in his hand, he studied the broken window. Dirt and shards of crockery lay scattered over the carpet, but it was the crimson trail leading across the floor that held his attention.

Taking a deep breath, he followed the bloody path. It led into Marisa's bedroom, disappearing inside the closet.

He stood there for several minutes, his heart pounding like thunder in his ears as he contemplated who, or what, waited behind the portal.

He flicked on the light and then, taking a deep breath, he opened the door.

At first, he didn't notice anything unusual, and then he saw the blankets. Not certain he wanted to see what lay beneath, he lifted the bedding with a trembling hand, shuddered at what he saw. Grigori lay curled up on the floor, as still as death. Dried blood stained his shirt and pants, made a dark pool beneath him. His left cheek had been badly burned.

Ramsey regarded Grigori for a long moment, wondering if the vampire was capable of feeling pain when he was lost in his deathlike sleep.

For one fleeting moment, he was tempted to drive a stake through the creature's black heart, to cut off his head, then burn the body, thereby assuring that this vampire, at least, would never rise to drink human blood again.

Muttering an oath, Edward shook his head. Though he hated to admit it, he needed Chiavari's help. It was a bitter thing to admit. He had hunted vampires all over the world. None had ever eluded him, or frightened him, as did Alexi Kristov.

With a last look at the vampire, Edward replaced the covers, and closed the door.

Needing to keep busy, he went to a lumberyard and bought a sheet of plywood to cover the broken window. When that was done, he set to work scrubbing the blood out of the carpet, an impossible task, but it gave him something to do.

Time and again he considered going in search of Antoinette and Alexi, but it didn't seem wise to leave Grigori alone and unprotected. He didn't know what had happened to Antoinette, didn't know if she would strike again.

When he was finished, he sat back and surveyed the results. He didn't think Marisa would be pleased when she saw the faint brown stains. Maybe a professional carpet cleaner could get them out.

At three, he called Marisa at work.

"Yes, hello?"

"Marisa, this is Edward."

There was a moment of silence: then he heard her take a deep breath. "What's wrong?"

"Is there any chance you can leave work early? I don't think we should be out after dark."

"What's happened?"

"Grigori was attacked."

"Attacked! By who? Is he . . . ?"

"No. He's hurt pretty bad, but I don't know what to do for him." He grunted softly. "As for who attacked him, my guess is it was Antoinette. One of the reasons vampires make revenants is because of their ability to move about during the day. How soon can you get away?"

"In about half an hour."

"Okay, I'll pick you up."

"No. I don't think you should leave him alone. I'll take a cab. I'll be home about four-thirty."

"Be careful."

"You too."

Marisa hung up the receiver, and then sat staring at the phone. Grigori was hurt. What did that mean, exactly? She knew he could be injured. She had seen the scratches inflicted by Alexi. But she'd also seen how rapidly he healed. . . .

She turned off her computer, called for a cab, then gathered her things together and went to tell Mr. Salazar that there was an emergency at home and she had to leave. She had told Grigori, in jest, that her boss was an ogre, but it wasn't entirely true. Salazar might be a tyrant where work was concerned, but he was extremely lenient with his employees.

"Sure, Marisa," he said, "take tomorrow off, too, if you need to. Donna can fill in for you."

"Thank you, Mr. Salazar."

"Sure, sure, no problem. Did you get the Wendall deposition typed up?"

"Yes, it's on my desk, ready to go."

"Good, good. Let me know if there's anything I can do."

"I will, thank you."

The cab was waiting when she left the building. She gave the driver her address, and then climbed into the backseat, fidgeting nervously as the taxi threaded its way through the heavy traffic on the freeway. She watched the sky turn from blue to gray and wished for summer and daylight saving time.

She felt like screaming by the time they reached her apartment. She paid the driver, then ran up the stairs, her eyes widening when she saw the plywood that covered the front window.

Her heart was pounding as she opened the door. "Edward?"

"Yeah?" He stepped out of the kitchen. "I thought I'd make dinner. Hope you don't mind."

"No, I don't mind," Marisa replied. "You'll make some woman a wonderful wife." She dropped her handbag on the sofa, muttering, "What the hell?" when she saw the faint brown stains on the carpet. "Where's Grigori?"

"In the closet in your bedroom."

"What's he doing in the closet?" she asked, the answer occurring to her before she had finished asking the question.

"I don't know if you want to see him."

"Why not?"

"He's pretty badly cut up." Edward shook his head. "He looks like somebody chewed him up and spit him out."

"That's how I feel, too."

Marisa looked up to see Grigori leaning against the doorjamb. She had often heard people say someone looked like death warmed over. In this case, it was the truth. His face was beyond pale, the skin dry and brittle-looking, like scorched paper. His shirt was in shreds, the cloth stained with so much blood she couldn't tell what color the material was supposed to be. The skin on his left cheek had been badly burned.

Nausea roiled in her stomach, making her feel faint. Her first instinct was to turn and run away as fast and as far as her legs could carry her. And he knew it. She read the knowledge in his eyes, dark black eyes filled with anguish, burning with rage and agony that was far deeper than physical pain.

"Come and sit down," Marisa said. She started toward him, one hand outstretched to help him.

"Stay away from me."

His voice slammed into her, halting her in mid-stride. She glanced over at Edward, who was standing near the front door, his crucifix clutched in both hands.

"Ramsey, take Marisa and get out of here."

"You said it wasn't safe for us to be out at night," she reminded him.

"You're not safe here, either."

"What do you mean?"

"Look at him, Marisa," Edward said, coming to stand beside her. "Come on, let's go."

"Are you crazy? He needs help."

"Ramsey, get her out of here! Take her someplace crowded and well lit. The mall. Buy me a change of clothes." He didn't need a new shirt or pants, he had an extensive wardrobe at home, but he needed to get them out of the house. He hoped that the errand would give them something else to think about.

With a nod, Edward reached for Marisa's hand. "Come on, let's go."

"No." She shook off his hand. "He needs help."

"He doesn't need our help," Ramsey said. "He needs blood."

She didn't want to believe it, but the truth was staring her in the face.

"He's right," Grigori said tersely. He clenched his hands; the scent of their blood, *her* blood, fanning the hunger that was roaring through him, demanding to be fed, demanding that he replace what had been lost so his body could heal itself.

Marisa stared at him, seeing past the wounds that crisscrossed his body, past the pain in his eyes to the hunger growing within him. From somewhere deep inside came the urge to go to him, to offer him the sustenance he needed. The thought appalled her even as it beckoned.

"No." Grigori shook his head. "Not now, Marisa."

And before she could decipher that cryptic message, Ramsey was pulling her out of the apartment.

Clinging tightly to his self-control, Grigori watched them go, watched her go. She had wanted to help him, wanted to offer him her life's blood. And he had wanted to take it, would have taken it save for the awful fear that, once he touched her, tasted her, he wouldn't be able to stop.

But there was no need for self-control now, and he shed it like a snake shedding its skin, surrendering to the pain that hummed through every inch of his body, loosing the hunger that clawed at his vitals. He felt the sharp prick of his fangs against his tongue, knew his eyes burned red with the need pulsing through him.

Ripping off what was left of his shirt, he tossed it into the trash, then staggered into the bathroom and washed the blood from his face and chest and arms. He looked at himself in the mirror, lifted a hand to his cheek, feeling the ragged edges of charred skin. It would be weeks before the burn healed. But it would heal and there would be no scar.

Shirtless, he left the house. Resting had restored some of his strength. He masked his presence from those he passed until he found what he was looking for, a healthy young man walking alone down a deserted street. Ordinarily, he never hunted in the same city where he slept, but now need overruled caution.

He blanked the man's mind, then bent over him, taking what he needed, drinking long and deep. The temptation to take it all rose up strong within him, but he took no more than the man could safely spare. He ran his tongue over the wounds to seal them, wiping all memory of his presence from the man's mind.

He ghosted through the city streets, taking his prey unawares. How much simpler it would have been to take one mortal and drain him to the point of death, to drink not only his blood but his life as well, but he had vowed, a century ago, that he would never take a human life again unless his own life was at risk.

It was after midnight when he returned to Marisa's apartment. He had expected to find Ramsey and Marisa asleep, but they were in the living room. Dialogue from a movie they weren't watching filled the silence of the room.

He felt the censure in their eyes as they watched him close and lock the door. When he turned around, they were both looking elsewhere. It made him feel as if he didn't exist.

For stretched seconds, no one spoke. And then Ramsey stood up. "Your clothes are in a bag in the kitchen."

Grigori nodded.

"I'm going to bed."

"Hold on, Ramsey. Where were you this morning?"

Edward let out a long sigh, and Marisa had the feeling that he had been waiting all night for this one question. And even as he seemed to gather the courage to answer, she wondered if things would have turned out differently if he had been at the motel that morning.

"There was a five-car pile-up on the freeway," Ramsey said, meeting Grigori's eyes for the first time. "Two fatalities. I got hung up in traffic."

Grigori nodded. "Good night."

Edward glanced at Marisa, then left the room.

"Well," Marisa said, not meeting his eyes, "I think I'll go to bed, too."

"Marisa."

"What?" She kept her head lowered, her fingers toying with the cross dangling between her breasts.

"Look at me."

She couldn't, she thought, she couldn't face him now, knowing where he had been, what he'd been doing.

"Look at me."

It was impossible to resist the power in his voice. Slowly, she lifted her head and met his gaze. "Does it hurt?" she asked, gesturing at his cheek.

"Yes. Why? Do you think me incapable of feeling pain?"

"I don't know."

"It doesn't hurt as much as the distrust in your eyes."

She glanced away, then met his gaze again. "Will I read about more dead bodies in the morning paper?"

"Not of my doing."

She said nothing, but he knew she didn't believe him.

"I haven't killed anyone, except to preserve my own existence, in over a hundred years."

She regarded him for a long moment. The hideous knife wounds were already healing. Some were no more than faint red streaks against his pale flesh. Only the burn on his cheek seemed unimproved, the flesh charred and black.

He wished suddenly that he had thought to stop at his resting place and put on a shirt, but he'd had other, more urgent matters on his mind. She was staring at his face. Seeing the revulsion in her eyes, he covered his injured cheek with his hand.

"Is there anything I can do for that?" she asked.

He shook his head. "The skin will rejuvenate, in time. Burns are always slow to heal."

"Oh."

"Marisa—"

"Don't."

"Don't what?"

"Don't look at me like that. Don't make me stay here."

"I'm not keeping you."

She drew her knees to her chest and wrapped her arms around them, staring up at him through eyes that were wide and frightened, eyes filled with doubt and confusion. And a reluctant concern.

"Did you want to be a vampire?"

"Yes."

"Why?"

"Because I felt it was the only way I could avenge the deaths of my children."

"How old were they?"

"My daughter was five, my son a year younger."

"I'm sorry."

"It was a long time ago," he murmured, "and yet the pain remains." He sank down on the floor, his back against the wall, one knee bent. He looked up at her, his expression bleak. "All these years, and still I have not been able to destroy him. I hunted him for a hundred years, and then, when I found him, it was too late. Silvano's family had interred him in the bowels of a church and I could not reach him. Now, he is here, and still I cannot find his lair, cannot get close enough to destroy him!"

His hands clenched. "In the past, I have been able to sense the presence of other vampyres, have been able to track them to their resting places. Why can't I find Alexi?"

She had no answer for him, could only stare at him, watching with disbelieving eyes as the lacerations on his chest continued to heal before her eyes, the red scars fading and then disappearing, until nothing remained but the ugly wound on his cheek.

"What is it?" he asked. "What's wrong?"

She shook her head in wonder, then pointed at his chest, his arms. "They're gone. The wounds, as if they were never there at all."

Grigori glanced down, then shrugged. "I told you, we heal quickly."

"I know." But it was still an amazing thing to watch. "Isn't it lonely, being a vampire? Not being able to tell anyone who you are?" Sort of like being Superman, she thought, always pretending to be Clark Kent.

"It can be lonely, at times," he admitted. In the beginning, he had missed his home, his family, but, gradually, he had grown accustomed to his solitary life, had even come to enjoy it. He had never lacked female companionship. The Dark

Gift carried an aura of power. Any woman he had desired had been his for the taking. He had seduced them, but he had loved none of them. He had traveled the world, watched the changes two centuries had wrought, seen things, done things, beyond the powers of mortal man.

"Eternity is such a long time. Doesn't life get . . . tiresome? How ever do you pass the time?"

He grinned at her. "Do you picture me lurking in the shadows, always on the outside looking in, wishing I could be part of humanity again?"

"Well, yeah, I guess so."

"It's not like that, Marisa. Think of people you know who work nights. What do they do?"

"I don't know. The same things I do, I guess."

He nodded. "I read. Books, newspapers, the classics, mysteries. I go to the movies. I've traveled the world. I stay at home and watch TV." He smiled at her. "All the good shows are on at night, you know?"

She couldn't help it, she smiled back.

"Not all of us are the evil monsters depicted in movies and novels."

"Like Kristov?"

Grigori nodded. "Like Kristov."

"Was he always like he is now?"

"I don't know. When I first met him, he seemed to be a fine gentleman. I couldn't understand why he wanted to spend time in our poor home."

But he knew now. It hadn't been his company Kristov had sought, but Antoinette's. And when she had refused him, he had lashed out in a rage, killing those she had held most dear. He could hear Alexi's voice screaming in his mind: *. . . she refused . . . to leave you or those brats. . . . Well, she* *doesn't refuse me anymore*. Pain clawed at him as he imagined Antoinette sharing a bed with Alexi, helpless to resist him, compelled to surrender to his every wish.

"Grigori?"

"What?"

"Where were you?"

"Remembering."

She nodded. Judging from the look on his face, they weren't pleasant memories.

"Have you ever made anyone else a vampire?"

"No."

"Why not?"

"No one has asked, and it is not something I would force on another."

"What's it like, to drink . . . to drink blood?"

"It is natural for me, Marisa. It is not repulsive. The taste can be—" he glanced fleetingly at the slender curve of her neck—"sweet, especially when it is offered willingly."

"It sounds as if you *like* being a vampire." She shook her head, unable to accept the idea. "I can't believe you don't miss being able to go out during the day, or eating a good meal, or . . . or—"

"For me, becoming Vampyre was a blessing. I was born in a poor village in Tuscany. I couldn't read or write, and had no hope of learning to do so, nothing to look forward to but a life of hard work and an early death. When I became Vampyre, it opened up a whole new world for me. Literally, a whole new world. The vampyre who made me taught me how to hunt, how to survive. And when she'd taught me all I needed to know to survive, she taught me to read and write. She taught me how to behave as a gentleman, to appreciate art and literature. When I realized I couldn't reach Alexi, I traveled to the far corners of the world, saw places and people I had never dreamed existed."

"How did you find her, the vampire who made you?"

"She found me." His lips twitched in what might have been a smile. "I used to go to my children's graves at night because I didn't like to think of them being there, alone, in the dark." The sadness of two hundred years flickered in his eyes. "My little boy was afraid of the dark."

"Grigori, I'm so sorry." Without realizing she had moved, she was off the sofa, kneeling beside him, drawing him into her arms. "So sorry . . ."

She held him close, one hand sliding up and down his bare back until, gradually, she was no longer comforting him, but caressing him. His skin was cool and firm beneath her fingertips; the muscles in his back and shoulders were corded and sharply defined.

He remained unmoving in her arms, quiescent as her hands slid down his arms, over his belly, threaded through his hair. He felt the first stirring of desire unfurl within her, heard the sudden catch in her breath as she realized that his body was reacting to her touch. Did she think him incapable of desire? Her blood warmed; a flush stained her cheeks.

When she would have pulled away, he slid his arm around her waist to keep her close. "Don't stop."

"I can't—"

"Because I am Vampyre." he said caustically.

"No . . . because . . . because I hardly know you

Because I—" The flush in her cheeks grew hotter and her gaze slid away from his. "I'm not, I don't—"

"You have nothing to fear from me. I don't have any diseases, Marisa," he said, reading the thoughts she couldn't put into words. "I can no longer father a child."

"Oh." She looked up at him then, and he saw the fear in her eyes.

Slowly, reluctantly, he released her. "I would not take you against your will, *cara*."

"You must have known a lot of women in two hundred years."

"Many," he admitted. "But when I'm with you, I can remember none of them."

"Except Antoinette."

"Yes," he said heavily. "Antoinette."

"She's still your wife, isn't she?"

He drew a deep, painful breath and let it out in a long, slow sigh. "The girl I married is dead. Nothing remains but an empty shell, a shadow of the woman I loved."

He looked past her to the window. "I must go. Be careful tomorrow. Have Ramsey drive you to work and pick you up. Don't go anywhere alone."

"Are you going to stay here again?"

"No."

"Where do you . . . sleep?"

"It's better if you don't know." He caressed her cheek with the back of his hand, his knuckles sliding over her skin, making her shiver with pleasure. "Be careful."

"You too."

"Always." He rose smoothly to his feet, then offered her his hand, pulling her up beside him. "Remember what I said. Don't go anywhere alone."

"I'll be all right." She smiled at him, then went into the kitchen, returning moments later with a brown shopping bag. "Don't forget your clothes."

He hefted the bag, certain he would not care for Ramsey's taste in clothing, which ran to dull browns and obnoxious plaids. "Thank Ramsey for me."

"I will. Would it have made any difference this morning, if he'd been there?"

She felt him tense as he considered her question. And then he nodded. "He would have killed her without a qualm."

"And you couldn't, could you?"

"No. Even knowing it was the only way to put her soul to rest, I couldn't do it."

"I'm glad."

"Are you? Why?"

"I just am."

"Does it make me less a monster in your eyes?"

"You're not a monster."

"You thought so not so very long ago."

She had no answer for that.

He placed his forefinger under her chin, tilted her head up, and brushed his lips across hers.

"Till tonight, *cara,*" he whispered tenderly, and then he was gone.

Chapter Fifteen

In the morning, before leaving for work, Marisa called Mr. Abbott and let him know she had accidentally broken a window. He told her not to worry about it and assured her that he would have it fixed as soon as possible. Next, she called and made an appointment to have her carpets cleaned, wondering, as she did so, what the chances were of getting the bloodstains out of the rug.

She thought about Grigori while she showered. She thought about him while she dressed, donning a blue jersey sheath with long sleeves and a high neck. She drew on her nylons, stepped into a pair of beige heels, and left the bedroom.

She thought about Grigori while she ate breakfast. She looked at the bowl of cereal on the table and imagined a bowl of blood. He had said consuming blood was normal for him, but the mere idea disgusted her. She lifted a hand to her neck, trying to imagine what it would be like to feel his teeth there. Was it painful, nourishing a vampire? He had said blood was sweet when offered willingly. Had there been many women who had offered him their life's essence?

She had known him such a short time, yet he

had taken over her life, her thoughts, her dreams.

Her life had never been in more danger, or been more exciting.

She was wondering if she'd have to go in and wake Edward up when he entered the kitchen looking bleary eyed.

"Morning," he muttered. "Got any coffee?"

"On the stove. Are you all right?"

"Yeah, yeah, I'm fine. Just catching a cold."

"You look awful."

"I feel awful." He poured himself a cup of coffee. "You ready to go?"

"Yeah. Just let me grab my purse."

He sniffled and sneezed all the way downtown.

"You'd better stop at the drugstore and get something for that."

"Yeah, I will." He pulled up to the curb in front of her office building. "I'll see you at five."

"Right. Go get some rest."

"Yeah, I think I will."

Shaking her head, Marisa watched him pull into the flow of traffic.

Ramsey stopped at the corner drugstore and picked up his favorite brand of cold medicine. He considered driving to La Habra to see if he could find some trace of Kristov, but by the time he pulled off the freeway, he was burning up. He'd take the cold tablets, lie down for an hour or two, and then search until it was time to pick up Marisa.

When he got to Marisa's apartment, he took a couple of aspirin for his headache, swallowed two cold tablets, and drank a glass of orange juice.

Going into the living room, he turned on the TV,

and then stretched out on the sofa. He'd just rest for a few minutes. . . .

Edward came awake with a low groan. How was it possible to feel worse after a nap?

Lurching to his feet, he staggered into the kitchen and took another couple of aspirin, washing them down with a glass of juice.

He looked at the clock on the stove, blinked, looked again, and swore under his breath.

Damn, he was supposed to be picking up Marisa, and he should have left fifteen minutes ago.

Going into the bathroom, he splashed some cold water on his face, then practically ran out of the house. If he hurried, if the traffic wasn't too heavy, he could still make it on time.

Grigori rose with the setting sun, his thoughts on Marisa as he showered. She would be on her way home from work by now. Stepping from the tub, he went into the bedroom. He grunted softly when he saw the shopping bag on the floor beside the bed. Curious to see what Ramsey had picked out for him, he dumped the contents of the sack on the bed, and knew immediately that it had been Marisa who selected the bulky dark blue vee-necked sweater and stretch jeans.

He dressed quickly in the clothes she had chosen, feeling as though he were slipping into her arms as he pulled the sweater over his head.

Leaving his lair, which was located in the guest house behind a rather expensive mansion, he headed for Marisa's apartment.

He knew immediately that she wasn't there. A wave of his hand opened the door, and he stepped inside to wait for her to return from work. He wondered how Ramsey had spent the day, whether he had learned anything of where Alexi took his rest.

He wandered through the apartment, noting that the front window had been replaced. The kitchen was clean and tidy, as usual. The spare bedroom smelled strongly of Ramsey. Ramsey, who was falling in love with Marisa. He cursed softly, annoyed because the very idea filled him with jealousy, because his first urge was to kill the man for daring to care for her.

Leaving the room, he slammed the door behind him.

He went into Marisa's bedroom, and her scent wrapped around him, warm with life. He ran his fingertips over the pillow on her bed, felt his awareness of her grow sharper as he imagined her sleeping there, imagined what it would be like to lie beside her, to make love to her through the night. . . .

His head jerked up, every sense alert, as he heard the front door open, the sound of familiar footsteps.

In the blink of an eye, he was standing in the living room.

"I must destroy you." Her voice, so different, yet the same.

"Antoinette, don't."

"I must."

"Remember, dammit! Remember who you are. Remember me."

She shook her head, the dark cloud of her hair floating over her shoulders. And then she lifted her hands. There was a pistol in the left, a very long, very sharp blade in the right.

He muttered a curse as she fired the gun. He felt the bullet pierce his chest, tearing through flesh and muscle and tissue. He reeled backward, slamming into the wall behind him, as she squeezed the trigger again.

With a wordless cry, he lunged toward her. He knocked the gun from her hand, wrested the knife away from her and flung it across the room. She fought him wildly, her nails raking his face, biting, kicking, but she was no match for his strength this time, and he wrestled her to the floor, one of his hands imprisoning both of hers, the weight of his body pinning her to the floor beneath him.

"Antoinette." He murmured her name, and then, with a low growl, he buried his fangs in her throat.

She cried out once, a cry filled with anguish and pain, and then she went limp beneath him.

As he drank, her essence spread through him, filling him, warming him. And with the blood came the knowledge of what her existence had been like for the last two hundred years. Empty years, with no memory of her past, no recollection of who she was. That, at least, was a blessing.

His tears fell onto her face like red rain as her heartbeat grew slow, lethargic, so faint he could scarcely hear it.

When he had taken enough, but not too much, he drew her into his arms and held her against him, his hand stroking her hair. And then he sank his fangs into his own wrist. Opening a vein, he pressed her mouth to the wound, telling her to drink.

Please, he thought, please let this work.

* * *

Marisa checked her watch for the third time. She had been standing out front, waiting for Edward, for twenty minutes. She was about to go back inside and call home when she saw her car pull up to the curb.

"About time," she muttered as she opened the door and slid into the passenger seat. "What took you so . . . Oh, my God."

She stared at him, wondering why she hadn't sensed his presence as she had in the past.

She grabbed for the door handle as the car spun away from the curb, but the door wouldn't open. It wasn't locked, but it wouldn't open.

"Please," she whispered, her heart in her throat. "Please."

"Sit back, my dear, and enjoy the ride."

Like a mouse mesmerized by a snake, she stared at Alexi Kristov, unable to draw her gaze away, unable to believe that it was really him. His skin, so pale when last she saw him, was now rosy with the illusion of life. His reddish brown hair, no longer lank, fell past his shoulders. He wore a pair of black pants, a loose-fitting white shirt with long, full sleeves, and a black velvet vest.

"Alexi." The name slipped past her lips.

He inclined his head in her direction. "The pleasure is all mine, my dear."

"Where's Edward?"

Alexi licked his lips in a way that could only be called obscene.

"You killed him?"

"Alas, no."

"Where are you taking me?"

"Someplace where Grigori will never find you."

"Please, don't—"

He laughed softly. "I'm not going to kill you, my dear."

"What have you done with Antoinette?"

"I sent her to kill Grigori, of course." Alexi cocked his head to one side, as if listening to a voice only he could hear. "She has failed. I fear she will be of no further use to me now," he mused with a twinge of regret. "Either he will kill her to free her from my power, or he will bring her over. Ah, well, she no longer amused me, and I tire of the game. And of this city."

He reached toward her, his right hand sliding down her arm and over her thigh. "Antoinette is lost to me, but you will take her place very nicely. And we will start a new game, in a new place."

The thought of being like Antoinette, a soulless, mindless creature, filled Marisa with horror. She grabbed the door handle again and gave it a desperate yank, but nothing happened. With a cry, she rolled down the window, intending to jump out of the car. Better to be run over and killed than face the fate Alexi had in store for her.

"No." His voice wrapped around her, holding her in place, as the window rolled back up, seemingly of its own accord.

Grigori, help me. . . . She sat back in the seat, unable to move. *Please hear me, Grigori, I'm so afraid. . . .*

Ramsey opened his eyes, surprised to find himself still alive. Wincing with pain, he sat up and looked around. There was nothing to see . . . no houses, no lights, no traffic of any kind. Where the hell was he?

Marisa!

He swore under his breath as he glanced at his watch. It was after six.

He lurched to his feet, only then realizing that the car was gone.

"Alexi, damn you!" He remembered now, remembered it all. He had been on his way to pick Marisa up from work when a cold chill had snaked its way down his spine. Knowing what he was going to see, he had risked a look in the rear-view mirror.

Terror had been a cold, hard lump in the pit of his gut when he saw Alexi staring back at him.

It was the last thing he remembered.

"Shit!" With both hands, he examined his neck, searching for the telltale signs, but there were no bites, at least none he could see. He examined both wrists, the bend of his elbow. Nothing.

Almost sick with relief, he started walking east, toward the city.

He was a dead man, he thought glumly, as surely as if Alexi Kristov had killed him. Because there was no way Grigori would let him live after this.

Chapter Sixteen

Antoinette regained consciousness slowly. For a long time, she stared at the man holding her, and then she smiled.

It was an expression he had thought never to see again, an expression of such love and devotion it would have broken his heart, if he'd still had one.

She lifted one hand to his ruined cheek. "What happened?"

"A burn. It's nothing."

"Does it hurt very much?"

"Not when you touch it."

She smiled at him again, then frowned. "Grigori, I had the most horrible dream."

"Did you, *cara mia*?"

She nodded. "You've been crying."

He didn't deny it, only held her closer, as if he would never let her go.

"What's wrong?" She glanced around. "Where am I? Where are the . . ." Her voice trailed away. Her eyes filled with confusion, and then she screamed. "He killed them! Alexi killed them!" She struggled in his embrace. "Let me go! I'll kill him! I'll kill him!"

"Antoinette, stop it."

At the sound of his voice, she stilled immediately. She was his creature now. She would do whatever he commanded.

He gazed deep into her eyes, the power of his mind calming hers.

"Listen to me, *cara*. You will never remember our children again, or anything else that happened that night. Do you understand?"

"Yes."

"You will do whatever I ask, tell me whatever I wish to know, won't you?"

"Yes."

"Where have you been staying?"

"I live in a small house off Hartdale Avenue."

"Does Alexi live there also?"

"No. I stay there alone, waiting for his bidding."

"Where does Alexi spend the daylight hours?"

"He told me never to tell anyone."

"But I am your master now. You must tell me."

"He sleeps in the wine cellar at our house."

"Our house?" Grigori frowned. The only house they had ever shared had been in Italy. He had gone back to his old hometown about thirty years before. All the houses in the vicinity, including his own and his Uncle Pietro's, had been torn down and replaced by a winery and acres of vineyards. "That's not possible."

She nodded. "He owns it now."

"Alexi owns the winery?"

She looked at him oddly. "We don't have a winery, Grigori."

"What is it like now, our house?"

"It is the same as it was when first you took me there."

He shook his head, trying to make sense of it. "When were you there last?"

She thought a moment. "Five days ago."

"What month was it?"

"November."

"And the year, do you remember the year?"

"Seventeen ninety-eight. Alexi woke me and said we were going to find you." A faint smile pulled at the corners of her mouth. "He said we were going through time to the year nineteen hundred and ninety-eight, but I did not believe him. It's not possible, is it?" She paused and glanced around the room, her gaze troubled as she saw the TV set, the stereo, the lamps. "And yet, everything is so strange here."

Grigori sat back, stunned. Alexi had traveled through time. How? He remembered asking Alexi where Antoinette was, and Alexi's reply: *Where you cannot find her.*

No wonder they couldn't find Kristov's resting place! He wasn't sleeping in the same city where he hunted. He wasn't even sleeping in the same century!

"Where is he now?"

She stared past him, her brow furrowed in thought, her expression blank. "He's gone back."

"Alone?"

"No. He has the woman with him."

"Is he planning to come back for you?"

"No. After I destroyed you, I was to destroy myself, as well." She spoke the words without feeling, as if they meant nothing to her.

Grigori swore under his breath, and then he stood up, drawing her with him. "How do you feel?"

"I don't know." She looked up at him, her eyes filled with confusion. "Am I dead?"

"No." He wasn't sure what she was now. In taking her blood and giving her his, he had broken Alexi's hold over her. She was bound to him now, until he died. Unless he brought her across and made her as he was. And that, he thought, was the only real answer, the only way she would ever be in control of her own destiny again.

But not now . . . not when he needed her help.

"Sit down, Antoinette. Relax."

"What are we going to do?" she asked.

"Do you know where Ramsey is?"

"Ramsey?" She thought a moment, then shook her head.

"Was Alexi going to kill him?"

"I don't know."

With a sigh, he went to the window and stared out into the night. He stood there, unmoving, still as only one who is Vampyre can be still, his thoughts churning. Alexi had Marisa. Antoinette was still alive. Ramsey was missing. Alexi had Marisa. . . .

Marisa. When had she become so important to him? She was a mortal woman, cut off from him by centuries of blood and death. And yet she had cradled him in her arms, made him feel things he had not felt in two hundred years.

He heard the rustle of Antoinette's skirts as she shifted on the sofa and felt a sudden stab of guilt. She was his wife, but she was no longer the woman he had loved. She would never be that woman again. And he was no longer the man she had married . . . no longer a man at all.

But she was still his wife, and he was responsible for her.

He stood there for an hour, staring into the night, his thoughts turned inward. Antoinette was safe for now, but Marisa . . .

He turned slowly as the front door opened and Edward Ramsey burst inside.

"Is she here?" Ramsey asked breathlessly. "Tell me she's here."

"Alexi has her," Grigori replied quietly, and it took all his self-control to keep from reaching for the other man, to keep from ripping him to shreds. "What happened?"

Ramsey sneezed and blew his nose. "I fell asleep. When I woke up, I got the car and started downtown. Alexi was in the backseat. That's all I remember."

Grigori took a step forward and Edward scrambled backward, his hand clutching the cross. He yelped as Antoinette came up behind him, her arms wrapping around him, pinning his arms to his sides. He struggled to free himself, but she was too strong for him.

Grigori approached Edward. Holding Ramsey's jaw between his thumb and forefinger, he turned the man's head from side to side, checking his neck for bite marks.

"I already looked," Edward said.

Eyes narrowed, Grigori stared at Ramsey, listening to the thunderous beat of his heart. There were no bite marks on the man's neck, but that didn't mean anything.

Ramsey glared at him, a kitten spitting in the face of a tiger.

"Go on, bloodsucker, do it!" Edward taunted. "You're no better than he is."

Grigori grinned at Ramsey's bravado. "I cannot help admiring your courage, Ramsey." He nodded at Antoinette. "Let him go."

As soon as Antoinette released him, Ramsey bolted across the room. "What have you done to her?"

"She's mine, now."

"You did that to her? To your own wife?"

"Would you rather she was still Alexi's creature?"

"What do we do now?"

"I've spent the last hour trying to decide. Nothing Antoinette says makes sense."

"What do you mean?"

"She says the reason we haven't been able to find Alexi is because he takes his rest in the wine cellar of our old house."

"What old house? Where?" Edward's eyes widened. "You don't mean in Italy?"

Grigori nodded. "But that's not possible. The house no longer exists. And yet . . ."

Edward held the cross in both hands, sliding it back and forth between his palms. "What? What are you thinking?"

"Time-travel," Grigori suggested.

"That's impossible!"

"Is it?" Grigori stared out into the dark of the night again. Khira had mentioned it once, saying that sometimes, when she grew sad or lonely, she went back to her old home. When he had asked her how she accomplished such a thing, she had shrugged and said she thought herself there.

He frowned, remembering. . . . *But you can only*

go back so far, she had warned, *only back to the time you were made. Beyond that you cannot go. Nor can you venture into the future.*

Was it possible? Could he do it? Could he go back in time? And if he could, what would be the point? Kristov had possessed the Dark Gift far longer than he. If what Khira had said was true, Alexi could go back in time over a thousand years, while Grigori could go back but two hundred years.

And yet what Antoinette said must be true, for he had built their house himself, built it the year they were married. Alexi must have taken perverse pleasure in taking his rest there, in keeping Antoinette imprisoned there all these years.

"You're not really considering it, are you?" Ramsey asked.

Grigori nodded. For Marisa's sake, he had to try.

"I'm going with you."

"Indeed?"

Edward stuck his chin out. "We're in this together, remember? If you're thinking of zapping yourself into the past, I'm going with you."

Grigori lifted one brow. "Are you? I don't even know if I can get myself there."

Ramsey grinned. "I've got faith in you, Chiavari. Hatred is a powerful motivator, and between us, we've got enough hate to accomplish a miracle."

"Perhaps." Grigori held out his hand. "Antoinette, come to me."

Like a sleepwalker, she went to his side and placed her hand in his.

"Ramsey, take her hand." Grigori smiled faintly. "If you know any prayers, this might be a good time to say them."

Edward held Antoinette's hand in one of his, his free hand clutching his cross.

"Scared, vampire hunter?" Grigori asked.

"Damn right."

Grigori laughed softly and then, taking a deep breath, he closed his eyes.

He thought of Alexi.

He thought of Marisa.

And then he focused all his thoughts, all his energy, on his home in Italy as it had been two hundred years ago in November of seventeen ninety-eight.

Blackness swirled around him, drawing him down, down, into an abyss deeper than the darkness that shrouded him while he slept. He had no sense of movement, yet he knew he was moving through time and space.

And then, inexplicably, he had a sense of time slowing.

He opened his eyes, knowing, even before he saw the house, that he had been transported into the past.

"Damn! It worked!" Ramsey was grinning like a fool as he glanced around.

Grigori swore under his breath. "He's not here."

"We'll find him."

"Will we? We don't even know if he came here." But he wasn't thinking of Alexi now. He was staring at the house, remembering. Memories rushed toward him, memories of his parents, of the day he had married Antoinette, of the laughter they had shared in the quiet of the night. He remembered how her body had changed, her belly swelling with the new life she carried beneath her heart, the wonder of holding his tiny newborn daughter in his arms, and then, a year later, his son. In his mind, he saw their smiles, heard the sound of their youthful voices calling, "Papa, Papa," and his heart, long dead within him, ached with renewed pain and grief.

"Chiavari, you okay?"

He swallowed the lump in his throat as he turned to face Ramsey. "Fine."

"So, where do we start?"

Grigori took a deep breath, inhaling the familiar scents of home—garlic and olive oil and oregano, the smell of sheep and goats and manure, the fresh, clean scent of the earth itself.

"Let's go inside," he said. "Maybe we can tell if he's been here tonight."

The house was as he remembered it: four small rooms sparsely filled with furniture, most of which he had made with his own hands.

He walked into the bedroom he had once shared with Antoinette. There was no sign of Alexi.

Turning on his heel, he left the room and went outside. The wine cellar was located behind the house. Lifting the wooden door, he descended the stairs. The cellar reeked of dust and stale air, of cork and grapes and old wine.

Of Alexi.

The vampyre had been there. He could see the outline of Kristov's resting place in the dirt. Grigori grunted softly. Alexi was an old-world vampyre, one who took his rest within a coffin.

But the coffin was gone. And so was Kristov.

"Find anything?" Ramsey asked when Grigori returned to the house.

"He's been here, but he's gone. I doubt he'll be back."

"He must have known we were coming."

Grigori glanced at Antoinette, who was standing in the middle of the parlor, her expression blank. How pretty she was, dressed in a red blouse and white ruffled skirt. Red. It had always been her favorite color.

"So how do we find him?"

Grigori glanced at Ramsey. "He will find us."

"I don't think I like the sound of that."

"You didn't have to come."

"Yes, I did. I just wish I knew what he was up to."

"He's playing the same game as before."

"Hide-and-seek, you mean."

"Something like that."

"So what do we do now?"

"We wait," Grigori replied. "Wait for him to come to us."

Chapter Seventeen

Marisa blinked against the light. She felt disoriented, confused. And then she heard the sound of laughter. Soft laughter, tinged with evil. It was a voice she recognized.

"You'll get used to it," Alexi said. He moved into her field of vision, his arms crossed over his chest, his malevolent gray eyes regarding her with amusement.

"What happened?" She glanced around. "Where are we?"

"Italy."

"Italy! That's impossible."

"For me, my sweet Marisa, nothing is impossible."

She looked around the room again. There was a small four-drawer chest of drawers, a commode with a porcelain pitcher and bowl, the narrow bed she occupied. She could tell by the faded outline on the wallpaper that there had once been a crucifix above the door.

She sat up, hugging herself against the chill in the room. "Is this your house?"

"It is now."

Something in the tone of his voice told her that he had killed the former owner.

She cringed as he moved toward her, flinched as his hand stroked her cheek.

"Such a pretty creature," he murmured, "but then, Grigori always did have good taste in women. Good taste." He laughed as his fingers closed around her neck, tilting her head back to expose the pulse in her throat.

Terror rose up in Marisa as she stared into Alexi's eyes. "Don't," she said with a gasp. "Please don't."

"Just a taste," he promised.

"No! I don't want to be like Antoinette. Please!"

"Antoinette . . . I loved her, you know." He made a vague gesture with his free hand. "Loved her as much as I was able."

"Is that why you killed her children and turned her into a mindless zombie? Because you loved her?"

"I asked her to leave him, to come away with me, but she refused." His gaze grew hot. "I fear I have a rather bad temper." His hand tightened around her throat until she could hardly breathe. "You would be wise to remember that."

She tried to speak, but couldn't, could only stare at him as he lowered his head. His eyes were changing, the pupils growing larger, changing color, until his eyes were red and glowing. His lips parted, and she saw his fangs.

"No!" She screamed the word as she felt his breath sear her skin. *This can't be happening!* She clawed at the hand locked around her throat, raked her nails down his cheek, screamed in helpless terror as she felt his fangs pierce her flesh.

Darkness rose up in her mind, a writhing miasma of evil and death.

And then, abruptly, he let her go. Reeling backward, he glared at her. "He has marked you as his!"

"What? What are you talking about?"

"He has taken your blood."

Marisa stared up at him. "No."

"Yes!"

"It's impossible. He never . . ." The words died in her throat. She had imagined Grigori bending over her late one night. But it had been a dream. Hadn't it? "It's impossible," she said again. "If he'd taken my blood, wouldn't I be like Antoinette?"

Alexi shook his head. Hands clenched, he paced the room. "He didn't take enough for that, nor give you more than a drop of his in return. Just a drop of his!" He screamed the words. "Only enough so that I could taste him like poison in your blood."

Alexi whirled around, his eyes blazing with fury. "I would have taken you and let him keep Antoinette," he raged, "but not now! Not now! Call him, Marisa. Call him to your side."

"I don't know what you mean."

"Call his name." He caught her arm and twisted it behind her back. "Call him! He will hear you."

She shook her head, too frightened to speak, her whole body churning in revulsion at the thought of Grigori giving her his blood. How could he have done such a thing without her knowledge?

She cried out in pain and terror, everything else forgotten, as Alexi gave her arm another cruel twist.

"Call him." The vampire's gray eyes burned into her mind, obliterating her will to resist.

"Grigori."

"Louder."

"Grigori! Help me!"

Sobbing, she cried his name over and over again, until her throat was raw, until fear and exhaustion carried her away, into darkness.

Chapter Eighteen

Grigori's head jerked up, his eyes narrowing as he heard Marisa's voice screaming in his mind.

"What is it?" Ramsey asked.

"Marisa."

"What about her?"

"I know where she is."

Ramsey stood up, his hands clenched. "How do you know?"

"Alexi has told her, and she has told me."

Ramsey stared at the vampire for a moment, and then he swore under his breath. "You drank from her."

Grigori met the other man's gaze, and then he nodded. "Not enough to hurt her."

"I can't believe you would do something so despicable. I can't believe she let you. Or did you first play with her mind?"

"I did what I had to do."

"Yeah, right."

"I marked her as mine," Grigori replied coldly. "And for this very reason."

Ramsey frowned, confused. "But she's not like Antoinette."

"No. I would not steal her mind, her will."

"But Alexi could do it, couldn't he?"

Grigori nodded. The older vampyre could make her a revenant, or force the Dark Gift upon her. Either one would negate Grigori's power.

Ramsey stared at him, his anger slowly fading. "So where is she?"

"Alexi has taken her to a small vineyard about three miles from here. It used to belong to my uncle Pietro."

"Three miles! That's a heck of a walk."

Grigori arched one brow. "We aren't going to walk."

"So what are we standing here for? Let's go."

"All in good time." Grigori looked over at Antoinette. She was sitting on the sofa, her hands folded in her lap. A puppet waiting for someone to pull the strings. It grieved him to see her so, she who had always had a mind of her own, who had been vibrant and alive. He thought of the high-spirited arguments they had had, the way her eyes had flashed at him when he had roused her temper, the delight of making up afterward.

Crossing the floor, he knelt before her. Lifting one hand, he stroked her cheek, let his fingers trail through her hair. "Antoinette, close your eyes."

She stared at him, trusting as a puppy, and then her eyelids fluttered down.

"What are you going to do?" Edward asked.

"Free her."

"What? Wait a minute, you don't mean to—"

"I'm going to bring her over." Grigori stared at Edward over Antoinette's head. "Have you ever seen anyone made Vampyre, Ramsey?"

Edward shook his head.

"Do you want to stay?"

Edward hesitated a moment, and then nodded.

Grigori took a deep breath and then he sat down on the sofa beside Antoinette. Enfolding her in his arms, he bent her back and kissed her.

Ramsey stood where he was, unable to move, as he watched the vampire tilt Antoinette's head to the side, gently brush the hair away from her neck. He sensed an energy in the air, a gathering of preternatural power, as Grigori bent over his wife's neck. Chills ran down Edward's spine as he imagined the vampire's fangs piercing the tender skin at the side of Antoinette's neck, and then, with revulsion, he imagined Grigori's fangs at his own throat, drinking his life's blood.

Edward wiped the cold sweat from his brow. There was no sound in the room save the rasp of his own breathing.

He stared at the vampire and the woman, his hand clutching his cross, the stake shoved into the waistband of his trousers feeling suddenly heavy. This was the perfect time to destroy Chiavari and the woman . . . to free the woman's soul from Chiavari's evil influence and send the vampire to hell where he belonged. But Edward couldn't move, could hardly breathe.

Chiavari seemed to loom over the woman like a great black bird of prey, yet he had not changed shape. Antoinette had gone limp in the vampire's embrace. Her face was turned toward Edward. She looked deathly pale; he couldn't tell if she was breathing.

A deep sigh rose from Grigori's throat. He drew back and Edward caught a glimpse of hell-red eyes and fangs stained with blood.

He realized he was holding his breath, that his

hand ached from holding the cross so tightly. He felt the bile rise in his throat as the vampire bit his own wrist, and then pressed the bleeding wound to Antoinette's mouth.

"Drink, Antoinette," Grigori urged softly. "You must drink."

A shiver of repugnance slithered down Ramsey's spine as he watched the woman drink the vampire's blood. He watched in morbid fascination as the color returned to her cheeks. Her hands clutched the vampire's arm, holding his wrist to her lips.

"It is done!" Grigori wrenched his arm from Antoinette and stood up. He ran his tongue over the wound in his wrist, licked the blood, hers and his, from his lips.

Edward Ramsey swore under his breath as Antoinette stood up, her cheeks rosy with life, her eyes filled with awareness and intelligence. And confusion.

She stared at Grigori uncertainly, and then smiled. "*Mi amore,*" she murmured. "I have missed you."

Grigori nodded. "And I have missed you." He stood there, waiting for her memory to return, and it would, all of it, everything that had happened. He wondered if she would hate him for what he'd just done.

"I feel so strange," she murmured.

He knew the moment her memory returned. He saw it in the horror in her eyes, heard it in the hoarse cry that was torn from her throat.

"Antonio," she whispered. "Martina." She ran out of the room.

Grigori followed her into the bedroom. She was

standing in the doorway of the room their children had shared, tears streaming down her cheeks.

"He killed them," she said. "And I shall kill him."

He saw her hands clench, heard the steel in her voice.

Slowly, she turned to face him. "What have you done to me, Grigori?"

"I have made you what I am," he replied. "What he is."

"And what is that?"

"You know," he replied quietly.

She stared at him, and he saw the knowledge grow within her. Would she accept the Dark Gift? Or would it drive her to madness?

She lifted one hand and studied it carefully. And then, slowly, her fingers curled into a fist. "I shall tear out his heart."

"And I'll help you."

She smiled at him then. "Thank you, Grigori, for freeing me."

"You don't hate me, then, *cara*?"

"I could never hate you. But tell me, how did you become Vampyre?"

He related the story quickly, and then told her everything that had happened since Alexi had escaped the carnival. "And now he's brought Marisa here," he said in conclusion, "and I've got to find her."

Comprehension flickered in Antoinette's eyes. "You love her."

He had not wanted to admit it, not even to himself, but he couldn't lie to Antoinette. "Yes."

She accepted it with a nod of her head. "What do you want me to do?"

"I'm not sure."

"We are three to his one," Antoinette said with determination. "He shall not escape us."

"Don't underestimate his power," Grigori warned. "My strength is not equal to his, and yours is less than mine."

"I am not afraid of him," Antoinette replied with a toss of her head. "I will not rest until I have avenged the deaths of my children."

"Nor I."

"I shall ask one thing of you, Grigori, and you must promise me you will do it."

A stillness rose within him as he waited for her to go on. He knew what she would ask. Knew he could not do it.

"When he is dead, when our children have been avenged, you will destroy me."

It was what he had been expecting. "*Cara*, do not ask this of me."

"Please, Grigori, I do not want to live in darkness. I cannot live on the lives of others. Promise me."

He hesitated a moment before he said, "I promise."

A long look passed between them, and then she smiled at him.

"He's at old Pietro's winery, and Marisa is with him," Grigori said. "Let's go."

"Are you crazy?" Ramsey exclaimed. "It's a trap."

"Don't you think I know that?" Grigori asked, his voice sharp. "But I can't leave her there. You know what he'll do if I don't come."

"He'll do it anyway!"

"Perhaps, but I told you once before, we'll never

catch him until he lets us. This may be our only chance."

"We need a plan," Ramsey said, his agitation rising. He clutched his cross, rubbing it between his palms.

"I plan to kill him," Grigori said.

"We are wasting time," Antoinette said.

"Right, as always, *cara*," Grigori replied with a wry grin. "Let's go."

Marisa woke to darkness. When she tried to move, she discovered that her hands were bound behind her back. Fighting down the fear that threatened to choke her, she sat up and glanced around. Nothing but blackness met her eyes. She struggled against the ropes that bound her wrists, but to no avail.

Where was Alexi?

Where was Grigori?

Where was *she?*

She had a vague recollection of waking in a small house, of lying on a bed while Alexi prowled through the rooms. Was this the same house?

With an effort, she gained her feet and then, one shoulder against the wall, she began to walk slowly around the room, searching for a door. She cried out when her knee struck something. Turning around, she felt the obstruction with her hands. It was a staircase. Moving carefully, she climbed up, grunting when she hit her head. She was in a cellar. She could see a sliver of dark blue sky through the crack in the heavy double doors above her head.

"Hello? Is anyone there?" She heard the edge of

panic in her voice. "Hello! Help me! Someone, please help me!"

"Someone is coming, Marisa."

The low voice startled her. She whirled around, her foot slipping on the stair. With a shriek, she tumbled down the steps to land in a heap on the earthen floor. The sound of soft laughter filled her ears.

"Grigori will come for you," Alexi said. "And then we will end the game. I will drain his life, and that of the vampyre hunter, as well, and then I shall make you mine."

"No!"

"Oh, yes, Marisa. Do not doubt it." He cocked his head to the side, and smiled. "Listen! They come!"

Grigori stood at the entrance to the cellar, his senses probing the darkness. Marisa was here, and so was Alexi. He glanced at Antoinette, standing serenely beside him, then at Ramsey. Tension flowed from Ramsey in waves, but he had his fear well in hand. Moonlight gleamed off the cross around his neck. He held a hawthorne stake in one hand, a hammer in the other. A bottle of holy water was tucked into his coat pocket.

Grigori blew out a deep breath.

There was nothing to be said. They would rescue Marisa and kill Alexi, or they would die.

He kissed Antoinette, and then he turned, took hold of the cellar doors, and ripped them off the hinges.

Marisa was lying on the floor at the foot of the stairs. Blood oozed from her cheek, her arm, her leg. The scent inflamed his senses.

"Alexi!"

"I am here, Chiavari."

"Show yourself."

"Come, find me."

"Coward."

"Come, come, Chiavari, play the game."

With a roar, Grigori launched himself down the stairs. Scooping Marisa into his arms, he carried her out of the cellar and thrust her into Ramsey's arms. "Get her out of here! Now!"

He didn't wait for an answer, but flew back into the cellar, his gaze piercing the darkness, his nostrils flaring, his fangs bared.

"I'm here," Alexi said, and before Grigori could locate the voice, Alexi was on him.

Grigori fell back under the other vampyre's onslaught. Alexi had fed recently, and the scent of blood teased Grigori's senses. Alexi clawed at his face and chest, his nails and teeth tearing through skin and flesh and muscle. Rage flowed through Grigori. His fangs lengthened, his own hands became claws, slashing through the air. The sound of Alexi's mocking laughter rang in his ears. The scent of his own blood filled his nostrils.

He felt the vampyre's teeth savage his neck, tearing at his throat. The thought of the vampyre drinking his blood filled him with fury, and he flung Alexi away from him, heard a satisfying thud as the vampyre slammed into the wall. Almost immediately, Alexi was back, his eyes glowing blood-red in the darkness, his lips stained with crimson.

Blood. It was everywhere. Marisa's. His own. Alexi's. The air was thick with the warm, sweet scent of it. Hunger rose up within Grigori like a bright crimson flame, blinding him to everything but the awful need that overshadowed everything else. He felt Alexi's fingernails tear at his throat again, slashing through his flesh, severing his jugular, and he fell back, his strength gushing out of him in a dark red torrent.

A shrill scream filled the air as Antoinette lunged toward Alexi. Grigori sat up in time to see her drive a fat wooden stake into Alexi's back. With a roar of pain and rage, Alexi whirled around to face her.

With a feral growl, Antoinette hurled herself at Alexi. All trace of humanity was gone from her eyes as she flung herself at the creature who had killed her children. Her arms and legs curled around him, holding on with iron tenacity.

Alexi reeled backward, his eyes blazing with pain, the wooden stake protruding from his back. He tried to shake her off, but somehow she managed to hold on. Her fangs sank deep into his neck. Her nails gouged his cheeks, his eyes. . . .

Grigori watched, helpless, as Antoinette and Alexi struggled. Even though Alexi was bleeding, even though she had driven a stake into his body, her strength, that of a newly made vampyre, was as nothing compared to Kristov's. A low growl rumbled in Alexi's chest as he sank his teeth into her jugular.

"No!" Gathering what little strength he had left, Grigori gained his feet and grabbed Alexi's arm, but the vampyre shook him off. Grigori stumbled backward, his head striking the edge of the stairs. He felt the skin split, felt a rush of hot blood flow down his neck.

"It's not over, Chiavari," Alexi declared, and

clutching Antoinette's limp body in one arm, he vanished into the night.

Grigori tried to stand up, but he had no strength left. Blood soaked his clothing, the ground beneath him. He glanced at the sky, judging the time, and knew he had to find a place to hide before the sun found him.

On his hands and knees, he dragged himself up the stairs and across the damp ground, searching for shelter.

Chapter Nineteen

"Edward, we've got to go back."

"Not now," he said firmly. "Not until the sun's up. Way up."

Marisa flinched as Edward washed the dried blood from the numerous scrapes on her arms and legs and face.

They had taken shelter in a small roadside chapel they had stumbled on in their flight. Edward dipped his handkerchief into the font of holy water again. She had objected at first, but he had waved away her protests, insisting that it would protect her from infection, and vampires.

Edward sat back on his heels. "Did Alexi . . . did he drink from you, or make you drink from him?"

"No." She rubbed her wrists, which were still sore from being bound. She looked down at her dress, which was torn and stained with blood. "I need a change of clothes."

"I don't know where you'll find any. Hell, I don't even know where we are."

"Edward, watch your language."

"What? Oh, sorry." He glanced around. The chapel was small. Built of dark wood and stone, it stood in the center of a small copse of trees. A statue of a sad-faced Madonna stood beside a rough-hewn altar. A single stained-glass window was set in the east wall. A large wooden crucifix hung below the window. It made him feel safe, protected.

"We can't just stay here," Marisa said.

"Oh, yes, we can," Edward said. He sat down with his back against the altar. "I've hunted vampires most of my life," he mused. "I've never met one as strong as Alexi. I wonder just how old he is."

"You don't think he's killed Grigori, do you?"

"I don't know. I hope not. I'd hate to have to spend the rest of my life in eighteenth-century Italy."

"Oh, Lord." She had forgotten, for the moment, that they were in the past.

"Yeah." He glanced at the stained-glass window, smiled when he saw the colors brighten and come to life as the sun rose behind the glass. Dust motes danced in reflected ribbons of red and gold and green light. "Let's go."

Marisa took off her heels, then peeled off her ruined nylons, glad that she wasn't wearing panty hose. Edward took her shoes and placed them in the pockets of his jacket.

Outside, the morning was bright and clear, the air fresh and clean. A faint breeze stirred the leaves.

Marisa's trepidation increased with every step she took. What would they find when they returned to the winery?

The sun was high in the sky when they reached the cellar.

"Stay here," Edward said.

Marisa nodded. She had no desire to see what, if anything, was left in the cellar.

Clasping his cross in both hands, Edward descended the narrow wooden stairs. The smell of blood filled his nostrils. He could see dark patches of it splattered across the walls and on the hard-packed earthen floor. It took only a glance to see that the cellar was empty.

"Edward?"

He ran up the stairs, taking them two at a time. The day seemed incredibly bright and beautiful and he took a deep breath, glad to be alive. "There's no one down there."

She stared at him, afraid to ask what it might mean. "What do we do now?"

Ramsey judged the position of the sun, then jerked a thumb over his shoulder. "Grigori's house is in that direction. There must be a town nearby."

"How far is it?" Marisa asked.

"His house? I'm not sure. I think Chiavari said it was about three miles from Pietro's." Edward grimaced as he contemplated the walk. "I should have spent more time working out."

"Come on, you wimp. Three miles is a piece of cake." The thought of food made her stomach growl. "Wish I *had* a piece of cake," she muttered, although it seemed wrong to feel hungry at a time like this.

"Yeah, me too." Ramsey shook his head. "Been a helluva night."

The town was located about a half mile from Pietro's. It was early and there were only a few people out and about. The people they passed regarded them with blatant curiosity. Marisa could hardly blame them. Their clothing alone would have made the people stare. Her dress was far too short for the mode of the day; worse, it was torn and stained with blood. Her hair was a mess; her face was bruised. Ramsey looked more presentable. His gray slacks were dirty, but his shirt and coat were remarkably clean, considering all they had been through.

It occurred to her, abruptly, that whatever money they had would not be accepted or recognized.

They passed a small bakery and her stomach growled loudly as the scent of coffee and freshly baked bread wafted through the air.

"Geez, I'd kill for a cup of that coffee," Ramsey muttered.

"Perhaps we could offer them something in exchange for breakfast," Marisa suggested.

"Yeah? Like what?"

"I don't know. My earrings, maybe?"

"It's worth a try."

"Let's just hope they speak English."

"I speak a little Italian," Ramsey said. "Picked it up in my travels."

Marisa combed her fingers through her hair and put on her heels. "How do I look?"

Ramsey grinned at her. "You want the truth, or a polite lie?"

"That bad, huh?"

"Well . . . here, put my coat on. It'll cover some of the blood on your dress."

Marisa slipped into his coat, and then they walked into the bakery.

It took a while, but eventually Ramsey managed to explain to the proprietor that they wanted to exchange Marisa's earrings for something to eat.

The man called his wife, who looked the jewelry over, and then nodded.

Marisa and Ramsey sat down at one of the tables. Marisa glanced around. It was a small place, a sort of combination bakery and café. There were no other customers.

A short time later, the proprietor's wife emerged from the kitchen bearing two cups of coffee and a plate of pastries. Marisa noted the woman was wearing her new earrings.

"What are we going to do when we leave here?" Marisa asked.

"Go back to the Chiavaris' and wait for them, I guess," Ramsey replied. "You got any better ideas?"

"Not really." She sipped the coffee. It was hot and bitter. She couldn't remember when she'd ever had any that tasted better.

"I watched him bring her over," Ramsey said.

"What?"

"Antoinette. I watched Chiavari bring her across."

"You mean you saw him make her a vampire?"

Ramsey nodded. "It was—" He shook his head. "I don't know how to explain it. It was awful, and yet—" He ran his fingertips over his cross. "It was kind of . . . I don't know . . . mystical."

"How did he do it? Is it like in the books?"

"Yeah, pretty much. He drank her blood until she was at the point of death, and then he slit his wrist with his teeth and she drank his blood."

Ramsey looked at Marisa, his expression troubled. "I felt like I'd just watched someone being reborn, but that's not right, is it? She's damned now."

"Is she?"

"You know she is! They both are. It's a life against nature. A life against God."

"I always wondered why drinking blood would make you a vampire. It doesn't go in your veins when you drink it, it just goes in your stomach. I'd think it would just, you know, just go out again."

"I often wondered that myself," Ramsey admitted. "As near as I can figure, once a vampire drinks, the blood isn't digested, like food. Instead, it's absorbed into the whole body."

"It's so bizarre, so hard to believe. How many vampires have you killed, Edward?"

"Thirteen."

"How can you do it?"

"Because it has to be done, and there's no one else to do it. There's no one else who knows, no one else who believes."

"What happened to your friend, to Katherine?"

"She fell in love with a rock musician. He was a vampire, newly made. I didn't realize what he was at first. The young ones can sometimes pass for human. He dressed sort of weird and she only saw him at night, but that didn't seem strange for a guy in a rock band. By the time I realized what he was, it was too late."

"And you killed him."

"I staked him through the heart and cut off his head." Ramsey's eyes blazed with fervor. "He won't lure any more young girls to their deaths."

Marisa swallowed hard. Edward's zeal left her feeling suddenly sick to her stomach. "Are you ready to go?"

"Yes." He took a deep breath. "I'm sorry, Marisa. I didn't mean to upset you."

"It's all right." She took the hand he offered her and they left the café.

For a time, they walked in silence. The touch of the sun on her back and the beauty of the countryside soothed her. For a moment, she pretended that everything was all right, that she was in Tuscany on vacation, that she knew how to get home again.

She delved into her memory, trying to recall what she knew about Italy. Famous names immediately sprang to mind: Dante and the Medicis, Michelangelo's *David*, the Pitti Palace set in the Boboli Gardens, the canals of Venice, the cities of Rome and Naples and Florence, *Firenze,* which was known as the city of flowers. There was the Ponte Vecchio, and the Leaning Tower of Pisa. Italy was the home of so many historic sites and works of art she had always yearned to see.

But not like this.

They turned a bend in the road and Grigori's house rose up before them. It looked picturesque in the early morning light. Set amid fallow fields, with a narrow stream running behind it and a sky filled with puffy clouds overhead, it reminded her of something out of a Disney cartoon. She almost expected to see Snow White standing in the doorway kissing Dopey on the head as she sent the Seven Dwarfs off to work.

It was quiet and dim inside. Where was Grigori? Had Alexi killed him? Wouldn't she feel it if he was dead?

She went into the kitchen and rummaged around until she found a towel and some soap.

Sitting at the wooden table, she began to sponge the blood out of her dress.

"Have you looked in the bedroom? You might be able to find something to wear in there."

"Oh, good idea." Rising, Marisa went into the bedroom. She found three dresses hanging on hooks behind the door. She selected one, lavender cotton with long sleeves and a round neck.

Slipping out of her blue jersey, she drew Antoinette's dress over her head. It was a little too long and a trifle snug on top, but other than that, it was a pretty good fit. And it was clean.

She changed quickly, thinking she would feel better once she was out of her ruined dress. She didn't. Wearing Antoinette's clothing made her edgy and uncomfortable.

"And with good reason," Marisa muttered. "You're in her house. You're falling in love with her husband—" She shook the thought aside. She would not fall in love with Grigori. When this was over, she would never see him again.

Returning to the living room, she found Ramsey sitting on the bench, his head cradled in his hands. He glanced up when she entered the room.

"I think I'm going to try to take a nap," she said.

Ramsey nodded. "Good idea. Maybe I will, too."

"Okay." She toyed with a fold of her skirt. "Do you think he's all right?"

"I don't know, but if he isn't, we'd better start learning to speak the language."

It took longer than usual to drag himself from the darkness. He sent his senses into the night, testing the air, searching for the presence of mortals. When he was certain he was alone, he emerged from the earth, burrowing upward until his head and shoulders were clear. Exerting even that little bit of energy left him feeling drained. Never before had he lost so much blood, or felt so weak, so vulnerable.

Closing his eyes, he delved deep inside himself, gathering what strength he had left. With an effort, he gained his feet, and then he began walking. Thoughts flashed through his mind like the changing colors of a kaleidoscope.

He needed sustenance. . . . Where was Alexi? . . . Was Antoinette dead? . . . Where was Marisa . . . ?

The hunger's dark need spread through him, clawing at his vitals, until his whole body ached with it.

As weak as he was, he still moved with greater speed than a mere mortal. A short time later, he stood outside the house he had once shared with Antoinette. Ramsey and Marisa were inside. He could sense their warmth, hear their beating hearts. The hunger fought for control, urging him to go into the house and take what he needed, to drink and drink until the deep, empty well of his need was filled.

He stood hidden in the darkness, a part of the night, death cloaked in the guise of a man. Stood there, his hands clenched, his nails digging into his palms, until he was in control, and then he opened the door.

Ramsey saw him first. Clutching his cross, Ramsey leaped to his feet. Like a warrior priest, he planted himself in front of Marisa. He held the crucifix in one fist, and raised his other hand, the one with the cross tattooed on the palm.

"Edward, what are you doing?"

"Protecting you," Ramsey replied curtly. "Look at him, Marisa! Look at him and see what he really is."

Marisa leaned a little to her right, peering around Edward. Grigori stood in the doorway, a vision from a nightmare. Bits of dirt clung to his hair and clothing; his skin was as pale as a shroud; his dark eyes burned like the fires of an unforgiving hell. His left cheek was still blackened where Antoinette's crucifix had burned him.

"Get out of here, Chiavari," Ramsey said.

"I can't. I need your help."

"It isn't help you need. It's blood. Go find it somewhere else. We have nothing for you here."

"Edward—" Marisa stood up.

"Stay back!"

"I won't hurt her," Grigori said wearily. "Or you."

"Yeah, right." Edward took a step backward, keeping himself between Marisa and the vampire. "Get out of here."

"You seem to forget, Ramsey, this is my house," Grigori replied, a faint note of amusement evident in his tone.

"Edward, he needs our help."

"Dammit, Marisa, look at him!"

"Yes, Marisa," Grigori said. "Look at me." His voice was low and deep, as it had been the first night she met him. An angel's voice, she had thought then. "Come to me."

She met his gaze, felt his voice wrap around her like a fine, silken web, felt herself being inexplicably drawn toward him.

Grigori held out his hand. "Come to me, *cara*."

"No!" Edward grabbed Marisa by the arm, but she twisted out of his grasp and darted toward Grigori, who quickly enfolded her in his embrace.

"Leave her alone, dammit!"

"Ramsey, calm down. I'm not going to hurt her."

Edward backed up until his legs bumped into the bench. Then, without looking back, he reached for one of the wooden stakes he had fashioned earlier.

"You don't need that," Grigori remarked.

"Like hell."

"Ramsey, listen to me. I will not take her blood unless she's willing."

Edward snorted. "Look at her! She's already under your spell."

"I will release her. If she refuses me, I will go elsewhere."

Edward's hand tightened around the stake. "I don't believe you."

Grigori cupped Marisa's chin in his palm. "Marisa?"

She looked up at him, and he broke the bond between them.

"Marisa, I need your help."

"What?" Confused, she looked over her shoulder at Edward. She didn't remember moving. How had she gotten here?

"Marisa?"

"What happened?" she asked, frowning. "How did I get here?"

"I summoned you."

She shook her head, bewildered. "I don't remember."

"He can control you now," Edward explained.

"Make you do things you don't want to do."

She looked up at Grigori. "Is that true?"

Grigori nodded.

"Because you took my blood. You did, didn't you? Alexi said so."

"I'm sorry, but it was necessary."

"Why?"

"I'll explain it all later. Right now, I need blood."

She knew what he was asking. Wondered *why* he was asking. Moments ago, she had been in his power. Why hadn't he just taken what he wanted? she wondered bitterly. He'd done it before.

Grigori smiled faintly. "Blood freely given is all the sweeter, and more powerful."

"And you want mine?" Revulsion churned in her stomach. She stared at his mouth, imagined his fangs tearing at her throat.

"Trust me, Marisa, I will not hurt you."

"Don't do it," Ramsey said.

Marisa stared at Grigori, trying to see the monster that Edward saw. But looking past the pale skin and the dark eyes that smoldered with a hunger she would never understand, she saw a man in torment, a man who could take what he wanted without asking, a man who could have killed her long ago. A man who had never hurt her at all.

"Marisa?"

She heard the need in his voice, remembered the kisses they had shared, the night she had held him in her arms. Slowly, she nodded.

"Marisa, are you sure you want to do this?" Edward's voice was filled with disbelief.

"It's all right, Edward. I know what I'm doing."

Grigori took her by the hand and led her to the

wooden bench. She sat down, and he sat beside her.

Edward stood nearby, the stake clutched in his fist.

"Relax, Marisa," Grigori said quietly. "I won't hurt you." He glanced over his shoulder at Ramsey. "If you're going to kill me, you'd best do it now, while you have a chance."

"Don't tempt me, Chiavari."

Grigori laughed softly, then turned toward Marisa. He brushed a lock of hair away from her neck, kissed the pulse beating there. He felt the hunger rise up within him, a darkness that threatened to overwhelm him, and he took a deep, calming breath. He could feel Marisa trembling in his arms, sense Ramsey hovering behind him.

His muscles tensed as he waited for the vampyre hunter to drive the stake through his back, into his heart, thus ending his existence once and for all. A long moment slipped into eternity. In that time, Grigori wondered what death would be like. Would his soul burn in hell for all eternity? Was there any chance he might find forgiveness on the other side?

He glanced over his shoulder at Ramsey, and then, with a sigh, he drew Marisa into his arms.

There was no pain. She knew he had bitten her, could feel the blood being drawn from her body, but she felt no pain, only a strange sense of weightless pleasure. She closed her eyes, and her mind filled with disjointed thoughts and images. . . . She saw Grigori as a young boy, saw him herding sheep, wrestling with his father, swimming naked in a small pool, kissing his mother good night. She saw him growing older, saw him sitting in a moonlit field with Antoinette, felt the excitement of young love, the awakening of passion as he kissed the woman who would be his wife. She experienced his pain, his rage, when he found the bodies of his children. She saw the vampire who had made him what he was, saw and understood why he had asked for the Dark Gift. Understanding, she discovered, was different from simply knowing.

"Marisa?"

She looked up at him. She had known Grigori was a vampire, she had seen the proof, heard it from his own lips, but only now did she truly realize what he was.

"Are you all right?"

She nodded.

He caressed her cheek, ran a finger over the mark his bite had left in her neck. He had taken no more than a few sips, yet the purity of her blood, her generosity of spirit, had taken the sharp edge off the hunger burning through him, filling him with a sense of warmth, a sense of light he had never known before. Never, in two hundred years, had he tasted anything so sweet, so satisfying, and yet the little he had taken wasn't enough to quench his thirst. He wanted to hold her in his arms and drink and drink, until he had taken all of her into himself. "Thank you."

Marisa nodded again, and then looked up at Edward. He was standing as before, the stake clutched tightly in his fist. There was pity for her in his eyes, revulsion and hatred for what Grigori was, what he had done to her.

"It's okay, Edward," she said, surprised at how

difficult it was to form the words, how weak her voice sounded. "I'm fine."

"Ramsey, get her something to drink."

"I'm not your slave," Edward muttered, but he went to do as he'd been told.

"What happened to Alexi?" Marisa asked. "Where's Antoinette?"

"Here," Edward said. He thrust a glass of red wine at Marisa. "Drink this."

She sipped the wine slowly, feeling its warmth spread through her.

"All right, Chiavari, spill it. What aren't you telling us?"

"He's got Antoinette."

"How do you know?"

"I know," Grigori said.

"What's he done to her?"

"He put a stake through her heart. Her body lies in a crypt behind the church."

"Then she's dead but not destroyed," Edward remarked.

"What do you mean?" Marisa asked.

"All we have to do is pull the stake from her body and she'll rise again."

"She does not wish to rise again," Grigori said quietly.

"How do you know?" Edward asked, and then wished he hadn't. The vampire looked at him through the eyes of one enduring the pain and damnation of hell.

"I know."

"She said she wanted to avenge her children."

"She is at peace now. It is time to free her soul, before she takes a life, before the darkness destroys the light within her." Grigori paused a moment. "The name on the vault is Amadeo. I want you to make sure she can't rise again; then see that she's buried properly." A sadness shadowed his eyes. "My children are buried there, under a tree near the back wall. Put her beside them."

"Me? Why me?"

"I thought you would be eager to do the job," Grigori retorted caustically. "Isn't that what you live for, destroying my kind?"

Ramsey nodded. He would do what had to be done, but it wouldn't be easy. He had never dispatched a vampire he had known personally.

"The church is located about two miles south of here. You can't miss it."

"I'll take care of it first thing tomorrow morning. Where's Alexi?"

"I don't know. Antoinette drove a stake into his back, but she missed his heart. I think he has gone farther into the past to lick his wounds."

"So, we've accomplished nothing," Edward muttered.

The words *nothing but Antoinette's death* seemed to hover, unspoken, in the air.

"I want to go home," Marisa said softly. She gazed up at Grigori. "Please take me home."

"Tomorrow night," Grigori promised.

"And until then?"

"Until then we stay here."

Chapter Twenty

"Well, I'm beat," Ramsey muttered. "I think I'll turn in."

"Good night, Edward."

"Don't fail me tomorrow, Ramsey."

"Don't worry. I'll take care of it."

Grigori nodded.

"See you tomorrow," Edward said. He started out of the room, then paused and glanced over his shoulder at Marisa. "Which room do you want to sleep in?"

Marisa thought of trying to sleep in one of the children's beds and knew she couldn't do it, couldn't sleep in a bed where someone had died. Nor could she bring herself to sleep in the bed Grigori had shared with Antoinette. "I think I'll sleep out here on the bench."

"Okay. Good night."

"Night."

Grigori went to the tiny window in the front of the house and stared out into the darkness. As clearly as if it were day, he could see the fields beyond, the weeds that grew in the furrows where he had once planted the crops that had sustained his family. He heard the beat of mighty wings as an owl plummeted earthward, talons outstretched, heard the terrified shriek of the bird's prey. The hunter and the hunted. Predator and prey. The endless cycle of life and death.

All these years he had thought Antoinette dead. In his mind, he had buried her and grieved for her when she hadn't been dead at all. She had lived as Alexi's creature for two hundred years, and now, because of him, she would have to be destroyed. He wished that he had the right to pray, wished he could go into the village chapel where their children had been baptized and light a candle for Antoinette's immortal soul. But he had no right, no hope of being heard.

"Grigori?"

Slowly, he turned around to face Marisa. What a rare and wonderful creature she was. Such a fragile being, wrapped in her humanity. And yet her life, her warmth, drew him like a hearth fire on a winter night, beckoning to him, inviting him to come in from the dark and the cold.

"I'm sorry about Antoinette."

"It's not your fault."

"It's not yours, either."

"Isn't it?" Grief and guilt settled over him, entangling him in a web of regret from which there was no escape. He had given her the Dark Gift. He should be the one to destroy her, yet he dared not go into the crypt at night, not when he might encounter Alexi again. He was not strong enough to withstand another attack by the vampyre. And, deep in his heart, he feared he lacked the courage to do what must be done. How could he cut out her heart, take her head? How could he desecrate the body of the woman who had shared his bed, borne his children?

"You should get some rest," Marisa said quietly.

"I'm fine."

"Sure you are."

"Marisa—"

"I'm here." She held out her arms. He looked at her a moment, and then, unable to resist the comfort she offered, he crossed the floor, felt the burden of his guilt ease a little as Marisa wrapped her arms around him.

They stood there for a long while, his forehead resting on the top of her head, her hand lightly stroking his back.

"I've got to go out," he said at length.

"Why?"

He lifted his head and gazed into her eyes.

"Oh, but I thought—" She lifted a hand to her neck.

"It was sweet, *cara,* but it wasn't enough."

"I don't think you should go out there. Can't you wait until tomorrow night when we're back home?"

"I am home."

"You know what I mean."

Grigori shook his head. "I can't wait."

"Why not?" She looked up at him, not understanding.

"I need to feed," he said, wondering how to explain it to her. "It isn't like the hunger mortals feel. It's . . . it's a need that won't be denied. Especially now. I need it, Marisa, in ways you can't begin to understand."

"Does it hurt, when you don't . . . drink?"

"You have no idea." *Hurt* didn't begin to describe it. He doubted if there were any words that could fully portray the agony that came with abstinence. The hunger was a craving that could not be denied, a need that went beyond mere physical agony, especially now, when he had been badly hurt, when his strength was at a low ebb.

"Then drink from me."

"No."

"Then take some of Ramsey's blood."

Grigori grunted softly. "Yes, I'm sure he'd like that."

"Well, this is an emergency. I don't want you going out there, not tonight. You're too weak."

He raised one dark brow. "You sound like my mother."

"You wait here. I'll go talk to Edward."

She didn't wait for Grigori's assent, but hurried out of the room.

Ramsey woke the minute she opened the door to the bedroom, his hand clutching his cross. "What's wrong?"

"I need your help."

"Sure." He sat up, wiping the sleep from his eyes. "What is it?"

"I want you to give Grigori some of your blood."

"Are you out of your mind? I'm not feeding that ghoul."

"Please, Edward. I don't want him to go out tonight. He's too weak. He'd never be able to fight off Alexi."

"That's not my problem."

"Oh, yes, it is. Have you forgotten he's our ticket back to the twentieth century?"

"Yes, I guess I did." He ran a hand through his hair, then shook his head. "I can't do it. I've spent my whole life destroying his kind. I'm not about to start feeding them."

"Please, Edward," she implored softly.

"You still care for him, don't you? How could you? You know what he is."

"I know," she replied miserably. "But I can't help it. He's so alone."

"Marisa—"

"Please, Edward."

He swore under his breath. "All right, all right, I'll do it. For you." Rising, he tucked his shirt into his pants, ran a hand over his hair. And then, grabbing a stake from the foot of the bed, he followed Marisa out of the room.

Grigori grunted softly as Ramsey emerged from the bedroom. Even if he hadn't been able to hear the conversation in the bedroom, the look on Ramsey's face would have said it all. He was doing this for Marisa, and for no other reason.

"Are you planning to use that?" Grigori asked, gesturing at the stake clutched in Ramsey's hand.

"If I have to. I don't mind being an appetizer, but I'm not willing to be the whole banquet."

Grigori laughed in spite of himself.

"It's not funny," Edward retorted. He sat down on the bench, his body quivering with tension, his eyes wary. "Go on, get it over with."

Ramsey flinched as Grigori sat down beside him.

"You don't have to do this," Grigori said curtly.

Edward glanced up at Marisa, and then back at the vampire. "Yeah, I think I do."

"Give me your left arm."

Ramsey grunted. "Sure you don't want to go for my throat?"

Grigori shook his head. Nuzzling Ramsey's neck was the last thing he wanted to do.

Ramsey took a deep breath, and then held out his arm.

Grigori rolled up Ramsey's shirtsleeve. He stared at the man's wrist, despising himself for his need, for the fierce hunger that could not be denied.

"It's not too late to change your mind," Grigori said, his voice gruff with the need churning through him. The fact that Ramsey knew what he was feeling only made it worse.

"Just do it." Edward hissed the words between tightly clenched teeth.

"Make a fist."

Edward did as bidden, watching, in morbid fascination, as the vampire bent over his wrist. Never, in a million years, had he imagined he would be nourishing one of the undead.

Grigori swore under his breath as he lifted Ramsey's arm. He could hear the rapid beat of Ramsey's heart. The scent of the man's blood, the fear he was trying to control, filled his nostrils.

He felt his fangs lengthen as he bent over Ramsey's arm.

Edward's right hand tightened around the stake until his knuckles went white with the strain.

Marisa stood across the room, her hand at her throat, feeling as though she were trapped in a living nightmare that had no end. Edward looked up, grimacing as he met her gaze. She tried to smile; instead, she felt tears well in her eyes. Tears of gratitude for Edward's sacrifice, tears of pity for Grigori.

After what seemed like an eternity but was

probably less than a minute, Grigori released Ramsey's arm and stood up.

"Thank you. I know how difficult that was for you," Grigori said stiffly. "You should get something to drink."

Edward rolled his shirtsleeve down. "Does this mean you'll be able to read my mind now?"

"I could always read your mind, Ramsey."

Edward stood up. He looked at Marisa, then at Grigori. "I'm going back to bed."

"Ramsey."

Edward turned around. "What do you want now, vampire?"

"Tomorrow," Grigori said, his voice ragged with pain. "Be swift. And merciful."

With a curt nod, Edward left the room.

"She won't feel it, will she?" Marisa asked, horrified to think that Antoinette might be aware of what was happening to her.

"I don't know. I hope not."

"Where will you sleep tomorrow?"

Grigori shrugged. "I don't know. I'll find a place, don't worry."

She went to sit beside him on the bench. "Have you ever regretted becoming a vampire?"

"No." He had enjoyed being a vampyre. He was never tired, never sick. He didn't suffer from the usual aches and pains that plagued mankind. He could move with preternatural speed. He had watched nations rise and fall, seen man leave the earth behind and take to the stars. And yet . . . His gaze moved over Marisa in a long, heated caress. "I've never regretted it," he said heavily. "Until now."

"Would you be mortal again, if you could?"

"I don't know, but it isn't possible, even if I wished it."

"Oh." Suddenly weary, she leaned back and closed her eyes, wishing, with all her heart, that she had never ventured out of her house on that rainy Halloween night.

Several minutes passed, and then she felt Grigori's arm slip around her shoulders. Grateful for his nearness, she snuggled against him, felt his hand stroke her cheek.

He was still holding her when she fell asleep.

She woke to the smell of coffee brewing. With a frown, she sat up. For a moment, she had almost imagined herself at home. Brushing the hair from her face, she stood up. It was then that she saw the dress lying across the foot of the bed. It was a pretty thing. The bodice was a rich, lustrous green silk with long, full sleeves and a square neckline edged in delicate rows of white lace; the full skirt was made of varying shades of light and dark green silk and satin. There was a note lying beside it. Curious, she picked it up. The message was brief: *You shouldn't have to wear another woman's clothes. I hope the shoes fit.*

Grigori's name was scrawled across the bottom of the paper.

How had he known it made her uncomfortable to wear Antoinette's clothes?

Slipping out of her borrowed apparel, she drew the gown over her head, smoothed it over her hips. The skirt fell to the floor in a whisper of silk. She found the shoes at the foot of the bed. They were half boots, actually, made of kidskin.

"A little fancy for every day," she remarked. But

the silk felt heavenly against her skin. The boots, she discovered, fit perfectly.

Feeling a little like Juliet, she went into the kitchen.

"Hey," Edward said.

"Hey yourself," Marisa replied with a grin. "I see you got a new wardrobe, too."

Ramsey grunted as he regarded his outfit. The shirt was stiff white linen with a fall of lace down the front. The trousers were mustard-colored, tighter than he normally wore. Grigori had provided a coat, as well. Made of dark brown wool, it was hanging over the back of a chair.

"Not exactly my style," he muttered.

"You look quite dashing."

"And you look like a princess."

Marisa stared at him, startled by the compliment. "Thank you." She glanced at the food on the table. "If I didn't know better, I'd think we had a fairy godmother."

Ramsey grimaced. "Grigori hardly qualifies for that position. Here," Edward said, handing her a cup of coffee.

"Thanks." She took a drink, feeling the warmth steal through her. She jerked her chin toward the pan on the stove. "You want me to do that?"

"No, sit down and take it easy. I'm almost done."

Marisa glanced out the window, trying to judge the time. It felt early. Sitting down at the table, she sipped her coffee.

"I hope you're hungry," Edward said.

Marisa stared at the plate he put in front of her. It was piled high with scrambled eggs, sausage, and sweet rolls. Edward sat down across from her, a cup of coffee cradled in his hands.

"Aren't you eating?" Marisa asked.

"No." A faint smile tugged at the corners of his mouth. "I made enough for the two of us, but I don't have much of an appetite."

"Did you . . . did you do it?"

"Not yet. I don't think it's something I want to do on a full stomach."

"I don't envy you."

He shrugged. "I've done it before. This is just the first time it's been a woman."

Marisa glanced out the window. The sky was blue. She could hear birds singing. "It's still so hard to believe," she murmured.

Edward nodded. It was difficult to accept. Even now, after hunting the creatures for almost thirty years, it seemed unreal. He had seen things no one should see, done things no human being should have to do. He stared down at his hands, wondering that they weren't stained crimson with the blood he had shed. He thought of Antoinette, of the life that had been stolen from her, the torment she must have suffered while being enslaved to Alexi. It was so unfair, and yet no one had ever said life was fair.

"Edward? Do you want me to go with you?"

"No." He drained his cup, then stood up. "Well . . ."

She looked up at him, wishing she knew what to say. *Good luck* seemed too flippant. "Be careful."

"Always." He put on his coat and stood there a moment more, looking unsure. Then he bent down and kissed her. It was a remarkably gentle kiss, filled with tenderness and uncertainty.

Marisa blinked up at him when he drew away,

wondering if she looked as surprised as she felt.

Edward looked embarrassed. "I'm . . . I'm sorry."

"It's all right."

"Marisa, I—" He shoved his hands into his pants pockets. "I guess I'd better be going."

"Hurry back," Marisa said. She stared after him as he left the room, her thoughts chaotic. She pressed her fingertips to her lips. Edward Ramsey had kissed her. She shook her head in amazement, wondering what ever had possessed him to do such a thing.

Ramsey called himself ten kinds of a fool as he gathered up his supplies and left the house. She probably thought him an old fool, and she was right. He was forty-two years old and he had never been in love. Never had time for love. He'd been hunting vampires since he was a teenager, traveling the world over, going wherever he was needed. He had seen most of the world, but he was abysmally ignorant when it came to women.

Ramsey couldn't help grinning when he saw the horse tethered to a bush outside the front door. Grigori was quite the fairy godmother after all, he mused. First he'd provided breakfast, now a ride.

Taking up the reins, he hauled himself into the saddle. He dropped the bag containing the stake, mallet, and cleaver over the saddle horn, and turned the horse south, toward the graveyard. Two miles, Grigori had said.

It was surprisingly pleasant, riding across the countryside in the early morning light. The horse seemed a tractable beast, plodding along at a fairly good clip. He had gone about a quarter of a mile when he passed a farmer walking along the road. The man waved at him, and Edward waved back. Farther on, he passed a woman drawing water from a well. She looked up at him and smiled. He saw a small herd of sheep, another of goats.

The church loomed in the distance, the tall wooden cross on the roof rising like a prayer to the heavens.

Edward rode to the rear of the small whitewashed chapel. Dismounting, he tethered the horse to the fence. Lifting his bag from the saddle horn, he made his way through the wrought-iron gates and into the cemetery beyond. A heavy stillness lay over the graveyard, broken only by the sound of his own footsteps.

He felt the hair prickle along the back of his neck as he went on, searching for the sepulcher that held Antoinette's body.

The crypt was located in the far corner of the cemetery, overgrown with vines. Taking a deep breath, he slung his bag over his shoulder, and then put his hand on the latch.

The door opened with a rusty creak, and he smiled in spite of himself. Perfect, he thought.

Standing in the open doorway, he saw Antoinette. She was lying on the floor. A wooden stake had been plunged into her heart. He knew, somehow, that it was the same one she had used on Alexi.

He stared at her for a long time, glad that half of his job had already been done. Left as she was, she would not rise again, but should someone come upon the body and remove the stake . . . He could not let that happen.

Taking a deep, calming breath, he withdrew the

cleaver from his bag. One swift blow would do it. She was a newly made vampire. Unlike older vampires, who did not sleep so deeply, who sometimes awoke when they sensed his presence, she was helpless, vulnerable. Totally immersed in the dark sleep, she would be unfeeling, unaware.

Bowing his head, he pressed his crucifix to his lips and uttered the ritual prayers that his father had taught him. The ancient words filled him with a sense of power, of peace. He felt the rightness of what he was about to do flow through him, strengthening him.

Crossing the floor, he stared down at her for a moment, and then he covered her face with a piece of cloth.

"May your soul find peace," he murmured, and lifted the cleaver.

Grigori came awake with a strangled cry of pain and grief and knew, in his heart, that Antoinette had been destroyed. As though it were happening to him, he felt the blade sever her jugular. He felt her soul depart her body, glimpsed the joy that would be forever denied him as her spirit was welcomed into paradise, where she would be reunited with their children. Unlike him, Antoinette had not sought the Dark Gift. She had not traded her soul for vengeance. Ever a loyal and devoted wife and mother, she would now reap the eternal blessings of having lived a righteous life.

With a sigh, he stared into the darkness that surrounded him. Tonight, he would go to her grave and bid her and his children a final farewell.

Chapter Twenty-one

Marisa felt her breath catch in her throat when she looked up to find Grigori standing in front of her.

Vampire.

She met his eyes, wondering if he was remembering that she had once told him he didn't look like one of the undead.

"Nice cape," she murmured.

He lifted one brow in a familiar expression of wry amusement. "Do I look the part now?"

She nodded. He was dressed all in black save for a white shirt that looked like silk. A long cape hung from his shoulders. He wore soft leather boots that reached his knees. He looked just like Frank Langella in *Dracula*.

Grigori's lips curved in a sardonic smile. "Let us hope I don't meet the same fate."

"Stop that," Marisa said. It was disconcerting, having him know her every thought.

He bowed, the gesture innately graceful. "Forgive me." His gaze ran over her in blatant admiration. The dress fit perfectly, showing off every slender curve. The rich green color made her eyes shine like emeralds. "You look lovely."

"Thank you." She smoothed her hands over the skirt's silky material. "I've never worn anything quite so fine. Wherever did you find it?"

"Paris."

"Paris! When were you in Paris?"

"Last night. Where's Ramsey?"

"He's looking after the horse." She grinned at him. "Did you find the horse in Paris, too?"

He laughed softly, and she thought how seldom she had heard him laugh. "No, he's a native Italian. I borrowed him from my neighbor."

"You must have had a busy night."

"Indeed. Where would you like to go for dinner?"

"I don't know."

"Paris? Venice? London?"

"Are you serious?"

He nodded. "You have only to name it."

She was trying to make up her mind when Ramsey entered the house.

"Well, the horse is bedded down," Edward said. "Damn, I'm starving. Where the devil is . . . oh," he said, his voice trailing off when he saw Grigori. "You're here."

"I was just asking Marisa where she wanted to go for dinner," Grigori remarked.

"I can't decide if I want Italian or French," Marisa said, grinning.

"I don't care what we have, as long as it's soon," Edward muttered. "I'm starving."

"I've always wanted to eat in a little outdoor café on the Boulevard St. Germain," Marisa decided.

"What year?"

"Are you serious?"

"Very."

"Eighteen seventy-five," Marisa said quickly. "January, eighteen seventy-five."

"Eighteen seventy-five?" Ramsey repeated. "Why?"

"That's the year the Paris Opera House was completed. I'd like to see what it looked like when it was new. Do you think we could go there after dinner?"

"We can even go to the ballet, if you like."

She smiled up at him, her eyes sparkling with excitement. Paris! Home of Notre Dame and the Louvre, the Eiffel Tower, and the Pantheon.

Grigori took her hand in his. "Let's go," he said, reaching out to take hold of Ramsey's hand, as well.

"You're kidding, right?" Edward's gaze darted from Marisa's face to Grigori's. "All this talk about going to Paris for dinner and the ballet—it's just a lot of idle chatter."

Grigori shook his head. "Ready?"

"You two go on," Edward muttered. "I'll wait for you here."

"I don't think that's a good idea," Grigori said, tightening his hold on Ramsey's hand. "Until we get back to your time, I think we'd better stay together."

"Yes, you're probably right." Ramsey glared up at Grigori. "That hurts, you know."

"What? Oh," he said, loosening his grip on the other man's hand. "Sorry."

Ramsey grunted, and then he looked over at Marisa and smiled. "You look beautiful," he remarked, his voice and expression softening as his gaze moved over her.

"Thank you."

Grigori felt a wave of jealousy sweep through him as Marisa returned Ramsey's smile. "Let's go," he said curtly.

Marisa closed her eyes as she felt herself caught up in Grigori's power. The world fell away, and she seemed to be spinning through an endless void where time as she knew it had ceased to exist, where there was nothing but darkness and the sensation of movement. She imagined herself going backward through a long, dark tunnel, and she seemed to hear voices from the past, her grandmother wishing her a Merry Christmas, her father telling her to drive carefully. . . .

Awareness returned with an abruptness that left her feeling slightly dizzy. "That was incredible," she murmured.

"It's damned disconcerting," Ramsey said tersely.

"But incredibly quick," Grigori remarked.

They were standing outside a small sidewalk café. It was the height of the evening and the café was crowded. Marisa looked and listened in wonder, fascinated by the quaint café, the lilting sound of the French language, the tantalizing aromas wafting out of the café.

"There aren't any empty tables," she said, glancing around.

"There will be." Grigori fastened his gaze on two young men who were deep in conversation at a nearby table. Abruptly, they both stood up and left. Grigori made a sweeping gesture with his arm. "Your table awaits, *mademoiselle*."

"How'd you do that?" Marisa asked as Grigori held out her chair for her.

"I didn't do anything."

"Don't give me that. I want to know."

"I simply planted the idea in their minds that they were ready to leave."

"Handy," Ramsey muttered as he sat down at Marisa's right.

"Indeed." Grigori sat down across from Marisa. She looked radiant. Her green eyes were alight with excitement. Her cheeks were rosy, her lips slightly parted as she glanced around, taking it all in. It pleased him beyond measure to have put that look in her eyes.

A waiter appeared. He spoke rapid French. Marisa looked at Edward and grinned as Grigori conversed with the man. The waiter smiled, then hurried away.

"I took the liberty of ordering for you," Grigori said.

"Not snails, I hope," Edward said with a grimace.

"No. *Boeuf bourguignon* and a bottle of red wine."

"It's so pretty," Marisa said. "I can't believe we're really here." She glanced at Ramsey, who sat beside her, glowering. "Smile, Edward. Try to look like you're having fun."

Ramsey grunted softly. "Sorry. I guess I'm just not in a fun mood."

Marisa reached over and covered his hand with hers. "I'm sorry, Edward. Of course you aren't. Maybe we shouldn't have come here. I didn't think—" She gave his hand a squeeze. How could she have forgotten so quickly what he'd done only hours before? She looked over at Grigori. "Maybe we should just go home."

"What's done is done, Ramsey," Grigori said. "Put it behind you for tonight."

"Easy for you to say," Edward retorted, his voice taut with anger. "You're not the one who took her head or cut out her heart."

Marisa gasped softly. She felt the color drain from her face as a quick image of a slashing blade flashed across her mind.

Grigori glared at Ramsey. "Enough!"

For a moment, the two men glared at each other, bristling like dogs over a bone.

Ramsey was the first to look away. "I'm sorry, Marisa."

"No," Marisa said, "I'm the one who should be sorry."

"There is nothing for either of you to be sorry for," Grigori said. He stared at Marisa's hand, still covering Ramsey's. Hers, small and honey brown, Ramsey's large and callused. It took every ounce of his self-control to keep from prying their hands apart. "Edward put Antoinette's soul at rest. It is what she wanted. She is free now."

Grigori turned to stare out at the street. A horse-drawn carriage passed by, the rich young couple inside carefree and happy. He envied them their youth, their innocence. His mind brushed against theirs, and he caught an image of bright lights and couples twirling around a dance floor. Antoinette had loved to dance. . . .

Antoinette. She would not have found happiness in the Dark Gift. She had ever been a pious woman, devoted to her family, to her church.

He looked up as the waiter arrived with dinner. Grigori caressed Marisa's cheek. "Enjoy your meal, *cara,*" he said softly.

With a smile, she reached for her napkin and spread it over her lap.

It pleased him greatly that she was no longer holding Ramsey's hand.

He sipped a glass of wine while they ate. The scent of their food rose in his nostrils, mingling with the aroma of the wine. And over all, ever tempting, ever tantalizing, was the smell of blood . . . blood warmed by wine. He could detect Marisa's scent above the rest, sweeter than life, more intoxicating than strong drink, more satisfying than anything he had ever known.

When they finished eating, Grigori transported them out of the café. Marisa had to smile as she imagined the waiter going back to their table, only to find his customers had vanished.

Moments later, they were in front of the Paris Opera House. Marisa could only stare at the magnificent edifice in wonder. She had seen pictures in books. Friends who had gone to France had sent her postcards, but none of them had done it justice. It was everything she had ever imagined, and more.

"Did you get tickets to the opera the same way you got our table?" she asked as they made their way toward the entrance.

Grigori smiled roguishly. "You learn fast."

"Did you pay for the tickets?"

He looked offended that she would ask, but she wasn't sure why. Was he offended because she had suggested he had paid, or that he hadn't?

"The manager was most happy to accommodate us," Grigori said, his smile widening. "He gave us his own box." He spoke to a man standing at the door, who fired off a rapid round of French, smiled at Marisa, and then gestured for them to enter. She glanced over her shoulder to make sure Edward was with them. He shook his head, obviously displeased with the idea of going to the ballet.

Inside, she couldn't help gawking like a typical tourist, her mouth agape as they walked up the staircase. She stared at the gaslights, at the paintings on the ceiling, at the chandeliers. Elegantly gowned men and women passed by on either side, and she stared at them, too.

Grigori took them to box five. Marisa couldn't help grinning as she sat down. Box five, indeed. The box that had belonged to the Phantom of the Opera. She grinned as she gazed out over the crowd. If vampires were real, maybe the mysterious Phantom had lived as well. Maybe, even now, he was lurking in the cellars beneath the opera house.

Her fanciful thoughts came to an end as the dancers took the stage. It was like a dream, sitting in a private box, listening to the music, watching the ballerina, who was so light on her feet she seemed to float across the stage like a feather blown by the wind.

At intermission, Ramsey went to get them something to drink.

"So," Grigori asked, "is it everything you hoped for?"

His voice slid over her like dark satin, all silky and smooth.

"Yes. It's beautiful."

"You are beautiful."

"I'm not." She shook her head, aware that she was blushing. "But I'm glad you think so."

He smiled at her. It was a sad smile, she thought, one that did not erase the pain that had lingered in his eyes since Edward had destroyed Antoinette. She wondered how many women he had loved, how many people he had cared for. How many he had watched die while he stayed forever young, forever the same.

He tipped his head to the side, meeting her gaze. "What are you thinking?"

"Don't you know?" she replied, her voice sharper than she intended. "Aren't you reading my mind?"

"No."

"Oh?" She smoothed her skirts, delighting in the sensuous feel of the silk beneath her fingertips. "Why not?"

"You asked me not to," he reminded her. "Besides, I don't think I care to know what's going on in your mind right now."

"Well, that's a first." She smiled to take the sting from her words and then frowned. "Why not?"

"The look in your eyes says it all."

"What do you mean? What look?"

"Pity," he said succinctly.

She shook her head. "I wasn't . . . I don't—"

He made an angry slashing motion with his hand, cutting off her words. "I don't want your pity, Marisa."

"What do you want?"

"I want you."

Three words. Softly spoken.

"It's impossible."

"Is it? Why? Because of what I am?"

She nodded.

"I chose to be what I am, Marisa, and I have no regrets."

"None?" She met his gaze squarely. "You were married. You had children. You seem to have loved them. Don't you miss that? Haven't you ever wanted to get married again? Have children again?"

He shook his head. "No."

She lifted one shoulder in a slight shrug. "I haven't been married. I want a home and a family."

"I can't give them to you, but there's no reason why you can't have both."

"So you just want an affair, and when it's over, I'm supposed to go find someone else. Is that what you're saying?"

"Marisa—"

"I'm sorry, I can't." Yet, even as she denied him, she heard his voice in the back of her mind: low and husky and edged with loneliness. *I want you.*

"I hope you like white wine," Ramsey said as he entered the box. He handed a glass to Marisa, offered one to Grigori, who waved it aside.

"Thank you, Edward," Marisa said.

Ramsey frowned, wondering at her sudden change of attitude. A few minutes before, she'd been bubbling like champagne. Now, she looked as deflated as yesterday's birthday balloons. He glanced at Grigori, but could read nothing in the vampire's expression.

Marisa sipped her wine, careful to avoid Grigori's gaze. She focused all her attention on the stage, but she was ever aware of Grigori sitting beside her. He shifted in his chair, and his thigh brushed her gown. The touch made her mouth go dry and her palms damp. What was there about him that affected her so, that made her want to take him by the shoulders and shake him until he admitted he was sorry he was a vampire?

She shook the thought from her mind. He was what he was and it couldn't be changed. She would not let herself love him, or care about him.

"Marisa?"

She looked up at the sound of his voice, only then realizing that the ballet was over.

"Are you ready to go home?" Grigori asked.

"Home?"

"Back to your own time."

"Oh. Yes."

"I know I am," Ramsey muttered. He stuck out his hand. "Let's go."

Chapter Twenty-two

Marisa blinked, and blinked again, relieved to find herself back in her own apartment. She reached for a light switch, but the two table lamps beside the sofa came on before she flipped the switch.

The lights came on in the kitchen, too, and then in her bedroom.

Slowly, she turned to look at Grigori. He gave her a shrug and an enigmatic grin.

Marisa glanced at the clock on the VCR. It was just after two A.M.

"What day is it?" she asked.

"Monday," Grigori replied.

"Monday!" It had been Wednesday when Alexi carried her off. She'd missed three days of work. What must her boss think? She went to check her messages on the answering machine. As she had expected, there were several from work, as well as one from her mother reminding her that she had promised to come for a visit over Christmas.

The lack of sleep and the events of the last few days caught up with her in a rush, draining her of energy. "I don't know about you two," she said, smothering a yawn, "but I've got to get some sleep."

"Yeah." Ramsey yawned, too, and then grinned at her. "I'm bushed. I'll pick you up tomorrow, at five."

Marisa nodded. "Okay. Good night, or good morning, or whatever it is."

Edward hesitated; then, placing his hands lightly on her shoulders, he kissed her on the cheek. "Sweet dreams."

"You too."

With a curt nod in Chiavari's direction, Ramsey left the apartment.

"He's sweet on you, you know," Grigori remarked.

"I know."

"What are you going to do about it?"

"Nothing. He's a nice man and I like him a lot, but that's all there is to it." She yawned again. "I'm beat. Are you going to stay the night?"

He nodded.

"You can't keep watch over me every night."

"Can't I?"

"Do you think he'll come back?"

"I don't know." He crossed the few feet between them and gazed down at her. "Go to bed, Marisa. We can talk about it later."

She stared up at him. He was going to kiss her good night. Just thinking of it made her heart begin to pound in anticipation. It seemed as if she could feel a thousand butterflies in her stomach, their wings beating frantically.

She gazed into his eyes, deep, dark eyes filled with power and knowledge, smoldering with desire.

His hand cupped the back of her head, and then he was bending toward her, blocking everything from her vision but his face. His lips touched hers and it felt as if the earth were falling away again, leaving her adrift in a black sea where there was no up or down, no right or wrong, just the incredible touch of his mouth on hers.

She swayed against him, hardly aware she had moved. Her eyelids fluttered down. From far off, she heard the sound of a woman's voice moaning with pleasure and realized, in a distant part of her mind, that the sound was rising from her own throat.

His arm went around her waist. It was the only thing keeping her on her feet.

She lost track of time. Had his mouth been moving over hers for a minute? An hour? A lifetime? She didn't know, didn't care.

He swung her into his arms, his mouth never leaving hers, and carried her down the hall to the bedroom.

He drew back the covers, and then, very gently, lowered her to the bed. "Rest well, *cara*." He brushed a kiss across her forehead and drew the covers up to her chin.

She was asleep before he turned out the light.

Taking a deep breath, Marisa stepped into Mr. Salazar's office. "Good morning."

He sat back in his chair and looked up at her. He was a handsome man in his mid-fifties, with wavy black hair and dark brown eyes. Working out kept him fit and trim.

He regarded her through narrowed eyes. "I trust you have a valid explanation for your absence."

"Yes, sir. I was called out of town rather abruptly."

He tapped his forefinger against the phone on his desk. "You couldn't call?"

"I'm sorry, sir, I know I should have called and explained, but there just wasn't time."

"Don't let it happen again."

"Yes, sir."

"I need to see the Walburg deposition this morning. And I'll need a copy of the Meekins bankruptcy. Oh, and call the Brownes and tell them I can't meet with them tomorrow afternoon. Ask them if Friday is all right."

"Yes, sir."

"And bring me a cup of coffee when you have time."

"Yes, sir."

He jerked his head toward the door. "Get on it."

With a nod, Marisa left the office, quietly closing the door behind her.

"Well, did he fire you?"

"No," Marisa said, grinning at Linda Hauf. Linda was married and had four sons. She had begun working for Salazar and Salazar two years ago, when her youngest son graduated from high school. It had started out as a part-time thing, but then Joe Salazar's secretary had quit and he had asked Linda if she wanted to work full-time. She and Linda had become good friends in the last year, although they didn't see each other much outside of the office.

"You're lucky," Linda said, rolling her eyes. "You should have heard him ranting and raving on Friday. I was sure you were history."

"He can't fire me," Marisa replied, laughing. "I know where all the bodies are buried." She regretted her choice of words as soon as she said them.

"So, where were you?"

"I got called out of town." Way out of town, Marisa mused. Standing here, surrounded by all the technology the world had to offer, her trip to the past seemed like a dream, but it had been all too real. "I'll talk to you at lunch."

"Right."

Back at her desk, Marisa located the Walburg deposition and the Meekins bankruptcy forms, poured a cup of coffee, no sugar, heavy on the milk. She delivered the papers and the coffee to Salazar, then went back to her desk and began answering the mail.

It was good to be back at work, good to be immersed in mundane, everyday matters.

She went to lunch with Linda. They ate at the mall across the street, and then wandered though one of the gift shops. Marisa bought a present for the office gift exchange, and picked out a delicate hand-painted teapot for her mother.

Returning to the office, she got caught up with the mail. She sat in on a meeting, taking notes. Salazar recorded all his meetings, but he still liked her to be there, to jot down pertinent points, to make note of their clients' reactions to things that were discussed.

Back at her desk, she typed up her notes, her mind straying, as it had several times that day, to Alexi. Where was he? Would he come back? What was she going to do about Edward and Grigori? She couldn't have them trailing after her day and night. Grigori had said Edward was sweet on her, and she didn't want to have to deal with that. Nor did she want to deal with Grigori. She was attracted to him in a way she'd never been attracted to another man, but he wasn't a man, he was a vampire.

She stared at the computer screen. She would tell them both tonight that she appreciated what they'd done, but that she didn't need them to shadow her every move.

She finished typing up her notes, dropped them on Salazar's desk, and bid him good night.

Edward was waiting for her outside. He was wearing a dark brown sweater, tan slacks, and loafers. He smiled when he saw her.

"I guess they didn't fire you after all," he remarked.

"No."

He opened the car door for her, then went around to the driver's side and slid behind the wheel. "So how was your day?"

"Fine. Busy." She smiled at him. "Lots of catching up to do."

Edward nodded. "Would you like to go out to dinner?"

"I don't think so."

His hands tightened on the steering wheel. "Got a date with Chiavari?"

"No. Why?" She turned sideways in her seat. "You're not going to . . . Tell me you aren't."

"He's a vampire, Marisa. We've got to kill them before they kill us. It's as simple as that."

"No! I owe him my life."

"Dammit, Marisa, the man is evil."

"I don't believe that."

"You're in love with him, aren't you?"

"No!"

Edward pulled up in front of her apartment and switched off the engine. "Listen to me. He's a vampire. He's taken your blood. He can read your mind. He can make you do whatever he wants, make you think you're in love with him. You can't trust him, Marisa. You can't trust any of them! They aren't human. They have no morals, no qualms about taking whatever they want."

"Edward, I appreciate your concern and everything you've done for me, really I do, but—" She blew out a deep breath. "I don't think I want to see you again. Or Grigori, either. I just want to forget this whole thing ever happened."

"I can't just abandon you. What if Alexi comes back?"

"I don't know. Maybe he won't."

"And what if he does?"

"I guess I'll just have to cross that bridge when I come to it. All I know is, I can't go on like this, being afraid all the time."

Edward sighed heavily. "All right, Marisa, if that's what you want."

"I'm sorry, Edward."

"Yeah, me too." He smiled at her, a melancholy smile that filled her with guilt. "Take care."

"I will."

"Would it be all right if I called now and then, just to make sure you're all right?"

"Of course." She unfastened her seat belt, then leaned across the seat and kissed him on the cheek. "Good-bye, Edward."

"You've got my number, in case you need me?"

"Yes."

"Don't hesitate to use it."

"I won't." She opened the door and slid out of the car. "Good night."

"Good night, Marisa."

She stood on the curb, watching him drive away, wondering if she had done the right thing.

Inside her apartment, she slipped the soundtrack to *Braveheart* in the CD player. The movie had been a little too bloody for her taste, but the music was beautiful.

Changing out of her work clothes, she went into the kitchen and opened the fridge.

"Well, Mother Hubbard," she muttered, "it looks like the cupboard is bare."

Closing the door, she grabbed her purse and headed for Angelo's. She wasn't in the mood to be alone, anyway.

"Hey, sweet cheeks, long time no see."

Marisa smiled at the waiter. "How are you, Tommy?"

"Fine, as always. You're looking good."

"Well, so are you. I don't need a menu."

"No? Well, what'll it be?"

"Just a plate of spaghetti."

Tommy nodded as he wrote it down. "And a glass of chianti?"

"Right."

"You've got it."

Marisa sat back in the booth and looked out the window. Christmas music came over the speakers. Brightly colored Christmas lights adorned the storefronts across the street. Where had the year gone? She'd have to get busy and do some serious Christmas shopping soon. Buy some Christmas cards. Paper, tinsel . . .

"Hey, Marisa, why the long face?"

"Just tired, I guess."

"Well, enjoy your meal."

"Thanks, Tommy."

"Give a holler if you need anything."

"I will."

"Pretty girl like you shouldn't be eating alone."

Marisa was about to reply when a deep voice said, "I agree."

Glancing past Tommy, she saw Grigori standing in the aisle.

"Mind if I join you?" he asked.

"I guess not." She took a sip of her wine as he sat down across from her.

Tommy looked at Grigori. "Can I bring you anything tonight?"

"Just a glass of wine. Red. Very dry."

"Wine again," Tommy remarked with a shake of his head. "Don't you ever eat?"

"When necessary."

Tommy frowned, shook his head, and walked away from the table, muttering under his breath.

"It seems we've done this before," Grigori said.

Marisa nodded. It seemed like years had passed since that night instead of only weeks. So much had changed since then. Her whole world had been turned upside down.

"Where's Ramsey?"

"I sent him away."

"What do you mean?"

"I told him I didn't want a bodyguard anymore." She took a deep breath. "And I don't think you and I should see each other anymore, either."

Grigori stared at her, one black brow arching upward. "Indeed? May I ask why?"

She took another sip of wine, hoping it would calm her rapidly beating heart. "I'm beginning to feel claustrophobic."

"What of Alexi?"

"He's gone."

"Is he?"

"Isn't he?"

Grigori shrugged. "For the time being, it would seem so."

Tommy approached the table and placed a glass of dark red wine in front of Grigori. "Anything else I can get for either of you?"

Grigori shook his head, his gaze focused on Marisa.

"No, Tommy, thanks." She stared at her dinner, and then pushed the plate away, her appetite gone.

"Alexi will come back, you know."

"I'll worry about it when it happens. Until then, I don't want to think about vampires, or vampire hunters, or—"

"Or me?"

"Or you." Taking her wallet from her purse, she placed ten dollars on the table and stood up. "Good-bye, Grigori."

"I'll walk you home."

"It isn't necessary."

He watched her leave the restaurant, and then, with a sigh, he followed her out the door, careful to mask his presence. He paused when she reached her apartment, his senses probing the area, but he perceived no threat. He waited until she was safely inside, and then he made his way up the stairs. She might think the danger was past, that Alexi had given up, but Grigori knew better.

With a sigh, he sat down on the top stair and gazed out into the darkness. So she wanted to be rid of him, did she? He smiled at the stars, because he was not yet ready to be rid of her.

Chapter Twenty-three

Grigori rose before sunset the following evening. By the time he had showered and dressed, night had fallen. A phone call brought him the information he needed. A contrived explanation as to why he must see the property at night, the promise of a quick sale, and it was done.

He met the realtor a half hour later. He had already explored the house from cellar to attic, but he walked through it again with the agent, and then gave her a check for the down payment. The house hadn't been lived in for several years. The paperwork would take thirty days, and then it would be his.

He bid the realtor good night, shook her hand, and watched her drive away. When he was certain she was gone, he went back up to the house. A wave of his hand unlocked the front door.

It was an old two-story house, probably built at the turn of the century. The exterior paint, once a dark shade of green, was faded and peeling. The shutters, once white, looked gray.

It had the musty smell of a house long empty. The place needed a coat of paint inside and out, a new roof, new carpeting. The kitchen and bathroom needed remodeling, but none of those things were important. What mattered was that it was a house surrounded by a high brick wall. A house that stood alone on an acre of land. Tall trees shaded the front and back, providing added privacy.

Starting at the basement, he walked through the house again, memorizing the location of every door and window between the cellar and the attic. As old as the place was, it was sound from top to bottom, save for the roof. It suited him perfectly.

Thirty days, the realtor had said. Grigori smiled faintly. As far as he was concerned, it was already his. The fact that there was no phone, no lights, and no running water mattered not at all. He had no need of those things.

He would take possession of the house that night.

Marisa glanced at the clock as she went to answer the door, wondering who would come calling so late. It was almost eleven.

"Who is it?"

"Grigori."

She rested her forehead against the door and closed her eyes. She hadn't seen him in over a week, and though she had missed him, she was relieved that he was out of her life. No matter how attractive she had found him, he was a vampire. Relationships with normal men were hard enough; she didn't need the added baggage of dating the undead.

With a sigh, she opened the door. "It's late."

"I know." He held out a bouquet of roses. "May I come in?"

"It's late," she said again. "I was just going to bed."

"Marisa . . ."

She looked up at him, not wanting to hear the loneliness in his voice, not wanting to remember the kisses they had shared, or the night she had held him in her arms.

"Please, Grigori—"

He thrust the flowers at her. A dozen perfect white roses, and in their center, like a drop of blood, a single red bloom.

"They're lovely," she said.

"As are you."

She recalled that he had said those very same words to her that night they had walked in the park together. She ran her fingertip over one of the rose petals. "What do you want?"

"To see you, nothing more."

"No." She shook her head. "I told you, I don't want to see you again."

She felt the anger that stirred within him. She remembered a line from a *Star Wars* movie, something about it not being wise to upset a Wookie. Obviously, the same warning applied to vampires.

"I told you once," Grigori said, his voice as hard as tempered steel, "I would never take you against your will."

"And I told you to stop reading my mind!"

"I'm sorry," he said softly. "I'm afraid I've become accustomed to having my own way."

She looked into his eyes, those deep, dark eyes, and in the back of her mind she heard Edward's voice warning her that Grigori could read her mind, that he could make her do whatever he wished. *They have no morals,* Edward had said, *no qualms about taking whatever they want.* Grigori could hypnotize her with a look, she thought. Perhaps he was doing it now.

She drew her gaze from him. "I think you'd better go."

"As you wish." His gaze caressed her, warming her skin. "Good night, Marisa."

"Good night."

She closed the door, and then leaned back against it, her nostrils filling with the scent of roses.

In the distance, she heard the melancholy wail of a wolf.

The dreams started that night—sultry, erotic dreams that made her toss and turn so that she woke drenched in perspiration; dreams that lingered in her mind long after she awoke; dreams that left her feeling as though she had done something wicked in her sleep. Dreams that made her angry because she knew he was sending them to her, knew it was his way of telling her that if she would not see him during her waking hours, she would see him when she was at her most vulnerable.

Even if she could forget the dreams—and there was no chance of that—he found another way to keep in touch. The day after the dreams began, he started sending her flowers at work. Always roses. White ones, red ones, pink ones, until her office looked like a florist shop.

He sent flowers to her house. Dozens and dozens of long-stemmed bloodred roses.

He sent her heart-shaped boxes of chocolates.

And more flowers.

Linda and the other girls at the office began to tease her about her new boyfriend, demanding to know his name and when they were going to meet him.

She was glad when Thanksgiving came. The office closed Thursday and Friday, giving her a long weekend. She intended to spend it finishing up her Christmas shopping. Her parents had asked her to come spend the holiday with them in Florida, but she just wasn't up to the trip. Linda invited Marisa to spend the day with her and her family, but she declined, deciding what she really needed was some time alone.

Being alone had seemed like a good idea on Wednesday after a busy day at work. Thursday morning she thought it stank. Everyone she knew was spending the day with friends and family, and she was going to be sitting home by herself.

Well, it was her own fault. She spent the morning wrapping Christmas presents, ate lunch, watched the Macy's Thanksgiving Day parade.

Later, bored, she did a load of wash. She was folding it when the phone rang.

She answered it on the second ring. "Hello?"

"Marisa?"

"Edward, how are you?"

"Fine. And you?"

"I'm good. I thought, well, I thought you'd probably left town by now."

"No." He didn't say why he was still in the city, but they both knew it was because he was worried about her. "I was . . . that is, I know you're probably busy, but I was wondering, if you're not doing anything . . . would you like to go out for dinner with me?" He said the last in a rush, as if he was certain she would refuse him and he wanted to get it over with as soon as possible.

"I'd like that," she said, surprising them both.

"You would? That's great. What time shall I pick you up?"

"Five?"

"I'll be there. And Marisa? Thank you."

"Thank you."

She was humming when she hung up the phone.

Edward arrived promptly at five, bearing a bouquet of flowers and a bottle of wine. He looked quite handsome in a light gray suit. She stared at him a moment, trying to figure out why he looked different, and then realized he wasn't wearing brown.

"Hi," she said, "come on in."

"Thank you." He handed her the flowers and held up the wine. "Shall I open this now?"

Marisa nodded. "I'm going to put these in some water."

He followed her into the kitchen and poured two glasses of wine while she pulled a vase from one of the cupboards.

"They're lovely." She arranged the bouquet in a cut-glass vase that had belonged to her grandmother, and then placed it on the kitchen table. "Thank you."

"You're welcome." He handed her a glass. "You haven't heard from Alexi, have you?"

"No. Why? Do you think he's come back?"

Ramsey shrugged. "I don't know, but if he does, you'll probably be the first to know it."

"That's a comfort. There haven't been any more

deaths reported in the papers." She read the *Times* every morning, always afraid she'd see those awful headlines that read *VAMPIRE KILLER STRIKES AGAIN.*

"Have you seen Chiavari?"

Marisa shook her head. "No." Except in my dreams, she thought. But she couldn't tell Edward that.

"So," Edward said, "where shall we eat?"

"I don't care. It's up to you."

"Do you want turkey and all the trimmings?"

"I'd rather have lobster."

They went to dinner at a seafood restaurant. Edward ordered fried shrimp; Marisa had lobster.

"How much longer will you be in town?" Marisa asked.

"I don't know. I rented a house down by the beach."

"You did!"

He nodded, somewhat sheepishly, she thought. "I really like it down there. I've never lived by the ocean. It's . . . I don't know, kind of peaceful."

"Kind of expensive, too, I'll bet."

"Yeah, but I can afford it."

"I never thought about it, but I guess there must be good money in vampire hunting."

"Yeah, it's a specialized field," Ramsey agreed. "People are willing to pay a great deal to get rid of a vampire."

"Do you have any family anywhere?"

"Here and there. I've got an old maiden aunt in Chicago, and a couple of cousins in Boston. What about you?"

"My folks live in Florida. They moved there two years ago when my dad retired. My brother, Mike, lives in Denver. He's a stockbroker. I haven't seen him since last Christmas."

"Christmas," Ramsey murmured.

"I'm going to Florida to spend it with my parents," Marisa said. "I'm not really in the mood, but they're expecting me. My brother and his family will be there. It's about the only time of the year we're all together."

"Must be nice," Edward remarked.

"What are you going to do?"

"I don't know. Maybe I'll go back to Chicago and see my aunt, get rid of my apartment, pick up my mail, change my address." He grinned crookedly. "Sounds like a fun holiday, doesn't it?"

"I'm sorry."

"Hey, no problem. I'm used to it."

"Maybe we can get together when I get back," Marisa suggested.

"Yeah, I'd like that."

They spoke of inconsequential things over dinner. Marisa mentioned she was getting a raise the first of the year; Edward said he was thinking of buying a new car.

"Would you like to go to a movie?" Edward asked as they left the restaurant.

"Sure, why not?"

They drove uptown. Marisa gazed out the window, admiring the lights and decorations that adorned the houses. Hard to believe it was almost Christmas, that another year was drawing to a close.

"You know, I still can't believe it was real," she remarked as Edward parked the car. "It all seems so bizarre."

"I know. Sometimes I can't believe it myself."

He got out of the car and came around to open her door. "It's just so unreal. I mean, here we are, going to the movies as if it had never happened. I can't believe that just two weeks ago, we were fighting a vampire. Tell me," she said as they walked toward the theater. "How do people get in touch with you? You don't advertise in the phone book, do you?"

He laughed at that. "Not quite. It's mostly just word of mouth. There are people throughout the country who know what I do. When they hear of unusual killings, they notify me."

He bought two tickets for the latest Mel Gibson movie and they went inside. "Popcorn?" he asked.

Marisa shook her head. "Not right now. I'm still full from dinner."

"Yeah, that lobster was almost as big as you are."

Marisa grinned at him.

They held hands in the show, went out for ice cream afterward.

"Thanks," Marisa said when they reached her apartment. "I had a really nice time."

"Me too. Maybe we can do it again."

"I'd like that." She looked up at him and knew he was going to kiss her good night.

"Marisa—" He put his arms around her and drew her close. There was nothing tentative in his movements now, no hesitation.

Marisa closed her eyes as his mouth covered hers. It was a pleasant kiss, evoking neither passion nor revulsion.

"Good night," he whispered.

"Good night. And thank you for a nice time."

He nodded. "See ya."

"See ya."

She watched him get into his car and drive away, and still she stood on the landing, staring into the distance, at the twinkling lights on the houses across the way, at the twinkling stars overhead.

She wished that she could love Edward, but she didn't feel passion for him, only affection. Maybe it was the age difference. After all, he was eighteen years older than she was, she mused, and then laughed out loud. Grigori was two hundred years older than she was and she didn't have any trouble whipping up a grand passion for him.

She crossed her arms over the railing and let out a long, slow sigh. Was that why she was feeling so melancholy? Because she missed him?

"Might as well admit it," she muttered. "Vampire or not, you're in love with him. But that's all right. You'll get over it."

"Get over what?"

She whirled around, her heart in her throat, at the sound of his voice. "What are you doing here?"

"I come here every night."

"What?"

"You heard me."

"What for?"

He lifted one dark brow in an all too familiar gesture. "Why the hell do you think?"

"I told you I don't want you here."

"I stopped doing what other people tell me to do a long time ago."

"Well, it's late. Good night."

"Sweet dreams, Marisa."

"Stay out of my dreams!" Unlocking the door, she went inside and slammed it shut behind her, only to find him waiting for her when she turned around.

"Marisa."

"Oh! I hate it when you do that." She threw her purse on the chair, and then crossed her arms over her chest. "What do you want?"

"I want you."

"Well, that's too bad."

"Tell me you don't want me."

"I don't want you."

"Liar."

She glared up at him, all her anger and frustration boiling to the surface. Before she realized what she was doing, she slapped him.

The solid smack of her hand striking his flesh seemed to echo and re-echo in the stillness that fell between them.

She stared at him, horrified by what she had done, by what he might do in retaliation.

"Feel better?" he asked quietly.

"No." She blinked back the tears welling in her eyes. "Please leave me alone."

"I can't."

"Why? Why are you doing this?"

"I told you. I want you."

"I can't. I don't believe in casual affairs."

"Is that what you think I want?"

"I don't know. I don't want to know."

"Marisa . . ."

His voice moved over her, whisper quiet, whisper soft. She shook her head, her heart fluttering like a kite caught in a high wind, as his knuckles caressed her cheek.

"Don't." She forced the word from a mouth gone dry.

"You want me, too."

"It isn't right." She swallowed hard. "It isn't natural."

She'd hurt him now. She could see it in the depths of his eyes . . . those devil black eyes that could look as soft as velvet or as hard as granite.

"There's nothing unnatural about what I want from you," he replied, his voice sandpaper rough. "Do you deny you've thought of it, wondered about it?"

She yearned to deny it with every fiber of her being, but she knew she couldn't lie to him. She could lie to herself as much as she wished, she could even voice the words aloud to Grigori, but it would be a waste of breath, because he could read the truth in her mind, the feelings in her heart.

Grigori held out his hand. "Come to me, Marisa."

"Please, don't ask me." He was close, so close. Too close. She shoved her hands in the pockets of her pants to keep from reaching for him, and yet, in spite of all she could do, she felt herself being inexplicably drawn toward him. Was it Grigori's own inherent power exerting its influence over her, she wondered, or was it her foolish heart overruling her mind?

Feeling as though she were moving in slow motion, she withdrew her hand from her pocket and placed it in his, felt his long, cool fingers curl around hers.

His arm slid around her waist, his touch light, yet she felt the latent strength in that arm, knew he could break her in half if he had a mind to. But there was no violence in him now.

Gently, ever so gently, he wrapped her in his embrace and covered her mouth with his. Magic flowed between them, cocooning them in a world that was big enough for only the two of them, a world where there was no night and no day, no wrong or right, only one man and one woman who should never have met.

She pressed herself against him, felt his arm tighten around her waist as he deepened the kiss. His free hand skimmed over her back, slid forward to brush the curve of her breast. Fire shot through her at his touch. Heat uncurled deep within her as every nerve, every fiber of her being, responded to his nearness, to the silent invitation of his lips. Never before, she thought, never before had she felt like this. She had been kissed, she had been caressed, but nothing had aroused her like the tender touch of Grigori's hands, the gentle persuasion of his kisses.

She felt the heat of passion warm her skin and flush her cheeks. She ached deep inside, ached for his touch, for his possession. He was the reason she had never slept with another man. She had been waiting, waiting for the enchantment that came with this man's touch.

"Marisa." His breath fanned her cheek. His lips feathered across her brow, the tip of her nose, the curve of her cheek. *"Cara mia, mi vita, mi amore."*

A low moan rose in her throat at the wanting in his voice, a wanting that thrummed through her with every beat of her heart.

She felt his lips at her throat, felt his tongue explore the pulse beating in the hollow there.

He groaned as, abruptly, he put her away from him. "I'm sorry," he said hoarsely.

"What's wrong?" She stared at him, still caught up in the passion that had burned so brightly between them.

"I think we shall have to postpone this for another time."

"Why?" Even as she asked the question, she knew the answer. He was staring at her throat, his nostrils flared, his hands tightly clenched.

"I should have known better than to come to you when I'm not fully in control." He dragged a hand through his hair, hating the Hunger raging through him, the images that chased themselves across his mind—images of Marisa enfolded in his arms, images of himself bending over her, his fangs bared. "Good night, Marisa."

"Good night," she replied, but he was already gone, leaving her feeling bereft and unfulfilled.

Chapter Twenty-four

She stayed up late that night. She told herself it was because she wasn't tired, that she wanted to watch Jay Leno because Mel Gibson was going to be on.

When the Leno show was over, she changed into her nightgown, then plucked a book off the shelf. She'd read it before, but it was one of her favorites. She managed to get through the first chapter before her mind strayed and she found herself wondering where Grigori was. She admitted then that the reason she didn't want to go to bed was because she didn't want to go to sleep.

And she didn't want to go to sleep because she knew he would come to her in her dreams, when she was receptive and vulnerable.

At two A.M., she knew she was fighting a losing battle. She slid into bed and stared out the window.

"Please, Grigori," she whispered. "Please leave me alone."

She was walking in the park in the moonlight, and she was afraid. Every drifting shadow held the threat of danger. Every sound sent her heart into her throat. She was afraid—afraid of the dark, afraid for her life.

She called his name, knowing he was the only one who could save her, called his name again and again until she was sobbing. And then he was there. Tall and dark and dressed all in black. The opera cloak he had worn in Italy fell from his shoulders, blowing about his ankles though there was no wind. His skin seemed to glow in the moonlight. But it was the hungry look in his midnight black eyes that held her captive.

"Why do you fight it?" he asked, and his voice was like distant thunder. "Why do you fight me?"

She stared up at him as he took a step toward her.

"We are connected, you and I," he went on. "Your blood flows within my veins. I know your thoughts. I can feel your desire." He held out his hand. "Come to me, Marisa; let me show you my world."

"What if I refuse?"

"Do not let your fears imprison you."

"I can't help it. I'm afraid of the darkness, of the unknown."

"Don't be afraid, Marisa. I won't let anything hurt you."

He took another step toward her, his hand still outstretched. "Come to me. It is what you want."

"Yes." She placed her hand in his, and felt the strength that flowed through him, the strength of two hundred years.

"Marisa!"

She lifted her face for his kiss. His lips seared hers, branding her, and she knew him. Knew him as she knew herself. She saw his childhood in Italy, knew he had loved his parents, been jealous of his older brother. She experienced his love for the land, his longing to travel to other parts of the world. She felt his joy and pride in his children, his grief at their loss, his guilt at Antoinette's death, his rage that he could not avenge himself on Alexi. And, over all, the Hunger that coiled deep within his belly, ever a part of him, coloring his thoughts, his needs. She was aware of the desire that heated his blood, felt it pounding in his veins, in the tension that caused his arms to tighten around her.

He lowered her to the ground, only it wasn't grass beneath her, but a coffin, and he was pressing her down, lowering himself over her. His hands and lips mesmerized her as they aroused her and she felt herself losing her identity, becoming a part of him, a part of his world.

She felt his teeth at her throat, knew that he was going to drink her blood, drink and drink until there was nothing left of her. . . .

She awoke with a start, her heart pounding like thunder, her body drenched in sweat. Flinging off the covers, she reached for the light and turned it on, relieved to find herself in her own bed, in her own house.

"A dream." She said the words aloud, comforted by the sound of her own voice. "Just a dream."

But she couldn't help wondering if maybe it was a warning of things to come.

Friday morning dawned clear and bright and cool. Marisa rose late after a restless night. She drank three cups of coffee, dressed, cleaned her apartment, which seemed suddenly large and empty.

She fixed a sandwich for lunch, wishing she had

some leftover turkey, but it was hard to have left-overs when one ate dinner out.

She turned on the TV and watched the last half of *The Way We Were*, and then, feeling melancholy, she went for a walk in the park.

She tried to sort through her feelings for Ramsey, for Grigori, but it seemed impossible to concentrate. She could think of nothing but the last time she had seen Grigori, the kisses they had shared. The dream that was, even now, all too vivid in her mind.

With a sigh, she sat down under a tree and gazed into the distance. She wasn't ready to make the kind of earth-shattering decision that becoming involved with Grigori would entail. She hadn't been deeply in love, or even in lust, with many men. In high school, she'd been active in sports and dance. She'd hung around with the "in" crowd, busy all the time. She'd gone to college, made new friends, and then started working for Salazar and Salazar.

She'd had her fair share of dates, but never met that one special someone. She knew she was something of an oddity, a twenty-four-year-old virgin, yet she hadn't met anyone she was willing to give it up for. None of them had tempted her as Grigori tempted her . . . but succumbing to his dark power could cost her so much more than her virginity. The cost could very well be her life.

That thought made her smile. One of the reasons she had avoided intimacy was the very real threat of AIDS. Sex wasn't something she was willing to die for . . . and yet getting involved with Grigori could be just as dangerous, just as life-threatening.

She fell back on the grass and stared up at the sky, which was, for once, clear of smog. Strange, that she seemed to attract men who were too old for her. Grigori was hundreds of years older than she was, though he looked no more than thirty. Edward was in his forties. Still, he was attractive in his own way, and one of the nicest men she had ever met. Too bad he was too old for her.

The sun was warm on her face. Feeling drowsy, she closed her eyes. . . .

Grigori stalked the dark rooms of his new abode, waiting for the sun to go down. For the last half century, he had been able to rise a little earlier each year, though he still succumbed to the dark sleep when the sun was high in the sky. Was it possible that, in time, he would not have to sleep at all? Had Alexi reached that plane of existence?

Alexi. Was he still in the past, licking his wounds?

Grigori moved to the window that looked out over the backyard. He could see the last splash of color against the western sky, feel the coming night creeping over the land, feel all his senses come fully to life. Awareness flowed through him. He could feel the energy of thousands of people pulsing through him, hear the pumping of their hearts, smell their blood. He could hear the barking of a dog a mile away, the constant hum of car engines, the hum of electricity through the wires. He knew it would rain before the night was over.

He knew Marisa was thinking of him.

He focused on her, felt his pulse increase as his heart began to beat in time with hers.

Marisa . . . she was a part of him whether she liked it or not.

He closed his eyes and her image leaped into his mind. How lovely she was, his Marisa, with her dark brown hair and vibrant green eyes. Her skin bloomed with the vibrant beauty of youth; her lips were warm and pink. He had dreamed of her last night. That in itself was a sign that his preternatural powers were growing stronger. Newly made vampires did not dream. Locked in the dark sleep, theirs was a dark and empty rest.

He recalled those early days when he had dreaded the hours of nothingness, when he had feared the darkness, feared the helplessness that had come over him, feared that some overzealous mortal would find him while he was vulnerable.

He recalled the nights when awareness had returned with a suddenness that left him feeling breathless with fear.

But those days were long gone. The dark sleep no longer frightened him, no longer held him powerless in a web of nothingness. He could move about during the daylight hours as long as he stayed out of the sun's light; even in sleep, he was aware of what was going on around him.

He was no longer afraid of anything. Except the touch of the sun, and the thought of losing Marisa.

When had she become so important to him? And what was he going to do about it? How was he going to convince her to look past the vampire and see the man?

Ah, he mused, but did the man still exist, or was he only kidding himself?

He felt his hunger stir to life as night fell, spreading a cloak of darkness across the land.

He changed his clothes, and then left the house. Blending into the shadows of the night, he went in search of prey.

It was dark when she woke. She scrambled to her feet, amazed that she had slept so long, but then, she wasn't getting much rest at night.

Dusting off her pants, she started walking home. It was only six o'clock, but it seemed later. Clouds hid the moon. Feeling suddenly nervous, she glanced over her shoulder, assuring herself that she was alone. The park, which had seemed beautiful and romantic when Grigori had been beside her, now loomed dark and foreboding.

Certain she heard footsteps behind her, she started walking faster.

She screamed when she felt a hand close over her arm.

"Shut up! I don't wanna hurt you, lady. Just give me your cash."

"I . . . I don't have . . . have any."

"Don't lie to me! And don't turn around."

"I'm . . . not . . . not lying." She was shaking all over. Her legs were weak, and she felt hot and cold at the same time. Fear congealed in her belly. She gasped when she felt something small and round and hard pressed into her back.

"I've got a gun, and I'll use it if I have to. Now, stop stallin' and gimme your money. All of it."

"Honest, I don't . . . don't . . . please . . ." She was going to die. And she wasn't ready. Please, not now . . .

His hand tightened on her arm, making her wince.

"Please . . . I didn't bring my wallet with me."

"I don't—"

His words died away in a choked sob and suddenly he wasn't holding her anymore. She heard what could have been a growl, followed by a sharp cry of pain.

Terror held her frozen to the spot. She told herself to run, but her feet refused to obey. It took all the courage she could muster just to glance over her shoulder.

She was sorry when she did.

Two dark shapes stood a few feet away, locked together in a macabre embrace. The taller of the two men was bent over the other one. She heard a muffled sob, caught a whiff of blood, and then she heard a voice, low and hypnotic.

"Leave this place and don't come back. You will remember nothing of this night. Nothing. Do you understand?"

She saw the shorter of the two men nod, then turn and walk away.

She was trembling violently when Grigori took her in his arms.

"Are you all right?" His voice was soft and soothing.

"Y-yes."

"Did he hurt you?"

She shook her head, knowing somehow that if she said yes, the man who had tried to rob her would die. "No. I'm just . . . just so . . . so cold."

Wordlessly, he swept her into his arms. Strong arms that would keep her safe. She buried her face in the hollow of his shoulder. There was a humming in her ears, a sensation of swift movement. She snuggled against him, her eyes closed, her heart pounding. She didn't ask where he was taking her. At that moment, she didn't care. He was warmth and safety. He would protect her.

Moments or hours later, she wasn't sure, he set her on her feet.

She felt a sense of power flowing past her, and the room was suddenly filled with the light from a dozen candles.

"Where are we?" Marisa asked.

"My home."

She glanced around. The room was large, with high, vaulted ceilings and old-fashioned leaded windows. Faded green drapes hung at the windows; a faded green-and-gold carpet covered the floor. The walls had once been pale yellow. A huge stone fireplace with a black marble mantel took up a good portion of one wall.

"You live here?" Her voice echoed off the high ceiling.

He nodded. "But it won't be legally mine for another week or so."

"Oh." She was trembling again.

He whispered her name as he took her in his arms. "Don't be afraid. You're safe now."

"He . . . he had a gun."

"Not anymore."

"You took it?"

Grigori nodded.

"You drank from him, didn't you?"

"Yes. And then I wiped it from his mind." She felt the muscles in his arms tense. "It troubles you, doesn't it?"

"A little." She smiled up at him tremulously. "But I'm getting used to it."

"Ah, Marisa, do you have any idea how much I need you?"

"You? Need me?"

He nodded. "Shall I wax poetic and tell you that I need you as a flower needs the sun, as a starving man craves sustenance? Shall I tell you how beautiful you are to me, how much I want you?"

She stared up at him, the mugger momentarily forgotten. Candlelight danced in the inky black of Grigori's thick black hair and cast golden shadows over his face. And his eyes . . . his eyes burned with a radiant heat that spoke more eloquently than words.

"I shall not rush you, *cara.* I shall not ask more of you than you wish to give. I ask only that you let me see you each night, and dream of you each day."

He lifted his hand, one long finger lovingly outlining the contours of her face. "Say yes, *cara mia*. I have lived alone too long."

It was tempting, so tempting. He needed her as no one ever had, ever would, and yet she couldn't forget what he was.

"I'm sorry." She whispered the words, afraid of hurting him, afraid of incurring his anger. "Please try to understand. I don't want to hurt you. I wish that I could—"

He placed his fingertips over her lips, stilling her words, and then, slowly and deliberately, he lowered his arms and took a step backward. "I understand."

"Grigori, please, just let me explain—"

"It isn't necessary," he said flatly. "I am Vampyre. I know your thoughts, Marisa, better than you know them yourself. Be assured, you have nothing to fear from me. Come, I will see you safely home."

Chapter Twenty-five

There were no more flowers after that, no more erotic dreams that filled her with both embarrassment and pleasure. She buried herself in her work, spent her weekends doing last-minute Christmas shopping. She mailed her Christmas cards, late as always, went to a holiday party at Linda's house and tried to pretend she was having a good time.

She checked the newspapers every morning and listened to the news each night, but there were no more vampire killings, no sign that Alexi Kristov had returned.

She went out to dinner and a movie with Edward a few times, and then Christmas week was upon them.

The office closed early on Wednesday, and Marisa packed her bags and went to Florida to spend Christmas with her parents and her brother and his wife and kids. She endured her mother's gentle urging to settle down, listened to her father complain about the fate of the nation, tried not to be jealous of Mike, who seemed to have everything: a lovely wife, four beautiful children, a new car, a thriving business.

It always amazed her how she became a little girl again as soon as she walked into her mother's house. Part of her resented it, but the other part, the part of her that had never grown up, would never grow up, was happy to let her mother fuss over her.

Christmas passed pleasantly. They exchanged gifts, went outside to watch the kids ride their new bikes. Later, they ate a big breakfast, followed by an enormous dinner, and then, too soon, the day was over. Mountains of paper and tissue and ribbon filled the trash cans. The kids, worn out after a day of playing and pigging out, went to bed early.

Marisa stayed up after everyone else had gone to bed. Sitting in the living room in front of the fireplace, she stared at the flickering flames. She wondered where Alexi had gone, how Edward had spent the day. She should have asked him to spend the holiday with her and her parents. It wouldn't have been any trouble to put him up, but she didn't want to encourage him, didn't want him to think that they could ever be more than friends.

Leaning back, she tried to focus on making New Year's resolutions. More exercise, less chocolate. Go to church. Help out at the soup kitchen. Call home more often. . . .

Finally, she gave up and let herself think of Grigori. How had he spent the day? Did vampires celebrate Christmas, or was it just another day in an endless string of days? Or nights.

How had he endured for two hundred years? What would it be like to be young forever, never to be sick, never to have to worry about dying? What was it like to know that everyone you knew would grow old and die while you stayed forever the same?

She closed her eyes, lulled to sleep by the lateness of the hour and the warmth of the flames. . . .

It was Christmas Eve and he was walking alone down a residential street. Dressed in the sweater and jeans she had picked out for him, he moved soundlessly through the night, oblivious to the bitter wind and the rain. Christmas lights twinkled from porches and housetops, shimmering with moisture. And all around him, he could hear the sounds of Christmas carols and laughter as families gathered together to celebrate the most joyous day of the year.

He walked for miles, his hands shoved into the pockets of his jeans, his face turned to the wind. She sensed his loneliness, his separation from the rest of the world. She felt his hunger, saw him pause outside an all-night drugstore, his nostrils flaring as he came upon an old man huddled in the doorway. She felt the hunger clawing at him, urging him to take what he needed, to satisfy his thirst. She felt his hesitation, and then, with a muttered oath, he passed the old man by, and she knew it was because it was Christmas, because the old man was on his way home to his invalid wife.

And then she saw him in the house he had bought, and she knew he had bought it because of her, that he had hoped she would share it with him.

She saw him walking through the dark, empty rooms, heard his voice whisper that he needed her, that his life had lost all hope, all meaning.

And then she saw him standing outside again, his head thrown back, his hands clenched tightly at his sides. He spoke her name, and then, riding on the wings of the wind, she heard the melancholy wail of a wolf . . . .

She awoke with a start, her heart pounding as she glanced around the darkened room. "Grigori?" But of course he wasn't here. He was back in L.A.

She lifted a hand to her cheek, surprised to find it damp with tears.

"Why do you weep, Marisa?"

She should have been frightened, or, at the very least, surprised. Instead, the soft, husky sound of his voice sent a warm glow pulsing through her. "Don't you know?"

"I'm trying not to read your mind, since it upsets you so."

"I was dreaming." She wrapped her arms around her waist and looked up at him. He stood beside the sofa. Wrapped in a flowing black cloak, he looked tall and dark and dangerous. The light from the fire haloed his hair. "But you know that, don't you?"

He shook his head. "No. What was it about?"

"It doesn't matter. What are you doing here?"

"What do you think?"

Her heart began to pound. Her mouth went dry. "I—" She swallowed. "I don't know."

He knelt beside her, the cloak settling around him like a pool of black ink.

"I missed you," he said quietly. "I came to see if maybe you had missed me, too." His gaze found and held hers. "Did you?"

She couldn't lie to him, not when he was looking at her like that. She could feel his loneliness as if it were her own. It made her feel powerful and humble at the same time, to think that he had come here. It was frightening, to know she had the ability to hurt him, to shatter his pride and wound his ego.

She looked at him and reminded herself that he was a vampire, but all she saw was a faint ray of hope in a pair of deep black eyes.

She looked at him and tried to see a monster, but all she saw was a man who had been alone too long, a man who needed her.

"Did you think of me at all while you were here?"

"Yes." She had thought of him constantly. At church on Christmas Eve, she had wished he could be there beside her. All day today, she had thought of him, lost in the dark sleep, alone, while the rest of the world celebrated the wondrous birth of the savior of the world.

"You missed me then?"

She nodded. "Yes. I didn't want to, but I couldn't help it."

The hope in his eyes burned brighter, its heat enveloping her. "Marisa."

"Merry Christmas, Grigori," she whispered, and held out her arms.

He could only stare at her, momentarily stunned by the love he read in her eyes, and then, with a cry, he drew her down into his lap and wrapped his arms around her.

"Marisa . . . Marisa . . ." He buried his face in the silky cloud of her hair and held her tight.

She clung to him, feeling the tremors that shook his body as he whispered her name over and over again.

"Aren't you going to kiss me?"

He drew back a little, a faint smile curving his lips. "As often and as long as you wish."

Happiness bubbled up inside her like champagne. "I wish," she murmured, "I wish you would kiss me now."

"Ah, *cara,*" he said fervently, "your wish is my command."

She closed her eyes as his head dipped toward hers, sighed as their lips met. She had yearned for this, hungered for this. Why had she fought it for so long?

Without taking his lips from hers, he turned her in his lap so that she was facing him, her legs circling his waist, her breasts crushed against his chest. His hands roamed over her back and shoulders, down her arms, along her thighs, tantalizing her with his touch, arousing her until she ached with needing him.

He burned with the same desire. She could feel it in every quivering muscle, hear it in the ragged edge of his breathing, in the rasp of his voice when he whispered her name.

She was breathless when he took his mouth from hers. "Grigori . . . have you always had this power over women?"

His knuckles brushed her cheek. "What power is that, *cara?*"

"You know very well what I mean. One kiss and I'm on fire."

"It isn't power, *mi amore.*"

"Magic, then?"

He smiled at her, his expression tender. "More like a miracle."

"A miracle?" She traced his lips with her fingertip, and then cupped his face in her hands.

"That you could love me."

"I do love you," she said, "but—"

He placed his hand over her mouth. "Let us not worry about the future tonight," he said. "Just let me hold you until the dawn."

She licked his palm, and he groaned low in his throat. "I can't believe you're here."

"You wanted me here, did you not?"

She nodded and snuggled into his arms, her head resting on his shoulder. "I think this is the best Christmas I've ever had."

His arms tightened around her. "For me, as well," he said, his breath warming her neck. "For me, as well."

They sat there for hours, content to hold each other close and watch the flames dance in the hearth. Grigori told her of his childhood in Italy, of his father who was a cobbler, of his older brother who became a priest. He told her of faraway places he had explored in centuries past, and she could see it all in her mind, the house where he had been born, Grigori as a young boy, tall and dark and handsome, even then. She saw the world through his eyes, the pyramids of Egypt and the canals of Italy, the great cathedrals of Europe, the jungles of Africa. How wonderful, to have lived so long and seen so much.

After a time, he grew silent, and she knew that dawn was drawing near. She stared at the hearth, only then realizing that, though they had never added more wood to the fire, it had burned all through the night.

"I must go." He pressed a kiss to her cheek. "When will you be home?"

"Sunday night. I wish you didn't have to leave."

He shrugged. "It cannot be helped. I will see you when you return, yes?"

"Yes."

He held her close, breathing in her scent, silently vowing that he would grant her every wish, fulfill her every desire, as long as she would let him stay by her side.

He stood up in a fluid motion, carrying her with him. "I'm afraid I've robbed you of your sleep."

She locked her arms around his neck and smiled at him. "I don't mind. I can sleep late tomorrow."

"Dream about me?"

She grinned. "I always do."

He kissed her again, long and hard, and then, ever so gently, set her on her feet. "Until Sunday night, *cara mia*."

"One more kiss?"

He swept her into his arms and kissed her until she was breathless, and then, in a swirl of black silk, he was gone.

Head whirling, heart filled with a dozen conflicting emotions, she made her way up the stairs and fell into bed.

She was in love.

With a vampire.

And it was the most exciting thing in the world.

It was a little after eight when the plane landed. Holding her purse and a small carry-on bag, she followed the other passengers up the ramp. It had been fun spending the last three days with her family, but she was glad to be home again. She couldn't wait to see Grigori.

The airport was crowded with people returning

home. Taking a deep breath, she told herself to be patient. She wasn't the only one in a hurry.

She was making her way toward the luggage carousel when she saw Grigori.

She smiled as he walked toward her.

"Welcome home, *cara mia,*" he said, and, taking her in his arms, he hugged her as if they hadn't seen each other for years instead of three days. It made her ridiculously happy to know he had missed her as much as she had missed him.

"What are you doing here?"

"I wanted to see you. Let's go get your luggage."

For the first time in her life, her bags were the first down the chute.

Grigori picked up her two suitcases and tucked them under one arm; then he took her hand. "Come, I rented a limousine to take you home."

"You're kidding, right?"

"No, it's right outside."

"But my car—"

"I drove it to your apartment last night."

"Why?"

"So I could hold you in my arms that much sooner."

It was, quite possibly, the most romantic thing anyone had ever said or done.

Marisa felt like a movie star as a sleek white stretch limo pulled up to the curb. The driver got out and opened the door for them, stowed her luggage in the trunk. Minutes later, they were on the 101 Freeway headed home.

Marisa snuggled against Grigori. "This is wonderful."

"Are you thirsty? Hungry?"

"No, I'm fine."

His arm tightened around her shoulders. "Did you have a good time with your family?"

"Uh-huh. My mom always cooks enough for an army. I probably gained ten pounds." She looked up at him. "I guess that's not a problem for you, is it?"

"No."

"Lucky."

"Indeed I am."

She felt a wave of heat flood her cheeks as his gaze moved over her, possessive, admiring. "The vampire diet plan," she quipped. "Liquid protein."

One side of his mouth lifted in a wry grin. "Don't knock it until you've tried it."

"No, thank you." And then she frowned. "Wait a minute. When we went to the North Woods Inn, you ate a steak." She grimaced at the memory. "A very rare steak, but you ate it."

"Did I?"

"Of course you did. I saw you."

He smiled indulgently. "I never ate it. I only planted the idea in your mind."

She punched him on the arm. "Messing with my head again."

He shrugged. "I won't do it anymore."

"Promise?"

"Yes."

"Can I ask you something?"

"Anything, *cara*."

"Did you take a walk on Christmas Eve?"

"Why do you ask?"

"I saw you."

Grigori frowned at her. "What do you mean?"

"I saw you in a dream. You were walking down a street, all alone. You passed a drugstore and there was an old man standing in the doorway. He was wearing a brown raincoat, and had a red scarf around his neck."

She felt the muscles in his arm tense. "Go on."

"You were going to . . . you know, but then you read his mind and saw that his wife was home alone, and sick, and he had gone out in the rain to pick up a prescription for her."

"You dreamed this?"

Marisa nodded. "You passed him by and then you went home."

His arm was like steel around her as he waited for her to continue.

She looked up, her gaze searching his. "You said life had lost its meaning for you, and then you called my name. And then—" She shivered as the sound of the wolf's lonely cry echoed in her mind.

"And then?"

"I heard a wolf howl, and I woke up. Was it real, or just a dream?"

A muscle throbbed in his jaw. He took a deep breath, and she felt the tension flow out of him. The arm around her shoulders relaxed. "It was real, *cara mia.* It happened just as you've described."

"Did you plant those images in my mind?"

"I told you I did not."

"That's why I dream about you, isn't it? Because you gave me some of your blood. Does that mean you can make me do anything you want?"

"I could always bend your will to mine, Marisa. The little bit of blood I gave you was only to mark you as mine, to enable me to find you, to allow me to speak to your mind."

"Alexi said he could taste you."

"Alexi." Grigori glanced out the window into the darkness, wondered where his old nemesis was hiding. Had he given up the game? Or was he merely biding his time, lulling them into a false sense of security before he struck again?

"Hey, where are you?"

He smiled down at her. "Here, beside you, for as long as you want me."

"That could be a long time."

His smile turned bittersweet. "I have a long time."

"What about Ramsey?"

"What about him?"

"He said he was going to destroy you."

"He would not be the first to try. He may not be the last."

"What do you mean?"

"I've been hunted before, in times past. Those who sought to destroy me are dead."

She was face-to-face with reality again. The other night, in front of the fire, it had all seemed magical, romantic, a fairy tale.

"You killed those others?"

"Of course."

"Would you kill Edward?"

"That choice is his."

"But how? If they come after you in the daytime . . . I mean, I thought vampires were helpless when the sun is up."

"No. It is natural for us to sleep during the day, but only the very young are helpless. I can sense the presence of others when I sleep. The instinct to survive is as strong with us as with you. I have yet to meet a mortal I could not defeat."

She shivered, suddenly cold clear through as

she pictured Edward bending over Grigori, his eyes blazing with righteous zeal as he plunged a wooden stake through the vampire's heart.

He didn't have to read her mind to know what she was thinking. Opening one of the side compartments, he withdrew a bottle of red wine. He filled two glasses, warmed one with his gaze, and handed it to Marisa.

"Drink this," he said, "and then we will speak of something more pleasant."

She did as he suggested. The wine warmed her, made her feel sleepy and relaxed.

He smiled at her over the rim of his glass. "Better?"

"Yes, much."

When she was finished, he put their glasses aside, and drew her into his arms. "We'll be home soon."

Home. Never had the word sounded so good.

They reached her apartment a short time later. The chauffeur carried her luggage up the stairs. Grigori carried Marisa. She had protested that she could walk, but he had insisted on carrying her. And now she was sitting on his lap on the sofa. He had started a fire in the fireplace simply by willing it to happen.

"You'd be great to have along on a camping trip," Marisa remarked. "I'd never have to worry about remembering to bring matches."

Grigori grunted softly. "I'm afraid I've never been camping."

"No, I guess not."

She slid her arm around his neck and rested her

head on his shoulder. "I wish I didn't have to go to work tomorrow."

"I thought you liked your job."

"Oh, I do. But every time I get a few days off, I start to get lazy."

"If you don't want to go, stay home."

"Yeah, right."

"I mean it. Quit your job if you are not happy there."

"I can't do that! I've got bills to pay, you know. Rent, things like that."

"Come live with me, *cara*. Let me take care of you."

She looked up at him as a new thought occured to her. "Where do you get all your money from? You don't seem to have a job."

He shrugged. "If one is wise, one can accumulate a great deal of wealth in two hundred years."

"I guess so."

"Come, *cara*, let me take care of you."

It was tempting, oh, so tempting. She considered it for all of sixty seconds, then regretfully shook her head.

"I'd like to, but I can't." She saw the question in his eyes and covered his mouth with her hand. "It's not because you're a vampire. It has nothing to do with you. It's me. I told you before, I don't sleep around."

He lifted her hand from his mouth and kissed it. "I'm not asking you to sleep with me." His tongue stroked her palm, sending shivers racing up and down her spine. "I'm only asking you to share my home, let me take care of you. There's no need for you to work."

"But what would I do all day?"

"Whatever you want." He caressed her cheek with the back of his hand, delighting in the softness of her skin. The siren call of her blood teased his hunger as surely as the warm womanly scent of her body teased his desire. "Go shopping. Sleep late. Employ a masseuse. Sit in the sun. Stroll on the beach. Take long walks in the park." He smiled at her. "In the morning."

She gazed up at him, her heart breaking because, even if she could accept his offer, he would never be able to sit in the sun with her, or walk hand in hand along the beach, or stroll through the park on a warm summer day.

"I appreciate the offer, really I do, but I can't. I'd miss working, and I like having money of my own. You're not mad, are you?"

"No, *cara*."

His lips grazed her cheek, the tip of her nose, then slid down to cover her mouth. His arm tightened around her waist as he deepened the kiss, and she forgot about work, forgot about everything but the man who held her so tightly, kissed her so completely, made her heart soar with happiness. She pressed herself against him, wanting to be closer, closer.

Grigori groaned low in his throat as he absorbed her heat into himself. The sound of her heartbeat roared in his ears; the very essence of her life called to him as the scent of her blood filled his nostrils. Hunger and desire warred within him. He felt his fangs lengthen as the hunger roared to life within him. Just a taste, he thought, what could it hurt? One taste of her sweetness. So easy, he mused, so easy to take her, to look deep into her eyes and let the power of his mind overshadow hers. She need never know. . . .

The tension radiating from Grigori penetrated the haze of passion that engulfed her. Feeling as though she were moving through thick molasses, she drew back, her gaze searching his face. "What's wrong?"

With great effort, he subdued his hunger, felt his fangs retract. "I think I'd better say good night."

"But it's early yet."

"You are far too tempting, Marisa." He stood up, and placed her carefully on her feet. "I shall see you tomorrow night."

"All right." She swayed against him, lifting her face for his kiss. "Thanks for picking me up."

"My pleasure." Tenderly, as though she were made of the most fragile spun glass, he cupped her face in his hands and kissed her. "Sweet dreams, *cara*."

"You too," she said, and then frowned. "Do you dream?"

He traced her lips with his fingers. "I didn't," he replied softly, "until I met you. *Buono notte, cara mia.*"

"Good night."

With a sigh, she locked the door behind him. Feeling giddy as a schoolgirl, she sat down on the sofa and gazed dreamily into the fire, a pillow clutched to her breast.

She was in love with Grigori Chiavari. The thought was both thrilling and frightening.

Marisa Chiavari . . . Mrs. Grigori Chiavari . . . Mrs. Marisa Chiavari . . .

Giggling, she kissed the pillow. She'd never felt

like this in her whole life. It was wonderful and scary, exhilarating and frightening, all at the same time. And, most of all, it was impossible.

How could she be in love with a vampire?

Chapter Twenty-six

Lost in thought, Grigori walked the dark streets. Before Alexi's escape from Silvano, before Marisa, his life had followed a set path. He had traveled the world, following winter, when darkness was long upon the earth. He was not a eunuch, not a monk. There had been women in his life. He had felt a warm affection for them all, but none had claimed his heart or spoken to his soul. He had pursued knowledge, embraced the arts, enjoyed theater and opera. His physical wants were few and easily satisfied.

But when Silvano had taken Alexi on tour, his peaceful days had been shattered. And then he had met Marisa . . . ah, Marisa, with her sun-kissed beauty and clear green eyes. Marisa, whose blood sang a siren song to his hunger, whose beauty tugged at his heart and soul even as her shapely form whispered to the desire of the flesh. But it was more than outer beauty or lust that drew him to her side again and again. It was the purity of her soul, her innate sweetness, the compassion that allowed her to look past what he had become and see the man he had once been.

Marisa . . . Could he hold her, make love to her

as he longed to do, and not destroy her? Since being made Vampyre, he had made love to many women, but never to a woman he loved.

A wave of guilt rose up within him. How could he think of loving Marisa when he had stood at Antoinette's graveside only weeks ago? And yet, she had been dead to him for centuries.

Awareness flowed through him and he whirled around, his eyes probing the shadows. "Come out, Ramsey. I know you are there."

A dark form materialized from behind a tree.

Edward Ramsey hunched his shoulders. Standing in the glow of a streetlight, he felt exposed, vulnerable. "Chiavari."

"Did you want to see me?" Grigori asked. And then he saw the bag hanging from Ramsey's shoulder. "Let me guess. Would you be carrying a hammer and a stake in that sack?"

Edward cleared his throat. Sweat beaded on his brow and pooled under his arms, but he kept his expression blank.

Grigori took a step forward. "Afraid, vampyre hunter?"

Ramsey lifted his chin a notch and shook his head.

"Liar." The softly spoken word seemed to hang in the air between them. "Did you perhaps think I would be foolish enough to lead you to my lair?"

Edward shrugged. He could feel his pulse racing. What was worse, he knew the vampire could smell his fear, hear the frantic beating of his heart.

"So," Grigori mused, "I take it you've decided you don't need me anymore."

"Alexi's gone. He's no threat now. But you are."

"I mean you no harm, Ramsey. You, or anyone else."

"You're a killer! You're all killers!"

"I've killed no one."

"Who's lying now?"

"Save for those who have tried to destroy me, I've killed no one in over a hundred and fifty years."

"I don't believe you."

"I don't care what you believe. It's true."

Grigori took a step forward. Edward stood his ground, one hand curling around the crucifix hanging around his neck. "Stay away from me."

Slowly, Grigori shook his head. "Edward, come to me."

"No." Ramsey took a step backward. "Stay away from me!"

"Why do you fight me? Your blood has nourished me, made you a part of me."

"No! No, damn you! Leave me alone." Tears of frustration rose in Edward's eyes as Grigori's voice drew him forward until, helpless, his whole body trembling with terror, Edward stood in front of the vampire, held in place by a pair of dark, impenetrable eyes.

Grigori folded his hand over Ramsey's left shoulder. He could feel the power thrumming through his own body, strengthening him. His fangs pricked his tongue as the Hunger rose up within him. Ramsey stood there, unmoving, as the vampire's fangs pierced his flesh.

Grigori drank quickly, sparingly, and then released his hold on Ramsey. "Go home, Edward. Go home and go to bed."

Ramsey nodded. "Yes," he murmured. "Home."

He blinked several times, then turned and headed back the way he had come.

Grigori watched him out of sight, wondering if he should have erased Ramsey's memory, wiped every recollection of their meetings from the man's mind. It was tempting, and he would have done it save for one thing: Ramsey had given him his blood when he desperately needed it. Like it or not, he owed the vampyre hunter a debt. He would not repay the man by stealing a part of his mind.

Grigori blew out a soul-deep sigh. Debt or not, he would do what he must to survive, and if that meant killing Edward Ramsey, then so be it. He would not let himself be destroyed, not now, when Marisa was almost his.

Edward woke in his bed the following morning with no recollection of how he had gotten there.

Sitting up, he glanced around the room. *What the . . .* And then he saw his bag on the floor near the door and it all came back to him. He had gone to Marisa's apartment in hopes that he would find Grigori there, had been exulting in his good fortune when the vampire sensed his presence.

Muttering an oath, Edward scrambled out of bed and ran into the bathroom. It couldn't be true. But it was. Turning his head to the side, he saw the two telltale marks on his neck. *Damn!* Grigori had taken his blood. Damn, it was one thing for the vampire to take his blood when it was offered, another thing entirely when he took it as though it were his right!

The thought made him feel cold all over, violated, as a woman who is raped must feel. Shivering, he grabbed his robe and slipped it on. He remembered now, remembered it all, the sound of the vampire's voice permeating his mind, bending his thoughts, until they were not his thoughts at all. As if he had no will of his own, his legs had carried him to the vampire. He shuddered as he recalled offering his neck to that bloodsucking monster, standing there like some mindless zombie while Grigori drank his fill.

A cold rage engulfed him. To think he had once given his blood to that monster freely, and this was the thanks he got in return. Ah, but it hadn't been freely, he mused ruefully. It had been at Marisa's urging. She had begged so prettily, smiled so sweetly. . . . He swore under his breath. *Marisa!*

He dialed her number, tapping his foot impatiently as he waited for her to answer the phone.

"Hello?"

"Marisa, it's Edward. Are you all right?"

"Of course, why? Is something wrong?"

"No, no, nothing. I was . . . uh, just worried about you. I haven't seen you lately."

"I went to Florida to see my folks, remember? I told you I was going."

"Yeah, right, I guess I forgot. Is everything okay?"

"Fine. Listen, I've got to go. I'm going to be late for work."

"Can I see you later? For dinner?"

"Gee, I'd love to, but I can't."

"You can't?"

"I'm sorry, I have a date."

"Oh?" He felt his mouth go dry. "Anyone I know?"

"Well, I'm expecting Grigori, if you must know."

Edward sagged against the wall. "Do you think that's wise?"

"I think it's wonderful," she replied, her voice soft and dreamy. "I've got to go. Bye."

He stared at the receiver, and then gently replaced it in the cradle. She thought it was wonderful. *Damn Chiavari!* He'd mesmerized her.

"You may have won this battle, Chiavari," Edward muttered. "But you won't win the war!"

She found herself smiling at the office Monday morning, humming while she worked. She typed up a bankruptcy report, but all she could hear was the sound of Grigori's voice whispering her name. She answered the phones, opened the mail, but always a part of her mind was thinking of him, counting the hours until she would see him again.

Grigori . . .

She skipped lunch and went shopping instead. She needed something to wear to the company New Year's Eve party, but what she really wanted was something new to wear for Grigori. She chose a slinky teal blue slip dress for the party. She tried it on, and knew she had to have it. She was leaving the department when a pair of black silk pants and a top caught her eye.

"Perfect," she muttered. She quickly found her size and carried the outfit to the salesgirl before she could talk herself out of making another extravagant purchase.

The next few hours went by in a blur, and then it was time to go home. She quickly shut off her computer, grabbed her handbag and packages, said a hasty farewell to Linda, and practically ran for the elevator.

* * *

At home, she took a quick shower, and then changed into her new outfit. The silk felt wonderful against her skin, smooth and sexy.

She had just finished spritzing herself with perfume when the doorbell rang.

Feeling as though a million butterflies were fluttering in her stomach, she ran to open the door.

Grigori felt his breath catch in his throat as he took her in his arms. *Bellissima!* His hands slid over her back, the feel of the warm black silk she wore making his palms tingle. An exotic fragrance rose from the dark cloud of her hair. Her lips tasted of sunshine and strawberries, the warmth and sweetness of which he had been denied for two hundred years.

He deepened the kiss, and she came alive in his arms, a living, breathing flame that threatened to consume him like the rays of the sun.

He drew her into his arms and carried her to the sofa. She heard a faint whoosh, and a fire sprang to life in the hearth.

Magic, she thought, vampire magic.

His arms held her close, his hands played over her body, his long fingers exploring the curve of her thigh, her breast, sliding up and down her back in long, shivery caresses that left her reeling, drowning in sensual sensation.

Her own hands moved restlessly over him, measuring the width of his shoulders, the rock-hard muscles in his arms, the solid expanse of his chest. Her fingers caressed his nape, slid up into his hair.

And all the while his lips never left hers. His tongue dueled with hers in a dance that was both old and new, and she was on fire, burning in his hands.

He bent her back on the sofa, his body covering hers, his hands and lips arousing her until she could scarcely think, scarcely breathe.

She opened her eyes and met his gaze, and the blatant desire she read there filled her with fear and exhilaration.

"Marisa. *Cara* . . ." His words were harsh, ragged with the need pulsing through him.

She blinked up at him, her beautiful green eyes dark with passion. "Grigori."

He blew out a ragged breath. "I want you."

Marisa stared up at him, incapable of speech, as a montage of jumbled thoughts and images raced through her mind: Grigori bending over Edward, taking his blood; Grigori as she had first seen him, tall and dark and mysterious; Grigori, lying on the floor of her closet; Grigori, his eyes filled with anguish as he begged Edward to be merciful. She thought of Alexi. He was a monster, a killer, a creature who delighted in death and misery. And she thought of Edward, who claimed all vampires were evil and should be destroyed.

"Marisa—"

"I want you, too, you know I do." She moistened lips gone suddenly dry. "I—"

He saw the hesitation in her eyes, heard it in her voice. Fighting the urge to take what he wanted, as he had been wont to do since he became Vampyre, he slid away from her, so that his body was no longer covering hers. But he couldn't let her go, not entirely.

Taking her hand in his, he waited for her to go on.

"I . . . I can't."

"You want me."

He lifted her hand to his mouth and his tongue stroked her palm, making her go all shivery inside.

She nodded, unable to deny it. "But wanting isn't enough."

His eyes narrowed. "Ah," he murmured, and wondered how he could have been so blind. "You want the words." His free hand caressed her cheek. "I love you, *cara mia*."

Anger penetrated the layers of passion. "Do you think I can be had for the price of a few endearments?"

He frowned. "What do you want of me?"

"I want more than empty words!"

"They are not empty, Marisa." He released her hand and sat up, his back toward her. "I have lived alone for two hundred years. I have not loved a woman in all that time, nor have I pretended to. I am not a eunuch, nor have I lived like one. I have taken women to my bed when it pleased me."

How many women? she wondered. How many in two hundred years?

Slowly, he turned to face her. "Save for Antoinette, I have never told a woman I loved her. I would not say it now if it were not true."

"Oh, Grigori, I'm sorry!"

He rose to his feet with the lithe grace of a dancing master. "Come," he said, offering her his hand. "I will take you to dinner."

She shook her head, thinking she had never felt more miserable or churlish in her life. "I'm not hungry."

"Do not pout, *cara*. It is most unbecoming."

"I'm not pouting. I didn't mean to hurt your feelings."

He smiled down at her. "I promised I would not rush you, nor force you to do anything you did not wish to do." He reached for her hands and drew her to her feet. "You look beautiful. I wish to take you out and show you off. Where would you like to go?"

"You're not mad at me?"

"No." He brushed a kiss across her lips. "Get your coat. It's cold outside."

He took her to the Velvet Turtle for dinner, sipped a glass of dry red wine while she ate. Marisa couldn't help noticing that Grigori caught the eye of every female in the room. Tall and dark, dressed in gray slacks and a white wool sweater, he looked as if he had just stepped out of the pages of a fashion magazine.

After dinner, they drove to the beach. Ignoring the cold, they took off their shoes and stockings, rolled up their pant legs, and walked along the shore. Marisa shrieked as a wave swirled around her ankles.

In an instant, she was in Grigori's arms. His eyes were like pools of liquid ebony in the moonlight, his mouth warm and moist as he kissed her. The heat of his lips chased away the cold, and she wound her arms around his neck, kissing him hungrily.

He held her effortlessly, his tongue sliding over her lower lip, delving into her mouth.

He kissed her, and it seemed as though skyrockets went off inside her head. All the colors of the rainbow came together, until she was engulfed in a bright white light. And Grigori stood in the middle of that light, his eyes burning like the sun.

She felt like a child who had been hopelessly lost in the darkness and was suddenly found. It was a most peculiar thought, for Grigori was a man born of darkness, as mysterious as the night that surrounded them, as elusive as the moonbeams that danced upon the sea.

"Marisa?"

"Tell me," she whispered. "Tell me you love me."

"Ti amo, cara mia. Mi vita, mi amore."

"Grigori." Her voice was husky, her breath warm as it tickled his ear. "Let's go home."

With a nod, he scooped up their shoes and socks and carried her to the car. Settling her in the passenger seat, he kissed her cheek, then went around and slid behind the wheel.

He felt her gaze on him as he drove home. Her hand rested on his thigh, as light as thistledown, warm and alive, keeping him in a constant state of arousal. She wanted him. He could sense it, smell it, feel it, taste it. Tonight, she would be his for the taking. She had banished whatever fears and doubts had troubled her and now she was ripe, like a peach ready for the picking.

She leaned across the seat and rained kisses on his cheek, his neck, his shoulder, and each touch was like a ray of sunlight burning his skin. "I love you."

Three words, spoken so softly a mere mortal would not have heard them. But they seared his heart, his soul. He let out a deep breath. She was his now, his for the taking.

And in that instant, he knew he could not defile her, knew he could not take her to his bed as if she meant no more to him than the other women he had used to satisfy the hungers of the flesh.

He was shaking with barely controlled need when they reached her apartment. He got out of the car and took a deep breath, then went to her side and opened the door.

She smiled up at him, a beautiful, sensual smile, as he took her hand and helped her out of the car.

He followed her up the stairs, his whole body quivering, every sense attuned to the woman before him, to the gentle sway of her hips, the curve of a shapely calf.

He unlocked the door, but didn't follow her inside.

Marisa frowned at him. "Aren't you coming in?"

Hands clenched at his sides, he shook his head.

"But I thought—"

"Not tonight," he said, his voice gruff. And then, calling on the strength of will he had developed over two hundred years, he kissed her good night.

"*Domani*, Marisa," he promised, and left her there, alone and untouched.

Domani . . . tomorrow.

Chapter Twenty-seven

"I have to go to my boss's house for New Year's Eve," Marisa said. She tucked her legs under her and sipped her wine. "Would you come with me?"

Grigori lifted one brow. "Do you think that would be wise?"

"Why not?"

He shrugged. "I should think that would be obvious."

"Please come."

"If you wish. What should I wear?"

"Suit and tie are de rigueur at these things."

"I shall be honored to escort the most beautiful of women."

"Flatterer."

"I only speak the truth."

They were sitting on the sofa in her apartment, sharing a glass of wine. Save for a quick kiss, he had not touched her since his arrival two hours earlier. They had watched an old John Wayne movie on TV, and he had been aware of her amusement at doing something so mundane with a man who was a vampyre. He had not meant to probe her mind, but when she sat so close, when her thoughts were centered on him, it was difficult to resist. He had known her almost two months, he mused, and though she professed to love him, there was a part of her that still thought of him as something less than human. She found it amazing that he walked in the park, read books, watched television, went to the movies, visited museums. She seemed to think his life should consist of little more than haunting the shadows wrapped in a long black cape, and frightening unwary mortals.

He took a deep breath, willing himself to be patient, to give her time. It wasn't easy, accepting something one had always thought impossible.

She was about to pour another glass of wine when the doorbell rang.

"Geez, I wonder who that is?" Marisa muttered. "It's almost eleven."

"Do you want me to get it?"

"If you don't mind."

He brushed his hand across her cheek as he stood up, and she felt a tingle of desire sweep through her. Tall, dark and handsome, she thought. He fit the description to a T. She watched him walk away, thinking again that she had never known anyone who moved the way he did.

Grigori crossed the floor, aware of Marisa's gaze on his back. He could feel the desire radiating from her. He was smiling when he opened the door. And then he frowned.

"It's Ramsey," he called over his shoulder.

"Tell him to come in."

Grigori stepped back. "A little late to be calling, isn't it, Ramsey?"

"You're here."

With a shrug, Grigori stepped back. "Come on in."

Edward stepped into the entryway, and Grigori closed the door. As soon as the vampire turned his back, Edward tackled him. Startled, Grigori hit the floor, face down. Moving quickly, Edward looped a thick silver chain around the vampire's neck and pulled it tight. There was an ugly hissing sound as the silver burned through preternatural flesh.

With an outraged roar, Grigori rolled onto his back, but Edward was ready for him. Straddling Grigori's legs, he laid a heavy silver crucifix on the vampire's chest.

Grigori went rigid as the silver burned his flesh. Though the cross was not heavy, he could feel it weighing him down, clouding his vampyric powers.

"Edward!" Marisa shrieked. "What are you doing?"

"Killing a vampire."

"Stop it!"

"Don't interfere, Marisa."

"Stop this, Edward! Are you crazy?"

"Look at him, Marisa! Come and see him as he really is."

Lips parted, fangs bared, Grigori glared up at Ramsey, but Ramsey refused to meet his gaze.

"He's evil, Marisa! A killer! He's got to be destroyed."

Grigori sucked in a deep breath. The silver burned his skin like a fine white flame. "Edward, release me."

"Your mind games won't work, vampire." Ramsey drew a stake and a wooden mallet from inside his jacket. "Not this time."

Grigori went suddenly still. Marisa, who had

been watching in horror, felt a palpable tremor in the air, a vibration, like static electricity, and knew that Grigori was summoning his power.

It was an awesome thing to see. Or not see. There was nothing tangible, nothing visible to the naked eye. Yet she sensed the power building within Grigori, bubbling to the surface like lava from the depths of a sleeping volcano. Why didn't Edward feel it?

She held her breath, afraid to watch, unable to look away.

And then Grigori lifted his arms, placed his hands around Ramsey's waist, and stood up in a single flowing movement, carrying Ramsey with him. The crucifix tumbled from Grigori's chest to the floor. He wrapped one hand around Ramsey's neck and lifted the man off the ground, then ripped the heavy silver chain away from his throat.

Marisa gasped when she saw Grigori's neck. It was raw and red.

Ramsey squirmed in the vampire's grasp, his face turning purple, his eyes bulging, as his breath was slowly choked off. The stake and mallet hit the floor with a dull thud, and he wrapped his hands around Grigori's, trying to loosen the vampire's deadly grip on his neck.

"Grigori, don't hurt him!"

"He was going to kill me."

"Please . . ." Marisa clasped her hands in an attitude of prayer, uncertain if she was asking Grigori to be merciful or begging for divine intervention. "Please."

Grigori focused his gaze on Ramsey's face. "Can you hear me, Ramsey?"

Edward nodded as best he could.

"You leave me no choice but to kill you."

Edward stared up at him, his eyes filled with resignation.

"Grigori, don't," Marisa pleaded softly. "Please let him go."

The vampire turned his head to look at her, and she felt his power slither over her skin. His dark eyes were filled with pain and rage. She wanted to look away, wanted to run away, but she stood where she was, knowing Edward's life depended on her. "Please don't hurt him."

Grigori gazed at her for a long moment, and then he lowered his arm, allowing Ramsey's feet to touch the floor. Wondering if he would live to regret what he was about to do, he relaxed his hold on the man's throat, though he did not release him.

"Look at me, Edward, and pay close attention to what I tell you. Do not cross my path again. You will not like what happens if you do."

His hand tightened around Edward's throat. "Do you understand me?"

"Y-yes."

"Don't make me kill you."

Grigori held Ramsey in his grasp a moment more, and then released him.

Edward gasped and stumbled backward, his hand massaging his throat, his eyes glinting with hatred.

"Edward, are you all right?"

Ramsey nodded, but he didn't take his gaze off the vampire. Never, he thought, never had he been so close to death. He thought of all the vampires he had hunted and destroyed, thought of the many times he had congratulated himself on ridding the world of evil. Only now did he realize how lucky he was to be alive. None of the other monsters he had destroyed had possessed the kind of power Chiavari possessed. If they had, he had no doubt that he would have been killed long ago. All this time he had thought himself a master vampire slayer. He knew now that all the creatures he had destroyed had been easy to find, easy to dispatch, because they had been young vampires, newly made, vulnerable.

Grigori jerked his head toward the door. "Get out."

Edward didn't meet the vampire's gaze as he backed toward the door.

A tight smile curved Grigori's lips as he willed the door to open. "Remember what I said, Ramsey. Don't cross my path again."

With a nod, Edward slipped out into the darkness.

Grigori stared after him a moment, and then closed the door. He took a deep breath, a little fearful of facing Marisa after what had happened.

She stared at him, at the horrible burns on his neck. The silver had burned through his shirt; she could see a dark smudge on his chest where the metal had burned his skin.

"Is there . . . is there anything I can do?" Her voice was faint, unsteady.

He shook his head, quietly cursing Edward Ramsey. Damn the man. His timing could not have been worse.

On legs that trembled, Marisa went into the living room and dropped onto the sofa. She wanted to pour herself a glass of wine, but her hands were shaking so badly, she didn't think she could manage without spilling it.

Uncertain as to what he should say or do, Grigori filled her glass with wine and placed it in her hand. "Drink."

She took several sips, then sat back and closed her eyes, willing herself to relax. It was over. Grigori was still alive. Edward was still alive.

"Marisa . . ."

She stared up at him, mute.

"Do you want me to go?"

"I don't know."

"You knew what I was. What I am."

Oh, yes, she knew, but in the last few days, she had managed to shove reality into a distant corner of her mind. He'd been so kind, so attentive. She had never dated a man who treated her with such tenderness, such respect, who listened so attentively to what she had to say, who valued her opinions, who needed her love so much. She had never known a man like this man, and he was not a man at all.

It wasn't going to work, Grigory realized. She would never see him as anything other than a monster, and why should she? To her, that was what he was. He had been a fool to think she could love him, accept him. A fool to think he could make any kind of life with a mortal woman.

He drew in a deep breath, held it for stretched seconds, then released it on a sigh. It was time to stop kidding himself, time to remember who and what he was. Time to go home, back to Tuscany, where he belonged.

"Good-bye, Marisa."

She looked up at him, her eyes narrowing.

There had been something final in the tone of his voice, as if he meant good-bye forever and not just for the night.

She stood up. The thought that she might never see him again overrode her doubts. "Where are you going?"

"Home."

"I'm never going to see you again, am I?"

"No." He slid his finger under her chin. Tilting her head back, he brushed his lips across hers. "Be happy, *cara*. Find yourself a nice young man. Someone who can give you lots of children." His knuckles caressed her cheek. "Someone who can grow old beside you."

He turned, and she knew that in moments he would be gone from her sight, gone from her life.

"Grigori! Wait! Don't leave me."

"It's for the best."

"No, no, it's not. Please." She couldn't bear the thought of never seeing him again, never hearing his voice, feeling his touch. Tears welled in her eyes, trickled down her cheeks. She dashed them away with the back of her hand. "Please, don't go."

"Ah, Marisa," he murmured, "do not weep. I cannot abide your tears."

"I love you. I've never loved anyone the way I love you. I don't care that you're a . . . a vampire."

"Don't you?"

She shook her head.

"*Cara.*" Slowly, he folded her into his arms. "*Cara.*"

"Are you upset because I didn't want to make love?"

"Marisa *mia*, you are so young, so innocent."

"I'm not young. And I'm not that innocent."

"Compared to me, you are a child." He kissed the top of her head. "Ah, Marisa, if all I wanted was your body, I could have taken you at any time."

"Then why are you leaving me?"

"Because what happened tonight made me realize this will never work. You may love me, *cara*, but I doubt you will ever be able to accept me for what I am. And I cannot change that, *mi amore*, not even for you."

"I can, I will! Promise me you won't leave." She blinked up at him through her tears. "You were going to be my date for New Year's Eve."

He felt his resolve weaken as he gazed down at her. How could he leave her? In two hundred years, he had told no one what he was, found no one he dared trust with the truth of his identity. Given time, perhaps she would be able to accept him wholly. Time . . . it meant nothing to him. What was another month, a year, to one who was Vampyre?

"Ah, *mi dolce amore*, please do not weep."

"Say you'll stay."

"Are you sure, *cara*?"

"Yes. Kiss me, Grigori—"

She pressed herself against him, and his arms tightened around her. Heat spiraled through him as her breasts were crushed against his chest. She was light to his darkness, sun to his moon. He would never let her go, not while there was a chance that she would yet be his, fully, completely his.

"Carissima!" He kissed her as he had not kissed her before, letting her feel the urgency of his desire, the fire of his passion. He let her feel the sav-

age hunger that rose up from the very depths of his soul, let her sense the pain that came from refusing to take the love he yearned for, the nectar of life that he needed to survive.

"Grigori—" She drew back, breathless, when he took his lips from hers. "How do you stand the pain?"

"It wasn't so hard to bear until I met you."

"I do love you."

His gaze moved over her face. She basked in the warmth of his eyes, took pleasure in knowing that he wanted her, that he found her desirable. That same knowledge also made her feel miserable because it caused him pain.

She tilted her head to one side, offering him access to her neck. "Drink from me, Grigori. I don't want you to suffer on my account."

"It's not a good idea, *cara*."

"Why not? You're hurting. I just want to help."

"Do you?" His gaze grew deeply intense.

"I just said I did."

"Will you be my woman, Marisa? Mine in every way?"

"What do you mean?"

"I want you to be mine."

"Are you asking me to marry you?"

"In a manner of speaking. I will pledge you my love and my protection for as long as you wish it."

"But—" She looked up at him, afraid to refuse, afraid of driving him away again.

"You want a real marriage, in a church."

She nodded. All her life, she had dreamed of a big church wedding, of walking down the aisle clad in a gown of pristine white satin. Her father would give her away; her mother would have tears in her eyes; Mike would smile with pride. Her friends from work would be there to wish her well.

"Marisa." He drew her into his arms again and held her close. "Do you want to marry me?"

She nodded. "Yes, if you'll have me."

"Do you know what it would mean, to be a vampyre's wife? There are so many things I cannot share with you. Think carefully before you agree. Once you are mine, truly mine, I will not give you up. You may soon tire of a husband who can share only half your life."

"How do you know you'll want to stay with me? How will you feel when I'm old and gray and wrinkled and you're still young?"

"I shall love you then as I do now."

She looked up into his eyes and knew it was true. "Will you marry me, Grigori? Will you stand beside me in church and vow to be my husband for as long as I live?"

"If that is what you truly wish. But think about it carefully, *carissima*. Think about what I said, what I am, what you want."

He kissed her lightly, savoring the sweetness of her lips, the way she swayed against him, softly yielding, and then he put her away from him.

"Tomorrow night," he said quietly. "Tomorrow night I will come for your answer."

Chapter Twenty-eight

She had trouble concentrating at work the next day. All she could think of was Grigori. She had asked him to marry her, but doubts crowded her mind. Oh, she had no doubt that she loved him, but was she strong enough to live with a vampire? He could not give her children, or do so many of the other, more mundane things husbands and wives did together. There would be no summer days at the beach, no bicycle rides through Griffith Park, no tennis games. He couldn't go to church with her on Sunday morning. . . .

The ringing of the phone jerked her out of her reverie. It was Edward, asking if he could take her to dinner.

"I'm sorry, I can't tonight."

There was a long pause. "You're seeing him, aren't you?" There was no mistaking the censure in Edward's voice.

"Yes."

"I don't understand you. How can you date him?"

Marisa blew out a long sigh. Might as well get it over with. "I'm in love with him, Edward. I know you don't approve, but I can't help it."

"What!"

"Listen, Edward, I can't talk now. Please, just try to accept it. Can't you be happy for me?"

"Happy? Are you out of your mind? The man's a vampire."

"Tell me something I don't know," she muttered. "I've got to go. Good-bye."

Marisa stared at the receiver. Strange as it seemed, Edward's call had helped her make up her mind.

She hurried home after work, took a quick shower, and slipped into a pair of white slacks and a green sweater. She ran a brush through her hair, checked her makeup. Her hand was shaking so badly, she could hardly put her lipstick on.

She knew he was there before she heard the front door open. He didn't need a key, she thought, and wondered what it would be like to be able to open doors with a thought, to read minds. To drink blood . . .

She stared at her reflection in the mirror a moment, and then hurried into the living room. "Hi."

His gaze slid over her, warm with admiration. "Hi."

She bit her lower lip, aware of a sudden tension between them. Usually, he took her in his arms, but not tonight, and she realized that he wouldn't touch her until she told him her decision. But surely he knew. He could read her mind . . . and then she remembered that he had promised not to invade her thoughts.

"Sit down." She waved a shaky hand toward the couch, wondering why she felt so nervous.

Grigori sat down, and she sat beside him. For a

moment, she toyed with the idea of teasing him, of making him wait, of pretending her answer was no. But then she looked into his eyes, those deep dark eyes that could be as impassive as a brick wall. They were not dark and unfathomable now.

"Marisa?"

"I love you, Grigori. I want to be your wife."

With a wordless cry, he swept her into his arms and held her close. He had hoped, but hadn't dared to believe. . . .

"*Cara!*" Holding her close, he kissed her. Kissed her until they were both breathless. "Are you sure?" He drew back a little so he could see her face.

"I'm sure." She smiled up at him, thinking how endearing it was to know he'd had doubts. "Did you think I'd change my mind?"

"I had prepared myself for the worst," he admitted. And because he had the power, because he had to know how she really felt, he let his mind brush hers. The love she felt for him burned like a pure white flame, brighter and stronger than the misgivings that plagued her.

"I'll do my best to make you happy, *cara mia*," he vowed. "I shall love you for as long as you live. Love you until my last breath."

"Oh, Grigori, you do say the sweetest things."

"When?" He kissed the tip of her nose.

"Is tomorrow too soon?"

"Not for me." He gazed into her eyes. "But I think you'll need more time."

"I suppose. I'll have to find a dress. And talk to Reverend Stacy about a date." Slipping out of his arms, she found a paper and pencil and began to make notes. "I'll have to call my folks and Mike.

And ask Barbara if she'll be my maid of honor. And Linda if she'll be a bridesmaid. Two attendants should be enough, don't you think? It's just going to be a small wedding. We'll need a photographer, and a cake. And I'll need to get some time off from work for a honeymoon. And—"

Grigori crossed the floor and plucked the pencil from her hand. "Make your lists tomorrow," he said with a growl.

She laughed as he swung her into his arms. "Bossing me around already, are you?"

"I have only a few hours to spend with you," he murmured, his breath warm against her ear. "I don't want to waste a minute."

"But we need to plan for our wedding."

"I shall leave that to you. Only tell me where and when, and I shall be there."

She wound her arms around his neck. "Is there anyone you want to invite?"

"No." He sat down on the sofa and cradled her in his arms.

"Don't you have any friends? Someone to be your best man?"

A deep sigh escaped his lips. "I've only been in this country a few months," he reminded her. But he could have been here for years and it wouldn't have made any difference. He was by nature a solitary creature, never trusting those of his own kind, hesitant to trust mankind.

"Maybe Edward," she mused, and then, remembering his phone call that afternoon, she shook her head. "Maybe not. I'm sure my brother and Mike Junior would be glad to stand up with you."

"If you wish."

"You don't mind?"

"No, *cara.*"

She snuggled against him, content to be in his embrace, to feel his arms locked around her waist.

"We'll have to go shopping," Grigori remarked. "I have a big, empty house for you to fill." He kissed the top of her head, knowing that it was not furniture that would turn his house into a home, but Marisa herself.

"It'll be expensive."

"Spend what you wish."

"Really?" She sat up a little, her eyes sparkling. "Do you like antiques?"

"I am an antique," he muttered.

"Very funny. I love antiques, but I could never afford to buy them."

"Now you can."

"Oh, it'll be such fun."

Grigori glanced around her apartment. "I suppose you'll do the rooms in blue." His gaze settled on the rug in front of the window. She'd had the carpet cleaned, but the bloodstains he'd left were still evident if one looked closely.

He stared at the darkness beyond the glass. What right did he have to marry this woman? He had entered her life and brought her nothing but trouble.

"Grigori?"

"*Cara?*"

"Where'd you go?"

He frowned at her. "Go?"

"You seem very far away. You haven't changed your mind, have you?"

"No, but perhaps you should change yours."

"Why? What's wrong?"

He felt the change in her, the increase in her

heartbeat as she stared at him, suddenly apprehensive. "I don't want you to be hurt, Marisa."

"Then don't leave me."

"I won't." He drew her head toward his. "I won't."

His kiss was ever so gentle, sweet and light. Her eyelids fluttered down as she surrendered to his lips. Warmth flooded her limbs; shivers of ecstasy engulfed her as his tongue slid over her lower lip.

"More." She whispered the word into his mouth. "More . . ."

With a low moan, he deepened the kiss. There was nothing gentle about him now. His arms were like bands of steel as he held her close. His mouth ravaged hers, bruising her lips. She felt the prick of his fangs, tasted her own blood on her tongue.

Grigori drew back instantly, his gaze searching hers. "Forgive me."

Marisa licked the blood from her lower lip, felt the sudden tremor in his arms. She stared into his eyes, saw the hunger that shadowed his gaze.

"Are you all right?" she asked.

"Yes. Did I hurt you?"

She shook her head. "Does it bother you?"

He didn't pretend he didn't know what she meant. He blew out a deep breath. "No, but—" He swept the tip of one finger over her lip, and licked the blood from his finger. "It tempts me in ways you cannot imagine."

"Oh. Do you . . . did you . . . you know?"

"Yes." His gaze was drawn to the pulse throbbing in the hollow of her throat.

"But you're still . . . ah, hungry?"

"In a way. I'm afraid the hunger for blood rises

hand in hand with my desire for you. I can't separate the two."

"So what does that mean, exactly?"

"It means I shall have to be very careful."

"You said it was painful when you went for a long time without . . . without, you know. Is it pleasurable for you, then, when you drink"—she forced the word out—"blood?"

"Very. And yours is the sweetest nectar of all."

It seemed odd to take pride in such a bizarre compliment, but she couldn't help it.

"How soon?" he whispered, his voice low and husky with desire. "How soon?"

"The sixteenth," she replied breathlessly. It would be rushing it, but a big wedding paled in the face of his need, her desire. She had only a few close friends, anyway. She didn't need dozens of casual acquaintances as witnesses. She didn't need a round of bridal showers. All she needed was Grigori.

The sixteenth was just a little over two weeks away. That would give her parents and her brother and his family time enough to get here. She would ask Mr. Salazar if she could take her vacation early. She needed to find a dress. Something long and white with a round neck and fitted sleeves. Satin, or maybe silk. And a veil. And white heels. And something old and something new, something borrowed, and something blue.

Two weeks and three days, and then she would he his.

He kissed her again, his hands feathering over her breasts, her thighs. She felt the rough satin of his tongue slide across her throat, felt his whole body quiver as he drew her up against him, letting her feel the proof of his desire. She ached deep, deep inside, ached with the need to hold him within the deepest part of her being.

Two weeks and three days . . . how would she ever wait that long?

New Year's Eve was cool and clear. Marisa stood in front of the mirror, trying to see herself as Grigori would see her.

The dress's teal blue made her eyes seem darker, deeper. The silk clung to her figure, outlining every curve, baring her shoulders and a good bit of cleavage.

A thrill of anticipation rose up within her as she heard the front door open. He was here!

She saw his reflection in the mirror as he entered her bedroom. Their gazes met and held, and she saw the admiration in his eyes, the love, the desire.

"Like it?" she asked.

He let out a long, low whistle. "*Like* is hardly the word."

She was a vision, an angel fallen to earth, a seductress come to play havoc with his self-control. Her hair framed her face like a dark silken cloud. Her green eyes were luminous, her skin the color of ripe peaches. His gaze moved over her softly rounded shoulders, over her breasts, the curve of her hips, down her long, shapely legs.

He swore under his breath as he felt the Hunger rise with his desire.

"You look very pretty, too," Marisa said, smiling.

"Pretty?"

She nodded. He wore a black suit that had obviously been tailored just for him, a white shirt, a tie of maroon silk.

"Wow," she murmured. "Wow. I'll have to beat the other women off with a stick."

"Indeed?" One corner of his mouth went up in a wry smile. "And I shall have to keep you close to my side lest some other man try to steal you away."

"That will never happen. I'm gonna stick to *your* side like glue." She smiled up at him, and reached for her coat. "Ready?"

The Salazars lived in what could only be called a mansion. Marisa was certain her whole apartment building, including the yard and the parking area, could fit inside. The rooms were luxuriously decorated, from the plush cream-colored carpets to the vaulted ceilings. Expensive paintings hung from the walls; there were glass shelves filled with costly crystal figurines and imported china.

A maid took Marisa's coat. Mrs. Salazar came forward to greet her, and after Marisa introduced Grigori, Mrs. Salazar gave Marisa a hug and told them to make themselves at home.

"This is quite a place, don't you think?"

"Indeed." Grigori glanced around, taking note of a painting on one wall. Either it was an original Picasso, or an extremely good copy.

"Look, there's Linda and her husband. Come on," Marisa said, grabbing his hand, "I want to introduce you."

Linda Hauf was a tall, slender woman with curly blond hair and bright blue eyes. Her husband, Jim, was in real estate.

Grigori murmured that he was pleased to meet

her, shook her husband's hand, engaged in a few moments of mindless small talk with the man while Marisa asked Linda to be her bridesmaid.

"Married!" Linda exclaimed. "Did you hear that, Jim? They're getting married." She looked at Grigori, as if judging his worthiness to marry her friend, and then gave Marisa a hug. "When did all this happen? Why didn't you tell me sooner?"

Jim Hauf rolled his eyes. "Come on, Chiavari, let's go get a drink," he suggested. "All this wedding talk could take hours."

With a shrug, Grigori followed the man to the wet bar. He ordered a glass of burgundy, then stood nursing his drink, listening as the man started talking about the upcoming Rose Bowl. Grigori nodded from time to time, but his attention was on Marisa. Soft candlelight caressed her face and shimmered in her hair. He watched her laugh, noting the way her eyes sparkled, the way she tossed her head, the way her hair floated around her shoulders. Even from across the room, he could smell the flowery scent of her perfume, the warm, womanly scent of her skin.

Once she looked over at him, her gaze catching his, and he felt such a rush of desire it almost brought him to his knees. In little more than two weeks, she would be his.

Dinner was served twenty minutes later. Opulent was the only word for the dining room. Crystal and translucent china and gleaming gold flatware reflected the light from the enormous chandelier that hung over the center of the table.

Grigori sat across from Marisa, sandwiched between an elderly matron with blue hair and a young woman he recognized as a television model. Conversation at the table was lively. There was a good deal of laughter mixed with the lobster bisque and the wine. The matron wanted to know if he was eligible; the model wanted to know if he was available later.

He caught Marisa staring at him and shrugged. *Not my fault.*

She grimaced at him, then turned to answer a question posed to her by the matron's portly husband.

The meal lasted over an hour. Grigori was uncomfortable, being in such close quarters with so many people. His senses reeled from the sound of so many beating hearts. His nostrils stung with the cloying scent of perfume and aftershave and perspiration. The smell of so much rich food, so many kinds of food, sickened him. He tried to recall the last time he had eaten, the last thing he had eaten, but the memory had been lost in two hundred years. He could scarcely remember what it had been like to eat solid food, to drink anything other than blood and an occasional glass of wine.

He realized Marisa was staring at him, and then he heard her voice in his mind. *Are you all right?*

He nodded faintly. *Yes, but I could use some fresh air.*

She looked at him, her eyes alight with mischief as she wondered what her companions would think if they knew there was a vampire sharing their table. But the most fun of all was being able to send her thoughts to Grigori, and being able to read his in return.

You're beautiful, carissima.

And you're very handsome.

I want to make love to you. . . .

She felt a wave of color wash into her cheeks. His words sounded so clear in her mind that she glanced around, certain Mr. Abercrombie and the others had heard every word. *Quit it. You're making me blush.*

And it's very becoming.

Grigori . . .

How long do we have to stay?

Until after dinner. We can sneak out then.

After dinner. He had rarely seen so much food at one meal. It just kept coming and coming, trays and platters and covered bowls. His village in Tuscany could have eaten for a week on the food that passed in front of him.

At last, the meal was over and the guests moved into the ballroom. As they filed out of the dining room, Grigori grabbed Marisa by the hand and led her outside, away from the crush of people.

He took a deep breath, filling his lungs with fresh air. And then he pulled Marisa into his arms and kissed her. And kissed her again. And yet again.

"Oh, Grigori, when you kiss me like that—"

"What?" He nuzzled her neck, feeling the pulse racing there. He closed his eyes and drew in a deep breath, inhaling the scent of her hair and skin, the fragrance of her perfume.

"Don't you know? Can't you feel what I'm feeling?"

"Yes, love," he replied thickly. He felt everything she was feeling, and more. The siren call of the blood flowing in her veins stirred his hunger. He ached with the need to taste her sweetness, felt his fangs lengthen in response to his thoughts.

She sighed and rested her cheek on his chest. "I'm not sure I can wait two weeks."

Fighting to suppress the dark need within him, he took a deep, calming breath, then kissed the tip of her nose.

"But wait we will," he vowed. "You will be my bride when I take you to my bed, *cara mia,* and once you are mine, I will never, never let you go."

She sighed as he kissed her again, certain that a lifetime in his arms would not be long enough.

Music drifted out onto the balcony as the orchestra began to play. Marisa swayed against Grigori.

"Dance with me?" she murmured, and the next thing she knew, his right hand was at her waist, his left hand was holding hers, and they were waltzing.

He danced divinely. It seemed his feet scarcely touched the floor as he twirled her around. He moved gracefully, effortlessly, leading her though the steps as though they had been waltzing together for years.

It was a glorious night. The sky was like a bed of black velvet strewn with a million twinkling lights. They danced for hours, oblivious to everything save each other.

There was a drum roll as midnight approached and the bandleader began the countdown.

Ten. Nine. Eight.

Marisa gazed into Grigori's eyes, wondering if he felt the same magic she did, the same sense of wonder.

Seven. Six. Five.

He stroked her cheek with his fingertip, and she felt the touch clear down to her toes.

Four. Three. Two.

One.

"Happy New Year, Grigori," she whispered.

"Happy New Year, *cara mia.*"

He kissed her gently. "Close your eyes."

"Why?"

"Close your eyes, *cara.*"

She waited, excitement flowing through her, as he took her hand in his.

"You can open them now," he said, and she watched him slide a ring over her finger.

"Oh, Grigori," she murmured. "It's beautiful."

She'd never seen a diamond so big in her whole life. She held her hand up, turning it this way and that, watching it reflect the lights from the ballroom.

"You like it?"

"I love it. I love you!"

"Ah, Marisa, when you look at me like that, I believe anything is possible."

"You're not having doubts about us, are you?"

Doubts? He had dozens, hundreds, but he shook them off. Marisa was here, in his arms. She had promised to be his wife, and that was all that mattered.

They spent the next few days shopping for furniture. Marisa was enchanted by the house Grigori had bought. The rooms were all large, with vaulted ceilings and hardwood floors. There was a large stone fireplace in the living room, smaller ones in all the bedrooms. There was a huge pantry in the kitchen, a solarium with large leaded-glass windows and a skylight, an old-fashioned music room.

Grigori approved of everything she picked out for the house: a beautiful antique oak bedroom set with a four-poster bed, a large round oak table and four chairs for the kitchen, another more formal table and chairs for the dining room, an intricately carved oak sideboard.

They bought sheets and towels, dishes and flatware. Money was never a problem. Several times, she by-passed what she really wanted and picked something less expensive, and every time Grigori insisted she buy the lamp or the table or the chair she preferred.

"You're a wealthy woman now," he reminded her. "Buy whatever you wish."

"You're going to spoil me," she muttered as they left an exclusive furniture store one night.

Outside, he took her in his arms and his lips brushed hers. "That, my sweet, is exactly what I plan to do."

Chapter Twenty-nine

The next few days flew by in a flurry of excitement. Marisa called her parents and her brother and listened patiently to their objections to her marrying a man she had known for such a short time. She spent three lunch hours shopping for a wedding dress; then she spent a Saturday afternoon with Linda picking out dresses for Linda and Barbara to wear. There wasn't enough time to order engraved invitations, so she sent out handwritten ones to a few close friends. She ordered a small cake, made arrangements for the church, made an appointment to get her hair and nails done. She spoke with Mr. Salazar, inviting him to the wedding and asking if she could have two weeks off for a honeymoon. He grumbled a bit, but, in the end, he agreed.

If her days were hectic, her nights were not. Grigori came over each evening and it was then, wrapped in his arms, that she found the peace that eluded her during the day. He never failed to bring her a gift of some kind: flowers—white roses by the dozen, yellow ones, pink ones, a single, perfect, bloodred rose; chocolates and perfume; a lovely silver filigreed heart on a delicate chain; a diamond necklace that was so beautiful it took her breath away.

"You don't have to bring me a present every time you come over," she chided one night, but he dismissed her objection with a wave of his hand.

"It pleases me to bring you things," he replied. And then he grinned at her, a sly, roguish grin that made her insides melt and her toes curl. "Besides, I like the way you express your gratitude."

Marisa shook her head. "Silly! I'd kiss you even if you didn't buy me extravagant gifts."

"Would you?"

"Of course. I kissed you tonight, didn't I? And you didn't bring me anything."

He lifted one brow. "Didn't I?"

"Did you?"

With a flourish, he reached into his pocket and withdrew a small square box. He handed it to her with a wink.

"What is it?" Marisa asked.

"Open it and see."

Stomach fluttering with excitement, she lifted the lid. A key rested on a bed of blue velvet. She looked up at him. "Let me guess. It's the key to your heart, right?"

He laughed softly. "No, *bella,* it's the key to your new car."

"New car! You bought me a car?"

Grigori nodded. "It's parked out front."

Marisa ran to the window, drew back the curtains, and looked outside. There were two cars parked at the curb. A sleek black Corvette, and a red Corvette convertible.

"You don't mean one of those?" she asked, glancing over her shoulder.

Grigori came up behind her and slid his arms around her waist. "Which one do you like?"

"Which one? You bought them both?"

He nodded. "I thought you would prefer the convertible, but you can have the other, if you like."

She didn't know what to say.

Grigori put his hands at her waist and turned her around to face him. "Would you rather have something else?"

"No. No. Who wouldn't want a Corvette, but—"

"But?"

"They're so expensive. And the insurance. I could never afford it."

"*Cara,* it's all paid for."

"But . . . it must have cost you a fortune to buy two cars, and insurance and—"

He placed a finger over her lips. "I have a fortune, *cara mia.* Let me spend it on you."

She looked up at him, wondering how she had ever thought him a monster. He treated her like a queen, spoiled her shamelessly, and not just by buying her presents. He was thoughtful of her wants, her needs. He valued her opinions, listened to what she had to say.

"Grigori, you're so good to me."

He smiled down at her. "Ah, *cara,* it is you who are good to me. It's been so long since I've had someone to care for, someone to take care of. I'd forgotten how wonderful it is."

"I love the way you take care of me," she murmured, and drawing his head down, she kissed him.

As always, the touch of his lips on hers flooded

her with heat, made her long for the day when she could be his, body and soul.

"Three more days," she whispered. Today was Wednesday. She had taken Thursday and Friday off to spend with her family and run a few last-minute errands. She had to pick up her wedding dress tomorrow afternoon; tomorrow night they were all going out to dinner so Grigori could meet her family. Saturday morning she had to pick up the flowers and get her hair done. The wedding was at six o'clock at the Methodist church around the corner.

"Three more days," he repeated softly, and the idea filled him with such longing, he thought he might die of the pain.

Three more days. He could wait that long. With an effort, he stilled the hunger within him. "So," he said, "which will it be? The red one, or the black one?"

"What? Oh, the cars." She smiled up at him. "The red one. I've always dreamed of owning a red Corvette." She tilted her head to the side. "But you know that, don't you?"

"What do you mean?"

"You've been reading my mind again."

"No," he replied. "It just looked like you."

"Honest?"

"Honest."

"My parents will be here tomorrow." She rested her head against his shoulder and closed her eyes. She loved her folks, she really did, but she wasn't looking forward to having them underfoot for the next three days. For one thing, she wouldn't be able to sit up late at night and neck with Grigori on the sofa, not with her father staying up to watch the eleven o'clock news. Her brother and his family would have to stay in a motel. There was just no room in her apartment for Mike and Barbara and their kids, unless she wanted to move out. Which might not be such a bad idea, she mused, if she could move in with Grigori.

She grinned at the thought. Tempting as it might be, she couldn't do it. Her parents would have a fit. They'd only be here for three days. She could stand anything that long. And then she would belong to Grigori forever.

"Come on," she said, grabbing his hand. "Let's go for a ride."

It was the most luxurious car she had ever seen. The interior was butter-soft leather, and it smelled as only a new car could smell. She fastened her seat belt, slid the key in the ignition, felt a thrill of excitement as the engine hummed to life. *Purred* might have been a better word, she mused as she pulled away from the curb.

"You like it?"

"I love it." It handled like a dream. "But why did you buy two?"

"One for you, one for me."

"I thought you just wished yourself wherever you wanted to go."

"Well," he admitted with a wry grin, "after I test-drove one for you, I sort of fell in love with it. I mean—" He shrugged. "I've never driven anything like it."

"Typical male," she muttered, and then laughed. There was nothing typical about Grigori. "What'll I do with my old car?"

"Whatever you want. Sell it. Junk it. Give it away."

She laughed then, laughed because she was happy, because Grigori was beside her, because, in three days, she would be his wife.

She was happy, so happy. She should have known it wouldn't last.

At seven-thirty A.M. Thursday morning, Edward Ramsey knocked at Marisa's door.

"Hi, Edward," Marisa said, yawning. "What are you doing here so early?"

"You haven't seen the papers, have you?" He thrust a copy of the *L.A. Times* in her face. "I think he's back."

She didn't have to ask who. Her hands were trembling as she took the newspaper and began to read.

VAMPIRE KILLER STRIKES AGAIN

The headlines screamed the news. She read the story quickly. The body of a young woman had been found in the Griffith Park area the night before. There had been no visible sign of a struggle, no indication of violence, save for the tiny wounds in her throat, and the fact that her body had been drained of blood.

Marisa stared at Edward, the paper falling, unnoticed, to the floor. He was back. Alexi was back. She folded her arms over her chest, suddenly cold clear through.

He was back.

"Is Chiavari still hanging around here?"

She nodded. "Come on in." Rubbing her hands over her arms, she went into the kitchen and poured herself a cup of black coffee.

Her parents were due in half an hour. Mike and Barbara would be arriving around noon.

She was getting married in two days.

Alexi Kristov had returned.

"After all that's happened, I can't believe you're still seeing Chiavari. The man's a vampire, for crying out loud."

"I love him." She took a deep breath. "We're getting married."

"Married!" Edward stared at her as if she'd just grown another head. "You're kidding, right? Tell me you're kidding."

Edward had picked up the paper on his way into the kitchen. Now he shook it in her face. "Vampire, Marisa! Does that ring a bell? He's no different from Kristov. Sure, he's handsome as hell, but he's still just a walking corpse. He's capable of murder, just like Kristov. You'll never be safe with him. Never! Some night he won't be able to control his hunger and he'll turn on you."

"Stop it!" She pressed her hands over her ears to shut out his voice. "Stop it! I won't listen."

"You will listen!" He dropped the newspaper and grabbed her hands, imprisoning them against his chest. "He's a killer. You know it. Stop thinking with your hormones and start using your head. Just because he comes in a pretty package doesn't change what he is. He's a vampire, and they're killers by nature."

"He's not! He told me he hasn't killed anyone in over a hundred and fifty years, except to preserve his own life, and I believe him."

"Then you're a fool. He wants you, Marisa, he's wanted you from the first, and he'll do anything, say anything, to have you."

She shook her head. "If he's what you say, he could have taken me at any time. He wouldn't have to marry me. He loves me."

"Dammit, Marisa, he's a vampire. He's incapable of love."

"No, no, no!" She tried to jerk her hands from his grasp. "Let me go, Edward."

"Not until you hear what I'm saying."

"I hear you."

"Do you?"

"Yes," she replied sullenly. "I hear you, but it doesn't change anything. I love him, and I'm going to marry him."

Edward stared at her a moment, and then, with a sigh of defeat, he released her hands. "It's your life," he muttered. "I guess you can throw it away if you want. But before you make a fatal mistake, ask him. Ask him how many people he's killed in the last two hundred years. Don't listen to that crap about not hunting where he lives, or only killing in self-defense. Just ask him flat-out. Ask him how many lives he's taken to sustain his own. And then ask yourself if you want to be next."

"Edward—"

She called after him, but it was too late. He was already gone.

The door had barely closed behind him when her parents arrived.

Chapter Thirty

"Marisa!" Her mother hugged her tightly, then stepped back and looked her up and down. "How well you look. . . ." The words trailed off. "No, you don't look well at all! What's the matter, Marty? Having second thoughts? Well, I can't say as I blame you. You just met the man—"

Jack Richards drew his daughter into his arms and gave her a bear hug. "Lay off, Marge, we just got here." He winked at Marisa. "You look fine to me. A little tired, maybe, but your mother looked like death warmed over two days before we got married. You got any coffee?"

"Sure, Dad."

Marisa went into the kitchen. Death warmed over. Interesting that her father would use that phrase. She glanced over her shoulder as her father entered the kitchen and sat down at the table.

"Terrible, these killings." He spread the newspaper out on the table, the same paper Edward had dropped on the floor earlier, judging by the wrinkles in it.

"Yes, terrible," Marisa agreed. She handed her father a cup of coffee and sat down across from him. *Ask him how many people he's killed. . . . I never hunt where I live. . . . Ask him how many lives he's taken to sustain his own. . . . I haven't killed anyone in over a hundred and fifty years. . . .*

"What is it, Marty? What's wrong?"

"Nothing, Dad, just wedding jitters, I guess."

"Where'd you meet this guy?"

"At a carnival just after Halloween."

Jack Richards laughed out loud. It was a good sound, deep and rich, reminding Marisa of camping trips and hikes through the woods, and birthday parties.

"Sorry," he said. "I didn't mean to laugh." He shook his head. "Do you love him?"

"Yes." *There's just one thing wrong with him. He's a vampire.*

"Does he love you?"

"Yes." *He thinks my blood is the sweetest nectar of all.* She shook the thought from her mind. "Where's Mom?"

"Unpacking." He reached across the table and took her hand. "If you love each other, truly love each other, everything will work out. Trust me. And if it doesn't, well, you know your mother and I are always here for you."

"I know, Dad. Thanks." She squeezed his hand, thinking how lucky she was to have this man for her father. He'd always been there for her. He'd taught her to ride a two-wheeler, taken her to her first concert, comforted her when she broke up with her first boyfriend, bought her her first corsage. He'd taught her to drive a car, persuaded her mother to let her shave her legs because all the other girls were doing it, slipped her an extra dollar or two when her allowance ran out, helped her with her homework.

"So, Marty, are we too late for breakfast?" her mother asked as she came into the kitchen.

"No, Mom. What would you like?"

"You just sit down and let me take care of it."

"Mom, you're my guest."

"Don't be silly. I'm not a guest, I'm your mother. You go get dressed, and I'll fix breakfast. What do you want?"

Marisa smiled at her parents, thinking how lucky she was. "Whatever Dad wants is fine with me."

"That's my girl," Jack said with a grin. "French toast and bacon. How's that sound?"

"Perfect!" Marisa winked at her father, and then left the room, smiling.

Mike and Barbara and their kids arrived a little after one. Marisa hugged her nieces and nephews. At ten, Mike Junior was the eldest; then came Nikki, who was eight, Mindy, who was six, and Danny, who had just turned two.

"I don't know why you live here," Mike complained as he gave her a hug. "The traffic is terrible."

"But the weather is wonderful."

"I guess. Couldn't you have gotten married in the summer so we could hit the beach?"

"Sorry, Mike."

"Yeah, yeah."

"Just ignore him," Barbara advised. "He's been complaining ever since the plane landed. You know how he hates to leave Colorado."

"How are you, Barb?" Marisa asked, giving her sister-in-law a hug.

"How am I? I'm pregnant, that's how I am."

"That's wonderful!" Marisa exclaimed, and in the back of her mind she heard Grigori urging her to marry a man who could give her children. She looked at Mike's kids. They were all beautiful, well behaved.

"Another baby!" Marge Richards rushed forward and hugged Barbara. "I thought Marisa would have the next one."

"Me too," Barbara said. "We really weren't planning on any more, but—" She shrugged. "Things happen."

Mike grinned. "Yep."

"Congratulations, son." Jack shook Mike's hand, then pulled him into his arms and hugged him. "Good thing you've got those three acres."

"There's room for you and Mom."

"No, thanks, my days of shoveling snow are over."

"Why didn't you tell us this at Christmas?" Marge asked.

"I just found out yesterday. I thought I had the flu."

"Can we watch a video, Aunt Marty?"

"Sure, Mindy. You know where they are."

"I don't want to watch TV," Mike Junior said. "Can Nikki and I play on your computer?"

Marisa smiled at her nephew. "Sure, Mike."

With the two younger kids settled in front of the television watching *Beauty and the Beast*, the adults went into the kitchen for coffee and conversation.

"So I can't wait to meet Grigori," Barbara said. "What's he look like?"

"A *GQ* model."

"Really?" Barbara grinned lasciviously. " 'Bout

time we had a handsome man in the family."

"Hey!" Mike exclaimed. "What about me?"

"You?" Barbara shrieked as Mike poked her in the ribs. "What about you?"

"I'm handsome. Aren't I, Marty?"

"Well . . ."

"Hey, come on, I'm your brother. You're supposed to back me up."

"Right. Like you backed me up when I asked you if Steve Renouf liked me, and you spread it all over the school that I had a crush on him."

"Haven't you forgotten about that yet?"

"No, and I never will."

"Okay, kids, settle down," Jack said. "I don't wanna have to send you to your rooms."

Marisa and Mike exchanged looks and then burst into laughter, and Marisa thought again how wonderful it was to have her family there, to feel the love they shared for one another.

They reminisced about old times, exchanged news, talked about the wedding. Before long it was time to get ready for dinner. Mr. Abbott's wife had agreed to come and stay with the kids while the adults went out to dinner.

Marisa ordered pizza for the kids, and then it was six o'clock.

There were millions of butterflies going crazy in her stomach by the time Grigori arrived. Would her parents like him? Would he like them? Would they notice there was something different about him?

He kissed her cheek when she opened the door. "You look lovely," he whispered, and his breath felt warm and intimate against her ear.

"Thanks. Are you ready to meet everyone?"

He nodded. "Worried?"

"A little."

He smiled down at her. "I love you, *cara*."

Words. They were just words. Ordinary words that were said every day, but they washed over her like a soothing balm, calming the butterflies.

"I love you, too." She took his hand and led him into the living room. "Hey, everybody, this is Grigori."

Was it her imagination, or was there a sudden lack of oxygen in the room? Her father and Mike exchanged glances she couldn't interpret. Her mother pressed a hand to her heart. Barbara murmured, "Oh, my, you were right."

Grigori slid a glance at Maria. "Right? About what?"

"I told them you looked like a *GQ* model."

"Ahhh."

She quickly introduced Grigori to everyone, including the kids, and then they trooped outside.

Mike let out a long, low whistle when he saw Grigori's Corvette. "Wow, nice wheels."

"You should see mine." Marisa tossed the words over her shoulder as she slid into the passenger seat. "Mine's red."

Mike looked at Grigori. "She's kidding, right?"

Grigori shook his head.

"But . . . but how?"

"And it's a convertible," Marisa added.

She grinned at the look of astonishment on her brother's face.

Mike, Barb, and her parents climbed into the van Mike had rented, and Grigori pulled away from the curb. He checked the rearview mirror to make certain her family was following, then gave her knee a squeeze. "You look like the proverbial cat that swallowed the canary."

"I can't help it." She grinned at him. "This is the first time I ever had a better car than Mike." She leaned over and kissed his cheek. "Thank you for that."

"You are most welcome. How was your day?"

"Fine—" The words died in her throat as she recalled Edward's visit that morning. In the rush of her family's arrival, she had forgotten all about it.

Grigori glanced over at her, noting the worry lines in her brow. "Is something wrong?"

"I don't want to talk about it now."

"As you wish."

They drove the rest of the way in silence.

Dinner went well. Marisa watched Grigori carefully. She recalled the time they had gone to dinner at the North Woods Inn. He'd ordered a steak and she would have sworn he ate it. She knew better now. He toyed with the food on his plate, but never really ate anything. Yet she knew that if she were to ask her parents about it later, they would assure her that he'd eaten a full meal.

Talk at the table was polite and restrained at first, but gradually everyone relaxed. They talked about the wedding; then Jack and Marge told about their wedding, and Mike and Barb reminisced about their own. Champagne flowed freely, as did the conversation and the laughter.

"So," Barbara said, "where are you two going for your honeymoon?"

"We're going to stay home."

"Home!"

Marisa nodded. "Grigori said we could go

wherever I wanted, but I want to stay home, in our own house, just the two of us."

"You always said you wanted to go to Italy for your honeymoon," Marge remarked.

Marisa looked at Grigori and smiled. "I've been to Italy."

"You have!" her father exclaimed. "When?"

"Not long ago. It was a quick, unexpected trip."

"Really?" Mike frowned at her. "You never mentioned it."

"Didn't I? I'm ready for dessert. Mom, what are you going to have?"

Grigori grinned as she neatly changed the subject.

It was late when they returned to Marisa's apartment. Mike and Barb picked up their kids, and then left for the motel. Jack and Marge bid Marisa and Grigori good night and went to bed.

Marisa sat down on the sofa and pulled a pillow into her lap. "Well," she said, "alone at last."

"Indeed." He regarded her thoughtfully a moment, and then sat down beside her. "Do you want to tell me what's bothering you?"

"Nothing, really."

"Really?"

She blew out a deep breath. "Edward came by this morning."

"I see."

"There's been another killing. Did you know that?"

He nodded. "Go on."

"He said a lot of foolish things. It doesn't matter."

"I think it matters very much. What did he say?"

Marisa glanced at the hallway. "We can't talk

about it here." She gasped as he took her in his arms and stood up. "What are you doing?"

"Going where we can talk."

Before she could protest, before she could ask where they were going, they were there.

He placed her on her feet, and then turned on the lights. "There's no one to overhear us now."

"I really don't want to discuss it."

"Don't you? Something's troubling you. I've known it all night. It's more than another killing. What is it?"

It was cold in the house. She wrapped her arms around her body, wondering if she was shaking from the chill in the air, or the coldness in Grigori's eyes.

He turned away from her. She saw him wave his hand, and in the next instant, there was a fire in the fireplace. He took several slow, deep breaths, and then turned to face her.

"Tell me, Marisa."

"He said I was crazy to marry you, that I should ask you how many people you've killed. He—" She wrapped her arms around her waist. "He asked me if I wanted to be next."

Grigori swore under his breath. "Dammit, Marisa, what do you want me to say?"

"I just want the truth."

"I've told you the truth. I've killed people. I told you that. Maybe I glossed over it to spare your feelings, but I never lied to you about it. There were times, in the beginning, before I learned to control the Hunger, that people died. I can't do anything about that. Their deaths haunted me then. They haunt me now. But I can't change the past."

He crossed the floor to the window. Drawing back the curtain, he gazed out into the darkness. "Maybe I'm just kidding myself," he murmured. "I thought we could make this work. Maybe I was wrong."

The anguish in his voice, the loneliness, tugged at her heart. She went to stand behind him. "I love you, you know I do."

He could feel her close to him. Her warmth engulfed him; her scent surrounded him. "Maybe that's not enough."

"What else is there?"

"Trust."

"I do trust you."

"Do you? Can you tell me, honestly, that you're not afraid of me, that there isn't a part of you that doesn't wonder if Ramsey is right?"

"Search my mind, Grigori, and find the truth for yourself."

"Marisa . . ." Slowly, he turned to face her. "If you're not sure, if you have any doubts, tell me now, before it's too late. I told you before, once you're mine, I will not let you go. There will be no divorce if you decide you've made a mistake." His gaze trapped and held hers. "Be sure."

He needed her. All her life, she had wanted someone who would love her unconditionally, someone who would need her, someone who couldn't live without her. "I'm sure."

With infinite care, he drew her into his arms. "I love you, *cara mia*. I will never love another."

With a sigh, she rested her head against his chest, felt his love wash over her, warm and sweet. This was right. This was where she belonged.

* * *

Friday was a pleasant day. Mike and his family came over for breakfast. Later, the kids watched TV while the adults played cards. It was just the kind of day Marisa needed. A time to spend with her family, to relax and have a good time with the people she loved most.

They discussed names for the new baby. It started out as a serious discussion and they suggested names like John and Mary. Eventually, as they tried to top each other, they were tossing out names like Heathcliffe and Hildegarde. It felt good to laugh.

They ordered pizza for lunch, and then went out for ice cream.

Back at home, Barbara put Danny down for a nap. Mike Junior and Nikki went to play on the computer. Mindy went into the bedroom to play with her Barbies. When the kids were all settled in other rooms, the questions started.

"So," her father asked, "what does Grigori do for a living?"

"He's a magician."

"A magician!" her mother exclaimed. "Really? I've never known a magician."

"Does he do children's parties?" Barbara asked.

"I don't think so."

"I've never heard of him," Mike remarked. "Does he use a stage name?"

"I don't know."

"You don't?"

Marisa shrugged. "I just assumed he used his own name. He hasn't been in this country very long. He's from Italy."

"You're not moving to Italy, are you?" Marge asked.

"No. Well, I don't think so. We never discussed it."

"I thought he'd be coming by today," Mike said.

"He had some last-minute errands of his own to run."

"I think he's pretty," Nikki said. She sat on the arm of the sofa beside Marisa. "Is he really a magician? Would he do some tricks for us?"

"I don't know, sweetie; you'll have to ask him. I thought you were playing "Doom" with Mike."

"He's hogging the computer. Is Grigori coming over later? I like him."

"Me too."

"You're not going to quit your job, are you?"

"No, Dad, why?"

"Well . . ."

"Well, what?"

"Well, can he support you? I mean, he doesn't seem to be working."

"He's got money, Dad. He just bought a big old house up in the hills. And who do you think bought my car? I certainly couldn't afford it. Not on my salary."

"I don't mean to upset you, honey, but you haven't known this guy very long. He seems nice enough, but there's something about him. I don't know what it is. I can't quite put my finger on it, but I think you ought to hang on to your job until . . . well, you know."

"Jack, Marty's a big girl now," Marge said. "She knows what she's doing."

"Thanks, Mom."

"You're welcome, Marty." Marge toyed with her necklace a moment. "Still, your Dad makes good sense."

"He always has," Marisa said. "I'm gonna get a Coke."

"Can I have one?" Nikki asked.

"Sure, sweetie."

Marisa went into the kitchen and pressed her forehead against the refrigerator door. She couldn't blame her parents for worrying about her. She had doubts, too. Marriage was a big step. She didn't want to be one of those women who changed husbands as often as they changed their shoes. She wanted it to be forever.

"Forever," she muttered. That was funny. Grigori really could give her forever, if she wanted it.

"You okay?"

Marisa straightened up and opened the door to the fridge. "I'm fine, Mike." She pulled out two cans of Coke. "Do you want anything?"

"No. Don't let Dad get to ya. He's just, you know, being a dad."

"I know." She closed the door, and then turned to face her brother. "It's all right."

"Well, you looked a little upset."

Marisa shook her head. "I'm not, really."

"Dad's right about one thing, though. You haven't known Grigori very long. Why the sudden rush to get married? I mean, you've waited this long."

"Not you, too!"

"Hey, I'm not criticizing, I'm just asking."

"I love him and I want to marry him. Why is that so hard to believe? Just because it took you and Barb two years to decide to get married doesn't mean it has to take me that long, too. Mom and Dad knew each other less than a year when they got married."

"I know, but—" Mike placed his hands on her shoulders. "Dad's right about something else, too. There is something strange about Grigori. He's different somehow."

"Mike, just drop it, okay? I know what I'm doing."

He squeezed her shoulders. "I know you do. We just love you, sis, that's all."

"I know." Their love was like a blanket, usually warm and welcome, but sometimes it smothered her.

Grigori arrived at sundown. Marisa was in the kitchen with her mother and Barbara, trying to decide what to do about dinner, when the doorbell rang.

A flutter in her stomach, a subtle change in the atmosphere told her it was Grigori even before she opened the door. As always, her first sight of him took her breath away. He was so tall, so incredibly good-looking. And his smile . . . a smile that was just for her, it made her insides turn to mush.

"*Cara.*" He bent down and brushed a kiss across her lips.

"Hi." He wore black slacks, boots, and a bulky gray sweater that emphasized his broad shoulders. "Come on in. We're trying to decide what to do about dinner."

His gaze slid over her face to the pulse throbbing in the hollow of her throat. He felt the sharp prick of his fangs against his tongue and wondered if he would be able to control his hunger for her once she was truly his.

Marisa's heart skipped a beat as his gaze moved over her. He didn't say anything, but she knew what he was thinking. Unbidden, unwanted, Edward's voice rose in the back of her mind: *Then ask yourself if you want to be next.*

She lifted her gaze to his. The sound of the evening news, the voices of her family, the traffic on the street, everything faded into the distance, ceased to exist, until there were only the two of them standing in the entry hall.

"Marisa . . ." He cupped her face in his hands, his fingertips moving lightly over her skin. "Give me a chance, *cara.* I'll make you happy, I swear it."

She didn't know what to say. His eyes were dark and vulnerable, filled with the pain, the loneliness, of two hundred years.

"I love you, *cara mia.*"

"I know you do." *Dammit, Marisa, he's a vampire.* Edward's voice rang out in her mind. *He's incapable of love.* She moved into Grigori's embrace and wrapped her arms around his waist. "And I love you."

"No doubts?"

"Just the usual doubts every bride has."

"That's all?"

She met his gaze again. "That's all. I'm not afraid of you, Grigori. I'm not afraid of what you are, only that I'll disappoint you."

"Never!"

He kissed her lightly, sweetly, and when he drew away, the world returned.

Because they couldn't all agree on what they wanted for dinner, they ordered pizza for the kids, Chinese for Marge and Barbara, and Italian for everyone else.

"So, Grigori, my daughter says you're a magician," Jack remarked.

Dinner was over and they were in the living room.

"Yes."

"Could you do a trick for us?" Nikki asked.

"What would you like me to do? Saw you in half?"

Nikki giggled. "No, I don't think so." She punched Mike Junior on the arm. "Maybe you could just make my brother disappear."

"I could," Grigori replied solemnly, "but I'm not sure I could bring him back."

"That'd be okay with me. Ouch! Mom, Mike hit me."

"That's enough, you two," Barbara warned.

Grigori glanced at Marisa. She grinned at him, one brow raised in amusement. Grigori grinned back, accepting the silent challenge in her eyes.

"I'll need an assistant," he said, rising to his feet. "Marisa?"

She rolled her eyes, then stood up and joined him in the center of the living room.

"Look into my eyes," Grigori said. "Forget where you are. We are alone in this room, just the two of us. Concentrate on the sound of my voice. . . . That's right . . . you are in my power now. You see only me, hear only me."

"I see only you," she murmured. "Hear only you."

"You will do whatever I tell you."

"Yes."

Grigori looked over at Marge and Jack, who were sitting on the sofa. "Would you get up, please?"

Marisa's parents exchanged glances, then stood up and went to stand near the fireplace.

Grigori lifted Marisa in his arms and carried her to the sofa. He laid her down, passed his hand over her face. "You will sleep now, Marisa, and will not awaken until I call your name."

Her eyelids closed.

He stood beside the sofa, and then, very slowly, he raised his arms, palms up. And she floated off the sofa to hover in the air.

"Wow!" Mike Junior exclaimed. "That's awesome!"

"Amazing."

"Impossible!"

"How can he do that?"

Slowly, Grigori lowered his arms. Light as a feather, Marisa landed on the sofa.

"Marisa," he called softly.

Her eyelids fluttered open and she sat up, blinking at him. "What happened?"

"He levitated you. Damn," Mike said, "how'd you do that? I've seen it done onstage, but . . . but I always thought it was done with wires." He shook his head. "I've got to hand it to you, that's the most amazing thing I've ever seen."

"Do me," Mindy said, tugging on Grigori's pant leg. "I want to fly, too."

"I don't think so." Barbara pulled her daughter into her lap. "You're not old enough to fly."

"Come on, man," Mike Junior said, "tell us how you did it."

"I'm afraid magicians are sworn never to reveal their secrets."

Barbara looked at her watch, and then stood up. "It's getting late. Kids, get your stuff together.

We've all got a big day tomorrow. Mike, are you ready to go?"

"Yeah, honey."

There was a flurry of activity as Mike and Barbara gathered up their kids and said their good-byes. A few minutes later, Jack and Marge went to bed.

"Looks like I cleared the room," Grigori said. "That would be a problem if I were a real magician."

"Did you have to do something quite so flashy? I mean, couldn't you have done something that could be explained? And why did you make me go to sleep? I've never been levitated before, and I missed it."

"I was afraid it would scare you."

Marisa tugged on his sweater. "I'm marrying a vampire," she said with a grin. "If that doesn't scare me, nothing will."

He couldn't argue with that, so he kissed her.

"I should go," he said.

"It's early."

"Get a good night's sleep, *cara.* I'll keep you up late tomorrow night."

She grinned up at him, her insides quivering with anticipation.

"*Domani,* Marisa," he whispered. "Tomorrow, you will be mine."

The heat in his eyes, the husky tremor in his voice, sent a shiver of pleasure down her spine.

Tomorrow.

Chapter Thirty-one

Her wedding day dawned bright and clear and beautiful. Happy is the bride the sun shines on, she mused as she slipped out of bed and pulled on her robe. She'd heard that old saying often. She hoped it was true.

Too nervous to eat, she drank two cups of coffee. She was starting on a third when her father entered the kitchen.

"Morning, honey."

"Morning, Dad."

"How'd you sleep?"

"Sleep? What bride sleeps the night before the wedding?"

Jack Richards laughed. "None, I guess. That was some trick Grigori performed last night. Sure would like to know how he did it."

"Yeah, me too. Is Mom up yet?"

"Nah, she's snoring away."

Marisa giggled. It was an ongoing joke between her parents, which one of them snored the loudest.

"You're sure about this?" her father asked. "If you're not, it isn't too late to change your mind."

"I'm sure, Dad."

"I just want you to be happy, Marty."

"I am."

"You'd better eat something."

"I can't." She checked the clock, quickly swallowed the rest of her coffee. "I've got to get going. My appointment's at nine-thirty."

"Take your time. I'll hold down the fort till you get back."

"Thanks, Dad." She kissed her father on the cheek, and then hurried into her bedroom. She took a quick shower, dressed, and left the apartment.

Her first stop was the beauty shop for the works—manicure, pedicure, wash and set.

From the beauty shop, she went to the florist's. She had picked white roses and baby's breath for her bouquet. Linda and Nikki were carrying pink roses and carnations. The florist would deliver the altar flowers to the church later that day.

At twelve-thirty, she met her mother and Barbara at the church. They put big white satin bows on the first three pews, checked with the minister to make sure the white runner would be in place down the center aisle, went over the songs that the organist would be playing.

It was almost two when they got home. Barbara left to go to the hotel to get the kids fed and dressed.

"You've got to eat something," Marge Richards said. "You sit down and relax a moment while I fix you something."

"Mom, don't bother."

Marge Richards shook her head. "I didn't eat on my wedding day, either. You could hear my stomach growling all the way in the back of the church."

Jack Richards laughed. "Yeah, she leaned over while the minister was talking and said she wished she had a Big Mac."

Marisa laughed. "You're kidding, right?"

Her father shook his head. "Nope. It's the honest truth."

"Are you sure you don't want something to eat?" Marge asked.

"Maybe later. I'm gonna try to take a nap. Wake me in an hour, okay?"

"All right, sweetie."

Marisa went into her bedroom and shut the door. Kicking off her shoes, she stretched out on the bed and closed her eyes. In a little over three hours, she would be Grigori's wife. . . .

Marisa, I, too, am counting the hours.

"Grigori!" She sat up, her gaze darting around the room.

Sleep, cara mia, *I will be with you soon.*

"Where are you?"

I am home, dreaming of you.

With a sigh, she turned on her side and closed her eyes. Moments later, she was asleep.

Marge Richards sniffed softly as she set the veil in place on Marisa's head. "You look beautiful. Just beautiful."

"Thanks, Mom. What time is it?"

"Five o'clock. Stop worrying. They can't start without the bride. Now, let's see . . . what've you got for something old?"

"Grandma's brooch."

"Right. Something new?"

"My dress."

"Something borrowed?"

"Hanky from Barb."

"Something blue?"

"The ribbon on my garter."

Marge Richards stood back and sighed. Marisa looked like a fairy-tale princess. Her gown was white satin, with a scoop neck, long fitted sleeves, and a full skirt. The veil was like a whisper of moonlight, pale and fragile.

"So, how do I look?"

"Perfect, honey, just perfect."

"Is Dad ready?"

"He's been wearing a rut in your carpet for the last twenty minutes. You know your father, always ready an hour early. I think the big question is, are you ready?"

Marisa nodded as she slipped her arm around her mother's waist. "Thanks for all your help, Mom."

"You did all the work."

"I don't mean just today. You've always been there for me."

Marge Richards blinked back her tears. "Be happy, Marty."

"I will be." Marisa blinked back tears of her own. "Let's go."

Mike and Barbara and the kids were waiting at the church.

"Is Grigori here?" Marisa asked. "Have you seen him?"

"He was here when we got here," Barbara said. "Lordy, you should see what that man does for a tux."

"Hey," Mike said. "What about me? I look darn good, if I do say so myself."

"Of course you do, honey," Barbara said. She looked at Marisa and rolled her eyes. "Men. They've got egos the size of the Grand Canyon."

"What about Linda? Is she here yet?"

"I haven't seen her."

"Geez, you don't think she forgot?"

"I'm sure she didn't," Jack Richards said. "Calm down, Marty."

At five-thirty, the organist began to play. Mike and the kids went to take their places. A few minutes later, Linda arrived at the church.

"Sorry I'm late. My baby-sitter canceled at the last minute and I had to get Jim's mother to come and stay with the kids. Marty, you look gorgeous."

They spent the next few minutes handing out flowers and making sure every hair was in place. And then her mother left to be seated.

And then they were playing her music.

"Ready, honey?" her dad asked.

Marisa nodded.

"No doubts?"

"No."

"Okay, then," he said, taking her arm, "here we go. Smile."

They paused in the doorway, and Marisa took it all in in one swift glance . . . the few close friends and coworkers sitting in the pews, the flowers on the altar, the minister, Linda and Barbara smiling at her, Mike and Mike Junior looking solemn and proud, and then she saw Grigori and everything else disappeared from her sight.

Save for his white shirt, he was a study in black, from his hair to his tux to his shoes. She felt the power of his eyes as he watched her walk down the aisle, felt the power of the man himself. It reached out to her, enfolding her in a lover's embrace.

Her heart was beating like a wild thing caught in a trap by the time she reached the altar.

She hardly heard a word that was said, was only vaguely aware of her father placing her hand in Grigori's. She felt Grigori's fingers close over her own, firm and cool, felt a quick jolt of electricity arc between them. And then they were exchanging the vows that would bind them together.

Grigori looked deep into her eyes as he placed his ring upon her finger and spoke the words that made her his wife. But it was the words he spoke to her mind that she heard.

I love you, cara. *I shall love and cherish you until your dying breath, protect you with my life. So long as I live, you will want for nothing.*

And then the ceremony was over. The minister smiled at Grigori. "You may kiss the bride."

She gazed up into Grigori's eyes as he lifted her veil. Gently, as if she were made of the most fragile crystal, he took her face between his hands and kissed her. There was a roaring in her ears. Heat exploded through her as he branded her with his kiss.

Her senses were reeling when he took his mouth from hers. The minister introduced them as Mr. and Mrs. Grigori Chiavari, and then they were walking down the aisle.

He kissed her again as soon as they were outside the church. There was nothing gentle in this kiss; it was filled with such passion and fire that she was surprised she didn't melt in his arms.

And then her friends and family were there, wishing them well, hugging Marisa, shaking hands with Grigori.

They went to the Hilton for the reception, which was small and intimate. Her father had insisted on paying for a sit-down dinner. The food was excellent; the champagne flowed like water. There was a band, and dancing, toasts to the bride and groom. They cut the cake.

Marisa hesitated as she offered Grigori a piece of their cake. Her gaze searched his, and then she heard his voice in her mind, assuring her that it was all right, that he could eat one small piece of wedding cake.

They posed for pictures, there were more toasts, and then it was time to leave. The wedding presents were loaded into the limo's trunk.

Marisa hugged her family, bidding them good-bye. Her brother and his family were leaving for home in the morning; her parents were going up to Carmel for a few days before going back to Florida.

She hugged her nieces and nephews, ignoring the tiny niggling voice in the back of her mind, a voice that sounded strangely like Edward Ramsey's, warning her that she had married a vampire and she might not live long enough to see her loved ones again.

A final good-bye, and Grigori swept her into his arms and carried her outside to a waiting limousine amid a shower of rice and good wishes.

They had decided to spend the night at their house instead of going to a hotel.

"Cara." He drew her into his arms as the car pulled away from the curb.

She smiled up at him, a riot of emotions roiling through her. He was devastatingly handsome. His eyes were dark, blazing with barely restrained desire. Soon they would be at his home . . . her home, too, now. It was her wedding night . . . how did vampires make love?

"Relax, Marisa, I'm not going to eat you."

He smiled at her, that incredibly sexy, heartbreaking smile, and all her fears dissolved. She snuggled up against him. "It was a pretty wedding, wasn't it?"

Grigori nodded. "Did I tell you how beautiful you are?"

"No." He hadn't spoken the words, but she had seen it in his eyes.

"*Molto bella*."

"Thank you." She frowned. "The pictures—"

"What about them?"

"Do vampires photograph?"

"I'm not a ghost, *cara*."

"Good. I'd look silly standing in front of the cake alone. The cake! Did you really eat, or was it just an illusion?"

"It wasn't an illusion, *cara*. Not this time." He did not tell her how distasteful it had been, or that, even now, he could feel that lump of sugar and flour and thick white frosting sitting heavily in his stomach.

They arrived at the house a few minutes later. Grigori and the driver carried the presents inside.

She stood in the living room, which was the only room in the house that lacked furniture. She heard Grigori bid the driver good night, heard the front door close, and then he was there, taking her in his arms, his dark gaze searching hers. There was passion in those deep black eyes, passion and a hint of fear.

Marisa frowned. "What's wrong?"

"Wrong?"

"You're looking at me as if you're afraid of me."

"Not of you. Myself. I'm afraid I might do something to hurt you, or"—he took a deep breath—"or frighten you."

"Frighten me?"

He smiled at her. "It's been a long time since I made love to a woman I cared for." He ran a finger down her cheek. "I'll try to be careful." He swore under his breath. "I've only made you more afraid, haven't I?"

She shook her head, but it was a lie.

"Have I told you how much I love you, how grateful I am that you're here?"

"No."

"If I ever do anything to frighten you, you must tell me."

She wished he would stop saying that.

His hands slid up her back and began unfastening the tiny cloth-covered buttons on her gown. Slowly, he drew the dress over her shoulders, down her arms, until, with a whisper of satin over silk, it pooled around her ankles. Her slip followed.

Grigori sucked in a deep breath as his gaze moved over her. Clad in a lacy bra, bikini panties, a white garter belt, stockings, and heels, she was the sexiest thing he had ever seen.

He started to remove her bra, but she caught his hand. "Not yet," she murmured.

He looked at her askance. "Change your mind?"

"No, now it's my turn."

She removed his coat and tossed it aside, then slowly unfastened his shirt. He wasn't wearing a T-shirt, and she let her fingers slide over his skin, felt him shudder at her touch.

She pulled his shirttail out, ran her hands up and down his back, and then tossed his shirt after his coat. She kept her gaze on his as she removed his belt.

He sucked in a deep breath as she began to unfasten his trousers. "You're playing with fire, you know."

"Am I?" She unzipped his fly and pushed his trousers over his hips, letting them puddle around his ankles. He wore a pair of black briefs that left little to the imagination.

"My turn again," he said. He brushed his lips across her cheek, and then knelt down, his hands sliding over her thighs and calves, caressing her ankles before he removed her shoes and tossed them onto the growing pile of discarded clothing.

Slowly, he rose to his feet, kissing her from her navel to her breasts. His hands were quick and sure as he unfastened her bra.

He wadded it up in his hand, his breath catching in his throat as his hungry gaze moved over her. Her skin was smooth and clear, perfection upon perfection, and he thought he had never seen anything more tempting in all his life.

The heat between them was potent, flammable. He started to remove his shoes, but she stayed his hand, then knelt down and removed his shoes and socks. She looked up at him, and he lifted first one leg and then the other so she could fling his trousers aside.

He took her hands and helped her to her feet,

his heart pounding wildly as she unfastened her garter belt and slowly, oh so slowly, peeled off her nylons to stand before him wearing nothing but a scrap of white lace.

"Marisa." His voice was warm and thick, like sun-warmed molasses, as he swept her into his arms and carried her up the stairs to the bedroom. He paused inside the door to rain feather-soft kisses over her cheeks, her nose, her brow.

He glanced at the hearth, and it blazed to life. The crackle of the flames was the only sound in the room as he carried her to the bed.

The covers had already been turned down. There was a bottle of champagne, a bottle of red wine, and two glasses on the bedside table, along with a slender crystal vase that held a single, perfect red rose.

He lowered her to the mattress, and followed her down, gathering her into his arms. "I can't believe you are here," he whispered, "that you are mine."

His eyes blazed with fervent heat as he kissed her, the touch of his lips igniting a fever of desire deep within her. Her arms twined around his neck, holding him close, as she returned his kisses. His hands caressed her, aroused her, until she writhed beneath him in sweet agony.

He tore off his briefs, removed her panties, and then hovered over her, his dark eyes intent upon her face. "Tell me," he said hoarsely, "tell me that you love me."

"I love you." She lifted her hips in silent invitation. "Love you, love you!"

"Ah, *cara*." He breathed the words as he made her his.

She gasped, then clutched him to her, trembling as her body stretched to accommodate him.

"Shhh, *cara,*" he murmured, "I'll never hurt you again."

She nodded, her face buried in his shoulder, as he began to move slowly within her, the tension melting away as pleasure built deep inside her. He whispered soft words in her ear, love words spoken in French and Italian. She felt his breath hot against her neck, felt his tongue sweep over her heated flesh. She moaned with delight, her body moving with his.

She closed her eyes, awash in a sea of pleasure, and he was there beside her, his breath harsh, his body slick with perspiration, his voice moving over her like black velvet. She was reaching, reaching, and he was there, lifting her higher, taking her where she wanted to go, until she was hovering on the brink. She cried his name, felt his teeth at her neck, and then she was flying, soaring, as wave after wave of ecstacy washed over her.

Slowly, like a feather drifting on the wind, she floated back to earth. She was smiling and couldn't seem to stop. Sleepy, yet wide awake. All her life she had waited for this moment. Had it been as wonderful for him as it had been for her?

She ran her hand through his hair, caressed his shoulder. He started to pull away, but she held him close. "Not yet."

"I must be heavy."

"No, I like it."

Resting on his elbows, he turned his head so he could see her face, frowned when he saw the tears in her eyes. "*Cara!*" he exclaimed softly. "Did I hurt you?"

"No. Oh, no. It was wonderful."

A smile of pure masculine delight curved his lips.

Marisa lifted a hand to her neck. Had she imagined it, or had she felt his teeth nipping at her throat?

She felt him stiffen as the thought crossed her mind.

His gaze slid away from hers. "Forgive me, *cara.*"

She caressed his cheek, ran her finger over his lips. "It's all right, really."

"I had hoped—" He shook his head.

"Hoped what?"

"I had hoped I could separate my love for you from the Hunger, but my desire for your sweet flesh arouses my thirst until I cannot resist." He ran his fingertips over the two tiny marks on her throat. "I took but a little."

She didn't know what to think, what to say. She tried to feel repulsed, betrayed. Instead, she felt a sense of fulfillment in knowing that she had nourished his Hunger and satisfied his desire.

She ran her hands down his arms, marveling at the latent strength she felt there. His skin was warm beneath her fingertips.

Grigori closed his eyes and surrendered to the touch of her hands. Her fingertips explored the muscles in his arms, traveled over his chest, massaged his shoulders, slid over his back, his buttocks.

He groaned softly, felt his body's quick response to the sheer pleasure of her touch as she continued her exploration. He drew a deep breath, fighting to keep his Hunger under control as she began to kiss his neck. Her breath tickled his skin; her breasts were warm and soft against his chest. And he wanted her again, wanted to hold her and kiss her, to bury himself deep within her, to drink in her sweetness again and yet again.

"Marisa . . ."

"Hmmm?"

He kissed her, kissed her until she was breathless, until she cried out for him to take her. He held nothing back this time, overcome by his need to possess her, to brand her as his forevermore. He brought her to the brink and carried her over, his mind melding with hers, making them one in mind and body, and when, at last, she fell asleep in his arms, he knew he would never let her go.

Chapter Thirty-two

He stood outside the house, his body lighter than air, filled with the blood of his latest victim. So, Chiavari had made the woman his wife. That was a rather interesting turn of events.

He had thought to end it quickly, to destroy Chiavari once and for all. Ramsey was no longer a threat. The woman could be taken at any time. But she was Chiavari's wife now. . . .

He stared at the house for a long while, his hatred growing, swelling, spreading through him. After the battle in the cellar, he had gone to ground to heal his wounds and nurse his rage. It had taken weeks for the gaping hole left by the wooden stake to heal. Ramsey, damn his soul to hell, had soaked the wood in holy water.

It was time to raise the ante, to bring the game to a close. He was weary of this modern world, of the constant rush, the noise, the pollution that stung his nostrils and burned his eyes. He yearned for the romantic days of the past, for the elaborate costumes, the pageantry, the ignorance of the common people.

Tomorrow, he mused, tomorrow he would send Chiavari a surprise, and when the vampire was dead, he would take the woman.

Chapter Thirty-three

Marisa woke slowly, a smile on her face, as the last remnants of a wonderful dream faded away. She had been making love to Grigori, and it had been the most amazing experience of her life. She rolled onto her side, came face-to-face with the man of her dreams, and knew it hadn't been a dream at all.

She pulled the sheet up under her arms and regarded the man sleeping beside her. How handsome he was! She smiled as she recalled the night past, glad that she had waited, glad that he had been the first man to make love to her. He had been so gentle, so tender, so eager to please and pleasure her. He had made love to her three times, and each time had been better than the last.

She had felt his mind probing hers, melding with hers. It had been incredible. She had felt every beat of his heart, every breath, knew the same excitement, the same ecstacy he did. Had he felt hers in return?

She glanced at the window. Dark green drapes lined with black shut out the morning light, reminding her that she had not married an ordinary man. She looked at Grigori again. He seemed to be sleeping, but was he, or was he trapped in some kind of darkness, unable to move?

She lifted her hand, hesitated, and then placed it over his heart. It was beating slowly, steadily, but he didn't move. Could he feel her touch?

"Grigori?"

His eyelids fluttered open. "What is it you wish?"

"Nothing, I just wondered—"

He raised one brow. "What?"

"I thought maybe . . . I mean, well—"

She started to draw her hand away, but he covered it with his own. "Is there something you need?"

"It's morning."

"I know." His body felt heavy, sluggish.

"I thought that—" She shrugged one shoulder. "How can you be awake?"

"It isn't easy," he replied with a wry grin. Indeed, he could feel the darkness calling him. "I must rest, *cara mia.*"

"Okay." She bent down to kiss him. "See ya later."

He pressed a kiss to her palm, and then his eyelids fluttered down.

She watched him a moment. His eyelashes were short and thick, his hair was mussed. He was beautiful.

Slipping out of bed, Marisa went to take a shower. Her body ached a little, reminding her of the night past. Making love to Grigori had been everything she had hoped it would be, and more.

He was deeply asleep when she returned to the bedroom. She dressed quickly, kissed him lightly on the cheek, and went downstairs.

He had been busy since the last time she had been at the house. The fridge and the cupboards were filled with food.

She opened the egg carton and found a note inside. She unfolded it. *I love you.* She smiled as she tucked it into her pants pocket.

There was a note inside the coffee canister: *I love you. You're beautiful.* Another inside the sugar bowl: *I am dreaming of you.* Inside the silverware drawer, she found his Mastercard, a couple hundred dollars in cash, and another note: *Go buy us some living room furniture, something we can snuggle on in front of the fire.*

She fixed breakfast, turned on the radio, and then sat down to eat. Maybe she would quit her job, she mused. She didn't have to work anymore. It might be fun to stay home. She could sleep late every morning, spend her days reading, or gardening, or shopping, or doing anything else she pleased.

She gazed out the window. The backyard was huge. There was a pool, a large covered patio, a gazebo, a rose garden. Of course, the yard was overgrown with weeds.

She put her dishes in the dishwasher, poured another cup of coffee, then went out to get the morning paper.

She was sorry the minute she opened it.

TERROR STALKS THE STREETS
VAMPIRE KILLER STRIKES AGAIN

Inside, she sat down and read the story. The body of a young man had been found in a ditch near West Road.

Marisa stared at the headlines. She had lost count of how many killings there had been. In the last two weeks, she had refused to think about Alexi, refused to let him or anything else intrude on what was supposed to be the happiest time of her life. But she couldn't ignore it anymore, couldn't forget that it had been the scent of her blood that had aroused him from a century of sleep.

How could she have gone blithely on, planning her wedding, having a good time, when people were being murdered, when she was partly responsible?

She had to do something. But what? If he returned to the past to rest during the day, they would never find him. And if Edward and Grigori hadn't been able to find him, what hope did she have?

And yet they had to find him, had to stop him. But how?

Feeling a sudden need to see Grigori, she put the newspaper aside and went upstairs.

Standing in the doorway, she watched him sleep. What was it like for him? she wondered. What was it like to live for hundreds of years? Did one grow weary of living, of being forever young? She had often wished she could live forever, and now the means was within her grasp. Would Grigori make her a vampire if she asked it of him?

She moved closer to the bed, watching the nearly invisible rise and fall of his chest. What would it be like to be a vampire, to watch her friends and family grow old and die? Would living forever be worth the price of losing everyone she loved? It might be fun, if she could go on as she was now, but that would be impossible. She would have to be always on her guard, never able to tell her friends what she was. There would be no more beach parties in the summer, no more Christmas mornings with her family. No more company Fourth of July picnics, or vacations at the lake. No children . . .

She felt a tug at her heart. There would be no children for her in any case, not as long as she was married to Grigori.

If she called his name, would he hear her? If she crawled into bed beside him, would he awake and take her in his arms?

"Grigori?"

She moved closer to the bed and called a little louder. "Grigori?"

His eyelids fluttered open and he gazed up at her. "*Cara,* is something wrong?"

"No. I was"—she shrugged—"lonesome for you."

He held out one arm in silent invitation and she slid under the covers.

"Does it bother you to be awake during the day?"

"No, but it is difficult, when the sun is high."

"Maybe I should let you rest."

"No." He hugged her to him. "I thought you would be out shopping."

"That's what I was going to do, but then I read the paper. We've got to do something, Grigori. We've got to stop him."

"Alexi."

"There's got to be a way. He can't be infallible."

"If he has a weakness, I have yet to find it." He smiled lazily as he took her hand in his and licked her palm. "I have a weakness, *cara mia*. Shall I tell you what it is?"

She shivered with delight as he licked the inside of her wrist. "I think I can guess."

"Can you?" He rained kisses on the inside of her arm, licked the bend of her elbow.

She leaned closer and kissed him, felt his free arm slide around her waist, and then she was lying on top of him, her breasts crushed against his chest. "I thought vampires were weak and vulnerable during the day."

"You make me weak," he murmured. "Weak with wanting you."

"Do I?"

"*Cara . . .*"

She ran her hands through his hair, feathered kisses over his brow, his cheeks. His hands slid restlessly up and down her back, and then he cupped her face in his hands and kissed her, his tongue teasing her lips until, with a low moan, she opened to him.

He caressed her out of her clothing, and then there was nothing between them but desire and his mouth on hers. She felt his power surround her, felt the world spinning away, until there were only the two of them, caught up in a magical sphere where touch was everything. Her whole body tingled with awareness, and then they were one, joined flesh to flesh and heart to heart. He carried her to the brink, and when she was teetering on the edge, she felt the touch of his teeth at her throat, heard him groan with pleasure as they plunged over the abyss together. It was like free-falling through a rainbow.

Breathless, she collapsed on top of him. He

murmured her name, his hands stroking her back. She felt his tongue whisper down the side of her neck and only then remembered that he had bitten her.

"Does it bother you?" he asked.

"Reading my mind again?" she asked, her tone mildly accusing.

"It is difficult not to, especially now." His arms tightened around her.

"Well, it's not fair. I should be able to read yours, too."

"You can, if you wish."

"Really?" She propped herself up on her elbows. "How?"

"I have given you my blood. You need only concentrate."

She couldn't help it. Remembering that he had given her his blood, that she had drunk it, even if she couldn't remember, made her shudder with revulsion.

He didn't move, but she felt him withdraw from her.

"I'm sorry."

He didn't say anything, only gazed up at her, his expression impassive.

"Alexi told me he could taste you on his tongue."

"It was necessary."

She glanced at his throat, wondering what his blood had tasted like. "Can I really read your mind?"

"Try."

Brow furrowed in concentration, she stared at him, then shook her head. "It isn't working."

"Don't try so hard. Just relax, let your thoughts touch mine."

It wasn't like before, when he had planted his thoughts in her mind. She tried to connect her thoughts to his, and failed. And then, as if he had opened a door, she heard his voice inside her head.

"You can do it, cara," he said, and his thoughts blazed a trail for her to follow.

"What am I thinking, *cara mia?*"

"That we should go to Italy again."

He smiled. "You see? You can do it."

"And all because you gave me a little of your blood." She traced the line of his mouth with her fingertip. "Didn't the idea of drinking blood repulse you when you first became a vampire?"

"No. Once the change took place, I craved it as a drunkard craves wine. It was sweet on my tongue, sweeter than anything I had ever tasted."

In the beginning, when the Hunger controlled him, when he feared he would never get enough to satisfy the craving, he had taken more than he needed, and in so doing, had taken lives as well. Eventually, he had learned to take less and thus spare the lives of those he used. The lives of those he had needlessly killed haunted him still.

"Cara . . . "

"Am I heavy?"

"No." He brushed a lock of hair from her cheek. He could feel the darkness creeping over him, dragging him toward oblivion. "I fear I must rest a little longer."

"All right." She kissed him, then slid out of bed. Gathering her clothes, she went into the bathroom and shut the door.

When she emerged, showered and dressed twenty minutes later, he was asleep.

* * *

She spent the afternoon at the mall. It was fun to wander from shop to shop, knowing she didn't have to check the price tags, that she could buy whatever caught her fancy. She bought two lamps and a painting for the living room, a new dress for herself, a black jacket for Grigori, a couple of compact discs for Mike Junior, a *Gone With the Wind* Barbie for Nikki, a baby doll for Mindy, a teddy bear for Danny. She bought a blue negligee for Barbara, and a black one for herself, picked up a sweater for Mike. She bought a couple of John Wayne videos for her father, a new bathrobe for her mother.

"Christmas in January," she mused as she stowed her packages in the trunk of the Corvette. "I could get used to this."

It was rather nice to be a lady of leisure, to sleep late, to make love to her husband in the afternoon.

Her husband, the vampire. The thought made her grin. She imagined going to lunch with Linda and casually dropping that bit of news into the conversation.

Sliding behind the wheel, she switched on the ignition and pulled out of the parking lot, wondering if Linda would believe her, or think she had gone completely insane. The latter, most likely. Still, there were people who believed in vampires. There were fan magazines and web sites, all dedicated to the undead. People showed up on talk shows, claiming to be vampires. She had always thought they were just a bunch of bizarre people looking for their fifteen minutes of fame, but now . . . maybe they really were vampires. Maybe the world was full of the undead. And if vampires existed, maybe there really were aliens and werewolves. Maybe all the creatures of myth and legend actually existed.

It was almost five when she pulled into the driveway of the house. Collecting her packages from the trunk, she paused a moment and studied the house, noticing, for the first time, that it looked a lot like the gloomy old houses Dracula haunted in the movies. Perhaps a paint job would brighten the place up, make it look less like a haunted house and more like a home. She stared at the peeling green paint, trying to imagine what the house would look like painted Dutch blue with white trim. The front yard was overgrown with weeds. Maybe tomorrow she'd buy some gardening tools and get to work. Or maybe she'd just hire someone to do it for her. Going up the front walk, she thought that she'd like to plant roses in the front yard, and maybe put some fruit trees out back.

Filled with plans for redecorating, she walked up the porch steps. She slid the key in the lock, but before she turned it, the door whooshed open.

She stood poised on the threshold, wondering if she should go inside, or turn and run. "Grigori?"

She took a step inside, ears straining. "Grigori?"

She heard nothing, sensed nothing. Surely if Alexi was here, she would know it.

Moving quietly, she put her shopping bags on the floor and tiptoed through the downstairs, turning lights on as she went.

Nothing.

For a moment, she stood at the bottom of the staircase, one hand on the banister, and then she started up the steps.

Chapter Thirty-four

"Grigori?"

She paused outside their bedroom, her hand on the latch. She knew, *knew*, something was wrong.

Taking a deep breath, she opened the door and stepped inside.

The heavy drapes at the window shut out the light, so that the room was nearly dark. As soon as she stepped inside the doorway, the overhead light went on.

Tension went out of her in a whoosh as Edward stepped in front of her.

"Edward! You scared me out of a year's growth. What are you doing here? Edward?"

The relief she had first felt at seeing him quickly turned to alarm as he stepped behind her and closed the door. "Edward?"

"Go sit down, Marisa."

"What's wrong?"

"Nothing, and everything."

"You're not making sense."

"You'll understand soon enough." He gave her a little push and she stumbled forward.

It was then that she saw Grigori. He lay still as death on the bed, bound by a heavy silver chain

. . . a chain that looked very much like the one that had once bound Alexi.

"What have you done to him?"

Edward pulled a syringe out of his coat pocket. "I put him to sleep, and then I bled him." He nodded at the basin on the table beside her chair. It was a large bowl, and it was filled with blood. Grigori's blood. Enough to weaken him. Enough to . . .

"He's not . . . not dead?"

"Not yet."

"Edward, please—"

He pushed her toward the chair in the corner. "Sit down, Marisa. Alexi will be here soon."

"Alexi! He's coming here?"

Edward nodded, his expression unutterably sad. "I'm sorry, Marisa."

She sat down heavily. "Why are you doing this?"

"I have no choice."

"What do you mean? Of course you do. . . ." The words died in her throat. "He's done something to you, hasn't he? Oh, Lord, you're like Antoinette."

"No. She had no mind of her own. Alexi has left me my mind, Marisa, but he has robbed me of my will." His voice was raw with torment. "This is worse. I know what I'm doing, and even though I don't want to, I can't refuse."

"Fight him, Edward! You've got to fight him."

"I can't." He began to pace the floor. "He's too strong." He stopped in front of her, his eyes wild, his hands clenching and unclenching. "He took my blood, made me take his. I can hear his thoughts in my mind. I can't shut them out!" He placed his hands over his ears and shook his head. "I can't shut him out!"

"He's going to kill us, isn't he?"

"He's going to kill Grigori. I'm afraid he has worse things in mind for you." Edward dropped to his knees in front of Marisa. "I'm sorry." He pulled a short piece of rope out of his coat pocket. "So sorry."

Instinct overcame fear. With a cry, she jerked her knee up. It caught him under the jaw. His head snapped backward and she kicked him in the chest with all her might. The air whooshed out of his lungs as he fell to the floor.

Jumping to her feet, she ran for the door. She screamed as she felt his hand close over her arm.

"Let me go!" she shrieked. "Let me go!"

She struggled against him, but he was too strong for her. Twisting her arm behind her back, he quickly tied her wrists together, then guided her back to the chair and pushed her into it.

"Marisa, I'm sorry."

She was shaking now, frightened beyond words. Alexi was coming. She felt a ripple in the air, a stirring against her skin, and knew that Grigori was emerging from the dark sleep.

Edward felt it, too. Reaching under his coat, he withdrew a sharpened stake.

"Edward, don't!"

"I won't. Not unless I have to." He glanced at her over his shoulder. "Alexi wants that pleasure for himself."

"Edward, please, please don't do this. Please. I'd rather be dead than become his creature."

"Marisa." A groan rose in Edward's throat. She saw him struggle against Alexi's hold on his mind, saw the torment in his eyes.

"Please, Edward. He'll make me like Antoinette."

He looked up at her, helpless, every muscle in his body taut. Pain flickered in his eyes, and she knew that Alexi was reading Edward's mind, knew the vampire was exerting his influence.

"I . . . I can't fight him," he said, panting heavily. "He's too strong."

Moving stiffly, he stood up and backed away from her. "I can't help you." Pain twisted his features and he bent at the waist, clutching his stomach. "Stop," he begged. "Please stop."

She watched him writhe in agony. What was Alexi doing to him? Fighting the urge to scream, to give in to the panic surging through her, she began to work her hands back and forth in an effort to loosen the rope.

Marisa . . .

Her head jerked up at the sound of Grigori's voice. She glanced at the bed. His eyes were closed. As far as she could tell, he hadn't moved.

Are you hurt?

No. Are you all right?

Weak . . . Alexi is coming. . . . You must be strong.

Are you in pain?

The silver . . . it burns . . . makes me weak . . .

What can I do?

Don't fight Alexi.

Are you crazy?

You are the one who is crazy, if you think you can defeat him. You are only a mortal, and a woman, at that. If you fight him, it will only be so much the worse for you.

So you just want me to submit? To let him kill

you and then turn me into some kind of zombie? I don't think so!

The very idea made her mad enough to spit. She was outraged that Grigori would even suggest they just give up without a fight. Adrenaline flowed through her as she tugged against the rope, and then, to her surprise, she felt the knots give, felt the rope loosen, just a little. The next thing she knew, one hand slipped free.

She glanced at Grigori again. He still hadn't moved, but she could feel him smiling in her mind.

Think you're pretty smart, don't you, she thought, getting me all riled up like that?

Your hands are free, aren't they?

Marisa swallowed a grin. He knew her much too well.

A sudden heaviness seemed to pulse through the air and she knew, with a sinking feeling of dread, that Alexi had arrived. The thought no sooner crossed her mind than he was there, in the room. Darkness seemed to trail in his wake, like a miasma of evil.

"So," Alexi said. "We are all together at last."

Marisa fought the urge to cringe in her chair. Clenching her fists, she stared at him, willing herself to be strong. Grigori's life depended on her now. Edward would be no help. Even now, he was kneeling in front of Alexi, accepting his master's terse words of praise for a job well done.

"Edward, it is time I made the woman mine. You will leave the room. Wait for me in the hallway." Alexi sniffed the air, his nose wrinkling as the smell of cold blood reached his nostrils. He jerked his chin toward the bowl. "Get rid of that."

"Yes, master."

Slowly, Edward rose to his feet. Moving like a robot, he picked up the bowl and started toward the door.

"Edward," Marisa cried, "don't leave me! Please, help me!"

"I can't." He tried to turn to face her, his whole being longing to help her, to strike Alexi down, but the vampire's power was too strong to resist. He told himself to stop, to turn, but his body refused to obey. One step after another, he moved toward the door.

"Edward!" The fear and anguish in her voice stabbed him to the heart. But there was nothing he could do. Nothing . . .

Ramsey! I've taken your blood, made you a part of me. Listen to my voice. Draw on my strength. You can fight him. Think! Combine your will with mine. Together we can defeat him.

I can't. Edward stared into the bowl, at the blood that was so dark it was almost black.

You can! Marisa needs help, help I can't give her. Damn you! Fight!

Cradling the bowl in one arm, Edward opened the door and stepped into the hallway. He heard Marisa's shriek of terror as he closed the door behind him.

Alexi leered at Marisa as he jerked her to her feet. Locking one arm around her waist, he caught her chin in his hand and kissed her, his tongue plunging into her mouth, choking her.

She struggled against him, the taste of him making her gag. There was a darkness in his kiss that seemed to smother all the light in her soul. She kicked him, but he only laughed. Shaking the rope from her wrists, she scratched his face, clawed at his eyes, but he only laughed harder.

"Fight me all you wish, woman; you cannot escape me. I will take you here, now, and there is nothing you can do about it. Nothing Chiavari can do to save you." Wicked laughter bubbled up from his throat. "I know the power of those chains. He does not have the strength to remove them. Even now, the silver burns his flesh and weakens his powers. Only a vampyre who has lived as long as I could withstand them. And he is but a babe compared to me."

He gazed down at her, his eyes glowing with hatred. "He took Antoinette from me, and now I shall take you from him. I will defile you, here, in his presence, and then I shall destroy him. And when that is done, you will be mine for a hundred years. And he will know it. In whatever hell he finds himself, he will know it."

He bent her back over his arm and licked her face, laughing when she shuddered with revulsion.

"It is time to end the game."

Grabbing her by the hair, he forced her to her knees. "Disrobe."

"No."

"Do it!"

Marisa shook her head. She slid a glance at Grigori. His eyes were dark with hatred. She could see him trying to summon his power, knew he was trying to get past the pain, the loss of blood, trying to find the strength to free himself of the heavy silver that weighed him down.

You can do it! I know you can. She tried to will

him her strength, rocked back on her heels as Alexi slapped her across the face.

"Do it!"

She was reaching for the zipper when the bedroom door slammed open and Edward burst into the room. Mouth stained with blood, eyes wild, he hurled himself at Alexi, the stake in his hand aimed for the vampire's heart.

With a cry, Marisa jumped to her feet. Hurrying to the bed, she lifted the heavy chain from Grigori's chest, and thrust her arm in his face. "Hurry!"

He didn't argue. She felt the prick of his fangs, the oddly sensual flow of blood from her veins. He seemed to drink forever, yet it was only a handful of seconds, and then he put her from him and rose to his feet.

He was wholly vampire now. His eyes blazed with a pure red flame.

Marisa watched it all, too terrified to move.

Edward and Alexi were locked in a fierce embrace. The stake had missed Alexi's heart. He pulled it from his body with a savage cry and tossed it aside. Unmindful of the blood that spurted from his chest in a dark torrent, he flung Edward against the wall, held him there with one arm while he jerked Edward's head to the side and buried his fangs in his throat.

A strangled cry rose from Edward's lips as the vampire began to drink.

And then Grigori was there. Like an avenging angel, he pulled Alexi away from Edward. With a triumphant cry, Grigori snatched up the stake and drove it through Alexi's heart.

A horrible cry of anguish and rage rose in the

vampire's throat. With a look of satisfaction, Grigori twisted the stake, driving it deeper, deeper. Alexi sank to his knees, his eyes growing dull. He tried to dislodge the stake, but he lacked the strength. A horrible hissing sound issued from his lips as he sank to the floor. His face turned a hideous shade of gray.

"Marisa, bring me the chain."

She stared at Grigori, one hand pressed to her mouth.

"Now, Marisa."

Unable to take her eyes from the horror before her, she picked up the chain.

"Drop it over him."

She did as she was told, though it seemed unnecessary. Alexi Kristov was truly dead this time.

"Marisa. Marisa!"

She blinked up at him, and then fell into his arms, sobbing. "Edward . . . what about Edward?" She looked over her shoulder at Edward, who lay sprawled on the floor, a gaping hole in his throat. "Is he . . . ?"

"Not yet, but soon."

"We can't let him die. Please, Grigori, you've got to do something."

"He won't like it."

"Please! He saved our lives."

"Very well. But you will have to take the blame."

"I will. Please, hurry."

"As you wish, *cara.*"

He let her go, and then put a hand on her shoulder. "Are you all right?"

"Fine. I'll be fine."

Sweeping her into his arms, he carried her across the floor and placed her in the chair. Yanking the bedspread from the bed, he covered her with it. "Rest." He brushed a wisp of hair from her cheek. "You might want to close your eyes."

She nodded, but she didn't. Hands clutching the bedspread, she watched as Grigori knelt on the floor and drew Edward into his lap. With surprising gentleness, he turned Edward's head to the side. She saw Grigori take a deep breath, and then he bent down, his long black hair falling over Edward's face, blocking her view. Several long minutes passed. The ticking of the bedside clock seemed very loud in the stillness.

Once, she glanced at Alexi's body, half expecting it to vanish into thin air. She wished Grigori had thought to cover it.

A movement drew her eye back to Grigori. She pressed her knuckles to her mouth as Grigori bit his own wrist, and then placed the bleeding wound to Edward's lips.

"Drink, Ramsey." His voice was soft yet compelling, as soothing as a mother's lullaby. "That's right, drink your fill."

And Edward was drinking, his mouth fastened to Grigori's wrist, his hands clutching Grigori's arm as if he feared it would be suddenly snatched away. His eyes were open, his expression one of near-rapture.

Grigori turned his head, his gaze meeting Marisa's.

This is what I am, what I have always been.

And Marisa met his gaze, unflinching, accepting him, loving him, for who and what he was.

"Enough." Grigori jerked his arm from Edward's grasp, ran his tongue over the wound in his wrist.

Edward sat back, looking confused. "What happened?"

Marisa leaned forward in the chair. Color suffused Edward's cheeks; the horrible wound in his throat closed, healed, in a matter of minutes.

Edward glanced from Chiavari to Marisa. "What the hell happened?"

"How do you feel, Edward?" Marisa asked.

"I feel fine," he retorted. "I want to know what the . . ." His words trailed off when he caught sight of Alexi's body. "Is he dead?"

Marisa shrugged. "I hope so."

"He's dead," Grigori remarked. He regarded Ramsey through narrowed eyes. "How do you feel?"

"Why do you two keep asking me that? I feel"—he frowned—"I feel funny." He looked at Alexi again. "I stabbed him, and then he—"

Edward lifted one hand to his throat. "He bit me. Ripped my jugular. I remember . . . what happened?"

"You were dying," Marisa said.

Ramsey stared at Grigori, a look of horror spreading over his face. "You didn't? For the love of all that's holy, tell me you didn't!"

"It was my idea," Marisa said. "He didn't want to."

"You told him to turn me into one of them? How could you?"

Marisa stood up, clutching the bedspread to her chest. "Would you rather be dead, Edward?"

He scrambled to his feet and backed away from them both. "Of course I would," he began, and then, shoulders slumping, he buried his face in his hands.

"Edward, I'm sorry."

Rising to his feet, Grigori went to stand beside Marisa. "Don't be sorry, *cara*. If he'd rather be dead, I'll be only too happy to accommodate him."

Edward's head snapped up. "Yeah, I'll just bet you would."

"It's your choice, vampyre hunter."

Edward snorted. "Not anymore. I guess you just put me out of business."

"Yes, I guess I did."

Edward lifted his hands, turned them this way and that. Crossing the floor, he stared into the mirror above the dresser. "I look the same," he murmured. "How can I look the same and feel so different?"

"You'll get used to it."

"I don't know what to say."

"You might thank Grigori," Marisa suggested, "for saving your life."

Edward turned around. "I was going to kill you, you know."

Grigori nodded. "I know you were going to try."

Edward gestured at Alexi's body. "What are we going to do with him?"

"I'll drag his body out onto the balcony. The sun will take care of the rest."

Edward shuddered, and then squared his shoulders. "Well, I guess I'll be going." He took a step toward Marisa, but then stopped, as if uncertain how she would receive him now.

Marisa held out a hand and smiled. "Keep in touch, Edward."

He took her hand in both of his and squeezed it. "I will. Good night, Marisa."

"Good night, Edward."

"Be careful, Ramsey."

Edward met Grigori's eyes, surprised by the genuine concern in the other man's voice. "You too. And . . . thanks."

Grigori nodded.

"Will he be okay?" Marisa asked when they were alone.

"That's up to him." He gave her shoulders a squeeze; then he dragged Kristov's body out onto the balcony, careful not to touch the chain coiled on his chest.

Marisa was sitting on the bed when he returned.

Grigori smiled at her. "Some honeymoon."

"Well, you can't say it hasn't been exciting."

"And are you still happy being Mrs. Chiavari?"

"I'd be happier if you were holding me." She slid off the bed and wrapped her arms around him. "Can we sleep in another room?"

With a nod, he pulled the blankets off the bed, swung her into his arms, and carried her down the hall into one of the other bedrooms.

Dumping the blankets on the bed, he sat down and cradled her in his arms.

"You are a most remarkable woman," he said.

"And you, husband, are a most remarkable man."

"I'm glad you still think so."

"I love you." She caressed his cheek. "Nothing will change that."

"*Cara* . . ."

"Do you think Edward will be happy being a vampire?"

"That's up to him. Life is what you make it, *cara,* whether you're a man or a vampyre."

"Are *you* happy?"

He nodded. Before Marisa, he had merely been content. He had accepted what he was, learned to live with it. He had made the most of the good things, and wasted little energy worrying over the drawbacks.

She cocked her head to one side, her eyes shining with love. "So, do you think I'd be happy as a vampire?"

"Marisa!"

"Do you?"

He stared at her, hardly daring to believe his ears. "You're not serious?"

She nodded. Until this moment, she hadn't realized how seriously she had been considering it, how desperately she wanted to share his life, all of it, how desperately she wanted him to share hers. There was only one way that could ever be possible. "Would you change me if I asked you to?"

"Only if you were certain it was what you wanted." He looked deep into her eyes. How many times had he dreamed of bestowing the Dark Gift on her? A hundred? A thousand? Yet he had never suggested it, certain she would refuse. "Is it what you want?"

"Yes, but not right away. I'd like to spend Easter with my family up at the cabin one more time, maybe go on vacation with Mom and Dad next summer, and spend one more Christmas with Mike and Barbara and the kids."

Grigori nodded. "There's no hurry, *cara.* We have all the time in the world."

"All the time in the world," she repeated softly. "I like the sound of that."

"Ah, Marisa, you'll never know how much you

mean to me. I wish I had words enough to tell you."

She gazed up at him, her lips parting in a sensual smile as she slid her arms around his neck. "You could show me."

And it was his pleasure to do so, not only that night, but every night for centuries to come.

ATTENTION
ROMANCE
CUSTOMERS!
SPECIAL
TOLL-FREE NUMBER
1-800-481-9191
Call Monday through Friday
12 noon to 10 p.m.
Eastern Time
Get a free catalogue,
join the Romance Book Club,
and order books using your
Visa, MasterCard,
or Discover®
Leisure
Books
Love
Spell